ITEM DAMAGE
Stains on edge

DATE
5/16/17   INITIALS

P9-DMU-221

TREASURE HUNT

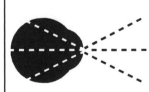

This Large Print Book carries the
Seal of Approval of N.A.V.H.

TREASURE HUNT

JOHN LESCROART

THORNDIKE PRESS

A part of Gale, Cengage Learning

GALE
CENGAGE Learning·

Detroit • New York • San Francisco • New Haven, Conn • Waterville, Maine • London

GALE
CENGAGE Learning

Copyright © 2010 by John Lescroart.
Thorndike Press, a part of Gale, Cengage Learning.

ALL RIGHTS RESERVED
This book is a work of fiction. Names, characters, places, and incidents either are the product of the author's imagination or are used fictitiously, and any resemblance to actual persons, living or dead, business establishments, events, or locales is entirely coincidental.
Thorndike Press® Large Print Basic.
The text of this Large Print edition is unabridged.
Other aspects of the book may vary from the original edition.
Set in 16 pt. Plantin.
Printed on permanent paper.

LIBRARY OF CONGRESS CATALOGING-IN-PUBLICATION DATA

Lescroart, John T.
    Treasure hunt / by John Lescroart.
        p. cm. — (Thorndike press large print basic)
    ISBN-13: 978-1-4104-2364-1 (alk. paper)
    ISBN-10: 1-4104-2364-6 (alk. paper)
    1. Private investigators—Fiction. 2. San Francisco (Calif.)—
Fiction. 3. Large type books. I. Title.
PS3562.E78T74 2010b
813'.54—dc22   2009042201

Published in 2010 by arrangement with Dutton, a member of Penguin Group (USA) Inc.

Printed in the United States of America
1 2 3 4 5 6 7 14 13 12 11 10

To Kathryn Detzer, Andy Jalakas, and
again (always) to Lisa M. Sawyer

It is one thing . . . that business between men and women, and there are many other more important things, including food.

— Alexander McCall Smith

1

The day he found the body, Mickey Dade woke up under a tree on Mount Tamalpais.

Sleeping outside a few nights a week had been going on as a regular thing with him for about four months now. He always kept a sleeping bag in his used Camaro's trunk anyway, and starting around mid-May, when the weather got nice everywhere but in San Francisco proper, he'd finish work and leave town in whatever direction struck his fancy.

Even in the urbanized, overcrowded Bay Area, there were innumerable places a guy could simply pull over, park, and crash on the ground under cover of trees or bushes or in the hollow of a sand dune in one of the city or county or even national parks, at the beaches, off back roads, even in the quiet "neighborhood watch" suburbs.

Monday the past week, while it was still light out he'd driven down to Woodside, an exclusive semirural enclave nestled into the foothills behind Palo Alto, and slept out under an old stone bridge over a dry creek bed. Two days later, he'd parked a couple hundred feet down an unnamed, little-used dirt track cut into the woods behind Burlingame around Crystal Springs Reservoir. Last night, he'd gone north into Marin County, got halfway up Mount Tamalpais, and pulled under an old low-hanging scrub oak in a forgotten and unpaved parking lot.

He always woke up at first light, so this morning he was on the Golden Gate Bridge by the time the sun cleared the hills behind Oakland. He had his iPod coming through his speakers. It was mid-September, and as usual this time of year, the coastal fog was taking a break. The morning clarity under the cloudless sky was startling. Mickey could easily make out the tiny dots of the Farallons twenty-some miles away over the deceptively still Pacific.

He exited the bridge and soon found himself on Marina, cruising through the streets. The closely set, well-maintained, beautiful low-rise homes stirred some vestigial gene he must have picked up somewhere. Just driving through a neighborhood of real honest-to-God stand-alone homes always filled him with something like contentment, although it wasn't quite that; it was more like hope that contentment and physical security were among life's possibilities.

This was something Mickey didn't have much personal experience with. He couldn't remember ever having lived in anything but an apartment house, although his parents had apparently rented a small bungalow in the Sunset before their divorce. His sister, Tamara, said she vaguely remembered that house. But she was two years older than he was. Mickey had been only two when his mom had taken them from their father and moved out.

But Mickey didn't get time to enjoy the Marina architecture this morning. A crowd was clogging the street up by the Palace of Fine Arts. At this location, he thought somebody was probably shooting a movie — the Palace had been a setting in both *Vertigo* and *The Rock,* among a host of other films. People loved the old domed structure that had been constructed for the Panama-Pacific Exhibition back in 1915. With its classical columns and its reflecting lagoon, the spot conjured both urban elegance and a hint of mystery. So he pulled into the Yacht Club parking lot, where he knew you could always get a spot at this time of the

11

morning.

When Mickey got out of his car, he was surprised that the noises carrying from down by the Palace seemed distinctly ominous and angry. Someone was giving harsh orders on a bullhorn. He heard a full-throated chorus of discontent — maybe actors and extras emoting, but he didn't think so.

Mostly, it sounded like a fight.

From the outskirts of the crowd, Mickey could make out at least three distinct groups, not including the vans from two of the local television stations.

The police, at least twenty of them, six of them mounted on horseback, held a line near the shoreline of the lagoon. The non-equestrian cops were turned out in "hats and bats" — full assault gear, helmets with tinted face masks, batons out. A larger, homogeneous, and clearly hostile group of maybe fifty citizens milled around on the sloping banks of the lagoon as if waiting for instructions to charge the police line. In front of them, a tall bearded guy in camo gear was right up in the face of the lead cop with the bullhorn. Finally, down by the water's edge, a smaller group of perhaps twenty people in the uniforms of the city's

Parks and Recreation Department huddled fearfully by a small fleet of rowboats laden with what looked like netting of some kind.

The camo guy started a chant, "Hell, no, don't let them go!" and in seconds the crowd was in full throat behind him, pressing forward toward the police line. The cops brought up their batons as the bullhorn exhorted the crowd to "Back away! Back away!"

"Hell, no, don't let them go!"

A white-haired man in a bathrobe and tennis shoes with his arms crossed and wearing a bemused expression stood on a lawn across the street. Mickey sidled up next to him. "What's going on?" he asked.

The man shook his head. "Idiots."

"Who?"

"All of 'em."

"But what's it about?"

The man looked over, askance. "You don't know about the ducks? Where you been?"

"What about the ducks?"

"They're moving 'em, or trying to." He shook his head again. "Lunatics. Stupid idea, bad planning, insane timing. But what else do you expect nowadays, huh? You really don't know about this? Moving the ducks down to Foster City?"

"Ahh." So that's what this was. Mickey

13

had read all about it over the past few months, but hadn't realized that it was coming to a head so soon. Now the whole story came back to him.

The city had approved a $22 million restoration for the Palace and its grounds, and part of that project included buttressing the remainder of the shoreline of the lagoon, most of which was already bounded by a low rock-and-concrete wall. But the rest of the shoreline, closest in toward the Palace itself, had become degraded over time — in the past year alone, a couple of kids had fallen in when the banks had collapsed under them. It wasn't so much dangerous as it opened the city to possible litigation issues, and so the supervisors had given the plan the green light, and put up $7.5 million to get the project started. The rest would, somehow, be funded by private benefactors. And lo, it had come to pass.

But to do any of this work, first the lagoon had to be drained.

Enter the ducks. And the San Francisco Palace Duck Coalition. And a former Berkeley tree sitter who, for the present campaign, had adopted the nom de guerre of Eric Canard. Mickey only now came to recognize the man in his camo gear. Usually he did photo ops in a full duck suit.

The Palace ducks, of course, along with its swans, herons, seagulls, and other birds, called the lagoon home. And if the lagoon were drained, Canard had argued to the Board of Supervisors, they would become homeless. Temporarily, but truly. And in a city that prided itself on being a haven to the homeless, this was simply unacceptable.

So the supervisors, caving in — to wide-spread derision in the media and on the street — had set about finding a solution to the problem. In spite of the fact that San Francisco had several nice and completely serviceable ponds, those ponds had their own populations of ducks whose environments, Canard argued, would be compromised by the wholesale relocation of the Palace ducks to their own home waters. So, eventually, the decision was made to relocate the ducks to Foster City, a residential community with Venice-like canals, and few permanent resident ducks, twenty miles south down the Peninsula.

This would have been a workable, though of course still wildly foolish, idea except for one thing: Six months before, Foster City had encountered its own problem with its indigenous ground squirrel population. These animals were burrowing in the city's levees and destroying them, threatening

15

homes with the very real possibility of imminent flooding. In response to this crisis, Foster City had decided to poison the levee-dwelling critters en masse. This slaughter passed largely unnoticed in Foster City itself, but did not escape the keen eye of Eric Canard. And when San Francisco announced its intention to remove its Palace ducks to Foster City, Canard had gone ballistic.

Surely, if the ducks were sent to Foster City, the heartless bureaucrats there would not treasure and protect them. These people had shown their true colors around the plight of defenseless animals and would obviously treat the ducks as they had treated their own squirrels if given half a chance. And Canard was not going to let that happen.

So he'd sued. And lost.

And had threatened to sue again. Which gave the city a window in which to make its move.

Across the street, the chant was wearing down, but Mickey could still hear a strong voice — undoubtedly Canard — yelling now at the lead cop.

"So how'd this start today?" Mickey asked the old man. "I thought it was still in the courts."

"No. The brains down at City Hall decided they'd just go ahead and round up the birds. The whole thing is nuts. And it's all moot anyway. They started draining the lake a couple of days ago before they were ready for the ducks — in secret, I might add, and that's never a good idea — so word got out to Canard and his people that something was happening down here, and the whack jobs started gathering before sunrise this morning. Uh-oh."

Off in the distance, the sound of sirens, police reinforcements on the way. Another news van pulled in, screeching to a stop.

The way this thing was developing, Mickey thought the story had a good chance to go national.

But Mickey had to get home, cleaned up, and to work. So he thanked the older man for his company, said good-bye, and crossed the street about a half block north of the crowd. Turning right, still hugging the shoreline, he followed it around to where it veered away from the view of the crowd.

Here the lower water level of the lagoon was much more obvious than it was up by the demonstration. The clumpy roots of the cattails shone black with the gunky bottom mud in the morning light. The low-hanging tree branches, which normally kissed the water's surface, now looked trimmed off a foot and a half or so above the waterline. An asphalt pathway came down to the water's edge off the parking lot, and Mickey took it as the shortcut back to where he'd parked.

But he hadn't gone more than a couple of steps when one of the tree roots sticking up from the brackish water stopped him in his tracks. It was funny the way these things growing wild in nature could so closely resemble shapes you'd expect to find in other species, in animals, even in people. Those roots, emerging from the water, could easily, he thought, be the hand of a man.

In fact, it seemed so near a resemblance that he forced himself to step off the pathway and look closer. He came right down now to the water's edge, where from this vantage he could dimly make out, six or eight inches under the water, an all-too-recognizable shape.

As Mickey stared in dawning belief, suddenly the water seemed to move and a trail of bubbles rose out from underneath the submerged form, turning it over and raising what was now clearly a body until its head broke the water's surface and the dead

18

man's eyeless face stared up at him, caught
and silenced in midscream.

2

At ten minutes past noon, Mickey walked up the single flight of stairs that led from the Grant Street entrance, in the heart of Chinatown, to the front door of his workplace, a private investigations firm called the Hunt Club.

Although the word *firm* was a bit of a misnomer, especially lately.

Six months before, the business had been successfully humming along in pretty much the same circumstances it had enjoyed for the first six and a half years of its existence. At that time, the owner — Wyatt Hunt — didn't seem to have too much trouble keeping himself and his two-and-a-half-person staff busy most of the time, working primarily for several of the city's well-heeled law firms.

Mickey's sister, Tamara, had held down the front-desk duties and often did light field- and interrogation work, especially when women witnesses or children were involved. A junior associate — Tamara's old boyfriend Craig Chiurco — had done the lion's share of the legwork locating witnesses, serving subpoenas, accompanying clients to depositions, and performing the other standard grunt work that made up the business.

Mickey, in addition to occasional subpoena service to the Hunt Club, had mostly driven a cab for a living, but was pretty much on call full-time to supply transportation to Wyatt or Craig should they need it, as they often did. In a city where parking was always so problematic, access to immediate transportation turned out to be a highly valued and oft-used service.

Wyatt Hunt himself was the computer whiz and the basic brains behind the organization. A natural-born marketer, Hunt also pulled in the actual jobs that kept everyone busy.

Until recently anyway. When bad luck, withering publicity over one huge failed case, a faltering economy, and possibly some questionable judgment had created a perfect storm that was threatening to shipwreck the enterprise.

Tamara had simply walked away from her job and had fallen into a profound funk from which she'd still not emerged. And with the exception of piecemeal work with the law firm Freeman, Farrell, Hardy & Roake, where Hunt had several close friends and one girlfriend — the business had all but evaporated.

Mickey, though, had not only stayed on with Hunt, he'd given up his more lucrative daily work in the cab business, quit most of his cooking classes, and taken over his sister's position at the front desk. He did this because Wyatt Hunt was not just a good boss. Hunt had literally saved the lives of both Mickey and Tamara when they'd been children.

So Mickey wasn't going to abandon Hunt. He'd stick it out until the job dried up and blew away. Or until it resurrected itself. Either way, Mickey was on board for the duration. He was still young, just twenty-seven. His own plans — to become a chef and open a world-class restaurant — could wait, since, like most American men his age, he was going to live forever.

Mickey the dutiful had, of course, called from the Marina three hours ago at the minute he'd realized he was going to be late for work, and had told the answering machine some of the story, but he'd of necessity left out a lot of it.

His discovery of the body had stolen the thunder from the demonstration. As soon as he'd run over and contacted one of the policemen on the scene, the television vans and a good portion of the crowd had swarmed to the other end of the lagoon to see the corpse in the water.

Now he let himself in to the Hunt Club's two-room office. A chair scraped in the back, and Wyatt Hunt appeared in the adjoining door on his right, just beyond the receptionist's desk. Tall and casually buffed, Hunt was dressed in slacks, a blue shirt, and darker blue tie. His sport coat, Mickey knew, would be hanging over his chair in his office in the back. "Just in time," Hunt said.

"For what? Tell me we've got some work."

"I'll play your silly game. We've got some work."

Mickey pumped a fist. "All right. You going out?"

"I am."

"Where to?"

"Lunch at Le Central."

Mickey whistled. Le Central was a white-tablecloth French restaurant down around the corner on Bush Street. This potentially meant that Wyatt had scored some deep-pockets client who would be footing the bill.

"Who's the client?" Mickey asked.

"Ah, the client. What client?"

"The one we're talking about."

"I'm afraid there is no client."

"So where's the work coming from?"

"What work?"

"The work you just said we had."

Hunt leaned against Mickey's desk and shrugged his shoulders. "Actually, truth be told, we don't have any work."

"But —"

"Hey. You told me to tell you we had some work, so I played along. In fact, though, I'm afraid we don't have any paying work." He turned a palm up. "At this stage, we'd better be able to joke about it, don't you think? And the good news is that I'm really going to have lunch at Le Central and was waiting for you. You eaten yet?"

"Not today. Other days, though, I have."

Hunt broke a grin. "Good for you. So I won't have to teach you how." He looked around the small space with a wistful air, as though he might not see it again. "Let's lock up and get ourselves on the outside of some grub."

Le Central had a notice on its daily-updated blackboard informing its patrons that its famous and delicious cassoulet had been

24

cooking now for 12,345 consecutive days. In spite of that, both Wyatt and Mickey agreed that it was too warm a day for the rib-sticking beans, duck, sausage, and lamb casserole, and instead both ordered the *poulet frites* — half a roasted chicken with fries. As an afterthought, Wyatt also ordered a bottle of white wine, by no means a common occurrence at lunchtime. When Mickey raised his eyebrows in surprise, he said, "Special occasion. You mind?"

"Not if you don't mind me falling asleep at the desk this afternoon," Mickey said. "But if you're okay with that, I'll force down a glass or two."

"That's the spirit."

"What's the special occasion?"

"Well, let's wait for the wine. Meanwhile, tell me about this morning. You actually discovered the body?"

Mickey launched into a truncated version of the day's events. The dead man, according to identification in his wallet, was Dominic Como, a prominent civic activist who'd gone missing about four days before. Even more startling, and depressing, from Mickey's perspective, was the fact that his grandfather, Jim Parr, had worked for Como as his personal driver. The dead man had been one of Jim's personal heroes. So now, if and

25

when he went home tonight, Mickey would be sharing his one-bedroom, nine-hundred-square-foot walkup with a grieving grandfather and a train wreck of a sister.

The waiter appeared with their wine. Hunt tasted it, pronounced it fine, and then waited for their glasses to be filled before he lifted his. "Here's to new beginnings."

"New beginnings," Mickey repeated. He hesitated, his glass poised in front of his mouth. "Why does that sound ominous?"

Hunt put down his untouched wine. "I've pretty much decided to close up the shop. Let you move on to your chef's career."

"What about you?"

"I'll be all right. Probably just hook up with one of the other outfits in town. Either that, or get a real job someplace. All these computer and marketing skills I've gotten good at ought to be worth something to somebody, I figure. Maybe a start-up."

"But you don't want to do that."

"Well, sometimes you don't get to do what you want. You, for example, don't really want to be a receptionist and gofer."

"That's not the same thing."

"Why not?"

"I'm a lot younger than you is one reason."

Hunt almost chuckled. "Forty-five isn't exactly one foot in the grave, Mick. People have been known to start over at that age. Goethe wrote *Faust* when he was eighty, so maybe there's still some hope for me."

"That's not it. It's not just the age. You love what you do."

"I sure as hell don't love sitting around the office waiting for the phone to ring."

"But when there's work . . ."

"Granted. It's a good gig. I'm not arguing. I like it a lot when it's working." He lifted his hands an inch off the table. "But you know what it's been like. I don't see how it's going to turn around. So I thought I'd give you a few weeks' notice — I'll keep you on the exorbitant payroll until I shut the doors for good, but I thought you deserved to know as soon as I made up my mind, and I pretty much have."

"Pretty much, or definitely?"

"Well, pretty definitely, unless something drastic happens. And I also wanted to tell you how much I've appreciated what you've done for me over these past months. But I can't ask you to hold on any longer when I don't really see any future in it."

Mickey finally noticed his wineglass. He picked it up and drank off a good swallow. "So what's the timeline?"

"Well, the lease for the office goes another two months from now and I've got to give a month's notice. So I guess it's formal in about thirty days, give or take."

"Unless something comes up to turn things around."

"I wouldn't hold my breath, Mick. I really don't see what could make a difference at this point."

Something jangled near Mickey's head and he swatted at the offending noise that had jarred him so violently from his afternoon sleep. The phone hit the floor in front of his desk and the receiver bounced across the hardwood.

Mickey jumped up out of his chair, yelling, "Coming. Sorry. Just a second." He came around the desk, grabbed the receiver, and, breathing heavily, managed to say he was sorry again before he realized where he was and said, "Hunt Club. Mickey speaking."

A man's voice. "Everything all right there?"

"Yeah. I just knocked the phone onto the floor. How can I help you?"

"You're Mickey, you said?"

"Yeah."

"Okay, hold on a minute. I've got somebody who wants to talk to you."

Mickey waited, then heard his grandfather's voice. "Hey, Mick, is that you?"

"Jim?"

"Yeah. Me."

"What's up? How you doin'?"

"Well . . . a little fucked up."

"Where are you?"

"The Shamrock."

"Are you okay?"

"Good. I'm good. But I'm going to need a lift home here pretty soon."

Mickey looked at his watch and let out a sigh. "Jim, it's only four o'clock. I'm at work at least another hour."

"I don't think Mose would let me drink for another hour."

"Who's Mose?"

"Bartender here. S'good guy." Slurring.

"How about you just have water or something? Would he serve you water?"

"I don't drink water. The things fish do in water. You don't want to know. Maybe he'd give me one more drink?" Sounding like he was making the suggestion to someone in front of him. "Maybe not, though. No." Back to Mickey. "He's shaking his head. Hold on just a second. Here he is again. Tell him I'll drink slow."

But the first man's voice came back on. "This is Moses McGuire. You know where the Shamrock is? Maybe you want to get

29

down here and pick up your old man. I don't know if I want to let him out of here by himself in the condition he's in."

"He's my grandfather," Mickey said.

"Whatever." McGuire lowered his voice. "Look, if he wouldn't have remembered your number just now, I would have had to call a cab, but he said he didn't want to take a cab, so I asked him how'd he feel about the cops, and I sure as hell don't want to do that. Meanwhile, I got a business to run. He's eighty-sixed here and you need to come down and get him right now. How old is he?"

"I don't know exactly. Seventy-four, I think, somewhere in there."

"That's too old for the drunk tank. You've got to come get him."

Swearing to himself, by now completely awake, Mickey said, "All right. Put him on again, would you?" And then, after a short pause, "Jim. God damn it. I'm going to call Tam first. You just wait. Maybe she'll beat me there and can walk you home."

"She's not home."

"Where is she?"

"I don't know. She went out."

"Well, I'll try her anyway. Meanwhile, you wait. Just sit there and have a club soda. Fish avoid club soda like the plague. The

30

bubbles make 'em fart."

Twenty minutes later, after double-parking around the corner, Mickey pushed his way through the door of the Little Shamrock, Jim's local hangout.

One of the oldest bars in the city, founded in 1893, the Little Shamrock started out very narrow up by the front door. A couple of large picture windows facing Lincoln Boulevard let in some natural light. A bar with a dozen or so stools ran down the left side of the room, and on the right, in front, an eclectic selection of memorabilia, including an antique bicycle, black-and-white photos, old election posters, and a grandfather clock that had stopped during the Great Earthquake of 1906 hung on the wall. Halfway back, the place opened up slightly to accommodate dart players and a jukebox, and in the very back, under the faux Tiffany lamps, the room took on the look of a dilapidated old living room, with a couple of sagging couches facing a cluster of overstuffed easy chairs.

Jim Parr sat at the far end of the crowded bar with an empty glass in front of him. Maybe the bartender had coaxed him into something nonalcoholic after all. Jim was staring at the television set. His cheeks were

31

wet. Excusing his way through the press, Mickey got back next to him and put a hand on his grandfather's shoulder, gathering him in a half hug. He kissed him on the top of his cue-ball head. "Hey."

Jim leaned into him for a second, then pulled away, grabbed the bar napkin, and wiped at his eyes. "How'd you get here so fast?"

"I ignored the speed limit. And I'm double-parked. You think you can walk?"

" 'Course. I could walk home if I needed to."

"Well, luckily you don't need to. You paid up here?"

"Paid as I went. Only way to live."

"So I've heard. Like a million times. Okay. Let's go."

The old man got his feet onto the floor and straightened up, leaning into Mickey. The bartender saw what was happening and gave Mickey an approving nod. He mouthed a silent thank-you.

Parr managed to keep upright as the two of them negotiated their way out of the bar and out onto the sidewalk. It was still a clear, warm day, and the sun was in their eyes as they made their way to the car. After Mickey poured Parr into the front seat, he went around and got in.

"This about Dominic Como?" he asked.

His grandfather, head back against the seat with his eyes closed, turned toward Mickey and another tear broke. "I loved that guy," he said.

Mickey facilitated his parking around the city by the judicious use of a handicap placard that he kept in his glove compartment and that he could put onto his dashboard whenever he needed it. His grandfather had given him this surprisingly valuable little blue item. In theory, only handicapped individuals had access to them, and there was nothing handicapped about Jim Parr.

And there had been nothing handicapped about Dominic Como, either, for that matter.

But Como nevertheless had always possessed a handicapped card for those special occasions when nothing else would do. When Parr had retired eight years ago, Como gave him one as a present. Como could get things that other people didn't seem to have access to. It had been one of his talents, and access to those things was one of the perks of Parr's old job.

So parking wasn't its usual awful and automatic hassle. Today Mickey pulled up into a spot by the emergency entrance to the UC Medical Center, only a couple of blocks from their apartment. By this time, Jim was snoring.

Fifteen minutes later, the old man was in his bed, still dressed except for his shoes, and with the covers pulled up around him. Mickey closed the bedroom door and, sweating from having basically carried Jim up to the second floor where they lived, he took a dispirited glance around the cluttered living room: Tamara's Murphy bed pulled down from the wall and unmade. Newspapers from several days scattered around. Coffee mugs on just about every flat surface.

He straightened up, and when he'd finished, he opened the door to his own bedroom, essentially a large closet with a window facing the wall of the apartment behind them. Here was his bed, a board-and-cinder-block bookcase, a small dresser/desk combo unit, a few prints on the walls.

But he didn't go into his room. Dead in his tracks, he stopped in its doorway. No wonder he fled from this place as often as he could.

This was no way to live.

The death of Dominic Como, now confirmed as a murder, led off the five o'clock news. The cause, as Mickey had suspected, was not drowning, but rather someone had hit him with a blunt object on the back of the head. Como had already been missing for four days by the time he was found partially submerged in the lagoon at the Palace of Fine Arts by . . .

Mickey, sitting in front of his television, came forward in mild shock as his own image appeared on the screen as part of the big story of the day. He had talked to several reporters that morning at the scene, of course, but never really believed that they'd run with any of the footage of him, since his own role in the larger story was at best only a footnote. But there he was on TV, describing how he'd come upon the body. He thought this was pretty cool in spite of how young he looked, and how disheveled, which he suddenly realized was what sleeping out under trees could do to you.

But when they identified Mickey as "an associate with the Hunt Club, a private investigating firm," it occurred to him that maybe his unshaven mug and slept-in clothing weren't the best advertisements in the world. That realization brought him up short — the idea that he might actually be a liability of some kind for Wyatt's business.

35

Maybe while he was cleaning up his apartment and his physical surroundings, he thought it wouldn't be such a bad idea to work on his own hygiene and appearance.

But then his image left the screen and Channel Four's perky anchorwoman was going on with more about the crime and the victim. Because of his grandfather's longstanding job as Como's driver, Mickey knew a lot about him, but he hadn't ever really focused on the breadth of his charitable work. Now he learned that Como had either founded or sat on the boards of no fewer than six major charities in San Francisco — the Sunset Youth Project (of which he was executive director), Braceros Unidos, the Mission Street Coalition, the Rainbow Workshops, the Sanctuary House for Battered Women, and Halfway Home.

The police investigation was continuing, but so far there were no suspects.

3

Cleanly shaven and showered, in slacks, a button-down dress shirt under a Mountain Hardware jacket, and tennis shoes, Mickey walked down to Golden Gate Park, then, in another quarter mile or so, found himself at the de Young Museum.

Off to his right loomed one of his favorite recent additions to the city's landscape. Adjacent to the museum, a strange-looking tower thrust itself nine stories up into the now-darkening sky. The exterior of the tower looked to be made of metallic panels — copper? — into which the builder had punched various imperfections, from bumps to indentations to holes. More unexpectedly, especially upon the first viewing, the tower twisted as it went up. What started as a rectangle at the base shifted as it rose until at the top it was a gravity-defying parallelogram. From the top — an enclosed viewing platform — Mickey had been pleased to recognize that the bottom of the tower was aligned with the east-west grid of the park, while the top's orientation was turned to match the grid of the city's downtown streets.

Inside now, he stopped a minute to listen to the jazz quintet playing in the lobby — a Friday-night tradition — then took the elevators up to the top. No charge. He'd been up here no fewer than forty times, and every time the place worked its magic on him. The windows were huge, both wide and tall, and through them the entire city revealed itself beneath and all around him. And since, because of the tower's twisting nature, it wasn't really obvious that there actually was a physical building under him, it always felt like he was floating.

The sun had just disappeared into the ocean and the purple western sky was now ablaze with gorgeous orange-red clouds. The Golden Gate Bridge was *right there,* just off to his right. And back behind him, the high-rises of downtown had just started to twinkle with their evening lights.

But tonight he wasn't here for the views. Because of its parallelogram shape, the floor came to a point on both the north and south ends. Mickey looked left and then made his way to the corner, where, as he'd suspected and hoped, his sister — in a cowl-necked sweatshirt and camo pants — sat on the floor, apparently mesmerized, hugging her knees.

"They just let you sit here all day?" he asked.

She looked up and shrugged. "I'm not bothering anybody."

Mickey went down on one knee. "Were you planning to come home sometime?"

"Sure."

"When?"

"Eventually."

"Good. Just so I know not to rent out your space." He paused. "Oh, and in case you were wondering, Jim's all right."

Now her head did turn toward him, quickly, in surprise. "Why wouldn't he be?"

"No reason. He's fine. Really. I mean, after I got him home."

"He went out? Where'd he go?"

"Shamrock. Then to drink-a-bye land."

"Why did he do that?"

"Maybe he wanted somebody to talk to. Maybe his roommate didn't tell him she was going out, and he didn't want to be alone."

"I don't have to tell him where I'm going, or what I'm doing. Or you either."

"Absolutely correct. I couldn't agree more. You're an adult. We're all adults."

"You don't tell us where you go most nights."

"That's true. I probably should do that. I may start now. Or I might start staying at home again." He changed his tone. "Jim's getting older, you know."

Her mouth turned down. "And your point is?"

"My point is he's getting too old to go out on his own and drink too much. The bartender said he might have had to call the cops if he hadn't reached me."

"Lucky he did, then."

Mickey let out a long breath and stared out over his sister's head at the last vestiges of the sunset. "I'd have thought you might relate to how he was feeling."

"About what?"

"About Dominic Como being dead."

She turned up and stared at him. "When did that happen?"

"Recently."

"And I'm supposed to relate to how Jim's feeling about that because . . . ?"

"Because Dominic was somebody he'd spent years of his life with? Kind of like you and Craig." This was Craig Chiurco, formerly of the Hunt Club.

At the mention of her former boyfriend, she blinked a few times in rapid succession.

40

A tear fell from her left eye and she wiped it away. Some of the tension seemed to go out of her shoulders. After another moment, she turned her head to face him. "What do you want, Mick?"

"I don't know, to tell you the truth. Maybe talk to you a little. Have you eaten yet today?"

Tamara's mouth softened, almost into a smile. "Food. Always food."

"Not always, but often. I figure it can't hurt."

"Probably not." She sighed. "And, no, I haven't eaten."

"All day?"

"Some cereal when I got up."

He gestured toward the city spread out below them. "Had enough of this view for today?"

"I suppose so."

Giving her shoulder a small, friendly, brotherly push, he said, "Let's go."

"So how much?"

"How much what?"

"How much weight have you lost?"

"I don't know exactly. Maybe ten pounds."

"More than that, I think. And you weigh yourself every day, Tam, so you know exactly, or pretty damn close. Don't scam a

41

scammer. How much?"

"Okay." She looked across the table at him. "Say eighteen."

"Eighteen pounds in six months?"

"Maybe twenty."

"That's way too much. Especially since you started at basically perfect."

"Not perfect enough, evidently." She tried a smile, but it didn't take. "I just don't have an appetite anymore, Mick. I try, but nothing tastes like anything."

"The pot stickers here will knock you out."

She shrugged. "Maybe. We'll see. It's not like I'm trying not to eat. It's just I don't think of it."

"Well, you need to." Mickey slurped at his cup of very hot tea. "I don't like to see you getting this thin, Tam. It reminds me of Mom."

Tamara's teacup stopped halfway to her mouth. "I'm not like Mom. Mom was on drugs. She overdosed."

"Yeah, but before that she didn't eat well either. And now, seeing you, you look a little like she did. And it brings it back clear as a bell. And that scares me."

"Mickey, I'm not going to die."

"Yeah, you are. But I'd prefer if it wasn't like soon. Otherwise, what's it all been for?"

"What's all what been for?"

"I mean, you know, Wyatt saving us. Jim getting his life together to raise us."

She pushed her cup around on the table. "Sometimes I think it wasn't for anything. It was just stuff that happened. And now we're all here and so what? Jim's probably going to die pretty soon. Wyatt's going out of business. Everything's a dead end."

Mickey put his own cup down. "Craig was that important to you? He's gone and now you've got nothing to live for?"

She shook her head. "It's not just him being gone. It doesn't even seem like it's so much him personally anymore. It's more the idea that I lived with this, this *illusion,* for all that time, thinking I was going somewhere, that he and I were going somewhere, and that all of it mattered." She leaned in across from him. "I mean, Mick, it all made sense. It hung together. I'm talking about the world."

"And now it doesn't?"

"I can't seem to find where my real life connects back in to it."

"You think you're going to find it sitting up in the tower?"

"I don't know where I'm going to find it."

"So you've given up looking? That's kind of what it seems like from here."

"Well, that's not it."

43

"No?"

Anger flashed in her eyes. "No!" Then, in a softer tone, "I am really trying not to lose it altogether here, Mickey. I don't think you can really understand what it's like when the rug's pulled out from under you like it was from me."

"Yeah," Mickey said. "I can. It got pulled out from both of us another time. And that was a lot worse than you losing your boy-friend. I remember it pretty well."

"What's your point?"

"My point is you're too young to give up. There's people out here in the real world who care about you — me, for instance, and Jim, and even Wyatt — and maybe you owe it to all of us to try to care a little back in return."

"I do care about all of you guys."

"You do? How are we supposed to tell? You quit working for Wyatt, you dump your job there on me, you disappear on Jim —"

"I didn't —"

"You did, Tam. Yes, you did. And we all felt bad for you, and still do." He reached a hand over the table and touched hers. "But you've got to come back now. You've got to start, anyway. Remember back before Jim even took us on, we swore we'd always call each other on it if we started down a wrong

44

road? Remember that?"

"Yeah, okay. Of course."

"Well, this is your brother calling you. You need to get out of this now, start going another way. Jim's going to need you these next weeks at least. I'm going to need you for him. Maybe even Wyatt will wind up needing you."

"Wyatt won't ever need me. He never did. And now he's mad at me."

"He's never said one word about being mad at you. If anything, he's worried. But not even slightly mad. He blames himself, is what I think. For hiring Craig in the first place, for keeping him on, for you guys getting together."

Tamara looked up at the ceiling and seemed to be gathering herself. She inhaled deeply and let the breath out in a long sigh.

The waitress appeared and placed a small dish in front of each of them, then a plate of six pot stickers down between them. "Kung pao shrimp coming right up next," she said.

Mickey picked a pot sticker up with his chopsticks and put it on the dish in front of his sister. "If you eat, you'll feel better," he said. "Promise."

45

4

Saturdays, Mickey went to his cooking class at La Cuisine, located in a large Victorian house on Webster Street between Clay and Sacramento. He was already halfway through his six-week Professional Series course — "Knives and Butchering," his eighth formal class in the past three years. At his present rate, he could expect to get his Certified Culinarian ticket, the lowest professional ranking, and possibly get hired to cut onions or sift flour for eight hours a day, in only another two or three years.

But it was working toward something that he loved. By the time he was thirty, if everything worked out, he'd be working in a kitchen; at forty he'd have his own place. Maybe a small one, but his own.

It was a timeline he could live with.

His class began at the stroke of eight o'clock, and if you were late, you weren't admitted. No excuses tolerated, even if you'd paid your entire tuition up front, even if you couldn't find a parking place, your uncle died, all of the above. Marc Bollet, the *maître,* locked the front door at show-time sharp, and didn't unlock it again for five hours. "You want the experience of working in a professional kitchen?" Marc said more than once in his still-pronounced French accent. "You must learn never, ever to be late. Never to be sick. Don't plan on too many days off, or vacations. *La cuisine* is not a career. It is a vocation, a sacred thing. Never be less than at your very best. Or you will find yourself without a job. Because there is always, always, someone who wants your chance."

Now Mickey, a full twenty-five minutes before class was to begin, courtesy of the best parking spot he'd ever found, got to the stoop with his cup of Starbucks and was somewhat surprised to see that, even this early, he wasn't the first of his classmates to arrive. Ian Thorpe looked up with an easy, crinkling, blue-eyed smile under a wispy blond mustache. He wore chef's clogs, a pair of stained khaki shorts, and a blue fisherman's sweater with white horizontal stripes. "Hey," he said. "I was hoping I'd catch you before class."

"Me? You caught me. What's up?"

"I saw you on the tube last night."

Mickey broke a small smile. "Me too," he said. "But only four times. After that it got boring."

"They identified you as a private investigator."

"I know, but they didn't get that part exactly right. I just work in the office, more or less the grunt. Answer phones, get the coffee, like that."

"Damn."

"What?"

Thorpe blew out. His eyes scanned the street behind Mickey for a moment. "Nothing, really. I was hoping maybe . . . well, maybe you could talk to your bosses. . . ."

"Boss. Singular. Wyatt Hunt. The Hunt Club. You need a private eye?"

"I don't know what I need, to tell you the truth, but somebody like your boss might be a good place to start. I need somebody who knows something about the law and how it works and who isn't a cop. And it's not for me. It's my sister. She worked for Dominic Como."

"She did? What'd she do?"

"She was his driver."

Mickey's mouth all but hung open. "You're kidding me?"

48

"No. Why do you say that?"

" 'Cause that's what my grandfather did for him too."

But just at this moment, another pair of their classmates showed up at the corner. "Maybe we can talk a little after class?" Thorpe said. "You be up for that?"

Mickey shrugged. "Sure," he said. "Why not?"

After class, back at the nearest Starbucks, Mickey removed the plastic top from his cup, blew over the coffee, and took a sip. "So," he said, "your sister."

Thorpe nodded. "Alicia."

"Younger?"

"Three years. She's twenty-five. Maybe I care about her so much because she's my only family, actually."

Mickey put down his cup. "I've got a sister who's pretty much my only family, too, except for a grandfather." He didn't see any reason to include his boss, Wyatt Hunt, an adopted foster child himself, who, on his own time, back when he'd been working for the city's Child Protective Services, had tracked down Jim Parr and convinced him to meet with his all-but-forgotten and abandoned grandchildren, a meeting that had eventually led to Jim's job as Dominic

Como's driver and then Jim's adoption of Mickey and Tamara less than a year later. Mickey went on. "Anyway, my dad disappeared for good when I was like two. My mom overdosed when I was seven. Heroin."

"Heroin," Thorpe said. "I hate that shit, and you're talking to one who knows." He lifted his eyes, his voice suddenly flat. "My dad shot my mother and then killed himself when I was twelve. It wasn't much fun."

"No. Doesn't sound like it." Mickey took a beat, let out a short breath. "That's a worse story than mine, or damn close. And I don't hear them too often. And now we're both training to be chefs. Somebody should do a study. Orphans and chefs."

"We want to cook for people 'cause there was nobody to cook for us."

"Good theory. So you guys didn't have other family?"

"One aunt in Texas. An uncle in Florida. Neither interested."

"So how'd you and your sister stay connected?" Mickey asked.

"Alicia, mostly, not giving up. We both bounced around a lot. Foster homes, you know? You too?"

Mickey shook his head. "We didn't have that. My grandfather — the one who drove for Como — showed up and took us in.

Saved us, no doubt. Maybe himself in the bargain."

"Well, Alicia and me, we got split up and farmed out to different families. I got into some bad behavior mixed with drugs and wound up at the youth work farm till I was seventeen. Alicia, she moved in with three or four different families, but she had some issues of her own — guys, mostly — and none of the family units took. But somehow she kept up on me, where I was, and finally talked me into the Sunset Youth Project."

Mickey nodded. "One of Como's charities."

"Right. Actually, the main one. So, anyway, between that place and Alicia keeping me honest, I eventually straightened out, got back into school, and then even college. A miracle, really."

"But now you say your sister needs a private eye around Dominic's death?"

Thorpe nodded. "She volunteered out at Sunset and got pretty close to him in the last few months. The cops came by and talked to her yesterday. She got the impression that she was some kind of a suspect."

Mickey sat with that for a moment. At last, he picked up his coffee and sipped at it. "How close was pretty close?"

"I don't know, not for sure."

51

"But what would you guess?"

Thorpe made a face, then shrugged. "I'd say it wouldn't be impossible that they were having an affair, though Alicia's always said she'd never go out again with a married guy."

"Again?"

"I told you, guys were always her problem. She's kind of pretty, and then of course having her father kill himself, she's got a few issues of abandonment and self-esteem. Wants to prove she's attractive to men. You'd think after the first fifty, the issue would kind of go away. But in Dominic's case, I didn't ask, and she didn't say. She did tell me, though, that she didn't kill him."

"You asked?"

He nodded. "Directly. I wanted to know what we were dealing with."

"And you believe her?"

"Absolutely. She wouldn't ever lie to me. I'm sure of that."

"Okay."

"Plus, you should see her. When it finally came out he was actually dead and not just missing, after you found him in the lagoon . . . I mean, she's been crying full-time ever since."

Even with his limited experience of criminal matters, Mickey had learned that crying

52

wasn't a guarantee of innocence or of much else. Wyatt Hunt had told him that most people who kill someone close to them spend at least some time afterward crying about it for one reason or another — genuine remorse for what they'd done, or self-pity for the predicament in which they'd put themselves. "So what would you want a private investigator to do for you?" Mickey asked.

"I'm not sure, to tell you the truth. I only thought of the possibility of it when I saw you on the tube and they said that's what you were. I know it's not much of a connection, you and me. But I thought you might be cheaper than a lawyer."

That drew a quick laugh. "That's true enough. Most of the time, we work for lawyers. That's basically the gig. So you're right, we'd be cheaper. Although we're probably not going to be what she needs."

"Well, I thought that at least you weren't a cop out to get her. I thought maybe you could find out the truth."

"Often not so easy. But you should know that the cops aren't going to be out to get her unless there's some evidence that points to her. And then after that, the truth might not be what you want to hear, in spite of what she's told you, or didn't tell you."

"I realize that. But I feel like I . . . I mean we talked about it, and both of us feel like we ought to do something. We can't just sit and let the cops build a case around her. Especially since it was somebody else."

Mickey's mouth broke into a smile. "So basically you'd want us to find out who killed him?"

"Or just eliminate Alicia as a suspect."

"Well, if she's really a suspect, what you really need is a lawyer."

"Except that's a problem too."

"Why?"

"Money." Thorpe came forward, elbows on the table. "I mean, we've got maybe a thousand or so between us, but that's at the outside. It would pretty much tap us both out."

Mickey sat back and turned his cup slowly on the tabletop. "Actually," he said at last, "if that's all the money you have, it's good news in a way."

"How's that?"

"You can't afford even the cheapest lawyer. And no reputable investigator would even start this kind of open-ended job for that kind of money. So you don't have to lose any of it. And if somebody — lawyer or investigator — offers to take you on with that little as a retainer, you know you're

54

dealing with a shyster."

Thorpe's shoulders fell.

"Another good-news moment," Mickey continued. "If Alicia does get charged, the court will appoint a lawyer for her for free. You know that, right?"

But Thorpe shook his head. "Her getting charged wouldn't be good news, no matter what. I spent some time in custody when I was younger. I think real jail might actually kill her. We can't let it get to that. She didn't kill Dominic, I promise you."

Mickey spread his hands in an apologetic gesture. "In that case, I doubt they'll get anywhere near an arrest. But I don't —" Suddenly he stopped as the germ of an idea occurred to him.

Dominic Como was a recent, high-profile murder. San Francisco's large and generous philanthropic community, and in fact many of the charities with which Como had been actively involved, could be expected to have a vested interest in apprehending his killer. But in general, precisely these very people had a deep-seated mistrust, if not actual hatred, of police and law enforcement in general. In this, the most left-wing big city in the country, better the murder of one of their own should go unsolved than that they should cooperate with the Man. Police, and probably the mayor herself, would be seeking a speedy resolution to the Como case, and at least an arrest. But a lot of the people who might know the most would be the least likely to talk to the cops.

What if, Mickey wondered, the Hunt Club could act as the clearinghouse between the people with information, the police who needed the information, and the institutions that had the cash that would be willing to pay for the information? What if he could pitch the idea of a "people's reward" for information related to Como's death?

This could in theory serve a host of purposes: It might provide valuable tips for the police; it would involve the wider community in the investigation; it could, of course, most importantly motivate an otherwise reluctant witness to come forward. On a more personal note, the Hunt Club could stay open servicing the reward hotline. If the reward was a significant dollar number, many a lunatic would also be contacting the charities who'd offered the money with spurious and/or just plain stupid or wrong information.

The Hunt Club might be of real value managing the flow of information to the police, forwarding any genuine leads, and gatekeeping against reports from the nutcase front. The process would save the cops perhaps hundreds of man-hours of unnecessary work winnowing out the wheat from the chaff.

This was work the charities would want done, but they would be ill-equipped to do it themselves, and he and Hunt could do it with their collective eyes closed. Mickey thought that there might be several prospective clients who could chip in to pay for the Hunt Club's services. Finding them would be a bit of a treasure hunt, but once Mickey did that, he might be able to give Hunt a couple of months' respite before being forced to go out of business.

The more he thought of it, the surer Mickey was that the money was out there; he just had to find it. And if they did the job right and met with success, it might even help to restore the reputation of the Hunt Club within the legal community. It could, in fact, be a new beginning for Hunt, and maybe even for Tamara. And Mickey, disposed to like Ian Thorpe because they shared such similar tastes and backgrounds, might even be able to set his and his sister's minds to rest.

All of this came to Mickey in a rush, his eyes glazing over. For those few seconds, he went still as a stone, until Thorpe tapped the table in front of him. "Mickey? You all right?"

He came back to himself with a small start, a fleeting smile. "You know," he said, "I can't really promise anything specific, but I don't see how it could hurt to talk to your sister, maybe give her a heads-up on how the next couple of weeks might go. If you think she'd talk to me."

"If I think she'd talk to you. Are you kidding me?"

Ian Thorpe already had his cell phone out. Was punching numbers.

5

Alicia Thorpe lived alone in the basement room of a gingerbread Victorian on upper Masonic, and although by now it was close to two o'clock in the afternoon, as she opened the door to her separate entrance around the back, it was clear that she hadn't really gotten herself moving for the day. It didn't take a trained investigator to see that she'd already spent some of the day crying, but the lack of any makeup and a blotchy complexion couldn't disguise the basic truth of Ian's description of her. She was, at the very least, kind of pretty. And obviously bra-less under a San Francisco Zoo T-shirt tucked into the slim waist of a pair of red-striped running shorts.

The day was warm, the sky clear blue, the air windless. A table with four chairs and a Cinzano umbrella graced the small brick patio area just outside her door, and after the introductions, the three of them gravitated there and sat down.

"So," Mickey began, "no cops so far today?"

"No."

"And how long did they talk to you yesterday?"

"About an hour. There were two of them, a man and a woman."

"Did you get their names?"

She shook her head no, but then said, "Wait," and suddenly jumped up, heading back to the house. She reemerged a few seconds later and handed Mickey two business cards.

"Well, this is pretty decent news," he said with a smile of genuine surprise.

"What?"

"I know these people. They're among the good ones. Devin Juhle is probably my boss's best friend."

"I don't see how that really helps," Alicia said.

"It helps because they'll probably talk to us off the record. They might be tempted to extend you a few courtesies, which normally isn't a big part of the arrest procedure. Every little bit helps. You'll see."

"I hope I don't see." Now her large eyes opened all the way — white showing around startling green irises — and she reached a hand over and touched his arm for a second. "So you think they're going to arrest me?"

Mickey backtracked. "No, no, no. I'm just saying it could be an advantage that we know the inspectors, that's all. And that they know us. It can't hurt."

Mickey didn't know that this was true. Certainly, if Alicia was the bona fide prime suspect, she had a good chance of finding herself in handcuffs the minute the homicide inspectors felt that they had a strong enough case to arrest her. And regardless of any personal relationship between Hunt and either of them, they would move swiftly to put her into custody.

On the other hand, Hunt had been known to play devil's advocate with Devin Juhle on other cases, which more than once had prevented Juhle from acting too quickly on his gut and arresting the wrong person. In one of Juhle's most recent homicide cases, though, *The People of the State of California v. Stuart Gorman,* Hunt's girlfriend, Gina, had crucified the inspector on the witness stand en route to getting her client acquitted, and this had severely strained the relationship between Juhle and Hunt. So the whole question of familiarity with the homicide pros was both nebulous and personal, but Mickey had seen times when it had worked to Hunt's advantage, and he'd like Alicia to believe that this could be the case now.

"Maybe it can't hurt knowing these guys," Ian said, "but it's kind of moot if Alicia's not going to be your client. So let's not get her hopes up."

"Why can't I be your client?" Alicia asked.

"There's a money issue," Mickey began, "but I've been thinking that over and maybe it's not insurmountable. I'd have to talk to Mr. Hunt and see what he says, but I think I see a way to investigate this thing on your behalf, which is what you both want, and get paid enough to make it doable, which is what we want."

"How would you manage that?" Ian asked.

Mickey temporized, since he wasn't yet exactly sure. "The first step is to hook up with some of the other charities Dominic was involved in, and see if any of them might want to chip in on a reward." Now he looked directly at Alicia. "Ian told me you'd gotten closely involved with him in the past several months. Is that true?"

She threw a quick glance at her brother, then came back to Mickey. "I was volunteering at the Sunset Youth Project. Getting involved in the process. I hope that's going to be my life's work."

"So you know these people? The people Dominic worked with?"

"Some better than others, but I'm familiar with most of them now, yes."

"So would you be willing to work with us if it turns out that this means we can help you out?"

She hesitated for only an instant, then met his eyes. "Whatever it takes," she said.

"All right," Mickey said. "Let me work out some of the details and run it by Mr. Hunt, see what he says."

Again, she put her hand on his arm. "Thank you," she said. "Thank you so much." Her eyes had gone glassy, perhaps a prelude to more tears. "I really didn't kill him," she said. "I cared about him a lot, okay? He was a great man, and maybe we were getting a little too close, but I really didn't kill him."

"I'm taking that as a given," he said. Mickey was also tempted to ask her what she meant by "a little too close," but if she became a client, there'd be time for all of those questions. He was far too aware, he realized, of how her hand felt resting on his arm, so he patted that hand in a professional manner, and pushed himself back from the table. Standing up, he took a business card out of his wallet and handed one to her and one to her brother. "If the cops come again, make me your one phone call and I'll at least be able to put you in touch with a good lawyer. Meanwhile, let me go see what I can do."

Wyatt Hunt's home was a unique environment incongruously existing in its light-industrial, south-of-Market 'hood. Less than three blocks away, San Francisco's Hall of Justice — a six-story blue-gray slab of concrete that would have been at home in East Berlin before the wall fell — set the tone for the surrounding area. The flat, dirty, perennially windswept streets weren't so much run-down or dangerous — like the Tenderloin district, for example — as simply depressing, and often deserted, especially now on a weekend.

Each street sported an abandoned store-front or two, some fast food, usually a bail bondsman's office, a Chinese dentist or acupuncturist, other businesses selling auto parts or advertising specialties or discount clothes. In every block you'd find a bar, or more often a venue that rented itself out as a club catering to a different clientele every night — Monday a hip-hop dance spot, Tuesday a lesbian pickup joint, then salsa after-hours, or karaoke on the Japanese tour circuit. Vagrants and changelings and explorers and the lost among the substrata of humanity that existed in the margins and mostly at night in one of the world's most glamorous and glittering cities.

In the midst of all this, in a former flower warehouse, Wyatt Hunt had created a kind of wonderland. Hunt had kept the original outer structure intact, so the first thing that hit you, if you entered by the door next to the garage entrance on the Brannan Street side, was the sheer volume of the space under the corrugated iron roof, perhaps twenty feet high, that spanned the building's nine thousand square feet.

Once inside, you'd probably next notice either Hunt's Mini Cooper parked by the garage door, or maybe it would be the NBA regulation half–basketball court he'd picked up for a song from the Warriors. When you crossed the court, you got to another play/work area filled with guitars and amps and desks with computers, and then you got to a door in a wall that ran from one side of the enormous room to the other.

Beyond that wall, Hunt had built his living area — bedroom, bathroom, library, den, kitchen — three thousand square feet. All white and pastel and modern, modern, modern. Lots of glass blocks in the wall to the alley out back, and above them high windows for natural light, the drywalled ceiling back here sloping down to fifteen feet or so.

Now, in natural light from the Brannan Street windows and the open garage door, Mickey was in a basketball game with Hunt, the sound of the bouncing ball and their grunts and the squeak of their shoes as they broke on the hardwood echoing off the non-insulated walls around them.

They were playing one-on-one, winner's outs, which gave Hunt a tremendous advantage since he was the far better player and, despite the age differential of over fifteen years, in better physical shape than Mickey. Winner's outs meant that every time someone made a basket, he got possession of the ball again at half-court. Early in the game, Mickey had scored four quick baskets, at one point each rather than two, but then Hunt had stolen the ball on him and put up an obscene twenty baskets in a row.

Mickey, by now feeling like a rag, dragged himself to center court just as Hunt brought the ball in, faked right, and broke left, a move that put Mickey ignominiously on his ass. Hunt then dribbled three times and laid up his game-winning twenty-first point with a triumphant shout. "Ha!"

■ ■ ■ ■

They were drinking lemonade, recovering their breath — Mickey rather more so than Hunt — sitting side by side on the stoop that led out from Hunt's kitchen to the alley behind his warehouse home.

"Twenty-one to four," Mickey managed to say between breaths. "How pathetic is that?"

"We should have done loser's outs. You would have had the ball more."

"Great. Remind me next time. If there ever is a next time, which right now I'm kind of doubting." Mickey chugged some lemonade, then rubbed the cold glass up against his forehead. "Why'd I let you talk me into this? I didn't come over here to get creamed in basketball."

"Yeah, but you got here and there I was, shooting hoops all alone. Talk about pathetic. You took pity on me, for which I'm grateful and in your debt."

"And because of that, you went easy on me, is that it?"

Hunt chuckled. "Perhaps not. That's not really my style. If I'm gonna play, I'm gonna beat you."

"I noticed. Congratulations. Mission accomplished."

Hunt nodded in acknowledgment.

"So in theory," Mickey added, "that means you still owe me, right?"

"Up to a point, in theory." Hunt sipped his drink. "You getting at something?"

"Not much except the reason I came by in the first place. You want to try to guess which cops pulled the Dominic Como case?"

Hunt sipped at his lemonade, wiped some sweat from his brow, then wiped his hands on his tank top. He looked up at the side of the graffiti-tagged building across the alley. "Okay, since you ask it that way, I'm deducing Devin's one of 'em. And Russo's his partner."

"You ought to do that stuff as a party trick. You know that?"

Hunt shrugged off the compliment, spread his palms. "Elementary, my dear Dade. But, if I may ask you, this is relevant to us because . . . ?"

"Because we might be able to talk to them."

"About Como? Why do we want to do that?"

Mickey took a breath and launched into an explanation of his strategy, about midway through which Hunt stopped him. "Wait a

68

minute. Nice idea, but the cops already have a unit to field reward calls."

"I know that. But the point is that we want the people who won't call the city, who won't call the cops."

Hunt said gently, "No offense, Mick, but that dog just don't hunt. And I mean that in the nicest possible way. We'd have to turn anything we get over to the cops anyway. So somebody calls us first, big deal. Eventually, they're talking to the police. We've got no privilege. We can't promise anonymity. We're just an extra phone call."

"Yeah, but the trick is to get 'em to call in the first place. Then we ease 'em into the process, which might not be too hard if it's a lot of money and they're not completely nuts. Maybe initially we don't ask for names. We can't disclose what we don't know. If it really looks like they've got something, we just explain that we'll have to give them up if they're going to get the reward. The whole point, Wyatt, is to get information from people who wouldn't normally give up anything at all. We can finesse the details later."

"So in your dreams, how much reward are we talking about?"

"I have no idea. Best case fifty, maybe a hundred thou, maybe more. I don't know how many hours we'll charge, but at least it would be work that could keep us solvent a while longer —"

"And how do we find these people who are going to offer a reward again?"

"Wyatt, c'mon, work with me here. I go by and talk to 'em. We create a groundswell movement among these people who are already so inclined. Como was large in half of these nonprofits, either as a consultant or an actual board member or director. He was the man. These people are going to line up to help find his killer."

Hunt got to his feet, paced across the alley, then turned around and leaned against the wall. He took a sip from his glass. "Has it occurred to you that the police might already be lined up to catch his killer too? And won't appreciate our involvement?"

"Well, that's where Juhle and Russo come in. We convince them of our value to their investigation."

"Assuming that Devin and Sarah are going to want to talk to me."

"I am assuming that."

"Well, sad to say, that's not too likely going to happen either." Hunt pushed off from the wall behind him. "I've tried to keep a low profile around this, but Dev and I kind of stopped hanging out together after Gina ate him on the stand on the Gorman case."

"Yeah, I remember. But didn't he eventually get the collar on the real killer in that one? Because of you and Gina?"

"He did."

"Well?"

"Well, I agree. He should have been overcome with gratitude at how we burnished his flagging career. But somehow he didn't see it that way. He kind of thinks I set him up and Gina screwed him. And she did make him look bad at the trial. No, worse than bad. Incompetent and stupid. And I helped her." He shook his head. "So, no is the answer. No to pretty much anything I've asked him since."

"But this is something new. And it will save him time and effort, maybe lots of both. He's got to see that. And if he doesn't, Russo will."

"Maybe." Hunt, now back at the stoop, lowered himself down again, finished his lemonade in a long swig, and placed the beaded glass on the cement between his legs. "I'll think about it. And I do appreciate you trying to keep us alive here, Mick, but I'm not sure this is the way. We need more than one case."

"Well, maybe not. We do good on one case, people might start remembering we do good work in general. What I'm just trying to do is get us back on the street. Get *you* back on the street, instead of sitting in the office waiting for the phone to ring."

Hunt let out a frustrated sigh. "Not to be defensive, Mick, but I've been doing a little more than that. A lot more. The way it usually works is your clients come to you. And nobody seems hot to let us play."

"So we make our own game. We can bring these people in, I know we can."

"How do you know that?"

Mickey took a breath, hesitating. Alicia Thorpe was the other foci in the elliptical orbit they needed to enter, and so far he'd left her out of it entirely. "There's a woman who may already be a suspect who knew Como and most of what he was working on. She can put us in touch with the people we need to talk to."

Hunt looked across at him. "She's a suspect?"

"She might be a suspect. Juhle and Russo talked to her."

"She got an alibi?"

"For when? Nobody's got a clue when Como actually died."

"So that answer would be no, no alibi," Hunt said. "And otherwise we know she's not guilty because . . . ?"

72

Mickey let out a breath. "She's not guilty, Wyatt. Originally, she wanted to hire us to find out who killed Como. She wouldn't have done that if she did it."

"There's so many arguments against that one that I don't know where to start." Still, Hunt held up his hand again and sucked on his cheek for a minute. "She good-looking enough to be affecting your judgment?"

"I hope not." Mickey turned to him, met his eye, nodded. "Possibly, but I don't think so. For the record, though, I would marry her tomorrow if she'd have me."

"Good to know. And she was involved with Como? Intimately?"

"Don't know. Maybe."

"But she didn't kill him?"

Again, Mickey hesitated. "Let's say that I think we can choose to believe she didn't and not have it come back and bite us. It's a calculated risk and also pretty much the only game in town. And meanwhile, she can put us in touch with people who will pay you to be back in that game. Maybe that's short-term, but guess what?"

"Tell me."

"No. You told me about ten minutes ago. If you're in the game, you're gonna win it. Or die or kill somebody trying."

Hunt chuckled. "That's flattering, Mick,

it really is. But that was basketball."

Mickey Dade shook his head, truly amused that his boss didn't seem to realize this fundamental truth about himself. "Don't kid yourself, Wyatt. That's any game you get yourself into."

6

At six o'clock that night, Mickey checked the coals in his Weber kettle cooker and then came back into his purple kitchen. He walked over and opened the refrigerator, atypically loaded with food. After leaving Hunt's, he'd gone down to the Ferry Building, and though it was by then late in the day, the various stores there still had a selection of foodstuffs that put to shame most of the other, regular grocery stores in the city. Now he pulled out the paper-wrapped leg of lamb he was going to butterfly and barbecue after smearing it with garlic, rosemary, salt, pepper, soy sauce, and lemon juice. He brought it over to his cutting board, where he'd piled up the ingredients you really didn't want to refrigerate if you didn't have to: heirloom tomatoes — green, purple, yellow — bunches of Thai basil, thyme and rosemary, two heads of garlic, a lemon.

He opened a bottle of Chianti and poured himself half a juice glass full.

Grabbing his favorite six-inch carbon-steel Sabatier knife off the magnetic holder on the wall, he honed it to a razor's edge with his sharpening steel. Then, whistling, he pulled the leg of lamb toward him and started cutting.

Five minutes later, Mickey laid the lamb out flat on the grill and covered it. Then, back in the kitchen, he took a saucepan down from its rung on the wall. He put it on the stove over high heat, throwing in half a stick of butter and some olive oil. In another minute, he'd added chopped shallots, garlic, thyme and rosemary, some allspice, and three cups of the chicken stock that he made from scratch whenever he started to get low. Some things you simply couldn't cut corners on.

He stirred a minute more, added a cup and a half of Arborio rice and some orzo, then turned the heat all the way down to the lowest simmer and covered the pan. This was his own personal version of Rice-A-Roni, the San Francisco treat, a simple pilaf, but he liked his strategy of first making the kitchen so fragrant that it drew his roommates to the feast whether they were inclined to eat or not.

And sure enough, here was Jim following his nose through the doorway from the living room. "That smells edible."

"Should be," Mick said, pouring wine into another juice glass and holding it out for him. "You ready yet for some hair of the dog?"

"That was one ugly fucking dog," Jim said, taking the glass, "but *salut.*" He and Mickey clicked their thick glasses and both sipped.

And then Tamara appeared in the doorway. "I'm not really hungry, but I might have a little of whatever that is."

"We call that a side dish, Tam. It goes with the other stuff that'll be ready in a half hour."

"Well, I don't know if I'll have much, but I'll sit with you guys."

Mickey handed her a half glass of wine. "Whatever," he said.

Tamara and Jim sat on the green benches on either side of the table, dipping the still-warm sourdough bread into a small bowl of extra virgin olive oil. The finished, medium-rare lamb rested under foil on the cutting board as Mickey finished cutting the tomatoes for "Donna's famous salad" (named after an old girlfriend and early cooking influence), which was going into his big wooden bowl and was composed only of tomatoes, basil, salt, and balsamic vinegar, no oil.

When the doorbell rang, Mickey turned away from the cutting board. "Tam," Mickey said, "you want to get that?"

She turned the knob and pulled the door open and just stood there. "Wyatt?"

"Hey, Tam."

"I don't . . ." She inhaled, then let out the breath. "I . . ."

"Mick didn't tell you I was coming over?"

"No." Another long exhale. "He knew if I'd known, I might have left."

"Why would you have done that?"

"Because . . . because I don't know. I didn't want to face you."

"You want," Hunt said, "I can go now."

"No. Don't be stupid. You're here."

"I can just as easily be gone, Tam. I don't want to cause you any pain." He hesitated. "Mickey should have told you he asked me."

"No," she said. "He was right not to. He's trying to force me to change the way I've been lately."

"How's that?"

"Isn't it obvious? Look at me."

"You look fine."

"No, I don't. I look like death."

"Death should look so good."

She snapped at him. "Don't bullshit me, Wyatt. If you're going to patronize me, then maybe you really ought to get out of here."

Hunt's gaze went hard. "And then what? I mean between you and me. That's just it?"

"Even if it is, what does it matter?"

"I hope you don't mean that." He took a breath. "It matters because, like it or not, you're family, and I don't have so much of it that I can afford to lose any of it. I love you, Tam. I'm always going to love you. Don't you know that?"

Looking down, she shook her head. "Sometimes I feel I don't know anything anymore. I thought you hated me."

"I could never hate you. Why would I hate you?"

"Because I left." She met his eyes. "I'm so so sorry. I just couldn't handle" — a tear broke and trickled down her cheek — "any of it."

"That was all right. I understood. It was fine." Hunt brushed the tear away with a finger. "You handled what you could and did what you had to do, Tam. You've got nothing to be sorry about."

"No? Then why do I feel like if I'd stayed on . . . maybe things with the business wouldn't have gotten so bad?"

"That was nothing to do with you. You in the office wouldn't have made any difference, wouldn't have brought in any clients. That's all on me and nobody else. What's gone wrong is because of me and the decisions I made."

Hunt stepped toward her. "Whatever you want to do, Tam, whenever you want to do it, I'm with you. I'm on your side. Really," he said. "Really and always."

She dropped her head and shook it one last time before bringing her gaze up to look at him, as something seemed to break in her. "Oh, Wyatt. I'm so sorry. I'm such a mess." And then suddenly she was in his embrace. Her shoulders let go, deep sobs racked her body, and she held on to him with all of her might.

Hunt brought his arms up tightly around her.

"It's all right," he whispered.

Her visible loss of weight had shocked Hunt when she'd first opened the door, and now, holding her, he couldn't help but be aware of how fragile she'd become. He would let her cry it out.

Gradually he brought a hand up to stroke her hair gently. "Shh," he comforted her after a time, as the sobbing abated and she was starting to settle. "Shh. It's okay. It's going to be okay."

While Tamara went into the bathroom for a minute to get the swelling out of her eyes, Hunt came into the kitchen, nodded a hello at Mickey, and slid in next to Parr. "What's a man got to do to get a drink around here?" he asked.

Parr nodded in commiseration. "He can be mighty light with a pour, that grandson of mine. I don't know where he could have picked up that bad habit."

Mickey, coming over with a fresh glass and the bottle of Chianti, said, "Yeah, well, what Jim here's not telling you is that he's still recovering from a few too many nonlight pours yesterday."

"A rare anomaly for which I've already endured too much abuse from my off-spring." Parr picked up the wine and filled Wyatt's glass, then poured a little more into his own. The two men clicked their glasses. "Mr. Hunt, it's good to see you."

"You, too, James. You too." Hunt put his arm around Parr's shoulders and drew him toward him. "You been keeping out of trouble?"

"Hah!" Mickey said.

"I had a few drinks yesterday in mourning

for my friend, Dominic Como," Parr said. "And the boy here decided he had to come drive me home from the Shamrock."

Mickey turned from slicing the meat. "He's leaving out the part about the bartender calling me at work, saying it was either going to be me or the cops."

"That would never have happened."

"Well, luckily, we didn't have to find that out, did we?" Mickey popped a slice of lamb into his mouth. "And this is all the gratitude I get."

"It's a heartless world," Hunt said. "I guess I shouldn't have talked Jim into taking in you and Tam all those years ago. You wouldn't have had all this aggravation."

"*He* wouldn't have had all the aggravation?" Parr said. "You want to talk aggravation, try living with two teenagers for any given week, much less the six or eight years it actually takes."

"Seven," Mickey said without missing a beat.

Parr turned on him. "Seven what?"

"Seven years. People are teenagers for seven years."

"If you want to grant that teenagers are people at all and not an entirely different species. And where do you get seven?"

Mickey held up fingers as he counted.

"Thirteen, fourteen, fifteen, sixteen, seventeen, eighteen, nineteen. Seven."

Parr turned to Hunt. "The boy is such a literalist."

"I've noticed," Hunt said.

Astonishingly, the warm weather was holding. After the dinner and its attendant accolades for the chef, Mickey suggested they take his bottle of homemade limoncello up to the roof, where there was a mellow dim light from a Japanese lantern, more room, a better view, and more comfortable chairs than the kitchen benches. So the three males walked up the outdoor stairway and out onto the deck that got used on every single one of the nineteen days a year that the nights were pleasant.

Everybody had helped bus the table, but at her insistence, Tamara stayed down to wash the dishes — she'd be up soon. So after they all got seated, Hunt checked behind him to make sure she was not coming up the stairs, then leaned in over the round deck table. "Is she seeing a doctor?"

Mickey shook his head. "No. She won't do that."

"Why not? How much has she lost?"

"At least twenty pounds, though she says less."

At this, Parr coughed. "That much? Are you sure about that?"

Mickey nodded. "I asked her yesterday. She said eighteen, maybe more, so I'm thinking probably twenty or twenty-five."

"That's too much," Parr said. "I knew she was losing some weight, but I should have seen it was that much."

"It's been gradual, Jim. I didn't see it myself until I happened to notice yesterday after all the time I've been staying away. So you don't have to beat yourself up over it. But you're right, Wyatt, it's serious enough. She says nothing tastes like anything."

"Well," Hunt said, "that lamb sure tasted like something, and so did the pilaf and that salad. Have you been making food like that every night?"

"No."

"Good. 'Cause if she had that in front of her and didn't eat it . . ."

"Well," Mickey said, "I haven't been home here a lot the past few months." He hunched his shoulders. "Without me, I think these guys live on macaroni and cheese, and not much of that."

"Hey!" Parr said. "I eat an egg every morning."

"Oh, sorry," Mickey said. Then, to Hunt, "And Jim here has a whopping large egg

84

every single day, which is why he's so fit, relatively."

"Tam doesn't make a big deal of it," Parr said. "She just doesn't put food in her mouth, or not much of it." Then, again, "I should have noticed."

"Well," Hunt said, "we've all noticed now."

And then Tamara was up there with them and everybody had their limoncello in front of them in matching little blue glasses.

And, finally, Hunt got around to Mickey's suggestion about Como. "I checked after you left, Mick, and you're right. Nobody's put up a reward yet."

"Are you working on that?" Tamara asked.

"Not yet," Mickey replied.

Hunt went on. "Mickey got the idea that we could drum up some business, go to some of these charities. The good news is I called the PD hotline number this afternoon, and there's nothing about Como. So, so far, at least, the PD doesn't have anything special going on around his murder. It's just an answering machine saying they'll get back to you. So the door may be open. The bad news is that the door might not necessarily be open for us."

"Have you talked to Juhle?" Mickey asked.

Hunt shook his head no. "I thought I'd

hit him at home tomorrow. I think his wife still might like me, although Connie's got that loyal-cop-wife gene and I can't be positive. But she and I have been through a lot together too. So it's a faint hope. Anyway, I'll find out soon enough."

Parr cleared his throat. "Who's Juhle?"

"Friend of mine," Hunt said. "Also the homicide cop who pulled the case."

"And why will you be talking to him, about this reward, I mean?"

"Because if we do have any luck drumming up this business, we'll have to coordinate anything we do with what they're doing. Sometimes cops don't like to share, maybe you've heard. Juhle might take some convincing that this could be helpful to him." Seeing the questioning look on Parr's face, he asked, "What?"

"It just seems a little cart before the horse is all. I mean, if there's no reward yet, what are you bringing to the party? Wouldn't your position be a hell of a lot stronger if you had something tangible to offer?"

"That's a good call," Mickey conceded. "Wait until we get some of these charities on board, then talk to Juhle."

"You could do that," Parr said. "Or just save yourselves a lot of time and go straight to Len Turner."

Hunt spoke up. "Who's he?"

"He's pretty much the Man around non-profits in the city."

"In what way?" Hunt asked. "I've never heard of him."

Parr chuckled. "Which is the way he likes it. He's a lawyer, pretty much at the top of the charity food chain. He represents most of the big ones and also runs the mayor's community outreach program. Back in the day, he was Dominic's right hand, and if anything, he's got even more influence now. You want something to happen around a reward, he's the guy you want to talk to."

"Len Turner, got it," Hunt said.

"And then you go get that bastard who killed Dominic."

Hunt threw a look across at Mickey, then over to Parr. "That's not exactly it, Jim. The main job would be fielding the calls. We wouldn't really be investigating on our own."

Parr leveled his gaze. "Well, you damn well should." He swallowed against some strong emotion, then looked again around the table. "It's just that Dominic saved this family. He didn't have to give me my job. Nobody else would have, not with my history. I mean, here I am, two strikes down . . . hell, we all know.

"But he believed I could straighten up and do the job every day. And because of that, I got to build a good life finally and let you kids have yours. And then somebody goes and kills him. That's just not right. It's not right." His watery eyes shone. "They got to be caught. That's all I'm saying, that it's personal. And if you're going to be in this thing, you might want to keep that in mind as you go about your business."

"Jim's right," Tamara said. "We get close, we ought to go after him."

"We?" Hunt said.

Tamara nodded. "And that's the other thing, while we're on this."

"I'm listening."

"Well, I don't know if you want to hear this after I've been such a flake for so long, but if you're out following up leads, Wyatt, and Mickey's out hunting up these people who are going to kick in more reward money, who's going to be answering the phones and keeping the office going?"

A silence hung for a long moment around the table between them.

Until Mickey said, "I guess, Sis, that would be you."

"Which would be special," Hunt said, "if there actually was a reward and someone was paying us to administer it. Notice the judicious use of the word *if.*"

Len Turner was listed in Mickey's telephone book under "San Francisco, City of" as the director of the Communities of Opportunity. At nine-fifteen P.M. on this Saturday night, after they'd come down from the roof, Hunt called Turner's number on Mickey's phone. He intended to leave a message that he'd like to make an appointment to meet with Mr. Turner early next week. He was somewhat surprised when Mr. Turner answered the phone himself; and dumbfounded when, after Hunt mentioned Dominic Como and his reward scenario, the man suggested that if Hunt were free, he might consider coming by to discuss the idea more fully right now.

Twenty minutes later, the night guard at the semidarkened City Hall let Hunt in, then directed him up the grand stairway where he'd find Mr. Turner's office to the right on the second floor, Room 211. This turned out to actually be a suite of rooms, the first of which was furnished as a barebones, windowless conference area with a large blond wooden table and sixteen chairs. A back door out of this room led to a hallway with a couple more side rooms, at the end of which was a heavy paneled dark wood door with a frosted glass window, and a light on behind it.

Hearing what sounded like a telephone conversation in progress, Hunt hesitated for a moment, then knocked and heard a cultivated voice tell him to come in.

Len Turner sat behind a busy but apparently well-ordered, old-fashioned carved-front desk. He held up a finger, indicating he was just finishing his phone call, and Hunt waited on the square maroon Persian rug that he estimated at about twelve feet on a side. The right wall was book-filled from the floor to the ten-foot ceiling. Behind Turner, a couple of large windows afforded a postcard view of the Opera House and the War Memorial. Along the left wall, decorated with dozens of framed photographs of the great and nongreat posing with Leonard Turner, a couple of low filing cabinets made the room's only concession to bureaucracy. By a low table with four upholstered chairs, there was also a half-size brushed-steel refrigerator and a table with an espresso machine, cups, glasses, and a selection of high-end spirits.

Turner, here in his office at nearly ten o'clock on a Saturday night, wore a light blue shirt and golden tie. His salt-and-pepper hair complemented a frankly handsome face of regular features, a strong jaw, an aristocratic nose. His voice, speaking on the phone, was businesslike and yet somehow soothing as he wound up the conversation. Now hanging up, he raised the wattage of his smile as he stood and came around the desk, extending his hand. "Mr. Hunt. Sorry to keep you waiting. Len Turner. Can I interest you in a good cup of espresso? I'm having some. Or water? Tea? A soft drink? Something stronger?"

"Espresso would be good," Hunt said. "I was a little surprised to find you still working at this time of night."

Turner nodded with a self-deprecating air. "A man who loves what he does never works a day in his life."

"That's a good way to look at it," Hunt said.

"Have a seat," Turner said, "and let me get this coffee going." He put two demitasse cups under a double-spigot on the high-tech machine and pressed a button. In thirty seconds, he placed one of the cups in front of Hunt and took a seat with the other one across the table from him. "Now," he said, holding his cup up in a toasting fashion, his face suddenly sober. "To Dominic."

Hunt raised his own cup, nodded, and sipped.

91

"A terrible thing," Turner said. "Terrible."

"Did you know him well?"

"He was my closest friend."

"I'm sorry to hear that."

Turner lifted his shoulders. "So when you mentioned what you wanted to talk about, naturally I thought it would be worthwhile to meet with you as soon as possible. I've been racking my brain to come up with some way to try to not only honor Dominic's legacy and memory, but actually to help bring some closure to this horrible situation. When you mentioned a reward, it struck me as a singularly right gesture."

"I'm glad to hear that. We thought it might be helpful to get more of the community involved if we could."

"Of course. That may be the only way out of this, from what I've gathered from the police. If somebody saw or heard something. It's a sad but unfortunately true fact that some people just don't trust the police."

Hunt nodded. "I've run into that."

"So you know."

"You've talked to them, then? The cops?"

"Just trying to gather some sense of what happened, which no one seems to have much of an idea of. Knowing Dominic as I did, I have to think it must have been some random mugging or robbery attempt or something. No one who knew him could have harmed a hair on his head." He sat back. "But regardless, finding the perpetrator has got to get some real priority now in the short term. More than it seems the police are giving it."

Hunt replied with some care. "I don't think it's that they're not giving it a high priority so much as that it takes them time to generate and follow up any leads. And that's where we thought we might be able to help."

"That's exactly what I was hoping too. Because the longer this whole thing festers, the more it can infect the entire community." He paused. "I'm talking about the nonprofit community here."

Hunt put down his cup.

Turner went on. "A man with Dominic's profile, there are going to be the inevitable rumors about what really happened, and why, and who's covering what up. And I think it's critical that these rumors don't gain currency, and that the wild speculations of people who may even sincerely be trying to help be somewhat controlled."

"That's how we were thinking to go, sir. If the reward gets large enough and does prompt a lot of calls, a good number of them are probably going to range from unlikely to ridiculous. Our idea is to identify those and save the cops time so they can concentrate on the valid leads."

"Of course. Sure. Of course. But I'm also talking about — if we're going to be working together here, you and I — I'm talking about keeping some kind of control over the flow of information that the public gets to see as well." Perhaps realizing how that sounded, Turner held up a palm. "I'm not saying we hide anything, of course, that's not what I mean at all. But you have to remember that there are any number of people in this city who see our work as wasteful or nonproductive or even unnecessary, and they'd like nothing more than to have ammunition to tear us down."

Hunt sat back. "Are you saying they'll find this ammunition around Mr. Como?"

"No. I strongly, strongly doubt that. Dominic devoted his whole life to the cause of easing poverty and helping the downtrodden. But even so, there are people who would smear him. And that's what I'm hoping you'll be able to exert some control over. How does that sound to you?"

Hunt felt that his own control over the precise parameters of his involvement, if any, with this man, had shifted to some degree. He wasn't at all certain that he could promise Turner what he seemed to be describing, or whether in fact it was even a reasonable approach. He just didn't know. The man was powerful and persuasive and clearly was going to have his own agenda, but Hunt didn't think that there would necessarily be a conflict he couldn't finesse. So after a moment, he nodded. "Doable," he said. "It sounds doable."

Turner clapped his hands. "Good. I really think this is an excellent idea, Mr. Hunt. Excellent. So how, specifically, were you planning to proceed?"

Over the next couple of minutes, Hunt gave him chapter and verse on Mickey's idea of contacting many of the city's non-profit organizations and soliciting them for inclusion in the reward fund. Turner nodded in agreement throughout, at the end volunteering to help with the solicitations — he knew all these people — in any way he could. In fact, what made the most sense, he told Hunt, was that there be a central command; that Turner himself could act as the escrow holder of the funds, after which he would administer the reward and, in consultation with law enforcement, decide on the reward recipients, if any.

He would be the liaison between Hunt and the various organizations in Hunt's efforts to keep the contributors informed. He would also be happy to consult with Hunt when there was a question of whether or not information should come out. "And finally," he rolled along, "I think we have to talk about your compensation for all of your efforts on this."

"I was thinking of me and my two associates billing at our regular hourly rate. I can get you our fee schedule first thing next week."

"That sounds fair."

"Great, but there is one other small thing. This whole concept really won't work unless we get a guarantee of a certain flexibility on the part of city government."

"How do you mean?"

"I mean, if the police or the district attorney decide to seize any- and everything we may get over the phone by search warrant as it comes in, then we're not going to get any calls."

Turner pondered that for a brief moment. "I could make a couple of calls and be of assistance in that respect. Meanwhile, I could have a contract drawn up in the next couple of days, but if you'd like to get started as soon as you can, we can be old-fashioned gentlemen and seal the deal with a handshake right now. How does that sound?"

Again, Hunt wasn't completely sure how it sounded, but what Turner was suggesting was certainly not unethical and it would put Hunt, Mickey, and Tamara to work at full pay immediately. And it wasn't unusual for a job to morph slightly or even greatly as its execution played out. He was sure he could stay on top of what were clearly Mr. Turner's priorities.

So, stifling his minimal scruples, he stood up and reached out his hand across the table. "That sounds like a deal to me," he said.

7

Wyatt Hunt hadn't been to Devin Juhle's home out on Taraval Street in a very long time. In the first years after Hunt had opened his office as a private investigator, he had nearly lived with Devin and Connie and their three children — Eric, Brendan, and Alexa. He and Juhle had been baseball teammates in high school, and they had still played games together, often including the children, whenever he came over — Ping-Pong, basketball, foosball, catch.

That was before *California v. Gorman*. It was also before the scandal involving Hunt's former associate that had knocked the bottom out of his business and essentially destroyed his credibility with the Police Department and most of the criminal law community.

Hunt wasn't kidding himself — this thing with Juhle wasn't simply a bridge to mend. It was a chasm to breach.

Now, at nine-thirty on a Sunday morning that had blown in blustery and cold — the three days of San Francisco's summer weather having exhausted their allotted run — Hunt parked his Mini Cooper on the street in front of Juhle's small stand-alone two-story home, made sure he was packing presents for the kids, and sat for a moment gathering the courage to go and face the music, the near-tragic opera, that he'd helped to compose.

Finally, unable to stall any longer, he opened his car door and walked across the lawn and up the four steps to the front door and rang the bell. The chimes rang within and he heard running footsteps and the door flew open.

For a horrible second, Hunt thought that Brendan, the middle one, age eleven or so, didn't even recognize him. He'd grown about four inches and had put on fifteen pounds. But the face suddenly broke a smile as he said, "Uncle Wyatt!" and the boy actually threw his arms around him. Then, calling back into the house, "It's Uncle Wyatt."

More footsteps from down the hallway that led to the kitchen in the back of the house, and here was Connie in green sweats, formidable and attractive as ever, drying her hands on a dish towel, her expression welcoming and warm, with just a trace of concern around the eyes.

"Well, look at who's here!"

He stepped into the house and they hugged, bussed each other on the cheeks. After which Connie held him out at arm's length. "It's so good to see you, Wyatt. So good." And then, her face clouding over, "Is everything all right?"

"Everything's fine." He looked around her and saw Alexa hanging back in the hallway, her body language quizzical and reserved. Hunt gave her a tiny wave and a "Hey, sweetie," but she only nodded and Hunt realized that it wasn't only Devin he was going to have to win over again.

Connie was going on. "Devin's off with Eric at soccer. Can you believe Sunday morning at seven o'clock? Is that obscene or what? But they ought to be back in a half hour or so, if you've got time to hang around for a while. Was he expecting you?"

"Unlikely. I wasn't sure I was expecting myself until I woke up." Hunt took a beat. Then, "You think he'll talk to me?"

She made a face and broke a half-smile that told him she wasn't too certain of that, but the actual words she said were, "Stranger things have happened. Meanwhile, how does a cup of coffee sound?"

"Like a fanfare of trumpets."

Amused, Connie shook her head. "I remember what I've missed about you."

They were catching each other up on their respective lives over the past months, the talk flowing as it always did with Connie, Hunt halfway through his second cup at the kitchen table, when they heard a noise and Connie said, "That's the garage door."

They fell then into a sudden and tense silence, waiting.

The garage connected to the kitchen. Eric was the first one through the door. Unlike his younger brother, he was about the same physical size as the last time Hunt had seen him, but his face had broken out with acne and his voice had a different pitch when, tentative yet polite, he nodded and said, "Hi, Uncle Wyatt."

"Hey, big guy. Good to see you."

"You too." He advanced and reached out his hand, which Hunt, standing, shook. He chose to take it as a good sign that they still called him "uncle," perhaps still considered him Juhle's brother on some level.

Devin evidently wasn't in any hurry to get in the house. He would have known Hunt was inside from the distinctive car parked out front. The connecting door closed shut behind Eric and they heard some sounds from the garage — Devin closing his driver's side door, throwing the duffel bag where it belonged.

Hunt found his breath snagged in his throat.

Juhle opened the door and stood for a second in the doorway, holding it open. Nodding first at his wife, then briefly at Hunt, he turned and closed it with an exaggerated gentleness. Turning back around, he leaned up against the counter and crossed his arms over his chest, nodding again, his face a mask. "Hey, Wyatt," he said with no inflection whatever. "What can I do for you?"

"I don't think so," Juhle said. "That's police work."

The two of them sat at either end of a sagging beige sofa in the downstairs family room, a converted half-basement where Juhle had his Ping-Pong/pool table set up, along with a dartboard and a foosball game area. A television rested on the middle shelf of a built-in bookcase mostly devoted otherwise to sports trophies for the kids, and Connie's washer and dryer reinforced the place's basic functional nature. Juhle's house wasn't big, and the family and their activities filled it all up, every spare inch.

"It's police work," Hunt countered, "that won't do any good. You won't get the calls we're going to get and if you did, you'll spend all your time screening out the nuts."

Juhle shrugged, shook his head dismissing the idea. "How many good tips you think you're going to get? Two? Three? Not even that. End of story."

"No, it isn't. Not if we get the reward set up and it gets big, and it will."

"What's big?"

"I don't know. Maybe a hundred grand, maybe more. Mick's shooting for the moon, and he's a charmer." Hunt came forward on the couch. "So we're not talking any couple of calls a day here. It's not impossible the reward might go to half a mil, and if that happens, the flakes come out of the woodwork. You know this and I know it, and you're going to spend half to all of your time either chewing your cud on nothing or running down ridiculous leads trying to identify one good one."

Another shrug. "That's what we do, Wyatt. Run down leads. It's police work."

Wyatt sat back, let out a breath. "This is getting a little circular, don't you think? You got any of these leads?"

103

Juhle paused, then spit out, "We got squat."

"That was my guess," Hunt said. "You know, time was this would have been a slam dunk for both of us, Dev. Win-win."

Juhle glanced down the length of the couch. "Time was a lot of other things too."

"You want to talk about some of 'em?"

"Talk's cheap, Wyatt. And bullshit walks."

"This isn't bullshit. This is something I can legitimately do to help your investigation. We are going ahead and contacting potential reward sources —"

"And who are these sources?"

"People connected to Como. Who want to see his killer get caught."

"None of them more than I do."

"Granted. But we can generate leads you can't. Calls from folks who would never call the cops. Most of what we get will be crap, sure, but if we even get one good tip you couldn't get, you're better off." Hunt sat back, spoke matter-of-factly. "This is a free gift to you, Dev. Call it an apology if you want. Sometimes the jobs we do, we're on different sides. It doesn't have to be personal."

This brought a cold smile. "And of course it's going to put money in your pocket for what you just admitted to me was mostly

104

going to be crap. For this I'm supposed to say thank you? You fuck with my career, my livelihood, and my family, and you tell me it's not personal?"

"It didn't happen that way, Dev. You could look at it that Gina and I saved you from being the cop who sent the wrong guy to prison. And then, P.S., she hands you the real guy, the actual killer. And you get the credit for that arrest. How's that hurt your career? You want to tell me that?"

No answer.

"Your feelings?" Hunt went on. "Okay. After what happened on the stand, okay. Sorry. But your career? Your livelihood? Your family? I don't think so."

Up one flight on the main floor, the television laid down white noise. Tires squealed and a car's horn sounded from outside on the street.

Juhle's jaw was set, the corners of his mouth drawn down. He stared in the direction of the bookcase wall across from him, then pulled himself upright on the couch and leaned forward, his elbows on his knees.

Hunt lowered his voice. "This is a done deal, Dev. I'm telling you as a courtesy. This is happening. But whatever you think of it, we will help you any way we can." Without a cease-fire, much less a peace treaty, in hand, Hunt got up. "Tell Connie and the kids it was nice seeing them."

Now that Hunt was on board with him, Mickey had all the excuse he needed to see Alicia Thorpe again.

They met at Bay Beans West, a coffee shop on Haight Street about midway between their two residences, got their brews, and realized it might be hours before they could find a place to sit inside. So they decided to walk instead, down to Lincoln and then due west into the teeth of the wind, out toward the beach.

For the first couple of blocks, they made small talk about the changing weather, Starbucks versus Bay Beans, how the La Cuisine classes were going for both Mickey and Ian, how everybody their age seemed to be doing one job for money, then all these other things that they seemed to like better for free — Alicia volunteering at the Sunset Youth Project, Mickey and Ian learning to cook.

"So what's your day job?" Mickey asked her. "When you're not volunteering?"

"It's kind of embarrassing."

"If it's work that pays you, it's not embarrassing. As my grandfather used to say, 'There is no work, if done in the proper spirit, to which honor cannot accrue.' "

A small contralto laugh. "That's good. Does that apply to being the hostess at Morton's?"

"Every job in the world, according to Jim. But especially hostess at Morton's," Mickey said. "Perhaps the most honorable of the service jobs."

"Well, thank you. I'll start trying to look at it that way. Instead of as six hours of mind-numbing tedium."

"There you go." They walked on in silence for a while, and then Mickey said, "Ian told me about your parents."

She cast a quick glance over at him. "Yeah."

"Did he tell you that pretty much the same thing happened to me?"

She stopped and faced him. "Your father shot your mother and then himself?"

"No. But my father disappeared and then my mother overdosed. Same result. No parents."

She closed her eyes, then shook her head. "I don't really remember it too much. It was just the way it was. I was only nine."

"I was seven, but I think it's the most indelible memory of my life — the shape under the sheet on the gurney, knowing it was Mom, as they wheeled her out."

"I must have blocked it," she said.

After a silence that lasted for half a block, Mickey cleared his throat. "So, about Dominic, all these charities he ran . . ."

"He only ran one. The Sunset Youth Project. And of course all the subordinate groups off that."

"Okay. So what are those?"

She shrugged. "Let's see. The art gallery, the two schools, the development company, the theater, the moving company, the Sunset Battalion . . ."

"Sunset Battalion sounds like a bunch of commandos."

"No. It's more like an urban Peace Corps. Mostly older guys, some of the girls, people who've been in the program awhile."

"So what do they do?"

Another shrug. "Pretty much whatever needs to be done. Tutoring, handing out pamphlets, bringing back the strays, working the neighborhoods. They're kind of the boots-on-the-ground people."

His understanding limited at best, Mickey nodded.

"Well, then, with this other stuff, what's the actual Sunset Youth Project do?"

"Sunset itself? It's the . . . I don't know what you'd call it. The umbrella. The administrative side."

They kept walking, and she must have noticed another question playing around on Mickey's face, because she said, "What?"

"I'm just trying to get my arms around this whole thing. I mean, if Dominic was only running one program, what's with the car?"

"Well, the one program has maybe two dozen sites in the city, maybe more. The main office and K through eight down on Ortega, the residential treatment center in Potrero, the outpatient center for adults by City College. Then the high school . . ." She stopped the litany. "You get the idea. I could get you the whole list if you need it, but the point is that Sunset's a huge organization. Huge."

"What's its budget? Do you know?"

"Total?" She thought a moment. "Fifty million a year, give or take."

Mickey stopped in his tracks. "No. Really."

"Really. I'm pretty sure it's somewhere in that neighborhood. It's in the annual report. You could check."

"Fifty million dollars?"

"Somewhere in there, I'm pretty sure. With everything, I mean all the programs, Sunset's probably serving five thousand people a day, all told, citywide. It adds up."

"I'll say. So where's all that money come from?"

"Everywhere, Mickey, are you kidding me? Individual philanthropists, foundations, tuition and other income from the schools, moving company fees and the sale of the redeveloped buildings. I mean, a lot of these things are profit centers in themselves. But also there's a ton of public health money from the city. . . ."

"This city? I thought we were in a budget crunch."

She nodded. "Always. But even if they cut way back, the Health Services Department is going to stay the single biggest agency in the city."

"Is that true? The biggest?"

Alicia shook her head. "I'm sure that's right. I think they're in for five million to us, just Sunset. But then there's also Ameri-Corps, which is federal and funds the Battalion, for another several mil. And then there's all the just day-to-day regular fund-raising."

"That gets you to fifty million?"

"Pretty close, most years."

"Wow."

"Yeah, I know. It's impressive."

"So, I've got to ask this, what was Dominic making running this thing? Does anybody know that?"

"Sure. It's public record again. You could look it up in twenty minutes." She broke a small smile. "But you don't have to because I already know. His salary was six hundred forty-eight thousand dollars."

"Every year?"

"Last year, anyway. And at least close to that the year before, and before that." She shrugged. "It's a major executive job, Mickey. He earned what he made. He deserved it."

"Still," Mickey said. "Six hundred and fifty grand. Makes me think I might want to go into charity work myself."

"I thought you wanted to be a chef."

"I do. But I'm flexible. For that kind of money I believe I could be tempted."

"No." She touched his arm again. "You don't do it for the money. You do it for the work. It's great helping people, it really is. Way better than standing in a restaurant saying hello with your smile on all day. That's why I got into my own volunteering. Although now with Dominic gone . . ." She stopped and visibly gathered herself as she threatened to tear up. "Sorry," she said. "I keep doing this." But wiping her hands over her eyes, she got herself back under control. "So I guess we're to that now. My relationship with Dominic."

"We can be if you're comfortable with it."

"I'm fine with it." The words confident enough that they carried with them almost the hint of a threat. "I've done nothing I'm ashamed of."

"Although the other day you said that maybe you and Mr. Como were too close. What did you mean by that?"

"I meant that there was some chemistry, physical chemistry, that we both acknowledged. But he was a married man and he wasn't going there. And neither was I. We'd even talked about me quitting so we wouldn't be around one another so much, but that just seemed like a needless hardship on both of us. And why did we want that? We liked being together. We joked and had little secret things we did that made everything fun. I mean it, in the middle of all this serious stuff he did, every day was fun. He was just a great guy doing great work. And that was the other side of it."

"Of what?"

"The job. The actual job."

"What about the job?"

She bit her lower lip. "This is the part where you laugh at me."

"I don't think so. Try me."

As they started walking again, she took a

breath of air. "I kind of want to go into politics and change the world. At least try to make it a better place."

"That's not a bad thing. The politics, maybe, but not the general idea."

"No, I know. But here I am with my little degree in political science, and I'm a hostess at Morton's. You know what I'm saying?"

"Sure. You wanted to do something more important."

She nodded. "And now you're thinking, 'So she gets a job driving a limo?' "

"I'm not thinking that. I'm listening."

"Okay. So the thing about this job with Dominic isn't so much about driving him around. It's about moving into another world where there's power and money and good things can happen." She was getting into it now and her voice came to life. "You know what happened to the last three of Dominic's morning drivers? This is in, like, the last two or three years." She held up one finger. "Jon Royce, now administrative assistant to guess who? Alice Tallent, city supervisor. Two, Terry McGrath, EMT school and fast-tracked to the Fire Department. Three, DeShawn Ellis, scout for the San Francisco Giants who got Dominic and me the best tickets I've ever seen last Opening Day."

"Connections," Mickey said.

She nodded. "I know it might sound crass and self-serving, and then, of course, it maybe looks like I'm using the relationship with Dominic to get a leg up on a career. But I'd already done a lot of volunteer time at Sunset when Ian was there, just to be near my brother. So it wasn't like I just glommed on to this opportunity to get ahead. And then this driving job came up, and I was kind of next in line, and I truly didn't know how I was going to feel about Dominic once I got to know him."

On the way back, by now chilled to the bone, they found themselves on either end of the back couch at the Little Shamrock, drinking Irish coffees. The place, late on a Sunday afternoon, had only two other customers playing a nearly silent and intense game of darts.

Alicia came back from the bar and put their second round down on the small table in front of them. Sitting back, she crossed one leg over the other and flashed a quick glance in Mickey's direction. "Here we've been doing all this talking," she said, "and I haven't really been completely straight with you."

114

"About Dominic?"

Shaking her head, she said, "No, not about Dominic. I've told you everything about Dominic." Hesitating, she drew a breath. "You know how I said I must have blocked out everything around what happened with my mom and dad? That's not really true."

"I didn't think it was," Mickey said. "I don't think anybody does that, not at nine years old. I was going to let it slide."

She nodded. "I noticed. And I thank you for that. But maybe I shouldn't be so defensive about it. Especially with somebody who's doing all this work for me and who's been through something so similar."

"I don't know how similar it really was, Alicia. Me and Tamara got a home out of it. I gather you and Ian didn't."

"No," she said. "They split us up. Not that they tried to, but Ian was, I guess, kind of gangly and sullen and all bad attitude. So it turned out not too many people were willing to take a chance on him."

"But they were with you?"

A shrug. "I was quieter, maybe more pliable. Just as angry as Ian was, I think. Maybe I still am, I don't know. But nobody saw it at first, although none of my homes really stuck either. Anyway, the bottom line is we got separated pretty quick, and he got into most of the drugs in the universe and some pretty bad behavior."

Mickey remembered. "He told me he spent some time at the work farm."

"Not really *some* time," she said. "Just about all the time from thirteen to eighteen."

"But you kept up with him?"

"Not so hard, really. His address didn't change." She reached for her Irish coffee and took a sip. "Anyway, I guess my point is that I was on my own and wasn't really too much of an angel myself. I don't like to think about how I was back then, but I don't want to pretend to you that I didn't have any reaction to what my dad did, and that I didn't act out because of it. Because I did. I was pretty rage-driven."

"Okay."

"No, not really okay. I was as bad as Ian was, not with all the drugs, maybe, but getting myself in trouble. And I kind of focused on older men, if you see where I'm going with this."

"Dominic."

She nodded. "If the cops look, they're going to think they see a pattern," she said. "But I wanted you to know that stopped a long time ago, and it was all long over by

116

the time I started working with Dominic. And it didn't start up again with him."

"I believed you the first time," Mickey said.

"Still," she said. She reached over and rested her hand for a second or two on his thigh, looked into his eyes. "I wanted you to know."

Mickey, his leg nearly burning where she'd rested her hand, reached out and grabbed his own Irish coffee, brought it to his mouth. "Well, while we're on this type of stuff," he said, "Ian mentioned something else I was a little curious about."

"What's that?"

"Jail." He put his glass down.

"What about jail?" Suddenly her voice became querulous, frightened. In her eyes he picked up a sense of the dark rage she'd alluded to earlier. "I'm not going to jail," she whispered at him. "You said you were going to keep me out of jail."

"And that's still our intention."

"I didn't do anything to Dominic. I really didn't."

"Easy, Alicia. I didn't say you did. I said we'd be trying to keep you out of jail. And just to try to prepare you for possible eventualities, maybe keeping you out of jail won't be possible after all. That's a major part of the job, but it's not the only part."

"No, that won't work. It's got to be the major part, Mickey. Don't you understand? I didn't do anything." Again, she emphasized her point by reaching over and putting a hand on his leg. "I can't go to jail."

"That's what Ian said too. He said he thought it would kill you." He looked over at her as now she pulled her hand away from him, came forward, and hunched over, her hands clasped in her lap. "I was hoping to reassure you that even if it came to that, you could get through it."

"How can you say that? How can you know? Have you ever been in jail?"

"No, but I know —"

She cut him off, her voice loud, and harsh. "I don't care what you know! You can't know until you've been there. It's not what you think, okay? They've got complete control over you. I can't go there again."

Suddenly the bartender was back with them. "Everything okay here?"

Alicia threw a look at Mickey, then up. "Fine. We're fine," she said. "Sorry."

"Just try to keep it down a little back here, then, huh?"

When he went back to the bar, they sat in silence for a long minute. Finally Mickey said, "Again?"

She was back to being hunched over, her breathing heavy.

"Alicia?"

At last, with a deep sigh, she straightened up. "The cops shouldn't have it. It shouldn't be on my record. I wasn't even eighteen. It's supposed to be erased. It was just a joyride and a stupid accident."

"Was anybody hurt?"

"No. Just me, a little. But the car belonged to the house I was staying in, the guy there's a fucking pervert, and I stole his fucking car, which ended that particular shot at my domestic bliss with stepparents. But the jail part was . . ." She stopped, looked pleadingly at him. "Nobody knows this except Ian."

"You don't have to say," Mickey said. "I've got a good imagination."

"I thought because there were only women on that side of the jail . . ."

Mickey moved over next to her, put his arm around her, and brought her in next to him. "Nobody's going to let you go to jail," he said. "That's not going to happen. I promise."

As soon as the words were out of his mouth, Mickey regretted them. You didn't promise when you couldn't absolutely deliver; it was one of the mantras he and

119

Tamara had lived by — a promise is a promise, they used to say.

But this particular horse was already out of the barn, and there was nothing he could do about it now.

8

When Wyatt Hunt opened his office door in Chinatown the next morning at eight forty-three, Tamara was at her old desk. She'd told him on Saturday night that if he'd take her back, she would be there, but actually seeing her in the flesh gave him a hopeful jolt of adrenaline. Maybe the firm would get back on its feet again and this was the first sign that things were turning around.

She glanced at her wristwatch, then up to her boss, her face alight. "I didn't realize that you'd changed your hours."

At a glance, she looked good, lightly made up with lipstick, mascara, and eye shadow. A black silk blouse under a multicolored scarf around her neck camouflaged her protruding collarbones. The overall effect was nothing like anorexia. She'd obviously lost some weight, of course, but Hunt might not have noticed anything amiss if he hadn't seen her and had his arms around her two nights before.

Still, reluctant to embarrass her on the one hand, or to scare her off with overeffusiveness on the other, he kept his greeting low-key. "So the cat actually did drag you in. For the record, I can't tell you how good it is to see you sitting there again."

"I can't tell you how good it feels to *be* sitting here again." She hesitated, then added, "I really want to thank you for letting this happen, Wyatt. I don't know too many other people who would be okay with taking me back."

"Anybody who'd had you working for them once would take you back in a New York minute, Tam. I'm the one who should be thanking you. And I do."

"Okay." She lowered her eyes, then raised them back up to him, a trace of her old impish smile playing around her mouth. "Do you think we can be through with all of this yucky stuff pretty soon?"

"Absolutely. No more yuck, starting now."

"Good. Mickey's already out on that Len Turner list you gave him. He'll check in when he's done or a little before lunch, whichever comes first. And Devin Juhle called. No message, just please call him back when you get in."

"Got it. And, Tam" — he stopped on his

way to the back office and stood by the side of her desk — "one last bit of yuck."

She sighed with some theatricality — one of her mannerisms from the old days which he loved. "Okay, one. What?"

Striking fast, he leaned over and kissed the top of her head. "Welcome back."

On his way to the Sunset Youth Project administrative offices at Ortega Street and Sunset Boulevard, Mickey couldn't get Como's $650,000 salary out of his brain. Or Sunset's $50 million-per-year operating budget. These dollar figures shifted his initial take on Como's murder. This much money around, it was likely in play.

And as far as this went, it was good news for Alicia. If she was of any interest at all to the police, it was not because of money, but because of her relationship to Como.

As Alicia had told him, information on nonprofits was a matter of public record, and hence easily accessible. With Len Turner's list to guide him, Mickey had done some computer research last night and verified that the three largest nonprofits where Como had a seat on the board — the Mission Street Coalition, Sanctuary House, and Halfway Home — each operated with a budget of over $30 million per year. Since

123

none of these quite matched the size and scope of the Sunset Youth Project, Mickey's first call was on Como's home turf.

The two-story building wasn't much of a scenic destination. The low, overcast skies didn't help much either.

Standing across the street, Mickey was struck by how sad and nondescript the place looked. The grounds took up an entire city block. Off to his left side, behind a twelve-foot cyclone fence with razor wire threaded around the top, were a deserted asphalt playground, four basketball hoops with no nets, a metallic climbing structure, and parking for half a dozen cars, including a Lincoln Town Car limousine.

Over the front doorway, a flag hung at half-mast.

Inside now, Mickey walked through the wide, low lobby — again, echoes of public schools he'd attended. A dozen or more young people loitered by the stairway on his right. He was headed toward a directory mounted on the wall in front of him, but noticed that the large office next to it, venetian blinds behind the glass, was lit up and obviously occupied, its door wide open. Stenciled on the glass were the words: Sunset Youth Project, Office of the Executive Director. Inside the large room, more loiterers stood around between the desks behind the counter. Mickey slapped on a smile and knocked. "Excuse me," he said, "I'm looking for Lorraine Hess."

The associate director stood behind the desk in her office and reached out a hand to shake Mickey's.

Dominic Como, Mickey was quickly learning, had an eye for lovely women. First the truly beautiful Alicia Thorpe, and now his assistant director. Solidly built, more than slightly overweight, and even in rimless eyeglasses, Lorraine Hess clearly at one time had been a babe and, except for the weight, wasn't so far from still being one. She wore a rust-colored woolen suit over a plain white blouse, the ensemble a few years out of style. Her hair, shoulder-length and mostly gray, was a riot of mismanagement, but not unattractive, and of a piece with the sultry, sunken bedroom eyes. Once, not so long ago, she might have been distractingly prettier, and might even be now if she'd give more thought to her appearance. But this clearly wasn't much of a concern to her. And especially not today, the first business day after the discovery of Como's body.

"As you can imagine," she was telling him, "we're in a state of complete numbness and disbelief around here. To say nothing of the personal devastation. None of us can understand how this could have happened, the random killing of such a wonderful man. Nobody who knew him could have wanted to do anything to harm Dominic. It's just such a loss."

"That's what I'm hearing from everybody," Mickey said.

"I'm not surprised. That's what I told the police when they came by. It must have been a random thing, a mugging maybe. It couldn't have been someone he knew, who knew him."

"Do you know who he was going to meet?"

"No. He never told Al. Mr. Carter. His driver."

"I thought Alicia Thorpe was his driver."

Hess made a little moue. "Ms. Thorpe was one of several daytime drivers. That shift ends at three. Al Carter drove the rest of the time. In any event, you were asking if I knew who Dominic was going to meet, and the answer is no. Al just let him off early near his house and that was" — she swallowed against her emotion — "that was the last time anyone saw him." She removed her glasses, rubbed her eyes, then replaced them, now looking at Mickey as though she were seeing him for the first time. "I'm sorry. You said you were with a private investigating firm? Is there something you came here to tell me, or any way I can help you?"

"Well, as a matter of fact . . ." And Mickey went into his prepared pitch on the reward, ending by telling her that Wyatt Hunt had cleared the idea with Len Turner, who would manage the reward fund.

"You mean you'll be working with Mr. Turner as well as the police?"

"Yes, ma'am. That's kind of the plan. We're assuming that once the idea gets out into the nonprofit community, the reward might become fairly substantial, and we'd then serve the purpose of evaluating the information received and passing the legitimate stuff along to the police. We're hoping to elicit information from people in the community who might not normally cooperate much or willingly with law enforcement. At the same time, we'd screen calls from cranks and publicity seekers, since we know there'll be some of them as well. Basically, we'd be acting as a clearinghouse. And of course validating the claimants for the reward, if any."

"But won't the police be investigating as well?"

"Sure. But Mr. Turner agrees that we could provide a valuable service by being a conduit to a community that doesn't always willingly interact with law enforcement. Even if they have very persuasive stuff. That's why you offer a reward. It's a little more proactive. And, as of last night, the police had no active leads they were working on."

Hess made no real attempt to disguise the stress and fatigue of the days since Como's disappearance. Now she leaned back in her chair, closed her eyes briefly, and let out a deep sigh. "And you've come to us, I presume, to sort of get the ball rolling?"

"Yes, ma'am. Mr. Turner recommended that you call him if you have any questions or misgivings. We're offering our services, that's all. We're trying to coordinate and facilitate the reward. But it's entirely your call."

"Well," Hess said, "I appreciate that, but I don't know if I have the authority to make that decision. As you know, with Dominic gone, we've got a huge vacuum at the top right now, and . . ." Again, she closed her eyes, shook her head wearily, brought them back to Mickey. "On the other hand, if Mr. Turner says . . . I know we want to do all we can, as soon as we can, to find out who could have been responsible for this. How much money were you thinking you'd need to start?"

"That would be entirely up to your discretion. But enough to incentivize somebody who otherwise might not be inclined to come forward. And as I've mentioned, Mr. Turner wasn't thinking you'd be in this alone. He told us that Mr. Como was on several other boards. Maybe you'd want to set an example for them to follow."

"I would have to go to our board, but —" Suddenly, she seemed to come to some decision. A bit of color came back into her cheeks and she slapped her palm down on her desktop. "Hell, at least we'd be doing something instead of just sitting here waiting for the police and twiddling our thumbs. Do you think twenty thousand would be enough? I'm sure I could go to the board with that much in mind. I could reach them all this morning by phone."

"I think that might be a good start," Mickey said, restraining an urge to let out a war whoop. In fact, he knew that this was about the maximum total reward that most professionals advised be offered. It was one thing, he knew, to offer $100 million for bin Laden, and another thing to dangle such a vast amount of money in a local case that it would serve as a distraction, attracting so many tips as to drown out any actual leads. But in this case, the idea was to generate every conceivable tip. Even paranoids have enemies, he knew, and even psychos sometimes possessed real information. But he kept his reply low-key. "That would give me something to go to the other charities with."

"Not till you hear back from me, though," Hess said. "I'll need the approval of our board."

"Absolutely," Mickey said. "If you'd like, I could wait."

It looked like a school because it still was a school, K through eight Sunrise School.

He got outside onto the asphalt yard just as the recess bell sounded. As the kids came flying out all around him, he let himself through a small gate in a fence, turned the corner of the building, and found himself in the small parking lot he'd noticed from across the street.

A tall, rangy, middle-aged black man was leaning back against the building, arms crossed over his chest, watching in a supervisory way as two other young men went over the limousine with sponges and hoses. On a hunch, Mickey sidled over to the area and caught the man's attention. "Excuse me," he said, "are you Al Carter?"

With a questioning expression, the man straightened away from the wall. He exuded authority. Except for a well-buzzed tonsure, he was bald, and the high, clear forehead spoke of intelligence and patience. His voice, when he spoke, was low-pitched, unhurried, educated. "I have that name," he said. "And you have the advantage of me."

Mickey extended his hand and introduced himself. "You don't know me," he went on, "but maybe you knew my grandfather, Jim Parr?"

At that name's mention, the closed-up face relaxed somewhat. "I certainly did know your grandfather. Is he still among the quick?"

"I don't know about that," Mickey said. "He's slowed down a little, but —"

Carter chuckled, shaking his head, cutting him off. "The quick, young man," he said, "in contradistinction to the dead. The quick and the dead. I was asking if Jim were still alive."

"As of this morning."

"Well, that's wonderful news. Tell him hello for me."

"I will." Mickey gestured toward the car. "So what are these guys doing?"

Carter cast a throwaway glance in their

131

direction. "We call this washing the limousine. It's one of their tasks."

"Are they being punished for something?"

A little half-laugh. "Punished? To the contrary, they're being rewarded. These two young men were handpicked by Mr. Como to do this job and if they continue to do it effectively, they'll be promoted to more responsible and important jobs." Now his expressive face did cloud over. "Or they would have been." Suddenly the eyes focused and he raised a finger in Mickey's direction. "You're the young man who found him."

"I am."

"And you are Jim Parr's grandson as well?"

"Right."

"That's an extraordinary coincidence."

"Yes, it is," Mickey said.

"So how is it," Carter asked, "that you've stayed involved in matters surrounding Mr. Como's death?"

"What do you mean?"

"I mean, you found his body. Your grandfather used to be his driver. Now" — he gestured to include their surroundings — "you're here. The connection eludes me."

"There's no mystery to it. I work for a private investigator. We're offering to coordinate a reward program."

"Ah, a reward program. I don't believe I've heard of that."

"It's in its early stages. Ms. Hess is hoping that the Sunset Youth Project here is going to put up twenty thousand dollars. With others of Mr. Como's charities kicking in, it could get to quite a substantial sum."

Carter's eyebrows went up, his head canted to one side. "So," he said, "the assumption being that there is information out there somewhere. Someone knows something he's not talking about."

"I don't know about assumption," Mickey said. "More like a hope. Maybe someone knows something but doesn't recognize its importance. The hope is that the money might get that person motivated to think a little harder about what they've seen or might have heard. You, for example, Mr. Carter. You were the last person to see him alive, if I'm not mistaken. Right?"

"No. That would have been his killer." Carter broke a sad smile. "A small, yet critical distinction, don't you think? But the police have already spoken to me and I told them everything I knew, which, I'm afraid, wasn't much. I left him off near his home on Tuesday night."

"How near?"

"A couple of blocks."

"And he never mentioned who he was supposed to be seeing?"

"Not by name, no. He said it was just an old acquaintance who was having problems. But old acquaintances of Mr. Como could fill the phone book, Mr. Dade. According to that criterion it could theoretically have even been your grandfather. And beyond that, it's possible that he had his scheduled meeting with the old acquaintance he'd told me about and then, after that, met with his killer. Or, as I think Lorraine would like to believe, it was a random attack by some mugger."

"But you don't think that?"

"No," Carter said. "No, I don't think I do."

"Do you have any specific reason for not thinking that?"

Carter shook his head. "I wish I did. I wish there was something I could point to, but it's just a nebulous feeling."

"Well" — Mickey, his wallet out, removed one of his business cards — "if it gets to be more than that, call this number. Or, of course, the police. The information doesn't have to come through us to qualify for the reward, if that's a concern."

"It isn't. I wouldn't be doing it for the

reward, Mr. Dade."

"No, of course not. I didn't mean to imply that you would. And remember that as we speak right now the reward sits at zero. But still," Mickey added, "if something does occur to you, or something new develops, it might be nice to know the money's sitting there waiting for somebody to claim it."

Carter nodded, his face set in grim stone. "I'll keep that in mind," he said.

9

First thing that Monday morning, Len Turner had talked to the mayor. The mayor had placed a phone call to the chief of police, who had personally called Devin Juhle and suggested — an order would have been inappropriate — that he extend "every courtesy" to the "concerned citizens who were assisting in the investigation" by offering this so-far nonexistent reward.

Devin Juhle told Hunt he'd be with his partner, Sarah Russo, at the Ferry Building's MarketBar restaurant at eleven A.M. They'd be willing to review the progress in the Como investigation to bring Hunt up to speed, with the understanding that if Hunt was successful in helping to get a reward established and funded, then when he got anything, he'd reciprocate.

In the normal course of events, they all would have met at Lou the Greek's, the city's legendary bar and eatery across the street from the Hall of Justice. But Juhle's choice of a lunch venue far removed from the normal haunt of cops and other court-house denizens drove home to Hunt the fact that he was still very much on probation, or worse, here. Juhle and Russo might co-operate with him and see how things went, but neither of them was ready to be seen with him in public.

Sarah was married to Graham Russo, a junior partner in the one law firm that was with some regularity still throwing Hunt the occasional bone of work. She was also a ten-year homicide veteran, and the mother of two boys. A freckled and athletic tomboy with Beatle-length dark hair, she looked about fifteen years younger than her actual age, barely old enough to drink. She and her husband and kids had been to a couple of case celebration parties at Hunt's warehouse/home, and as far as she was concerned, Hunt was okay. She agreed that the reward idea was at best stupid and at worst distracting, but she pointed out that it was no more stupid or distracting than half of the political things that San Fran-cisco's Police Department had to put up with every day. She was willing to go with the flow.

Down on the Embarcadero, the morning

cloud cover had lifted and mostly dissipated. Now a gauzy sunlight bathed the outdoor tables as Sarah was gearing up on her summation. "So we've got nothing on his activities after five forty-five last Tuesday. The wife, Ellen, didn't even call to say she was worried about him and hadn't seen him until almost seven o'clock on *Wednesday* night . . ."

"Apparently," Juhle put in, "he frequently stayed out late at some fund-raiser or another, got home after she was asleep, and was up and out the next morning before she got up."

"Didn't sleep in her bed? Or in their bed?" Hunt asked.

"Evidently not," Russo said. "Or not that she noticed."

"America's fun couple," Hunt said. "So where was she Tuesday night, then? The wife?"

Russo didn't have to consult her notes. "She walked up to Chestnut and went to a movie, *The Reader.* It checks. At least, that's what was playing there that night. Still is, for that matter."

"She went alone?"

She nodded. "That's what she says. Got home around nine-thirty, read for a while, went to sleep around eleven."

The waitress arrived with their food. All of them were having the Cuban pork sandwiches and iced tea and the young woman put the plates down, saying, "And today's award for most original order goes to . . ."

Everybody got a little chuckle out of that.

And then the waitress was gone and Hunt took a bite of his sandwich and said, "But nobody saw him on Wednesday all day, right? He didn't come into work?"

"Right," Juhle said.

"So it was Tuesday night?"

"That's close enough," Russo said. "ME says he can't be sure, but it's not a stretch to say he didn't come home Tuesday night because he was already dead."

"How about his phone?" Hunt asked. "Who'd he talk to?"

"Lots of people," Juhle said. "And I mean like forty different numbers in or out the last day. All of whom we've called, by the way, and most of whom we've reached. But the last completed call in or out was at nine-forty. After that, it all went to voice mail. And the cell site information says he's where his driver said he left him."

Russo held up a much-scribbled-upon computer printout for Hunt's edification.

Juhle stopped his chewing. "Police work."

"And a darned fine job of it too," Hunt

139

said. "And what did all these good cell-phone-talking citizens have to say?"

"Everybody so far," Russo said, "has had a completely plausible reason to have talked to him, and about half of those are verified by Como's calendar anyway. No ancient acquaintances that we've come across."

"Maybe it wasn't true, what he told his driver."

"Maybe that," Russo conceded. "Or maybe the driver — Al Carter — didn't tell us the truth about what Como told him."

Hunt put his sandwich down, looked across at Russo. "Any sign of that?"

She shook her head. "Not really, no. Carter got the limo back to Sunset's headquarters, where they keep it parked, at six-thirty, when it was still light out. Three witnesses there agree with that timetable. And there's no motive for him anyway. Carter's loyal as a dog. He's been driving Como around for something like eight years."

"But wait," Juhle suddenly said. "Let's back up to the first thing Wyatt asked about that. Maybe what Como told this guy Carter wasn't true. Maybe he wasn't meeting an old friend after all."

"Devin likes the idea of a woman being involved," Russo said.

"Who's that?" Hunt asked, all innocence.

"Young girl," Juhle said. "Really, really beautiful young girl, I think even Sarah will agree. . . ."

Russo nodded. "Even Sarah admits she's very pretty."

"In fact" — Juhle leaned halfway across the table to Hunt — "she is so incredibly beautiful she'll make your teeth bleed. Alicia Thorpe. Twenty-five or so, volunteering at Sunset —"

"— and Como was having an affair with her?"

"That's the problem." Juhle shook his head sadly. "If he was, they both were damned discreet."

"And so," Hunt asked, "how would she be involved then, exactly?"

Russo let herself chuckle. "Probably not, is your answer. And Devin's answer after we talked to her. And mine, too, while we're at it. And Dev so badly wants an excuse to go look at her again. I told him if he kept it up I'd have to tell Connie."

"Hell," Juhle said, "I've already told Connie. Now she wants to see her too. I'm thinking of taking Connie out to Morton's and spending a million dollars just so we can both look at her."

"Morton's?" Hunt asked.

"She's the hostess there," Russo told him.

141

Hunt looked over at Juhle. "Is she there Tuesday nights?"

Juhle pointed back at him. "Not the last one. She could have been anywhere."

"Did you ask her?"

Juhle threw him a withering gaze. "Oh, I must have forgot. What a good idea." Then, "Of course I asked her, Wyatt. She, like Mrs. Como, was home alone watching television. Except if she really was out with Como."

"But alas," Russo said, "we have nothing like any evidence on her."

Hunt's cell phone went off and he brought it to his ear and had a short conversation. When he closed it, he said, "Well, I'm glad you took this opportunity to get me caught up on all the excellent police work and progress you've made so far. That was Tamara from my office and it looks like we're going to be in business together for a while."

Jaime Sanchez came up from the Mission Street Coalition offices to downtown to have lunch with Len Turner at the Olympic Club, a venue in the grand tradition of old San Francisco. The spacious, high-ceilinged dining room conveyed a tone of gentility and leisure. Here all voices were well-modulated, controlled; there was no un-

142

seemly hurry or vulgar clothing on display. Almost all of the male diners today — and today, as every day, they were mostly male — wore conservative dark business suits and ties. One could order, of course, nearly anything from the waitstaff, but the buffet was so staggeringly laden with all manner of foodstuffs — from cold cuts to chicken three ways; from smoked salmon to poached and sautéed fish; pastas and potatoes and a carving station with leg of lamb, prime rib, and fresh ham — that most guests availed themselves of that opportunity.

Sanchez wore his own personal uniform — unpolished brogues, a pair of well-worn khakis, a blue blazer with some years on it, and a light orange shirt with matching woolen tie. He enjoyed flouting this bastion of privilege with his inadequate attire. He caught a glimpse of himself in the mirror, and his relatively short physical stature, along with the general swarthiness of his complexion, didn't make for much of a presentation, either, at least in this crowd.

To hell with 'em, he thought. He knew he was here because of what he represented.

His partner, Len, on the other hand, couldn't have looked more natural here, and couldn't have fit in more easily. Sanchez thought that he had probably come here as a child, on his father's knee. He knew not just the greeter and the waiters by first name but the bussers behind the buffet.

Well, he told himself, this was why Len was so valuable to have as a partner. The man was not only a skilled negotiator (and lawyer), but he cultivated an ease that inspired confidence, the sense that everything was as it should be, and under control. Even in rarefied settings such as this one, Len was always at home. Tall, aristocratic, fit, and tanned. Could it all be just genes? That, to Sanchez, was a scary thought.

Now they were returning from the buffet. In contrast to Sanchez's overheaping plate of fettuccine, green beans, French fries, Caesar salad, and prime rib, Turner's plate held a small bit of petrale in lemon-caper sauce, a few slices of scalloped potatoes, and three spears of asparagus.

As they sat down, two of them at their four-person, white-tablecloth table, Sanchez forced a laugh. "I've got to learn to control myself around a buffet like that. I see all that incredible food and I swear to you, Len, I want all of it."

His elegant colleague offered a small smile. "That's what it's there for, Jimi. You want more, when you're done, go back and get it. Nobody's going to say a word." He forked himself a bite of fish, savored it, nodded in mute approval, then directed his attention back across the table. "Thanks for coming up on short notice."

"No problem," Sanchez said. "Always better to talk in person anyway. You said it was urgent."

"Well" — Turner waved a hand — "maybe the urgency is relative. But I thought it would be worthwhile if you and I, first, came together on a consistent game plan for this reward idea, which basically I like, and then talked a little about strategy for the succession at Sunset, which is going to be a huge deal."

"Don't I know," Sanchez said.

"Yes, I'm sure you do. But first things first, huh?"

"Always. So what do you have?"

Turner put his fork down. "Nancy Neshek called me as soon as she'd gotten off the phone with Lorraine. What Nancy understands, and you I'm sure, while perhaps Lorraine doesn't, is what a great fundraising opportunity this reward scenario is for all of us." He lowered his voice and leaned in over the table. "Here's Dominic Como, fallen hero, champion of the people. Every organization where he's on the board — that's yours and Nancy's and at least three others I could name — we announce we're ponying up 'x' number of dollars for the reward. It's going to be a city-wide, concerted effort to find his killer, because the police have run out of leads. But, you're asking, aren't these charities running on lean budgets anyway? Where's all that money going to come from?"

For Sanchez, the picture suddenly snapped into sharp focus. "Our generous contributors."

"Right. We make a special, one-time appeal for emergency funds to cover the reward we're offering. So we commit, let's say, a couple of hundred grand between us, maybe more — it doesn't really matter, chump change, whatever it turns out to be. We print up special pledge cards, get 'em out to your mailing lists and into the community, make a pitch on TV. It could easily bring in two, three million, maybe more."

The number lit up Sanchez's eyes. This was the kind of plan that could make the nonprofit world so incredibly lucrative. Turner was proposing that he and Nancy Neshek and a few other executives could invest thirty or forty thousand dollars each on the reward and its attendant publicity, and conceivably bring in a million or more each for their efforts. And that wasn't even including private foundation and grant money, which — given Dominic Como's personal connections with these groups — Sanchez thought would flow like water.

Never mind that none of the charities might ever actually have to pay a cent of that reward, since it was far from a certainty that anyone could provide the information that would lead to an arrest in the Como case. Nevertheless, this one-time, special fund-raising campaign would raise money that no one in the real world would ever audit or follow up on in any way. This was because once they gave, contributors simply tended to assume that the funds would be used either for the express purpose of the campaign, or to buttress another needy area in the charity's charter.

"This is one of those 'opportunity knocks' moments, Jimi. We'll want to get this reward up and posted as soon as we can."

Sanchez brought a hand up to his mouth, placed two fingers on his lips against the urge to smile. "Of course," he said. "That goes without saying. I was going to put up twenty-five, same as Sunset."

"That sounds about right. Nancy's in at that level too. And I'm sure I can talk to a couple of other colleagues and get the total up to over a hundred, which is about the minimum we'll need for credibility. As soon as we get to that number, I thought I'd announce the press conference, put things in motion. Then we can sit back and just watch the money start to pour in."

Sanchez went back to the buffet for dessert, and sat down again across from Turner with a wedge of cheesecake and a brownie sitting under a scoop of vanilla ice cream. Both men waited while their coffees were refilled, and then Sanchez waded into the turbulent waters of the succession question at the Sunset Youth Project. "I realize that there'll be an open evaluation and hiring process, Len, but I don't think anyone could object to my qualifications. I've been running Mission for seven years. I'd be a logical and natural choice."

Turner dabbed his lips with his napkin. "Well, that's what we need to discuss, Jimi. I'm all for supporting you, and for advancing your candidacy with the board, but there are still some unresolved issues that aren't so obvious."

Sanchez clearly hadn't anticipated this objection from his colleague. His brow went dark. "Like what?"

"Like, first, Lorraine Hess."

"Pah! She's —"

But Turner raised a hand, stopping him. "Lorraine Hess is a woman with ten years' hands-on experience with the nuts-and-bolts stuff, Jim. She knows the place inside out. She's going to have a good deal of support from the board. And she's made no secret of the fact that she's going to want to be in the running and deserves the job. And did I mention she's a woman? We've never had a woman director. That could prove to be more important than everything else put together." Len offered half a smile. "You're damn lucky she's not black."

Sanchez was shaking his head. "She's not executive material, Len. You and I both know it. She's a worker bee. She'd be best staying where she is. I don't think she even has a clue what Dominic actually did."

This brought a tight smile. "Did anybody?"

"I like to think I've got a pretty good idea of it."

While he shoveled a bite of cheesecake and washed it down with some coffee, Turner said, "I'd be interested to hear that. We can look on it as part of your interview process."

Sanchez swallowed. "Fair enough," he said. "But saying what he did first of all entails what he didn't do, and that is any

149

actual work with Sunset's organization. He was just totally above it. Which, by the way, is why Lorraine wouldn't be any good at his job. There wasn't really anything to Dominic's job at all, except to do favors and collect money. I think she's still under the impression that he actually had some function within the organization, when in fact he didn't."

"No. I agree. That was his genius."

"Call it that if you want. But if some new hire goes waltzing into there thinking he or she's going to be doing something, as opposed to simply peddling and trading influence, there's going to be anguish and gnashing of teeth, believe me."

Now Turner leaned in over the table. "Well, frankly, Jimi, that's exactly the concern that some of us on the board have about your interest in the job. You have actually been in charge of running your programs day-to-day at Mission, keeping track of your people, mandating profit centers. To use your phrase, you're a bit of a worker bee yourself."

Sanchez allowed himself a small nod. "I've been biding my time, Len. I'm ready to move up to a new level. I think I've paid plenty of dues."

"And then who takes over your place at

Mission?"

"It's good you asked that. You know that my wife has been in the office and on the payroll almost since the beginning. She'd be the natural choice, I'd think, and would serve to demonstrate our commitment to gender equality."

Turner sat back with a look of appreciation. "You know, Jimi," he said, "all this time we've worked together and I had no idea you were so ambitious. Those two jobs, yours and Lola's, they'd bring in what?"

"Round it off to eight hundred."

"Don't you think that might draw a little scrutiny?"

Sanchez put down his fork. "I make two hundred now, Len. Lola's at around one fifty. No one raises their eyebrows. If I move to Sunset and Lola moves up at Mission, no one will even notice. The important thing is that Dominic's work continues, that our people keep getting elected. And how does that happen? You know how that happens."

Turner did know.

In fact, as counsel to Sunset, Turner had come to understand the power that Dominic Como had held. Not only did he control the purse strings on his $50 million-per-year budget, he directed those funds to

151

where they could wield the most political influence in the city. For the great secret of the nonprofit community, especially in the incredibly corrupt environment that was San Francisco, was its intimate connection to the political, and hence the business, community.

Como's genius lay in the fact that he'd positioned himself as the broker between all of the elements. He was the go-to guy for problems among the families of the power elite. If a judge's son needed rehab, for example, Como's wide-ranging connections in the social service community made it possible for a spot to open in a facility in Arizona, say, or Los Angeles, rather than in San Francisco where the boy's presence could be politically embarrassing for the father. If a supervisor's daughter needed a job, Como could find her a place with the Muni bus system. In fact, if a politician was having trouble with any one of San Francisco's constituencies — unions, Hispanics, gays, immigrants, city employees — Como had been the de facto intermediary, greasing the wheels of governance through the judicious application of money or personnel.

For the simple fact was that election laws in the city forbade any individual giving more than $1,150 to any single political candidate, for whatever position, be it district attorney, city supervisor, mayor, or any other elected position. On the other hand, there was no limit at all to nonprofit charity giving, which could also be written off on taxes.

Len Turner's position functioned entirely upon this axis. His clients, for the most part developers of multimillion-dollar, long-range city projects, found it in their hearts to be charitable to worthy foundations such as the Sunset Youth Project because the money that found its way into Dominic Como's coffers could then be applied to the election of city officials sympathetic to these projects. Armies of volunteers, ostensibly on their own time, manned phone banks, handed out pamphlets, packed rallies, and — on a darker note — sometimes disrupted their opponents' events. While technically illegal and certainly unethical, these practices continued unchecked because the people whose job it was to oversee these activities were among the very people benefiting from them.

Now Turner pushed himself a bit back from his table, crossed one leg over the other, and reached for his coffee cup. He met the eye of his companion and nodded.

153

Jaime was telling him that he knew how the game was played, and signaling that he was ready to try to take his own game to the heights that Como had scaled. It was true that he wasn't as polished as Como had been — but then who was? "Well, listen," Turner said. "I appreciate your frankness, Jimi. Let's let things settle for a few weeks — hell, Dominic's not even buried yet — and then see how we stand. It's good you've given me this early warning of your interest. I'll pass it along to some of the board. Meanwhile, let's get this reward up and running, take advantage of the opportunity that's right in front of us. How's that sound?"

"Good. That sounds good, Len. But I did want you specifically to know that my interest in taking over Dominic's job at Sunset isn't going away. If it wasn't for the unfortunate choice of words in this situation, I'd be tempted to say I'd kill for that job."

10

Tamara heard Hunt's cry of delight from back in his office. She jumped up at her station, went to the connecting door, and opened it to see her boss standing up behind his desk, arms outstretched above him in the classic touchdown signal.

"I'm guessing good news," she said.

Hunt brought his hands down, but his eyes still danced. "That was the wife, Ellen, who had just got off the phone with Len Turner. You want to guess?"

"She confessed?"

"No."

"She gave you a list of suspects?"

"No, but she does want to talk to us. Meanwhile, how about if she puts up fifty grand on her own?"

"Fif*teen?*"

Hunt's smile wouldn't go away. "Five-oh, Tam. Fifty. She didn't want people to think she didn't care as much as any of the nonprofits. She's the most hurt. She's been damaged the most. She wants the killer to be caught more than anybody else. I feel terrible for her, but in all other ways, I've got to say that I'm starting to feel pretty good about this whole thing. Your brother is too much, you know that?"

"I do, but don't tell him. He'll get all swell-headed."

"Don't tell me what?" Mickey appearing as if by magic behind her in the doorway. "I promise, my head will stay the same size it is now."

His sister half turned to face him. "Ellen Como just came in for fifty thousand, which brings us up to — you're not going to believe this — two hundred twenty-five thousand dollars."

Mickey's mouth dropped. "No way."

Hunt nodded. "The phone's been ringing off the hook. Ten here, fifteen there, a couple more twenty-fives. This was a brilliant idea."

"Uh-oh," Mickey said. "Tam's right. I can feel my head getting bigger." He pushed on the sides of it with both hands. "Stop," he cried in mock desperation, "stop." Then, smiling, "It's no use. I'm going to have to buy a new hat."

"You don't have a hat," Tam replied. "I've

never seen you wear a hat."

"Whew! That's lucky. I could have been out a perfectly good hat."

"I'll buy you the damn hat," Hunt said.

When the telephone rang again, Tamara pushed her brother to the side and ran over to her desk. Hunt came up to stand beside Mickey at the door, waiting to hear what was coming next.

"The Hunt Club, Tamara speaking. How can I help you?" A pause, then, "Yes. Yes, we are. Uh-huh, that would be us. Just a minute, Mr. Hunt is handling that. I'll let you speak with him." She covered the receiver and looked over. "It's somebody from Len Turner's office," she said. "You're not going to believe this, but the Board of Supervisors just voted to pitch in."

By the time Hunt left the office, the city had pledged thirty thousand dollars and the total reward from still other nonprofits had grown to three hundred thousand.

It was a lifeline.

So he was in high spirits as, following Ellen Como's phoned instructions, he pulled his Mini Cooper into the sandstone driveway in front of the mansion on Cervantes Street. Getting out of the car, he looked up at the façade in front of him, marveling at

157

the way some people managed to live. He loved his giant old warehouse, of course, but that was industrial and mostly his own handiwork.

This place just took his breath away. Looking as though it had only yesterday been painted a rich Tuscan orange, it might have been plunked down whole and set here from the hills outside Florence. An actual turret rose over a circular entryway, giving the place the feel of a castle. One side of the face of the second story was a picture window that would, he knew, command a view of the Marina, the bay, and the Golden Gate Bridge beyond. Over the garage directly in front of him a riot of bougainvillea bloomed, and above that, apparently another entire wing stretched to the property line at the side and well into the back.

He took the fifteen curving steps up through a flowering garden of herbs and brightly colored blossoms and stopped at the top to check out the view behind him, which was, if anything, grander and more expansive than he'd imagined. Even the entry floor here was higher than the tops of the residences across the street, so the vista included the dome of the Palace of the Legion of Honor (in the lagoon in front of which Mickey had found Como's body) and, beyond that, the greenery of the Presidio.

He tarried a moment longer, taking it all in, and was just about to turn and ring the doorbell when the door suddenly opened behind him.

"Mr. Hunt?" Ellen Como waited expectantly. "I didn't hear the bell but I saw you standing out here."

Hunt shrugged an apology. "I'm afraid I got mesmerized for a minute. This is quite a view you have."

Cursorily glancing behind him, she nodded. "I tend not to notice it much anymore. It never changes, you know. But, please." She stepped back and pulled the door with her. "Do come in."

They sat on matching chairs with a table between them. The table held a plate of chocolate chip cookies, a floral pitcher of water, a coffeepot, sugar and cream, two cups and saucers, and two glasses.

Ellen was very nearly beautiful, obviously fit, and exquisitely turned out. Here in the midafternoon, she wore a demure, dark brown, tailored evening dress. Not a perfectly dyed reddish-brown hair on her head was out of place. Hunt thought it was possible that she'd had a face-lift and maybe other cosmetic surgery, particularly around the eyes, but if so, the work was all but undetectable. He noticed her hands — usually a giveaway of age — and they were smooth and graceful-looking. She might equally have been thirty-five or forty-five and, at whatever age, a product of wealth and breeding.

"Before we get started," Hunt began, "I wanted to express my condolences to you. I realize that this must be an incredibly difficult time, and if at any point you don't feel up to talking . . ."

She acknowledged him with a small nod, a tiny lift of her cheekbones that might have been an attempt at a smile. "Thank you, but I asked you here, if you recall. I'm very grateful to you for coming out."

"Of course. So how can I help you?"

She gathered herself, drew in a breath, folded her hands together on her lap. Her shapely legs were crossed at the ankles under her chair. "You said you'd be looking into tips you got from people who might want to claim part or all of the reward?"

"Right."

"Well, I thought to do that efficiently you might need to have background on Dominic, on what he was involved in, who he was involved with."

Hunt decided to come out with it right

away. "Are you talking about Alicia Thorpe?" He'd already gotten the report from Mickey that Ellen had sent Juhle and Russo to talk to Alicia, to consider her a suspect.

Ellen Como narrowed her eyes, perhaps surprised by the question. "I mentioned her to the police," she said, "and they didn't seem too interested. They seemed more concerned with where I was, my so-called alibi."

Hunt was canted forward on the chair, comfortable. "They did go and interview her," he said. "I think the problem is that they don't have any physical evidence yet. The murder weapon, anything like that."

"So you've been talking to them too? The police?"

Hunt gave her what he hoped was a reassuring look. "Last time, just about three hours ago. We're in pretty close communication."

"When you saw them, did they mention that girl?"

"As a matter of fact, they did. I think they're considering her a person of interest at this time, but as I say, since there's no actual evidence . . ."

Her eyes flashed in sudden anger. "What do they need? There's plenty of evidence

161

that she and my husband . . . I told them this, but they won't do anything."

"I'm sure they would if they could, ma'am. They're under a lot of pressure to make an arrest soon. If they get something on anybody, they'll move quickly on it."

She now came forward herself. "Listen to me. I'm telling you for an absolute fact that my husband was infatuated with that girl. He told me so himself. He thought it was only fair that I should know." She coughed out a bitter laugh. "He said they hadn't done anything, if you want to believe that. Lorraine Hess as much as told me that she caught them in flagrante in the office. And she said it wasn't the first time. As if that mattered. He said he was 'just kind of in love with her,' whereas he loved me. That was the real thing, where with her it was just something he was going through, he was sure he'd get over it, but he wanted me to know. He wanted to be honest, whatever that meant. It was all so civilized. He didn't want to hurt our marriage."

"So what did you do when he told you that?"

"What did I do? I didn't do anything for a while. I was just numb. Here was my husband of thirty-two years telling me he was in love with another woman, but somehow that didn't mean he didn't love me too. Or even more. So for a couple of weeks, I think I just sleepwalked around the house, trying to understand." She let out a long breath and straightened up with her back against her chair. "Then I came to my senses and told him that I just couldn't take this any longer, that he had to fire her."

"When was this?"

"I'm not sure exactly. Not the exact day. But recently, anyway. In the last week before he . . . he disappeared."

"And what did he say to that? Your demand that he fire her?"

"He said he didn't know if he could. It wouldn't be fair to her." Suddenly, she slapped her palm down on her lap, and again, and again. "Fair, fair, *fair.* As if what he was doing to me was fair. All that talk of fair, it made me sick. Literally sick. *He didn't know if he could.* Can you imagine?"

Hunt could only nod.

"He kept saying that because they weren't *doing anything,* and by that he meant having sex, that he was still faithful to me, that he wasn't cheating. But I didn't even know what he meant by having sex. I mean, since Clinton, who knows what that means anymore? Maybe they were doing everything but. . . ." She blew out heavily. "Oh, listen

163

to me. It doesn't matter what they were doing. He was in love with her. That was the important thing."

Hunt gave her a few seconds to get herself under control. Then he spoke quietly. "So what finally happened? How did you leave it?"

Her head nodded several times. "Last weekend, his last weekend, I mean, I told him I was kicking him out if he didn't fire her. That was it. I couldn't take it anymore. We had a terrific fight."

"And?"

"And he agreed."

"He agreed to fire Alicia?"

"Yes. I told him it was me or her, and for once he made the right decision."

"And this was just before he went missing?"

Another nod. "A day or two before."

Hunt mulled this over for a moment, then raised his eyes to meet hers. "Ellen, did you tell all this to the police?"

She hesitated. "Not all of it," she said, then went on. "They made it clear they thought it might have been me who killed him. They wanted to know what I had done the night . . . the Tuesday night. They kept going on about was I sure what I'd done and what time I'd gone to sleep, and why

164

didn't I report him missing until the next day." She sighed. "Anyway, it was just clear to me that they thought it must be the spouse, it was always the spouse. They weren't going to look too closely at the Thorpe girl, no matter what I said, they already thought it was me. But then I got to thinking that maybe I didn't tell them what they'd need if they talked to her. I was just mad, and not thinking too clearly, since they'd only just told me they'd found Dominic."

Hunt paused again. "So did he, in fact, fire her?"

"Yes." She tightened her lips. "On that Tuesday, he called me at home to tell me specifically that he had told her it was over. She was done working for him." She gathered herself, drew herself up. "Then I'll tell you what happened. Then she met with him that night to beg to get her job back, and he told her he couldn't give it to her, and she went into a rage and killed him."

Hunt let out a breath. This was a compelling and believable enough scenario. Unfortunately for Ellen, there was an equally compelling argument to be made that everything had been exactly as she had described it except for Dominic actually firing Alicia. Instead, perhaps Ellen had followed him to the Palace of Fine Arts, and heard him tell Alicia he was leaving his wife to be with her. If it was going to be either Alicia or Ellen, Como might have said, it would be Alicia. And so by the time Alicia left, Ellen had worked up enough of her own jealous rage to kill him herself.

But Hunt only said, "Do you mind if I go back to the police and give them the parts of this story you left out?"

"Not at all," she said. "I wish you would. I should have told them the first time. I just wasn't thinking clearly."

"They may want to come back and talk to you again."

"That would be fine," she said. Then she added, "I know if they look, they'll find something on her." Then, suddenly, as though someone had thrown a switch, she broke a really beaming smile, wiped her palms on her dress, and stood up. "I've already sent Len my check," she said. Crossing back to one of the sideboards, she turned. "This is going to sound a little funny," she said.

Hunt got up on his feet as well. "What's that?"

"If it turns out that that girl did kill Dominic, and I'm certain that it will, and it's on

166

my information that they get her, I'm going to claim that reward. All of it."

11

The press release went out at 3:45 and Tamara got the first call at 4:08.

"You-all ain't cops, right, 'cause I ain't talkin' to no cops."

The caller identified herself as Virginia Collins and she lived alone on a thirty-foot sailboat named *Delightly,* berthed in the Marina. She'd heard the announcement about the reward on KNBC's four o'clock news on her radio, and she wanted to know who she could talk to to give her information. She wanted to make sure that there was a record of exactly who she was and when she had called so that if her information checked out, she would get the reward.

She'd heard all kinds of stories, she told Tamara, about where they'd announce a reward and then deny payment to the person who really helped get the arrest and conviction because they weren't connected and didn't know anybody who had to do with releasing the reward funds. And also, she wanted to know about the conviction part. What if they just arrested the person you'd helped to identify, and then they couldn't convict? Did you still get the money? Or any part of it?

And while she was at it, did Tamara know how hard it was to get convictions on anybody in San Francisco? It was common knowledge that juries in this town never convicted. Virginia's brother John had been an attorney for a while, working for the DA, this was back in the eighties, and even then it was nearly impossible to get a jury to convict somebody.

And what if there was a plea bargain? Did that count? They should definitely give some portion of the reward for the arrest itself. And then a bonus for the conviction.

"What about if they arrest the wrong person?" Tamara had to ask.

"That never happens," Virginia replied. "They arrest somebody, you can pretty well bet that they did it."

"But you see the problem," Tamara persisted. "They arrest somebody and give you half the money or whatever, and then they find somebody else actually did it and they've already lost the payment. Then what? That's why they've got to have the conviction along with the arrest."

"Okay, that's a good point. But even so, I want to make sure there's a record I called and what I told you, and when. Like if I'm first, that ought to make a difference. A big difference."

"I'm sure it will," Tamara said. By now she had concluded she was talking to, if not a certified lunatic, then certainly someone light on a few critical synapses. "Can you tell me briefly the nature of your information?"

"Are you kidding? I don't think so," Virginia replied. "Not on the telephone. They're all tapped, you know. The cops. I give you the information. They solve the crime, take all the credit, I don't get no reward. I ain't talkin' to no cops."

"I don't think all the phones are tapped," Tamara countered. "Not anymore."

A brief harrumph. "Well, if you believe that . . . if I were you, I'd just be a lot more careful. Somebody's listening in, I can tell you that for a fact. You're not on a cell phone there at your office, are you?"

"No. We've got a landline."

"Well, maybe that's a little better. At least they can't pluck it out of the air, but they can tap a landline just as easy. Especially an investigator's office like yours."

"I'll try to be careful what I say, then. Maybe you can give me a few more details on your contact information, at least, and we can have someone call you back, or set up an interview."

"I wouldn't have them call."

"No. Right. Of course. You said you were down on a boat at the Marina?"

Mickey had actually been out on real work, serving a subpoena on a dental hygienist named Paula Chow who had worked in the offices of Bernard Offit for six years, ending her employment with him a couple of years before. It seems that while treating female patients for TMJ or, in layman's terms, clicking of and pain in the jaw, Dr. Offit had developed a technique that included massaging the breasts of these women. Eventually, fourteen victims of this questionable treatment came forward and pressed charges. Dr. Offit's defense attorney, contending that this technique was indeed not just defensible but therapeutic, needed to call witnesses, such as Ms. Chow, who would testify that Dr. Offit was a fine man and a good boss, and would never have done anything so tawdry for his own sexual gratification. And, more particularly, that she had seen him administer this treatment, and that none of the patients had complained at the time, nor had there been any sexual component to it.

Mickey found Ms. Chow at her new place of employment at a dentist's office on Clement Street, and served her for a court date the following week. He then called his sister at work to check in. She told him that right at this moment, Mickey was needed to go talk to a possibly crazy woman who lived on a boat in the Marina.

"What makes you think she's possibly crazy?"

"You'll see."

So he drove out Park Presidio and around to the same Marina parking lot he'd used last Friday morning, parked, and came to the gate leading down to the boats. The sun was out by now, although the wind was brisk, and the bay was a kaleidoscope of sails skidding along over the whitecaps.

A woman stood just inside the gate with her arms crossed and an impatient look on her face. Wearing a yellow slicker over painter's pants and boat shoes, she seemed to be in her late fifties or early sixties, with windblown hair the color and consistency of straw. "I'm Virginia. Are you the Hunt Club?" she asked him with some asperity.

Mickey flashed his disarming smile. "Not

the whole thing, just pretty much its top operative."

"Well, good," she said. "I need someone with brains. Got some ID?"

"Yes, ma'am." Mickey flashed her his driver's license and gave her a Hunt Club business card. This was a long way from identifying him as a private investigator, but it seemed to satisfy her. Only after she'd perused the card for a long ten seconds did she reach into her pocket for the key to the lock. While unfastening it, she shot him a squinty look. "Can't be too careful, you know."

"Yes, ma'am. I couldn't agree more."

"There's a lot more rape going on than people report."

"Right."

"People look at me, fifty-seven going on thirty I always say, and tell me I shouldn't worry about rape, I'm too old. But you know, rape's not a sexual crime. It's not about sex, it's about hate and anger. There was a woman last month, sixty-two, over in Berkeley, in a wheelchair, can you believe? Mugged and, as they say, sexually assaulted, which means raped. Anyway, that's why I like it down here, behind this fence. Nobody gets in here doesn't know one of the boat owners."

"Good policy," Mickey said.

She looked him a good hard squint in the eye for a second or two, possibly to see if he was fooling with her, but again he must have passed her scrutiny because with a "Follow me, then," she turned and led him down to a badly misused sailboat near the end of the pier, which she stepped onto.

Then she and Mickey were seated on cracked and slightly damp cushions around the wheel. Virginia had some laundry drying, hung with clothespins from the guylines on the seaward side. From inside the galley came the sound of talk radio.

Mickey had already decided that Tamara's call on this woman was correct, but crazy people could have good information. Still, he didn't want to take more time than was necessary chatting here, so he crossed a leg, casual and relaxed, leaned back against the seat, gave her a smile. "So, Virginia, I understand you have some information you think might be helpful about the Dominic Como murder?"

"I think I do, yes. Do you need anything to verify the time we're talking? Is there some official form or something we sign that I can keep a copy of?"

Mickey, feeling that maybe Tamara hadn't sufficiently prepped him here, figuratively put on his tap dancing shoes. "Well," he said, "I'm sure we could have you come down to the office and we could write up a statement for you to sign, and have it notarized, if it comes to that. But why would you want that exactly?"

"The reward," she said simply. "So someone don't steal the reward from me."

"Ah."

"An' nobody tells the cops who I am. I come up with something first, and then next thing you know everybody knows it, *because I told it,* and suddenly nobody remembers where it first came to light. Pretty convenient, if you ask me."

Mickey nodded, taking all of this very seriously. "All right, Virginia," he said at length, "I'll tell you what we'll do, if it meets with your approval. You tell me what your information is and if we both decide it's significant or important enough, I can take you down to the office right away and we can draft and notarize your statement. Then copy it and send you back here with your copy. How does that sound?"

She gave him the thousand-yard stare again, considering. Then, making up her mind, she nodded. "I'm glad they sent somebody with brains."

■ ■ ■ ■

The three of them — Mickey, Tamara, and Wyatt Hunt — sat with their knees all but touching at a small table in a blessedly quiet corner of the Quiver Bar at the Epic Roasthouse, Pat Kuleto's gorgeous new place on the Embarcadero, right at the water's edge. It was a cocktail hour of celebration about the new work they'd picked up, Hunt springing for drinks at the end of the day.

"She was absolutely lucid," Mickey was saying. "No question about what she saw and what it meant. And I must say, I don't think any of us would have even thought of it."

"So what was it?" Hunt asked.

Mickey sipped at his beer. "You really ought to guess. If only to get a feeling for how far off we all were."

"She saw the limo out there," Hunt said, "after it was supposedly back at Sunset."

"Not close. Tam?"

"She heard something."

"Nope. Way more obvious."

"She saw something," Tamara said.

"Good."

"From her boat?"

"Getting warm," Mickey said.

"Wait a minute," Hunt put in. "So it happened out by the boats?"

Mickey was enjoying the moment, leading them on. "I told you, think outside the box. We would never, ever, have thought of this. We're not even in the right area code. And we know it happened because she saw it with her own eyes."

For a long moment, all was silence. "Okay," Hunt said, "he actually met somebody on one of the boats. They had a fight out there . . . but, no, that's too far from the lagoon. Nobody's carrying a dead guy three blocks. Or even from the boats out to the parking lot."

"No. No carrying involved. No boats involved either." Mickey tipped up his beer again, put it down, gave a last-chance look to his colleagues. Theatrically, he sighed. "We can call Devin Juhle and close the case as soon as I tell you guys," he said, "but I thought, obvious as it is, we might want to talk about it a little first, before we bring in the cops." One last triumphant glance around the table. "Okay, you know the blimp, the tourist blimp?"

Hunt, very slowly, nodded. "Airship Ventures," he said with caution. "The *Eureka.*"

"Right. That's the one. Well, Virginia was out on her deck Tuesday night, late dusk,

177

just enjoying the peace and serenity out there, and she notices the *Eureka* coming back from out over the Golden Gate. Beautiful, if you like blimps, and who doesn't, just floating around up there. But whatever, it was a warm night and she just watched it sail pretty much straight overhead, a couple of blocks south, but really, darn close. And then, suddenly, she's looking up at it and she sees something — I'm not making this up — she sees something fall out of the thing. At first, she can't believe what she's seeing, but then she realizes it looks like a body, and it just falls and falls until it goes out of sight just over the trees, about where the lagoon would be."

"Lucky they drained it," Tamara said. "He might have killed a duck."

"But he hit the lagoon before it was drained," Mickey said, "and he didn't hit a duck anyway."

Tamara smiled brightly. "Well, that was lucky too."

"You're right," Hunt said drily, "we never would have thought of that."

"He fell into the lagoon?" Tamara asked.

"Absolutely."

"How'd he wind up at the one end, tied up in all the roots and stuff?"

"Must have been the tide," Mickey said.

178

"There's no tide in the lagoon."

"Hmm," Mickey said. "There's a slight snag in the story."

"Here's another one," Hunt said. "She saw this and didn't call the police?"

"Ah." Mickey held up a finger. "That one's covered. She thought the police might think she had something to do with it if she reported it. She was going to wait until it was in the paper or on the radio and learned more about it, but then they were obviously covering it up somehow. At least until she heard about the reward, and realized what it must have been. Which was Como."

Tamara put down her Cosmopolitan. "Wow."

"I know," Mickey said. "I was impressed. So now I'm wondering how many calls like this we're going to get. Wyatt, maybe we could figure out a better weeding-out process."

"Not if they won't talk on the phone," Tamara said. "They're all tapped, you know, and I don't think Virginia's the only one that knows it."

"Heck," Mickey said, "even I know that. But really. Wyatt?"

Hunt finished his Scotch. "Well, let's see how many of 'em we get. We told Devin half our work would be weeding out the wackos,

179

maybe more. And if we don't get some live ones, I'll be interviewing them too."

"Not that it wasn't a good time," Mickey said.

Hunt made a face. "No. I hear you. Sounds like it."

12

At ten after six, Hunt walked into the homicide detail and over to Juhle's desk. The inspector looked up and Hunt opened a leather folder and extracted several sheets of paper.

Juhle didn't exude joy at the interruption. "What's this?" he asked.

"Eleven reports. One guy didn't give his name or address, but we included a summary of his statement. Nine people gave statements, eight to Tamara over the phone. They're in order from least obviously crazy to most crazy. One lady wouldn't talk on the phone, so I sent Mickey out to talk to her. She saw Como fall out of a blimp. And I had a chat with Mrs. Como, who mentioned a couple of things she forgot to tell you when you interviewed her. Don't look at me like that — I'm just the messenger. That's ten in two hours, Dev, plus Mrs. Como." Hunt paused. "It's something," he said.

Juhle raised his eyes. "Tell me about the blimp lady."

At a quarter to seven, Hunt and Juhle had baseball gloves on (Hunt owned several) and were playing hardball catch, soft-tossing, alongside the basketball court in Hunt's warehouse, both of them dressed in street clothes.

"What pisses me off," Juhle was saying, "is people telling you stuff that they didn't tell me and Russo when we talked to them. What'd they think we were doing, just dicking around?"

Hunt caught Juhle's toss and threw it back. "People don't trust cops. Either that or they're scared of 'em."

"Me and Russo? She looks about fifteen and scares no one, trust me. And I can't even scare my own kids."

"It's what you represent. You're involved with the cops, everybody knows that basically you're in some kind of trouble. You talk to me or Mickey, or even Tam, it's just a conversation. Besides, you didn't want to talk to the blimp lady. We saved you from that."

"I'm grateful. You guys are my heroes."

Juhle threw. Hunt caught.

Hunt threw. Juhle caught.

182

Juhle said, "Ellen Como. We talked to Ellen Como for like an hour, maybe more. She told us basically nothing helpful, and she gives you the store."

"She got the feeling you thought she was a suspect."

"Well, she wasn't all wrong there. She *is* a suspect. Note the clever use of the present tense. What'd she think? She doesn't call to report her missing husband for a whole day? She lives two blocks from where they find his body? He got left off outside their house? No, no, it can't be her. What can we be thinking?" He unleashed a fastball.

"Hey! You're gonna throw the arm out again. Easy." Hunt demonstrated, a nice soft sixty-foot toss. "So anyway," he concluded, "Ellen's pretty sure it's her. Alicia."

"She said he fired her on that day?"

"The very one."

"Well, the girl said there wasn't anything physical between them."

Hunt caught the next throw and shrugged. "Maybe there wasn't."

"I've seen her, if you remember. I'd bet there was. But even if there was, so what? That doesn't mean she killed him. And you realize that Ellen could have just been trying to deflect the investigation away from herself?"

"You're kidding," Hunt said. "I never would have thought of that."

"Yeah, well. The thing is, they both had a reason, and she's the spouse, so she gets top billing until we find some evidence leading someplace else."

"And on that front . . . ?"

Juhle shook his head no. "Somebody must have dragged him to the lake, or even went in with him and got him tucked under the trees, but there's no sign of struggle on any of the banks. We've just got the body with the bump on the head."

Hunt threw. "What caused the bump? Any idea?"

"ME says no pattern injury. No definite shape or weight to the weapon. Other than that, something hard. A rock, a piece of lumber. Hell, a baseball bat, an anchor, a sap, a gun? Who knows? Maybe somebody will call you and give you a hint, and then you can tell us. Did I mention that this pisses me off?"

"I think so."

"You dangle three hundred grand out there — and by the way, that's obscene in its own right — and suddenly you've got witnesses, you got people just dying to be good citizens. You think any one of 'em might just think to pick up the phone and tell what they think they know to the police? You think that maybe could happen just once?"

"You want the truth?"

"Always."

Hunt caught Juhle's toss and kept the ball in his mitt, signifying the end of the catch. "I wouldn't hold my breath."

Hunt met his girlfriend, Gina Roake, for a late dinner at Sam's Grill. Sam's was a hopping power room during the lunch hour, but settled into a more intimate groove as the evening wore on. Now, closing in on nine o'clock, Roake and Hunt sat in one of the booths back by the kitchen. Their waiter had pulled the curtain on them after he'd left their dinners, and there might as well have been no one else in the restaurant.

Roake was older than Hunt, closing in on fifty, but as an inveterate exerciser and outdoors person, she was in excellent shape. After twenty-five years in the practice of law, she'd just recently had her first legal thriller, *Brief Deception,* accepted for publication, and she was thinking about her next one.

Most of the dinner, they'd talked about what that one might be about, and of course the marketing for the first one. Would they want her to go on tour? What about her law practice when she was out of town? Should she spend her own money on advertising? Did she want to use the same character in the second book, or break in an entirely new one? Maybe she should go to nonfiction, write up one of the real cases she'd seen or worked on? God knows, there had been some good ones. Did she have a big enough theme? Did it have to be a murder case?

Hunt nodded. "Got to be murder."

"They're always murders, though. All these books."

"Right. You know why? Any violent crime that's not a murder has a living victim. And the victim can tell you what happened. You could write a book, but it would probably be pretty short, and it wouldn't be much of a mystery."

She smiled.

"Besides, people don't care so much about bicycle theft, or other lesser crimes. Except maybe rape, now that I think of it. You could probably do a rape case, but you'd have to kill people in it eventually anyway. And if you're going to be knocking people off, might as well make it a murder case to begin with."

"Maybe you're right." She put her fork down, reached across the small table, and took his hand. "Have I been monopolizing the conversation?"

"Very charmingly."

"But that means yes. I'm sorry."

"Nothing to be sorry about. It's all been interesting."

"And yet, in spite of that" — she broke a smile — "you seem slightly distracted."

"Maybe a little," he said.

"Maybe a little," she repeated. Then, "What?"

"Actually, it's been a hell of a day."

"Good? Bad? I was thinking bad, and didn't want to ask. You'd get to it."

"Well, in fact, in a remarkable and unexpected change of pace, it's been nothing but good. Pretty amazingly good, in fact." He ran down the events for her, from Tamara's appearance in the office this morning, to Mickey's idea and the miraculously ever-growing reward, the reprieve on his business, short-term at least. Ending it with El-len Como and the tragicomic relief of Virginia, now and forever to be known as the Blimp Lady. The victim's fall from the sky into the lagoon, "which," he concluded, "we've pretty much discounted as improbable."

"Good decision." Gina shook her head in gentle amusement. "This town." But after another minute, her expression grew serious. "So in effect you're investigating this murder?"

"Not exactly. Passing what we find, if anything, along to Juhle, is all."

"He's talking to you again? I'm glad to hear that."

"Me too."

"I felt a little guilty, I *still* feel a little guilty, about driving you guys apart. Does he know you're still seeing me?"

"I assume so. He's a cop. He knows everything. But that doesn't matter. It wasn't you and him. It was me and him. Although he's not too thrilled that people seem to be coming to me now and not him."

"Is he offering them money too?"

"That's what I told him. It wasn't much consolation."

Gina sipped wine, put her glass down, something obviously still on her mind.

"I can hear the gears turning from over here," Hunt said.

A fragile smile. "I just worry about you getting in the face of these murder suspects. That's not exactly the same thing as surveillance, or rounding up witnesses, or subpoena service."

Hunt downplayed it. "I'm not really getting in anybody's face, Gina. Just passing along information."

188

"Didn't you just tell me you went and saw Ellen Como?"

"Well . . ."

"And isn't she a suspect? Isn't she, in fact, like, the prime suspect even as we speak?"

Hunt couldn't reply.

"All I'm saying," Roake went on, "is that the thing about people who have actually murdered someone, there's always some small chance they'll feel the need to do it again."

"I don't think that's going to happen."

"Most victims don't, babe, that's kind of the point. Until that last little 'uh-oh, I should have seen this coming' moment. After which, 'Oh, well, too late now.' " She picked up a piece of sourdough, looked at it, put it back down. "I don't mean to sound paranoid, Wyatt, and maybe I wouldn't if all this wasn't around Dominic Como, but since it is . . ."

"Since it is, what?"

Stalling, Gina moved a few more items around — twirled her wineglass, adjusted the placement of her knife. Finally, she raised her eyes. "I really don't want to slander the dead, especially a dead well-respected and apparently well-loved community leader, but let's just say you don't get to be a power broker in this town on

Como's level if you don't have a whole lot more going on than meets the eye."

"Like what, specifically?"

"I can't give you specifics. I don't know any. Which is how he wanted it. All I can tell you is that things just happened because Dominic Como laid his hands upon them. Or didn't happen if he didn't. Do you know Len Turner?"

This got all of Hunt's attention. "I do. He's handling the reward. What about him?"

"He's handling the reward? That's perfect. What about him is that, cutting to the chase, he's ruthless and unethical, as well as all but invisible to the general public. He's also counsel, or was, to Como and several other of our most successful service-oriented non-profits. Some have been known to call him consigliere. Want to hear a story?"

"Sure."

"Okay. Twenty years ago, Len Turner's a young attorney with Dewey, Cheatham and Howe — not their real name . . ."

"I got it," Hunt said.

"I thought you would. Anyway, Turner's got a client who owns this tiny little four-acre parcel of land down by China Basin that would be worth about a zillion dollars except for the slight problem that back in World War Two and through the fifties it

190

was a U.S. Navy munitions and fuel storage facility, which means that now it's essentially a toxic waste dump down to about a hundred feet. But now there's starting to be talk that the Giants are going to move to China Basin, which, as you've noticed, they have, and the whole area's going to be a redevelopment gold mine. You with me so far?"

Hunt nodded. *"Sí."*

"Okay, so Turner gets hired to change the zoning and get it approved by the Board of Supervisors. This turns out to be not as difficult as you might think, because Turner's clients had a lot of money to begin with. So he simply found experts and hired them to write fraudulent environmental impact reports. He then paid off one of the supervisors, Frank Addario, to support it and shepherd it through the board. But, and this is my favorite part, the best move he made was anticipating resistance from the Conservancy Club, which coincidentally had about forty-nine other questionable sites all over the state they were fighting to save. He bribed them — their president, actually — to the tune of a million dollars, to forget this one spot in what was already a severely polluted city environment. So what would it hurt?"

191

"So what happened?" Hunt asked.

"So the zoning got changed and everybody won. Except, of course, the city as soon as a buyer appeared and got about two months into the cleanup and discovered that the land essentially could never be used."

"Didn't they sue?"

"Sure. And they even won, in the sense that the sale got rescinded. But, and this is the truly great part, Turner and his clients then turned around and sued *the city* for approving the zoning change in the first place. They hadn't done their due diligence, et cetera. And finally, the city settled with these cretins to the tune of like ten million dollars."

"Can this guy Turner be my lawyer?" Hunt asked.

Gina gave him a sweet smile. "No, because I'm your lawyer. But you see what I mean? And the story isn't over yet."

"I'm listening."

"Okay, before the settlement, while all the stink is going on over this deal and the lawsuit, needless to say all the supervisors who voted for the zoning change are taking a lot of heat. At about this time, Como enters the picture. Or this particular picture."

Hunt cocked his head. "How do you know

192

all this?"

Roake hit him with a level gaze. "Mostly David." This was her former fiancé, David Freeman, who for forty or more years before he died had been one of the city's legal titans. "He was counsel for the Conservancy Club."

"Aha. Okay, back to Como."

"Como sees an opportunity here, and starts pumping money that certain development interests had been donating to the Sunset Youth Project into the campaigns of the supervisors who are running to unseat the scoundrels who have helped perpetrate this fraud on the city."

"That's got to be illegal."

"Oh, it's illegal, all right. But illegal only matters if someone is going to pursue it criminally. And back then in the DA's office, perhaps because the DA had a son who was having rehab issues himself, there didn't seem to be the will."

"This is getting good," Hunt said.

"I thought you'd enjoy it. And so, to continue, guess what? A majority of new supervisors got elected. And those are the folks who, to avoid the cost and hassle of litigation, for the good of the city and to put this ugliness behind them, approved the settlement. In other words, it all just went away. Oh, and one other thing."

"Hit me."

"This was also when the city signed over the decrepit and abandoned former Ocean Park Elementary School to the Sunset Youth Project to use as their headquarters."

"Wow," Hunt said. "Nice ending."

"You see why I think it might be smart of you to watch out and pay attention around this thing? It might have been Como's wife, or something else personal, all right. But it might also have been something altogether different. In which case, there are interests you don't want to get in the way of."

"Well" — Hunt went back to his meal — "you made your point. But I still think there's a big difference between these financial shenanigans and people actually killing other people over them."

"You do, huh?"

"I do."

"Well, then, I better not tell you about Addario and Ayers — the supervisor and the Conservancy Club president."

"I bet you're going to, though."

She nodded. "Before the settlement got announced, Addario apparently committed suicide, and Ayers was apparently the victim of a hit-and-run."

"I notice you said *apparently* twice in there."

"Right." Solemn, Gina nodded again. "Good word, isn't it? *Apparently* is the new *allegedly.*"

13

Tamara opened her eyes before the alarm went off, while it was still dark out, and for a moment could not exactly place herself, although she had slept in the same Murphy bed that she'd been using for the past six months. She turned to look at the digital clock on the windowsill and saw that it was 4:42.

At 5:01, and wide awake, she tossed the blankets off and sat up. She'd been sleeping in plaid flannel pajamas that had once been Mickey's, and they swam on her, even with the string on the pants pulled as tight as it would go. Quickly she made the bed, then lifted it, gently folding it up into the wall so it wouldn't wake anyone.

After a quick trip to the bathroom, she looked in at where Mickey slept and felt a surge of relief and love when she saw his gangly form splayed out on top of his bed. Closing the door softly, she went into the kitchen, turned on the one light, and set up the Mr. Coffee for eight cups. While the coffee gurgled and dripped, she rummaged in the refrigerator, pulling out a plate covered with strips of leftover lamb, then some polenta, butter, a carton of eggs.

Five minutes later, she poured her first cup of coffee, added heavy cream and — what the hell — three sugars, then scooped her three-egg concoction onto her plate, smothering it with ketchup.

The first bite was so delicious that it brought tears to her eyes.

The Hunt Club's office was over a Chinese gift shop on Grant Avenue. The door was around the corner on Sacramento and at 8:10, twenty minutes early because they were excited about the possibility of more leads coming in by phone, Mickey and Tamara were just getting to that door when, coming from the other direction, they almost literally ran into the two women who were about to turn into the same doorway. And upon recognition — it was Gina Roake and another, younger attorney from her office, Amy Wu — the exclamations and hugging commenced.

"We heard from Wyatt you were back!"
"We're so glad it's true!"

197

"We've missed you so much."

"I missed both of you too."

Mickey, standing to one side, said, "Me too," ambiguously, and Wu came over and gave him a conciliatory buss on the cheek and about half a hug. "We would have missed you, too, Mickey," she said, "except you just wouldn't go away."

Hunt showed up early, too, but it was still after everyone had gone upstairs and gotten the office opened up, the coffeemaker going, the shutters open. The three employees were acutely aware of the number "7" blinking at Tamara's phone, but waited until Roake and Wu left to go back to their own offices before they encircled the desk while Tamara pressed the playback button.

"Hi, the Hunt Club. This is Cecil Rand, three eight one, two two eight four. I believe I've seen something that might have to do with the Dominic Como murder. I'm not sure if it's anything and I don't want to have the police think I'm just trying to waste their time, so maybe you could call me back. Thanks." He repeated his number, and hung up.

"Hello." A tentative woman's voice. "Is anybody . . . ? Hello? My name is . . . well, never mind. I guess I'll just call back when you're there."

"Oh, super," Mick said. "Unless you die in the meantime."

Next was another woman, no greeting. "This is Nancy Neshek. I'm the executive director of the Sanctuary House. My name may be familiar because my organization has also put up twenty-five thousand dollars for the reward, so I won't be calling to claim any part of that, but I did have a question if one of you could please call me back, either at home or my office, sometime tomorrow. It's somewhat important." She then left both of her numbers, said thank you and good-bye, and rang off.

"Hey. I'm Damien Jones, over here at the Mission Street Coalition, and uh . . . well, there's just some stuff goin' on here that ain't right. I mean, they say we getting all this foundation money s'posed to pay for room and board and food and stuff and then they take it out our pay. I don't know how Como did it over there at his place, you know, Sunset, but if I can get moved over there, I'm applying."

Next: "My name is Eric Canard with the San Francisco Palace Duck Coalition and I just wanted to inform you that I'll be going to the media myself in the next day or two to expose this obviously fraudulent murder you've got everybody talking about, and the even more blatant attempt to deflect attention from the situation with the displaced ducks from the Palace Lagoon, which is now, as I'm sure you know, just about completely empty. I don't know who's putting up all this supposed reward money, but I think I can prove that there is both no dead man and no money that will actually be paid for any reward. If the Hunt Club is even in fact your real name."

After that hang-up, Hunt's mouth twitched. "Well, Mick, that's at least one for you."

The penultimate message was from a real client, another of Roake's junior associates calling about scheduling a deposition for the first two days of the following week, and would Wyatt call to verify his availability.

Finally, the tentative woman again, maddeningly repeating her first message almost verbatim — she'd call back later, when they were there.

"Leave a message!" Mickey actually yelled at the telephone. "Leave a goddamn message. What's the matter with you?" He looked at his sister. "What's the matter with her? She afraid somebody's going to jump through the phone and bite her?"

But Tamara could only shrug and turn to

her boss. "How do you want to divide these up?" she asked.

Hunt decided that calls number one and three — Nancy Neshek and Cecil Rand — were worth his time and energy, and that Mickey would take the other ones, leaving Eric Canard to Mickey's own judgment as an obvious flake and publicity hound, but one who in fact had probably spent a significant amount of time in and around the lagoon and might have seen something, and who would never, ever, under any circumstances, talk to the police.

For his own part, Hunt first called Nancy Neshek's home number and left a message. Then, still before nine A.M., he called Sanctuary House, which had apparently not yet opened its main office for the day. Leaving another message there, he next called Cecil Rand, who picked up on the first ring and told Hunt he'd meet him at Johnny Rockets Diner on Chestnut Street in the Marina District. Rand told Hunt he was old and black and run-down-looking; "you'll think I'm a bum, but I'm not." And he would be wearing an almost-new Raiders jacket. Hunt said he'd be in his Cooper if Rand was outside waiting.

Hunt made it down there in about fifteen

minutes and saw a man fitting that description standing in the doorway to Johnny Rockets. He was rolling down his window to say hello and ask if he was Cecil Rand when the man pointed at him, said, "Hunt?" and got a nod in return. He jaywalked, stopping the traffic, through the opposite lane, passed in front of the car, over to the passenger door, and got in.

"Cool car," he said, fastening his seat belt. "I've always wanted to ride in one of these. Bigger than it looks, isn't it?"

"Yeah, I love it," Hunt said. "Plus, you wouldn't know to look at it, but it's a rocket ship. The thing hauls." He looked across at his passenger, who came exactly as advertised. "So where we going?"

"Hang a right. The lagoon."

Hunt gave him another quick glance. His clothes were worn but clean, and he exuded a kind of raw confidence that made Hunt glad he'd included Cecil as among the legitimate tipsters. And his saying that they ought to go to the lagoon was promising. It was, after all, if not the scene of the crime itself, then, nevertheless, a venue of significant interest.

They'd just turned off Chestnut when Rand volunteered that he almost hadn't called, probably wouldn't have if it hadn't been about Dominic. "Although if it turns out I get some of the reward, you know, that wouldn't hurt none either. But even then, if it wasn't Dominic, I don't know if I'd have bothered. But whoever killed him, they got to get caught."

"You knew Mr. Como?"

"Yeah. The guy saved my life."

The phrase struck Hunt, since he'd heard so many other people use it in recent days. "How's that?" he asked.

"I did some time growing up. Down at Corcoran. You know that's a prison."

"I've heard of it."

"Lot of folks haven't, you'd be surprised. Well, you get out of prison, it's hard to find work, maybe you've heard that too." His unshaven face wrinkled. He obviously thought he'd uttered some kind of witticism. "So I got nowhere to go when I get here, back to the city I mean, and I'm in town maybe two weeks, standing in line outside the Divisadero kitchen, the money they give me out of the joint just about all gone, and I'm thinking, 'Shit, what now?' And suddenly up comes this limo and pulls in and this guy — it turns out it's Dominic but I don't know it then — he's dressed up like a banker, better'n a banker, he gets out and he's smiling, talking to people, right at

203

home with brothers, all like that.

"So by the time I'm inside, he's there, too, his jacket's off, and he's actually serving up food on my tray and I'm thinking this is some strange dude, and I don't know why but I stop there in front of him and the Lord speaks to me and tells me to ask him if he knows where an ex-con like me can get myself a job. And he just stands there lookin' at me a minute and then says don't let him leave without snagging him again.

"So I don't take my eyes off him, and then he's putting on his jacket and I get up and he actually comes over to me and asks me what I want to do and when can I start. And I tell him anything and right now. And I can see he likes that 'cause he says come on out with him and he drives me in his limo out to this house they're rebuilding over on Fell and next thing I know I'm carrying drywall and learning how to put it up. Got pretty good at it too."

"I bet you did."

Rand nodded, satisfied. "So there it was. Steady work with his rehab people until I learned what I was doing and then Dominic caught me onto a regular crew, I mean real construction work. Saved my life. Here, pull over here."

They'd come all the way up to the north

end of the lagoon, near where Mickey had found Como's body. By now, the only water left was visible as little more than a sinuous puddle that ran down the middle of the mud slick that used to be the bottom of the pond.

"Now, before we get to it, maybe I should have said this first." Rand put a quick hand on Hunt's arm, stopping him from getting out. "I want to keep it that my name don't get out in front of the police on this thing. If it turns out it's somethin', then it's what it is, is all. But I don't want anybody telling the police who got you here and how'd I see it when nobody else did. Good?"

Hunt didn't like to make promises he wasn't sure he could keep, but he didn't want to shut Rand down either. So he nodded ambiguously and let him continue.

" 'Cause you know," Rand went on, "they get somebody like me done time, next thing it's how'd he know where to look? He must have been part of it. You understand what I'm sayin'?"

"I do."

A brusque nod. "Least not till they doin' the reward, when it's over."

"I hear you."

"Okay, then." And they both reached for the door openers.

As soon as they got out of the car, Hunt could smell rotting vegetation and gas. And he noticed that all along the opposite shore, the degraded shoreline had been fenced off, no doubt in preparation for the improvements, the new rock-and-concrete wall.

Cecil Rand came around and led him across the street, then down across the grassy lawn to the old retaining wall. They were still quite a ways from the water-hugging trees that marked the exact site where Como had been found, but Rand didn't seem to know or care about that, and stopped perhaps fifty yards short of it, and on the street side.

"Okay, now," Rand said as they stood looking out over the mud. The sky today was heavily overcast and the gray morning light flat and without glare. "Now, I ain't saying this is absolutely somethin', it's just what it is."

"All right," Hunt said. "What are we looking at?"

Rand moved in closer next to Hunt and pointed slightly off to his right. "I was walking by here last night before dark and stopped right here. Seen it and started thinkin' on the reward. Put my stogie out here to mark the spot, so I'd get it right."

Hunt looked down and saw the carbon X

on the low wall. Then his eyes came up, following where Rand was pointing.

"Just this side of the last of the water," Rand said. "It's still there."

"What, though?" And then Hunt squinted. Maybe ninety feet away from where he stood, and still ten feet on this side of the puddle, the smooth flat surface of the mud yielded an instantly recognizable shape, out of place among the smattering of roots and bottles and rotting algae. It looked like two sticks crossed at perfect right angles, but Hunt knew what it was even as he said, "I see it. You mean the tire iron?"

Rand was nodding and nodding, the corners of his mouth turned up in satisfaction. "I'm seein' that ol' thing in the mud last night and thinkin' I be lookin' at what got used on Dominic."

14

The headquarters for the Mission Street Coalition's moving company occupied two large warehouses and an office that was little more than a shed in the light industrial neighborhood a couple of blocks off Cesar Chavez Boulevard between the 101 and 280 freeways.

Mickey, clueless, drove out to the Coalition's residential home on Dolores, got there at about nine-thirty, then asked around and at the desk for Damien Jones. The administrative bureaucracy at the home wasn't the most organized system Mickey had ever encountered, and it took him nearly a half hour to hunt down Damien's likely whereabouts, and he only succeeded then because, inadvertently, he had run into the executive director of the program, Jaime Sanchez, and his wife, Lola.

Identifying himself for what he was, an associate with the Hunt Club, Mickey had explained that Mr. Jones had called the reward hotline number at the office yesterday and apparently had some information relating to the murder of Dominic Como. This seemed to surprise and slightly displease both of the Sanchezes. They couldn't imagine what that might be or why Damien hadn't told them first. But nevertheless Mr. Sanchez directed Mickey to the moving company's headquarters, where he arrived at ten-twenty only to discover that Mr. Jones was out with a moving crew on a job at Forty-second Avenue, almost to the beach, and a good half hour's drive, or more, from headquarters.

Before he started that drive, though, Mickey took a frustration break and called his sister at the office, giving her the play-by-play of his morning so far, which had produced nothing at all even in the limited realm of eliminating spurious claims to the reward money. "So now I'm off to Forty-second Avenue! Forty-second Avenue! That's like five blocks before you leave the continent, do you realize that? The way this morning's going I'm not even going to lay eyes on this Jones guy until noon, and that's if he's not on his lunch break someplace else. And all for what? So I can get to meet another Blimp Lady, except this guy's a guy? This is dumb. Isn't there somebody else I can check out? Did that girl ever call back? I can check out Damien Jones when he comes back home tonight, if he does. If his name's even Jones, which now that I think about it, it probably isn't. Well?"

"Well, what, Mick? Did you ask me a question?"

"I bet I asked you a hundred in there."

"Try one again. One."

"Okay. Have we gotten any new calls?"

"Yes."

"Great. Who? Hang-up Lady?"

"Not her. Not yet. But actually, we've gotten three more. The bad news being that they all sound to me like Wyatt's going to give them to you. If I had to bet."

"Are they closer than Damien Jones? I mean physically closer? Maybe I can see one of them on the way out to see him. Or all of them."

"I think maybe you should wait until Wyatt decides, don't you?"

His sister's voice of calm reason finally made an impact. Mickey let out a deep sigh into the telephone and said, "Probably." He took another breath. "Speaking of which, you get any word from him?"

"As a matter of fact, I have. The guy he met this morning? He thinks he might have come up with the murder weapon."

"Yes!" News of success on any front pumped Mickey right up. "What is it?"

"A tire iron they found in the lagoon. He's called Devin and they should be over there by now."

"That is so great," Mickey said. "Do you think this reward thing might actually work, Sis? Would that be cool, or what?"

"Very cool, Mickey, very cool. But let's just see what happens. See if the tire iron . . . I mean if they can tell. And then where it leads, if anywhere. But at least it's something. Some real evidence. Maybe."

"Okay," Mickey said.

"Okay, what?"

"Okay, I'm motivated again. We'll keep doing it this way. Meanwhile, what are you doing for lunch?"

She hesitated. "I haven't really thought about it. I had a huge breakfast, you know, this morning."

"I remember. But they've got this new theory where you can eat two, or even three, meals in one day, and it won't kill you. In fact, it might even be good for you."

"Don't worry. I'll get something," she said.

"You'd better. There'll be a quiz on what it was when I get back."

■ ■ ■ ■

Damien Jones, at long last.

Mickey got the strong impression that Damien's boss wasn't happy to give him time off for this interview, but Mickey had told him the half-truth that Mr. Sanchez had directed him how to find Mr. Jones, intimating that the big boss himself wanted the interview to proceed.

Now Mickey and Damien had walked a few houses down the street from the move-in job site and were sitting on concrete steps leading up to one of the other houses. Out here, the gray cloud cover was thick, but high enough that it wasn't quite fog. In spite of that, every few minutes, the deep bass of a foghorn punctuated the early afternoon stillness.

Since Mr. Jones had called with information that seemed to have at least an oblique relevance to the investigation, Mickey found that he had to summon all of his patience as it quickly became obvious that Damien was under the influence of some kind of controlled substance. During the first few questions, trying to establish a rapport with the young workman, it wasn't even obvious that Damien remembered the substance of his call to the Hunt Club the previous night.

So Mickey gently prodded. "You said something about the fact that the foundation was supposed to pay for your room and board, but now you were paying. And it wasn't fair."

"Right. Right."

"And that Mr. Como didn't do the same thing at his place. The Sunset Youth Project."

"Okay."

"Okay. And that this somehow had something to do with his murder."

Damien sat on the step with his elbows on his knees, staring straight in front of him, to all appearances stumped. After a minute, he laughed softly to himself, hung his head, and shook it. "Seemed like I had it all worked out last night, but that wasn't exactly it, what you just said."

Mickey nodded, all understanding. Although he knew that if this was all he was going to get after the four hours he'd spent tracking this bozo down, he'd be sorely tempted to kill him. Still, he reined himself in and managed to sound sincere. "That's all right," he said.

"But that don't mean it isn't true."

Mickey wasn't clear what antecedent Damien was referring to here and, in fact,

213

was reasonably sure that Damien couldn't identify it himself. But all he said was, "No, I know."

"I mean, it's a racket, you know."

"What is?"

"The whole, you know, the rehab thing."

"A racket?"

"Yeah."

"How's that?"

"Well." Damien looked up the street, making sure he was still out of earshot. The foghorn sounded, and he continued. "You know, they collecting money from the foundations. Big money."

Suddenly Mickey felt a chill raise the hairs on his arms. Unbidden, the discussion he'd had with Alicia Thorpe the other day about the Sunset Youth Project's funding from the city and from other foundations came back to him in sharp detail, particularly her disclosure that the city's Health Services Department was the biggest single line item in the city's budget. And now here was Mr. Jones, no relation to Mr. Einstein, referring to the same thing. Which didn't necessarily mean anything, except for the rather salient fact that Mr. Jones, addled as he might be or might have been last night, somehow was introducing this funding issue into a discussion about Dominic Como's murder.

214

And now, it seemed, Jones had found a scent. And it was Mickey's job to keep him on it. "Right," he said. "So the Mission Street Coalition gets money from the city. So what?"

"So what is they s'posed to use that to keep up the program. But it don't go to no program."

"So where's it go, Damien?"

"Now, that I wish I knew." He clucked in disappointment. "But, oh, yeah, this what I was sayin'. The whole thing is, they get me, 'stead of jail, into the program here, okay?"

"Right."

"Okay, the thing is, they ain't no *program* to the program. You know what I'm sayin'?"

Thinking, *Patience, young Jedi,* Mickey said, "Not exactly. Maybe you can tell me."

"Okay, here's the thing. We here for the rehab, you know. Otherwise, we maybe in jail, right? Right. So we get here, ain't nobody doin' that twelve-step shuffle, ain't nobody urine testing, we just come in and say, 'No, we ain't doin' no shit,' and sign this form, and then we done. Except they make us work."

Getting a little wound up now, Damien Jones's expressive face went into a deep frown. "Hey! Look at me, now. Whatchu think I been doin' all day 'cept humping these loads? And the company, the Coalition, they chargin' the same as like Bekins, you know, the moving people. And they s'posedly payin' us fair, but we don't never get to see no money. See what I'm sayin'? *That's* the money goes for rent and food, *my* money. Not no foundation money. So where's all that foundation money go? That's what I want to know. So bottom line is they got me workin' for a year, payin' all the bills 'here, and meanwhile I don't do every little thing they ask, I'm out of the *program* and back in jail. You want to know the truth, they got theirselves a bunch a slaves workin' here, nothin' less, and I'm one of 'em. And that ain't right."

"No, it isn't," Mickey said. "And I'm glad you decided to tell me about all this. But you called last night originally about the reward, and I'm afraid if this doesn't have anything to do with the murder of Dominic Como . . . well, you know what I'm saying, don't you?"

For a long minute, Mickey thought he'd lost Damien for good. The faraway stare came back, the exhausted elbows-on-his-knees posture. Methodically, he bobbed his head as though listening to his own private soundtrack. Then, when at last he spoke, Mickey could barely hear him. "You know

216

them Battalion people out there?"

Again, one of Alicia's references, "sort of an urban Peace Corps," and Mickey snapped back to full attention. "What about them?"

"Well, brothers I know in there, they gettin' paid, all right, and they don't do no real work, so I'm thinkin' how's that happen and how do I get some of that?"

"What do you mean, they don't do work?"

Damien rolled his eyes, explaining the obvious. "I mean work like I'm doing. Humpin' loads, cleanin' up, sweepin', kitchen work, like that."

"So what do they do?"

"Whatever Dominic Como says."

"Ah." The explanation didn't really turn any light on for Mickey, but now at least Como was overtly in the conversation. Now the trick was to keep him there. "So you're saying what, exactly?"

"Well, first, I want to get me some of that."

"That might be a little difficult, Damien, since Como's dead now."

"Okay, yeah, okay. But I'm talking if . . ." Here his eyes brightened, his whole demeanor perked up, and he snapped his fingers. "Here it is! Here it is! Thinkin' on the reward now, what I got last night!"

"Hit me."

"Okay, I'm in that Battalion, right. Like the most I got to do is wash a car or pass out some pamphlets or answer some phones, some shit like that, basically nothing, you with me?"

"So far."

"So say I fuck up a little, maybe go off the rehab, something small — maybe a doob or a beer one time. You know they test out there, not like here. Anyway, who knows why, I get on Como's bad side and now he's tellin' me I'm done with the Battalion, I'm back in the shit, workin' like I'm doin' here. Or say, even better, I'm close to done with my time, and he says he's gonna violate me back to jail, out of the program. See what I'm sayin' now?"

"Still not completely, I'm afraid."

"Hey, he kicks me out now, I am fucked. I can't let that happen. I got to stop him before, you know?"

"So you kill him?"

Damien Jones threw his hands up in celebration, flashed Mickey his brightest smile. "Now you got it. That's what I'm talkin' about." He kept nodding as though making sure that the strands of his argument, if that's what it was, held together. "That's what I'm *talkin'* about." Now he looked straight at Mickey. "That's where you look, at them Battalion people. It's one of them, hallelujah, and you know where to find me."

Suddenly and thoroughly deflated, Mickey all at once came to the full-blown realization that in spite of Damien's enthusiastic narrative, he was in his own way another variant on the Blimp Lady. If not nuts, then certainly and fundamentally unhelpful.

By now just about completely baffled by trying to fathom the solution that Damien had apparently reached and was sharing with him, Mickey leaned in toward the young man. "And, just so I'm sure I understand, Damien, you're saying you think Mr. Como's killer is one of these Battalion people?"

"I'm saying you look there I bet you gonna be happy you did."

"And if we do, after that, why exactly do we need to find you, then?"

Damien straightened his back, put on a look of surprised indignation. "What we been talkin' 'bout all this time? First, I get his place in the Battalion out there, the killer's, and second, 'cause then you got to give me that reward."

Hunt had called Devin Juhle and Sarah Russo within minutes of his initial sighting of the tire iron, but they'd been in the field on another matter and hadn't checked back in with him until lunchtime. Meanwhile, he'd taken down Cecil Rand's vitals and promised to keep him anonymous at least until it was determined if the tire iron out in the mud was tied in any way to the death of Dominic Como.

After Rand had gone, Hunt then tried again to reach Nancy Neshek, but she hadn't come in to her office at Sanctuary House this morning — evidently a regular occurrence, what with her fund-raising duties and/or women in crisis situations, and she still wasn't answering at home.

He'd then checked in with Tamara to see about any new leads. He decided that talking to two more people who identified themselves as members of Canard's Palace Duck group probably wasn't even worth Mickey's time, and he himself wasn't inclined to call Belinda (no last name), a psychic who, if put in close contact with Como's body, could re-create his last hours, and thus probably shed enormous light on the murder.

And reluctant to abandon his post lest someone come and remove his possible evidence while no one was guarding it, he put his back up against a tree and waited.

Now, finally, Juhle and Russo stood with Hunt at the concrete edge of the mud flat that had once been the lagoon. The cloud cover had mostly burned off and now the mud had a dull shine, making identification of anything somewhat problematic. "And even if I see it, which I don't," Juhle was saying, "how do you know it has anything to do with anything?"

"I don't. But it's there, all right," Hunt said. "And since it might be evidence in a murder you're investigating, I thought you'd call those fine upstanding people from Crime Scene Investigations to collect it for you."

"I'm going to go look at it," Russo said.

"Are you shitting me?" Juhle asked. "It's knee-deep mud out there, Sarah. And you can't touch it till CSI gets here anyway."

"I'm not going to touch it. But we're not calling CSI if it turns out it's a pipe that's been in this lagoon for a hundred years. You guys watch my shoes." And she sat on the wall and started removing them.

"All right." Juhle sat next to her. "God damn it. I'll do it."

"Aw, Dev. You're so cute when you get all guy-protective." She held out a hand to him. "But, I'm good, really. I'm a mom, after all. I've already waded through tons and tons of shit. And this is only mud. I'll think of it as a spa treatment. But you, Wyatt," she added, "you better point me straight at it or I'll arrest your sorry ass on any charge I can think of or even one I make up."

Hunt turned to Juhle. "She's a little harsh, don't you think?"

"You want to see harsh, point me even a little bit the wrong way." And so saying, she finished tucking her socks into her shoes. Next she rolled up the bottoms of her pants and swung herself around, lowering herself into the mud, into which she sank as far as her ankles. "For the record," she said, "this is not warm spa mud." After a good shiver, she added, "Okay, Wyatt, point."

Hunt stood at the charcoal X that Rand had drawn with his cigar the night before. He had a decent idea of the location of the tire iron and pointed out a tree on the opposite bank that Russo should head for. "It's ten or twelve feet before you get to the water. You can't miss it."

She turned back to him. "I'd better not, 'cause I tell you right now I'm not going to spend a lot of time mucking around looking for it."

It was, truly, one slippery step at a time, and she walked gingerly. When she was about halfway there, Hunt said, "I'd have thought you'd have dragged this lake already."

"We did. We took out six Dumpsters of shit."

"So how'd you miss this?"

"I don't know. Murphy's Law." Juhle grunted. "Anyway, we're here now, for all the good it's going to do us."

"Why wouldn't it?"

"Because the water washes away the trace evidence. Except not all of it, not all the time. We'll see."

Just at this moment a black-and-white police car pulled to the curb above them and emitted a short one-note blast of his siren. Hunt and Juhle turned and saw two uniformed policemen coming out of the car and down the grass, looking stern and ready for action. "Excuse me, gentlemen," the lead cop said, "would you mind telling me . . . ?"

But Juhle already had stepped in front of Hunt with his ID out. Introducing himself, saying the magic word *homicide,* Juhle instantly transformed the cops into two nice guys who wanted to know if there was anything they could do to help.

"She's got it," Hunt said.

And sure enough, Russo was straightening up out in the middle of the mud, waving her arms.

Juhle turned back to the cops. "Actually, guys, you can help. One of you please call dispatch and have 'em get CSI down here as fast as they can move. Tell them it's the Como one eighty-seven."

Lorraine Hess, associate director of the Sunset Youth Project, stood wringing her hands in her office doorway, facing the two police inspectors. "But you're saying you don't know if it's from the limousine yet, is that right?"

"That's right." Sarah Russo, naturally taking point with the obviously distracted woman, nodded and spoke in her well-modulated, educated, nonthreatening voice. "All we've done so far is sent the tire iron itself directly down to the police laboratory for analysis. And all we know so far is that it's the basic kind of tire iron that comes standard on a lot of cars, including the Lincoln Town Car. There's a small chance, if it was the murder weapon, that it will still have at least traces of Mr. Como's hair or blood or something recoverable through DNA, although maybe not. In any event, though, the thing's a mess and it's going to take some time, maybe a lot of time, to find out what we're dealing with there for sure." She trotted out her professional smile, which looked entirely genuine. "In the meanwhile, Inspector Juhle and I got to talking and realized that it would probably be worth our while to see if there was still a tire iron in Mr. Como's limousine."

"But why?" Hess asked. "I thought the limousine was back here by the time he was murdered. That's what we've heard."

Juhle decided to speak up. "That may be true, but —"

"It is true, I believe, Inspector."

"Well, be that as it may, if the tire iron is in fact missing" — Juhle shrugged, nonchalant — "it at least opens the door to the possibility that someone from here at Sunset might have been involved in the murder."

"But the tire iron could be gone from the limo and still not have been the murder weapon."

"Yes, of course," Sarah said. "And by the same token, if it isn't gone, then we're pretty much back where we started. It could be any tire iron from any one of hundreds of cars in the city. Anyway, the point is, with your permission we'd just like to look."

Hess brushed a vagrant hair away from her forehead. "Well, sure. I mean, that goes without saying, but don't you need a warrant or something like that?"

Juhle flashed a glance at Russo at the unexpected question. He cleared his throat. "A warrant would give us the absolute right to take that car apart and look all through it," he said, "and I'm sure we could get one in short order. But we thought we could save some time and energy trying to find Mr. Como's killer by just coming out here and asking if we could check the trunk, that's all."

"Right," Hess said. "Of course."

"Parked along the side, right?" Russo asked. "Do you have a set of keys?"

"Yes, and, yes, I'm sure I've got a spare bunch of them here somewhere, or maybe in Dominic's office. Can you give me a minute?"

Russo nodded. "All the time you need."

Hess turned and went back into her office, opened a drawer or two, sighed, closed the drawers again, then came by the inspectors again and walked across the lobby and into Como's office.

"A little nervous, don't you think?" Juhle whispered.

"She doesn't want to think it's one of her people."

"I'd think she'd be happy for the chance to prove it's probably *not* any of them. I mean, if the tire iron's there . . ."

"I know what you're saying. But the more I think about it, what does that really mean? If it's there, it means nothing. If it's not there, by itself it means nothing either."

"It means somebody took it out."

"Big deal. When? Six months ago? Yesterday? And even if our very own tire iron from the lagoon is what killed him, how do we know it's that particular limo's tire iron after all?"

"We don't. That's what makes this job so much fun. But it might, in fact, narrow the field. And you agreed to come out here, if you remember."

"I just don't know what we're going to do if we find it's gone."

"If it is, it'll lead to something. You just watch."

"Great," she said. "Words to live by."

And then Lorraine Hess emerged from Dominic Como's office, holding up a set of keys, wearing a smile that managed to be hopeful and fearful at the same time.

After swearing that she'd walked down to Union Square and bought a hot dog with lemonade and fries for lunch, Tamara gave Mickey the three names on the phone when he called in after the complete strikeout with Damien Jones.

But hearing about the duck people and Belinda the psychic, Mickey decided he'd be damned if he was going to talk to any of them. Getting together with nutcases who at least had some kind of a whacked-out story — Damien or the Blimp Lady — was one thing; but wasting his time with automatic fruitcakes like Belinda, for example, wouldn't help the police or the Hunt Club. There was such a thing as an automatic, commonsense pass on certain people, and he'd make that point to Wyatt the next time he saw him. Meanwhile, he told Tamara to call him if the mysterious Hang-up Lady or any more or less legitimate crazy person called back and needed to have their evidence debunked, but meanwhile he was going to try to call on another source for inside information about Dominic Como.

"Say hi to her for me."

Dang. How did she know?

But Alicia didn't pick up when he called her on her cell phone, so he left a message and then tried her brother and got another strikeout. It was turning out to be that kind of day. So he drove back on Lincoln alongside Golden Gate Park, a plan for the next couple of hours developing in his mind.

When he got to the Panhandle at the east

end of the park, he found a parking spot and walked back to the bocce court that hid itself very effectively beneath the cypresses. Maybe his luck was changing, because there, as he'd hoped, in the company of three other old geezers was his grandfather, lining up a shot. Mickey waited until he'd thrown — a damn good roll that stopped inside all the other balls and only a couple of inches from the jack. It must have been the last shot of the round, since it drew enthusiastic applause from Parr's team and good-natured snarling obscenities from the other men as all of them started walking down the court to pick up.

When they turned back, Jim saw Mickey and raised a hand. "You see that shot?" he asked. "I'm on fire today. We're up eight three this game. You know all these reprobates?" As Mickey nodded all around, Jim asked, "Everything all right? Tamara okay?"

"Yeah, she's good. She loves being back at work, I'll tell you that. Otherwise, everything's fine except nobody in the world is home, which makes it hard to hook up with people. So since I've got the time I thought I'd go get something for dinner and then I thought I'd stop by and see if there's anything you especially felt like."

Jim shrugged. "You make it, it's going to

be good, so it doesn't really matter."

"Even goat?"

Another shrug. "Never had it. Can you just go out and buy goat?"

"Sure. Bi-Rite's got it. They can get anything. You'd really eat goat if I made it?"

"I'd eat anything, Mick. You know me. You might check with Tam, though. She might have some thoughts on goat."

"I'm thinking of inviting somebody else over too."

"Whatever," Jim said. "I'm easy."

One of the bocce players called over and Jim told him to keep his fucking shirt on, then came back to his grandchild. "So how's the case going?"

"Decently, I guess. Tam thinks Wyatt might have found the murder weapon. Meanwhile, I'm eliminating the bad tips and getting to meet a really fun whole new class of people that I'd never otherwise get to know."

"What's that?"

"Apparently sane whack-jobs."

"No, not what's the fun new class of people, Mick. What's the murder weapon?"

"A tire iron, maybe."

Jim Parr's face hardened. "Bastard. You getting any closer to who did it?"

"Not that I know of. Maybe there'll be

fingerprints or something on the tire iron, but that would be a long shot. So probably not."

"Shit. Maybe I should just go out there."

"Where?"

"Sunset."

"And do what?"

"I don't know. Talk to some people. See if they'd talk to me. Find out what was really happening."

"I've got a better idea, Jim. Don't do that."

"Why not?"

"Because it's a really dumb idea, that's why not."

"Well, it's hard for me to believe that nobody out there knows anything at all. I mean, Dominic just has a regular day of work and then goes home and meets somebody who kills him? Somebody must have known or seen something, don't you think?"

"Yeah, I do. But we can't seem to get started down any trail that leads anyplace."

"All I'm saying is maybe I could."

"Right. And why is that? Because you're a trained investigator?"

"Hey, smart-ass, I'm as trained as the next guy. If I heard something important, I know for damn sure I'd recognize it. I know those people out there."

"But we don't know it's one of them."

"Well, that just goes to show what you know."

"What does that mean?"

"It means, it's staring you right in the face and you don't see it."

"What is?"

"The plain, simple truth about Dominic, which is that Sunset was his whole life. He lived and breathed it, morning, noon, night, weekends, holidays. His. Whole. Life. Get it? If somebody killed him, and it wasn't completely random, it had to have something to do with Sunset. Period. Maybe only a little bit. But something. Which means it's probably right there if you know what to look for."

This speech, since there was little to refute in it, shut Mickey right up. He took a few deep breaths through his nose, his mouth a tight line. "You might be right about that," he said finally, "but you going out there is still a dumb idea."

"Oh. Okay, then. I won't."

"Jim."

"No. You convinced me. I promise I won't go out there."

"A promise is a promise, you know."

"Absolutely. Scout's honor too. Now listen, I've got to get back to kicking some ass in my game, and you've got to go buy some goat. I'll see you tonight, all right?"

"Right."

15

Once upon a time, in the early days of the current administration of District Attorney Clarence Jackman, Gina Roake had been an original member of his "kitchen cabinet," advising him on municipal and legal matters while he grew into the position to which — much to his surprise — he'd been appointed. The cabinet remained in its informal existence, meeting almost every Tuesday for lunch at Lou the Greek's for about a year, and during that time, its members found that they had formed strong bonds with one another. Defense attorneys like Roake, her partner Dismas Hardy, and her then-fiancé David Freeman somehow managed to find common ground with the likes of Jackman, the city and county's chief prosecutor, and Abe Glitsky, then deputy chief of inspectors of the San Francisco Police Department.

Also among the members of the cabinet

was Jeff Elliot, the writer of the *Chronicle*'s popular CityTalk column. Elliot had contracted multiple sclerosis as a young man and over the years had gradually declined to the point where he now only rarely left his wheelchair or his desk in the basement of the *Chron*'s building at Fifth Street and Mission. Bearded, decidedly heavyset, and with thick graying hair grown well over his ears, he was nevertheless as sharp as ever, a repository of pretty much everything that could be known about the city, its residents, or its institutions, public or not.

Now, unable to allay her concern about her boyfriend Wyatt Hunt's nonchalance in his attitude toward both his investigation into Como's death and the presence of Len Turner in the mix, Gina Roake was sitting on a hard wooden chair catercorner to Elliot in his tiny cubbyhole of an office.

It was four-thirty on Tuesday afternoon.

"Actually," Elliot was telling her, "if I believed in coincidences, I'd say it was quite a coincidence you happening to come by here today with that question."

"Why is that?"

"Because just today, I . . ." Rummaging around on the surface of his desk, he extracted a sheet of paper from a small pile of them. "Well, here. Troglodyte that I am, I

235

still ask for and get hard-copy galleys. They hate me for it, but what are they going to do? I'm a star. So, anyway, this is tomorrow's column. You might find it somewhat interesting."

CityTalk
BY JEFF ELLIOT

Everyone knows that the murder last Tuesday of community activist Dominic Como has left his flagship Sunset Youth Project ("SYP") in a precarious state. But CityTalk has learned from sources in the city's Health Services Department that its troubles may have begun before Mr. Como's death. The sources, who wished to remain anonymous because the reports they spoke about were not due to become public until later this week, portrayed an organization rife with political intrigue and corruption.

Roake looked up from the page. "Let me guess," she said. "Como and his pals were lining their pockets with grant money."

"Damn," Elliot said. "You stole my scoop. Who woulda thunk it?"

"Okay, so let me go double or nothing. Just a wild guess. Somehow Len Turner's in

236

this up to his eyes."

Elliot sighed. "You're psychic."

Gina shrugged. "It's a small talent." She went back to the column.

According to documents released by the federal government last Friday, the SYP is to be barred access to federal grants and contracts for up to one year due to its unauthorized use of AmeriCorps funds. AmeriCorps has contributed over $4.6 million to SYP over the past four years. According to its contract with AmeriCorps, SYP agreed to use these funds to pay tutors at its Ortega campus, to redevelop certain selected properties to be used as residential treatment facilities, and to assist with marketing and operations in SYP's other subsidiaries, such as its moving company, art gallery, and theater.

Instead, the documents list a number of violations against Mr. Como, including:

- Misuse of AmeriCorps funds for his personal benefit, including paying several different drivers to take him to personal appointments, wash his car, and run personal errands.

- Unlawfully supplementing the salaries of

instructors at the Ortega campus with federal grant funds by enrolling these instructors in the AmeriCorps program and giving them federally funded living allowances and education awards.

- Improperly using AmeriCorps members for political activities, such as pamphlet distribution and telephone solicitation.

- Misusing AmeriCorps members as janitors and clerical personnel at the Ortega campus, not as tutors.

"So how'd they find out?" Gina asked. "Tell me someone in the organization ratted him out. I love it when the vipers turn on each other."

"Nothing so dramatic. At least not that we know of. Someone with the federal Corporation for National and Community Service caught some irregularities. You gotta see the full report. It's pretty blunt."

"Bean counters," Gina said. "You gotta love 'em."

Elliot nodded. "Keep reading. Now comes the juicy local stuff and affirmation of your psychic power."

In a closely related matter, just this past

weekend the San Francisco Board of Supervisors released its yearly budget analysis of the Communities of Opportunity ("COO") program, headed by Len Turner. Mr. Turner, apart from this mayoral-appointed position, also serves as legal counsel to several service-oriented non-profit organizations, including the Mission Street Coalition, the Sanctuary House for Battered Women, and, notably, the SYP, among several others.

The COO program has supplied nearly $4 million, mostly foundation money from private sources, into community redevelopment for some of the city's most poverty-stricken neighborhoods. But the just-released budget analysis has revealed that despite this influx of cash — earmarked for after-school tutoring, health care, addiction rehabilitation, and job placement — the program has essentially nothing to show for its efforts over the past two years.

"So," Gina said, "the Supes found out this was coming?"

"Looks like it."

"And they were shocked, *shocked,* that there was gambling going on at Rick's."

"Exactly."

"So where did the money go?"
"Read on."

Below is a partial listing of questionable expenses so far unearthed: conferences for community development professionals ($602,335), theatrical and musical events ($136,800), consultants and public relations ($477,210), program office and community staff ($372,000), and community outreach ($256,780). Beyond these "expenses," nearly $2 million went to "community-based organizations and other services" — i.e., to the very nonprofits who were charged with administering the COO funds. And finally, in the COO program alone, Mr. Turner pulls down a salary of $370,000 per year.

Revelations such as these lend credence to the pejorative term sometimes used to describe these professional fund-raisers and community activists: "poverty pimps." They like to describe themselves as people who are "doing well by doing good." They are doing very well indeed. In fact, judging from the financial improprieties apparent in these two recent reports, it seems that in San Francisco, nonprofit is in fact a high-profit, big-money game. And taking into consideration Mr. Como's murder, it may also be a deadly one.

Gina Roake handed the galley sheet back to Jeff Elliot. "Looks plenty grafty to me," she said. "Not to mention slightly dangerous, which is exactly the message I've been trying to get through to Wyatt."

"It's a good one. Isn't he getting it?"

"Not clearly enough, I don't believe." She paused. "So, off the record, what do you think the odds are that these two reports" — here she indicated the article she'd just read — "had nothing whatsoever to do with Como's death?"

Elliot leaned back and scratched at his beard. "Fifty to one. Maybe a hundred to one. I'd be stunned if they didn't."

"I would be too. The timing's just too perfect. So the question is, why exactly would someone want to kill him over this?"

Elliot broke a smile. "You going for the reward?"

"Not specifically, although if we came up with something really good right here and now, I'd be happy to share with you."

"Okay. Deal." Elliot stretched out a hand and they shook. "Now give me a second." Sitting in his wheelchair, he closed his eyes, head back. "Theory number one takes a bit of a stretch to start out, but ends strong."

"Let's hear the stretch part."

"All right. We assume that Como either didn't know about or wasn't hands-on responsible for any of the stuff from tomorrow's column." He held up a hand. "I said it was a stretch. But let's assume . . ."

Roake made a face. "Okay, but only for the sake of argument."

"Fair enough. Como is a bona fide saint who doesn't know that scandal is about to blow up all over at Sunset. Somebody else, let's call him Turner for lack of a better word, has been screwing with the books and playing loose with the rules for three years or more —"

"Try twenty," Roake said.

"Okay, twenty. Anyway, so last week Como gets wind of let's say the AmeriCorps problem cutting off his federal grants. So he goes to Turner, his corporate counsel, and realizes that it's got to have been Turner behind the cooking of the books and the misuse of the funds. So he meets him alone and calls him on it, says he's going to fire him, get him kicked off the COO program, all of the above. Turner can't have that happen, and voilá. He whacks him."

"Yeah, but Turner knows this stuff's going to come out anyway."

"Sure, but if the community hangs together, Sunset loses some federal funding for a while, but otherwise nothing happens. Nothing changes. On the other hand, if Como makes a stink, Turner's in deep shit with the whole nonprofit world, which is his entire income. Not to say life."

Roake chewed on it for a moment. "Possible," she said, "if you can buy the premise, which I'm afraid I can't."

"Yeah," Elliot said. "I don't know if I can either. I mean, it would be hard to argue that Como didn't know he had some drivers taking him around places, you know?"

"I know. So where's that leave us?"

"We need a second theory, and I got the first one, so it's your turn."

"All right." Roake closed her own eyes. "Okay, how's this: One of those private interests that provided the funding, they got pissed that Como was essentially stealing from them, personally."

"So they killed him?" Elliot was shaking his head. "Doesn't sing for me at all. And besides, that's the COO money you're talking about, and that report — the budget analysis — was coming out right about the time somebody killed him. So if it was about money, the timing says it was about the federal money."

"And Turner, somehow, don't you think?

All right, how's this? They both knew about the money problems. Are either of them looking at prison time over this?"

"I don't know. You're the lawyer, you should know this, right? Me, I'd say not impossible."

"Okay, let's go with that for the moment. Say Turner knows he's going to jail if it's him and Como each pointing fingers at each other. Except if Como's dead, then it's Turner's finger and that finger's only pointing in one direction, at Como. Como stole the money, misappropriated the money, it's all his fault."

"That's good," Elliot said.

"Yeah, but . . . if that were the case, I'm surprised Turner didn't even try to make it look like a suicide — Como knows he's going down for this, and decides to kill himself. But still, in general terms, I think it flies. Or" — Roake's eyes lit up — "even better . . . you're going to like this . . . Turner's got some rehab and paroled people in these residential units and he hires one of them to take Como out. They don't do it, he violates them back, and they go to jail. And, hell, what do they care about Como anyway?"

"So it's a hit?"

"At least it's a theory that works. And

we've got to have something involving both Len Turner and the money, right?"

Elliot clucked. "It's tempting to think so. Maybe Hunt ought to talk to him."

"Thanks, Jeff," she said, "but that's pretty much exactly what I came here to talk him out of. He's basically working for Turner, but he doesn't want to be messing with him. Besides, Turner's controlling the funds for the reward."

Elliot raised his eyebrows. "So you're telling me Hunt gives Turner a pass? He's not going to look at him at all?"

"That's my hope. They're just supposed to be a clearinghouse for information going to the police."

"So what do your psychic powers say?"

"Unfortunately," she said, "they say I'm whistling in the wind."

When they looked in the trunk of the limo out at the Sunset Youth Project, they found that its tire iron was in fact missing. Now, back at his desk in the homicide detail, Devin Juhle hung up his telephone and looked across his desk and then the desk of his partner, Russo, where she sat with the tip of her tongue sticking out through her lips as she labored over the typed transcription of an interview they'd done on another

245

of their cases.

Picking up a paper clip, he tossed it across, and she looked up in exasperation.

"What?"

"You'll never believe who that was."

"George Clooney."

"Nope. Guess again."

"If it's not George Clooney, I don't care who it was."

"Yes, you will."

She picked up the paper clip, unbent it, bent it back. "It couldn't have been the lab already with the tire iron."

Juhle nodded with satisfaction. "Mr. Como must have been more important than even we thought he was. And they found a trace of his DNA. Strong profile, and no doubt about it."

"How'd the lab even find the DNA after that soak in the lake?"

"Probably that prayer to Saint Jude I said."

"But really?"

"Really. Hair follicle stuck to the tire iron. It settled into the mud and the mud covered it up so all of it didn't wash away. In a million years it might have been a hair fossil if we'd have left it alone." Juhle leaned back, linked his hands around the back of his head. "You know what this means? Warrant for the car."

Russo's shoulders sagged as she let out a sigh. "And I suppose we're going to want to do this tonight?"

"Get the warrant tonight, impound it tonight before anybody can get it any cleaner, do the search first thing tomorrow." He gestured to the marked-up paperwork on his partner's desk. "Sarah, what's got into you? Look what you're working on when the game's afoot. The trail's heating up. I can feel it." Now he was on his feet. "Let's go find us a judge. You with me? I know you're with me."

She sighed again, with perhaps exaggerated weariness. "Yes, kimosabe, I'm with you."

16

Much to Hunt's delight, Tamara had fielded three calls in the afternoon from previous clients who all seemed to have developed amnesia about the last six months. Or maybe Hunt had served sufficient penance for his transgressions and his firm's name in the newspaper suddenly announced to the legal world at large that he was back in business. If the city's well-connected service-oriented charities were entrusting him with work, then clearly his name was no longer anathema, and his firm no longer a pariah.

All three of the clients were law firms located in buildings that were within a short walking distance from Hunt's office, and by seven-thirty on this Tuesday night he was walking out of the last one at Market and Spear, now wrestling with something that had been the least of his worries over the past months — staffing. In the past two and a half hours, he'd just reestablished personal relations with these big-time litigators who needed private investigators to sit in on their depositions or serve subpoenas or locate and deliver witnesses. Everybody he'd talked to seemed genuinely enthusiastic that he was back in business — had they actually thought he'd closed up? — and all of them had work that, of course, couldn't wait. After all, this was the law, where nothing could wait. Everything had to be done yesterday latest. When could he start?

But he only had Mickey, who didn't have any kind of license besides the one that he used to drive, and Tamara, ditto, who'd been back on the job for a whole two days now. Thinking it never rained but it poured, but basically happy about it, Hunt headed back to his office to make some calls to see if he could line up a few underemployed, licensed stringers that he could bring on to do some work for him temporarily.

When he got inside the main door, though, he noticed the message light blinking "1" and pushed the button to hear Juhle pass along the news that Hunt's anonymous source might be in line for part of the reward after all, since the police lab had discovered Dominic Como's hair on the tire iron they'd retrieved from the drained lagoon. And what did Hunt think of that?

Hunt thought first that Cecil Rand would be happy to see some money at the end of this, and second that it was not too surprising, finding the murder weapon near the scene of the crime, although the speed of the police lab's analysis was nearly unprecedented. He also didn't think any of this was overwhelmingly important. It didn't identify a suspect, not unless there were fingerprints or other identifying marks on the tire iron, and there couldn't have been or Juhle would have mentioned them.

Hunt went back through the door behind Tamara's station, switched on his light, and, pulling the chair up behind his own desk, sat down and started going through the notes he'd taken at his various meetings, estimating his personnel needs for the next couple of weeks. Touching his mouse, he awakened the computer screen in front of him, and he pulled up his address book.

And then suddenly he wasn't looking at the screen anymore, but had slumped back in his chair, some barely registered thought nagging at him. For a minute, maybe more, he didn't move except to squeeze the skin around his lower lip.

Finally, he got up and walked outside again to the reception area, over to Tamara's desk. There, on her yellow pad, she'd written the names and telephone numbers of the reward callers, and up near the top was Nancy Neshek, who hadn't been either at work or at her home all day. Hunt had tried for the fourth and last time just at five o'clock, before he'd gone out for his first meeting, and neither had her workplace heard from her nor had she answered her home telephone.

Hunt sat down in Tamara's chair and punched in the Neshek home number. On the fourth ring, the answering machine picked up again and Hunt waited and then, on the off chance that she was monitoring her calls and would pick up when she heard him, he left a brief message identifying himself. He then waited again to give her time to reach the phone, until at last, when it was clear she wasn't going to answer, he hung up.

And sat still again.

She had called and left a message here last night, saying it was somewhat important and that he could reach her either at her home or office the next day. She'd been very specific. He could reach her either at home or her office. And he hadn't been able to do so. Of course, something could have come up. She might have made other last-minute plans, but . . .

It had been bothering him at some sub-conscious level since late in the afternoon, and now suddenly it struck him as truly significant. Five minutes later, Hunt had used his computer wizardry and discovered her home address on Seacliff Avenue, and was in a cab on his way home.

There he picked up his Cooper. It didn't take him fifteen more minutes to pull up outside Nancy Neshek's house on the cliffs overlooking Phelan Beach. When he got out of his car, he was struck, in spite of the size and stunning architecture of the homes, by how deserted the street felt, and how strongly the gusts blew off the ocean a hundred or more feet below. In the deepening dusk, the two-story Neshek home still exuded a pale yellow glow, although through its lower windows, all was dark inside. Hunt first went to the front door and rang the doorbell, hearing the chimes echo back through the house.

He checked his watch. It was just eight o'clock. Abandoning the front porch, he walked down the driveway and around to the side of the garage, where a quick look revealed a car parked inside. Next, he crossed over a perfectly manicured gravel path and climbed the six steps up to the back door, a thick slab of oak whose large window let Hunt look into a kind of mud-room behind what appeared to be the kitchen.

Going back to the car for his flashlight, he also slipped on a pair of gloves, his heart now pounding in his throat. He knew that he could be shot or restrained or arrested now as a cat burglar and no one would blink an eye. Returning to the back door, he tried the handle and verified that it was indeed locked. He shone a fast beam of light into the mudroom and kitchen and saw nothing unusual or out of place.

Back down those rear stairs, he followed the gravel path again along the back of the house until he came abreast of another bank of windows. Stepping through the garden and getting to them, he saw that they made up the back wall of the dining room.

In the neighbor's house twenty feet over, a light came on, and he froze. An outside door opened over there, then slammed shut. Another gust rattled the trees and hedges behind him. Drawing a slow breath, he got back through the garden and now followed the lawn next to the gravel path — reducing the noise of his footsteps — around the side of the house, where the neighbors had just turned on their lights.

Hunt estimated when he'd cleared the dining room windows and stepped up to the next bank of them. A dog barked somewhere in the neighborhood as he risked another brief beam from his flashlight. He shone the light over the floor and the leather couch, the rattan rug in the center of the living room, and then the matching chairs over on the piano side.

He would never have seen it if he hadn't caught a glimpse of a river stone fireplace mantel and leaned in at the window to follow the play of his beam over the stones. And there, with the side of his face pressed against the window, on the floor he saw a hand and a portion of an arm before the rest of the body disappeared from his angle of vision.

Mickey rubbed the boneless goat-leg roast with olive oil, salt, pepper, rosemary, and thyme. He inserted fifteen cloves of garlic into slits he'd made in the meat, and now the smell of the thing cooking with root vegetables in the oven infused the entire small apartment.

Alicia sat on one side of the fold-down table, Tamara and Jim Parr on the other, and after throwing together a beet, arugula, and goat cheese salad, Ian had boosted himself up onto the kitchen counter. Mickey was just stirring the polenta into the pot of boiling and salted water. Ian had explained with no embarrassment at all that he was an addict and an alcoholic and couldn't drink, but everyone else was having cheap rosé in heavy juice glasses.

They were talking about surfing, which was what Alicia told them she had been doing all day out at Ocean Beach.

"How did you not freeze?" Tamara asked.

"Oh, you never go without a wetsuit. It's not like surfing in Hawaii or even down south. If you didn't have a wetsuit, you couldn't last five minutes."

"How about the sharks?" Mickey said.

But Alicia was shaking her head. "Not here. Up in Bolinas, maybe, but not here."

"Famous last words," Ian put in. "I tell her she's surfing around the general vicinity of Seal Rock. You know why it's called Seal Rock? Right. You know the preferred diet of the great white shark? I rest my case."

But Alicia just shook her head. "I've never even seen a shark out there, Ian."

"Most people who get eaten don't see 'em, either, except from the inside."

"Well, I'm not planning to get eaten. Besides, you've got to take risks sometimes if you want to do what you want to do."

Suddenly she turned back to face her ta-blemates. "Am I right, Mr. Parr?"

Flattered to be included, Parr nearly choked on his wine and then, coughing, was shaking his head up and down, laughing at himself. "No guts, no glory," he said. "That's my motto, and I managed to get myself old living with it."

"You're not old, Mr. Parr."

"Jim, please."

"Jim, then. Who is not old in spite of a life of risk." Then Alicia whirled back on her brother. "See?" And finally, to the rest of them, "Ian doesn't want me sleeping out in my car either. Too dangerous."

"It *is* dangerous," Ian said. "There's all kinds of nuts out there."

Mickey turned away from the stove. "You sleep out in your car?"

Alicia nodded. "Sometimes. Last night I did. I wanted the early morning waves."

"Actually in it?" Mickey asked.

And Tamara clarified, adding, "Mickey's been spending about half his nights sleep-ing outside."

"Mostly on the ground, though," he said. "I can't stretch out in my car."

"She can," Ian explained. "She's got a Honda Element. She can run laps in the damn thing if she takes the seats and her surfboard out."

"Why do you do it, Mick?" Alicia asked. "Sleep out, I mean."

He stirred the polenta for a moment. "I don't know exactly," he said. "It's not structured. It's peaceful. You feel free. You wake up with the sun." He shrugged. "I just like it. How about you?"

She sighed. "Well, here's the thing. I get two days off a week, Monday and Tuesday. Otherwise, I've got to be in a dress and nylons and high heels and makeup. And sometimes, a lot of the time, I guess I feel like I'm trapped. So I drive off and sleep where I stop, and I don't feel so . . . I don't know, so regimented. Like I can still make some of my own decisions, and I'm not stuck in a life I don't want to live. I mean," she added, "look at all of us — maybe not you, Jim — but the rest of us. We're just all marking time, trying to get into something that's going to feel like our real lives, you know. You guys going to chef classes, and, Tamara, you starting your day job again.

"Maybe I sleep out to remind myself that my real self is still there, I've still got time, I've got game, I'm going to be doing something that's really me someday, that *matters,* and as long as I'm still that person who can just jump up and go sleep out somewhere, then that's someone I recognize. I'm still here." As though surprised by how much she'd revealed about herself, she ducked her head a bit into her shoulders and looked around at her audience. "Sorry," she said. "TMI." Too much information. "It's my inner nerd. I can't shut her up."

"That's all right." Tamara grabbed a bite of arugula from the bowl in front of her. "We're a tolerant household. The nerd's welcome too."

Mickey was looking in at the goat and now pulled it out of the oven, setting it on the top of the stove. He covered it with aluminum foil, then turned back to the table. "Ten minutes to let the meat rest while the polenta cooks, then we eat. And you said it better than I could, Alicia. That was pretty much exactly it." In spite of her no-nonsense style of dress tonight — she wore old jeans, a plaid flannel shirt, and hiking boots — Mickey had been fighting the temptation to stare at her since she'd come in. But now he braved a quick surreptitious look and noticed a faraway glaze and glassiness in her eyes. "Alicia? Are you okay?"

Biting her lip, she nodded. "Just, you know, dealing with the Dominic thing again. That whole doing-something-that-matters is looking a little more distant right now, that's all. But I'm okay. Really."

Parr tipped up his glass, then poured himself some more. "What about Dominic? Did you know him too?"

"Did she know him?" Ian asked.

And for the next twenty minutes, until the dinner was halfway gone — everyone loving the goat — they covered the common ground between Jim and Alicia as Como's drivers, some of the life and politics up at Sunset, how things were the same, and how they had changed. "Yeah, but even with all the changes," Parr was saying, "everything I hear is that what Dominic did was essentially the same. He drives around, talks to people, helps wherever he can. Serves food. Drives nails. He was just a hands-on guy. I'm never going to believe Dominic was stealing money. And irregularities? A business this big, there's always going to be paperwork problems. But if somebody was taking money, it wasn't Dominic."

"But do you think that's what this is about?" Mickey asked. "Somebody taking money and Dominic found out?"

"This is what's been getting to me," Alicia said. "I can't *imagine* what it's about. Given who Dominic was, the man he was, it just defies belief."

"Well."

All eyes went to Parr.

"But I promised my good-cooking grandson I wouldn't go out there and ask around."

Ian was sitting in the visitor's chair at the end of the table. "And what would you ask about?"

Parr put his fork down. "Just what we've all been talking about here. Somebody taking money. Maybe somebody who just wanted to take over. I mean, look at it. Dominic's been doing it his way forever. So long as he's there it's going to keep getting done the same way. But now there's more money and more organization all around, am I right? More decisions that he's got to take part in, but he's not really interested. He wants to be on the street 'cause that's who he is."

Mickey, though, was shaking his head. "It's a good theory, Jim, but let's not forget that Dominic wasn't exactly Saint Francis of Assisi living with a vow of poverty. Just his legit salary was six hundred and fifty grand a year in this job." He held up a hand at the expected opposition around the table. "Not that he didn't earn it, but he was also the rainmaker who brought in most of that money."

"And is that a bad thing?" Alicia asked.

"Not at all. But let's remember that whoever took him out killed the goose who kept laying the golden egg, year after year. Alicia, Jim here is talking about serving food and driving nails, but how often did Dominic do fund-raisers too? Almost every day, right? At least four days a week?"

"At least," she had to admit.

Mickey shrugged. "I'm just saying I haven't seen any sign he was slowing down in the job. In fact, the more we talk about this, the more I'm inclined to start with what Al Carter said — Dominic was meeting somebody he knew over how he could help him. That sounds like Dominic, doesn't it? Hands-on, one-on-one. Even if the appointment was just an excuse to get Dominic alone, at least he believed it."

"Maybe you should talk to Al Carter again, Mickey," Alicia said.

And Mickey nodded. "The thought has crossed my mind."

Hunt had sat in his car and pondered for most of fifteen minutes, then had placed a call to Gina Roake. She advised him to leave the scene and to make an anonymous call to the Police Department reporting what he'd seen. Maybe even disguising his voice. He wanted, she had told him, nothing to do

261

with discovering the body of Nancy Neshek, if indeed it was she, which he did not doubt.

But they both knew he could not do that without running the risk of losing his license. More than that, he just didn't see himself operating like that. So about twenty minutes ago, he had called Juhle and then gone back to sit in his car at the curb.

The first police vehicle to appear was a black-and-white SFPD squad car. This might turn out to be a dicey moment, Hunt realized, since his precise role here was nebulous at best. Especially when the crime was murder and the scene was a locked-up, darkened mansion in one of the city's most expensive neighborhoods.

Nevertheless, there was nothing to do but brazen it out, so he flashed his lights briefly at the squad car as it pulled up, and emerged from his Cooper into the lights of the squad car with his identification held out in front of him. "I'm a private investigator named Wyatt Hunt," he announced. "I'm the one who called Inspector Juhle."

One of the officers — the name badge over his pocket read "Sorenson" — jerked a thumb in the direction of the house. "There's a body in there?"

"Yeah."

"How do you know?"

"I saw it from the window." He didn't want to go into too much detail about which window and what he'd been doing out here in the first place. Maybe they wouldn't ask.

"You're sure?"

"Reasonably, yeah."

"Okay." The cop opened the back door of his squad car. "Please have a seat and we'll be right back."

This sounded like a request, but Hunt knew that squad car doors didn't open from the inside when you were in the backseat and that a cage separated him from access to the cop's stuff in the front. He was being detained in the nicest possible manner.

Sorenson said, "Let's go, Lou," and they walked together up to the now-dark front porch where Sorenson tried the door, rang the bell, and called out "Police" a couple of times, to no response. Meanwhile, his partner was shining a flashlight beam through the windows on either side of the front door. After a short discussion, they walked back to the squad car and opened the door.

"It's all locked up."

"I know."

"The back too?"

"Right."

"We didn't see anything," Sorenson said.

263

Hunt got out. "It's farther to your left," he said. "Way over by the corner."

"You saw something over there? We didn't see a thing."

"It was lighter out."

Hunt was starting to wish he'd taken Gina's advice and placed an anonymous call when another figure approached on the street to his right. "Excuse me," the man said. "I live just across there. What's going on here?"

But Sorenson was within hearing and moved a few steps down the pathway to the door. "Would you please stay back, sir? This is a potential crime scene."

"A crime scene. What happened?"

Sorenson had the neighbor and Hunt both in his flashlight now. "We're not sure," he said, as another car pulled up behind Sorenson's squad car.

"Here's the sergeant," his partner said.

"Let's hope so."

Eventually Juhle arrived in his personal Camry, but not before another squad car, a van from Channel 3 that must have picked up the dispatch call, an ambulance (in case the person wasn't in fact dead and needed medical attention), and six other locals — neighbors who had materialized out of the once-deserted street. By the time Juhle got there, none of the other five policemen on the scene with their flashlights, and looking through the door and front windows, had been able to spy the body.

Hunt knew he was going to have to admit he'd been over to the side window, snooping, and was starting to get a bad feeling about it.

It was a windblown night and late, now at least two hours since Hunt's original phone call to his friend. Within five minutes after Juhle had arrived, and after trying to finesse what he'd actually done for a little longer, Hunt had finally directed Juhle to the side window, where he'd seen enough of the body to authorize a break-in. Then, after a brief discussion, deciding they could just crawl in and get inside the house if they could unlock and open a window, Sorenson had punched out a small pane of glass from the bay window on the ground floor opposite the room where the body lay. Within a minute or so, someone had climbed through the window, turned on some lights, and opened the front door.

And, of course, discovered the completely dead body of Nancy Neshek.

Meanwhile, breaking the window had set

off the burglar alarm, which brought apparently all of the rest of the neighbors out — they numbered at least thirty — along with four more squad cars to control the crowd. Hunt leaned back up against the hood of his Cooper, arms crossed, freezing in his light jacket.

He knew that one day he would laugh about this entire scenario, since to the tune of the deafening school-bell alarm, there were now six squad cars, two of them with rotating blue and red strobelike lights, thirteen cops not including Juhle, three paramedics and their ambulance, and another news van and its crew capturing the absurdity as it unraveled.

But there wasn't anything really funny about it now.

Finally, the alarm company managed to turn off the bells — the sudden silence like a vacuum in the night.

"This sucks. It really does," Juhle said.

"I'm not so wild about it myself," Hunt replied.

By now it was midnight.

Nancy Neshek's body still lay in the living room where someone had hit her more than once with a fireplace poker and where she had subsequently died. The crime scene technicians were working and still photographing the scene. The coroner's assistant was in with them, waiting until they were finished before she would order the body moved. For the moment, she was having a conversation with Sarah Russo, who'd finally arrived an hour ago in high dudgeon from her night impounding the limo and an interrupted late dinner. She very obviously didn't even want to see Hunt, and not so much Juhle either.

So Hunt and Juhle sat outside in the van that served as the mobile command center for SFPD, away from the action and the hostility.

"Neshek actually called you on this reward thing?" Juhle asked.

"Last night. But not to give information. To ask a question."

"And you don't have any idea was the question was?"

"Not a clue." Hunt shook his head. "Except I'm pretty sure it wasn't if I knew how to compute the circumference of a circle."

"Pi-R-squared," Juhle said.

But Hunt kept shaking his head. "Nope. That's the area. I think it's pi-D, but that wasn't what she called about anyway."

Juhle hesitated. "So what got you out here?"

Hunt ran it down for him — the original call with its sense of urgency, her lack of availability at both of her phone numbers during the whole day. "But really, bottom line," he concluded, "it was just a hunch."

"Hunches are good."

"I've got another one, then. Whoever did this, did Como."

"Not impossible, maybe even probable." He indicated the house. "Let's see if whoever it was left something for us in the way of evidence. And by us I mean the police, not you and me."

"I thought we were all about share and share alike."

"Wrong. In fact, you're lucky you're not sitting in an interview room downtown, and you know it." As far as it went, this was probably true. Who was to say that Hunt hadn't in fact come out here to speak to Neshek and had gotten inside the house, where for some reason he struck her down with the poker, then set the house alarm, locked up, walked out, and called Juhle? Certainly, both Juhle and Russo had been overtly aware enough of this possibility that they hadn't permitted Hunt to enter the house and thus have a ready and benign explanation if they found trace evidence of his presence there — a fingerprint, a hair

268

follicle. Hunt had spent time answering questions in police custody before, and knew that the only thing that stood between him and another interrogation room right now was the forbearance of Juhle and Russo. "And in any event," Juhle went on, "I'll want a taped interview from you by tomorrow, let's say high noon."

"Dev, come on, it's —"

"It's the only offer you're getting from me, Wyatt, and it's a damn good one. I'd suggest you take it before I get Sarah involved and ask her opinion, which I think would be somewhat less lenient."

Wyatt came forward on his chair. "You realize, Dev, that I didn't even have to call this in. I could have gone home and let somebody else discover the body in three days or a week or whenever."

"You could have, but that would have been a crime. A private eye sees a body, he's supposed to report it. It's kind of like our rule that if you find a body, we're going to want a statement. It's all about having a complete file. This really isn't negotiable, Wyatt. And it's a favor I probably shouldn't even offer. But really, really, in my heart, I don't see you killing our victim out there."

Hunt managed to chortle. "Thank you so much."

"You're welcome. So, tomorrow, noon."

Hunt gave it a last try. "You know Como's memorial service is tomorrow at eleven? I was planning to go to that, see who showed up, talk to a few people."

"The whole world's going to show up."

"Yeah, but my point is that I'll be in the Green Room at the War Memorial when high noon rolls around."

"Well" — Juhle's smile had no humor in it — "then in that case we'd better get your statement before eleven. In fact, keep talking much longer and we'll drive downtown right now and get it all polished up before dawn if you'd like. Good?"

It didn't sound good to Hunt. He'd heard the best offer he was going to get. So he stood up, shook Juhle's hand, told him he'd be there before eleven, and said good night.

17

"I know it's early," Hunt began when Mickey picked up his phone at around seven o'clock the next morning, "but —"

"No sweat," Mickey replied. "We saw City-Talk and figured, 'Whoa.' Tam's in the shower now and as soon as she's out, we're on our way down. Unless you've got something for us to do out here."

"No. We need to talk first before we do anything. You guys are great. Have you heard yet about Nancy Neshek?"

He hadn't, and Hunt told him.

Mickey paused to take in the enormity of it. "This thing's heating up pretty good, isn't it?" he said at last.

"It's not cooling down, that's for sure," Hunt said.

Hunt pulled a chair for himself from the back room, and forty minutes after Mickey had hung up the phone at his apartment, the three of them were all seated and gathered in the tiny reception area at the Hunt Club.

"We've got some huge issues to deal with today that weren't here yesterday," Hunt began. "First, Tam, I've got a list for you and I've got to put you on calling in some freelance troops to do some hourly work for us. Evidently, with the reward, word's gotten out that we're in the private investigations business again, and I'm not about to let the opportunity pass because we don't have enough people. If I give you the assignments and deadlines, you think you'd be comfortable doling 'em out?"

This was a significant increase over any of the responsibilities Tamara had shouldered in the past, but Mickey could see that the idea hit her like a shot of adrenaline. Hunt clearly was trying to motivate her to stay on, take more ownership of her job, get back to the way she'd been before the meltdown. And this appeared to be an effective way to do it. "If you think I can."

"I know you can. Get 'em in here so you can see them in person, make sure they're not stoned or drunk, get an idea of what they're capable of, tell them what we'll pay, and parcel out the individual gigs. Good?"

"Good."

"All right. Now. We got three new calls this morning, but the first two sound like crazies to me. We all agree?"

Nods all around. And no wonder, with one call being from Belinda the psychic again — apparently she was hot on the scent now — and the other from a guy who used to know Dominic at one of the projects and had seen him walking around near Japantown yesterday — he was sure of it.

"But the Len Turner call," Hunt went on, "I'm going to have to talk to him again. He'll be at the memorial service today. As you heard on his phone message, he's pretty pissed off. He thinks we had something to do with the leak to CityTalk, if that's what it was."

Mickey raised a finger. "What do you think it was, Wyatt?"

"I think these reports were due to come out anyway and both Turner and Dominic knew about them in advance somehow. Beyond that, I think he's a dangerous guy who thinks that since he's paying us, we'll do whatever he wants. Now, I don't know what they did about these reports, if anything, but obviously somebody's playing fast and loose with this community money. And meanwhile, I want to protect our position vis-à-vis the reward, and Turner's clearly the guy to see about that. But first I've got to waste a couple of hours this morning talking to Juhle and Russo about finding Neshek's body. So, Mick, we're going to want to change our strategy."

"Okay. Sure. Whatever."

"This isn't clearinghouse stuff anymore. Which is why we've got to be careful with Mr. Turner, since it's not what he thinks he's paying us to do. We don't want to give him a reason to pull the plug, agreed?"

"Of course."

He looked over at Tamara. "See why I love this guy?" Then, back to Mickey. "Okay. Even if we haven't had any reward calls, you and I are both going to get in a quick look at this Neshek thing, if only because then we can eliminate suspects on Como."

"How's that?" Mickey asked.

"If somebody's got an alibi for Monday night, two nights ago, when Neshek got killed, then odds are they didn't kill Como. Assuming, of course, which I am, that the same person killed both of them."

"Do Juhle and Russo think that?" Tamara asked.

"They won't say so, at least not to me, but they'd be dumb if they didn't."

Mickey sat, his arm resting on the back of his chair, apparently relaxed. But he

274

couldn't stop tapping his foot. "So what's the plan?"

"The plan is that I go to the memorial service this morning and concentrate on the Como people and see if there's any I can eliminate. If, say, Mrs. Como had a bridge group over or went to Napa or something on Monday night, then she's clear. Same with Al Carter. Or even your friend Alicia."

Mickey shot a quick — angry? defensive? — glance at his sister, then said to Hunt, "What about Alicia? You're not telling me she's really still a suspect in this."

"Well, she's a person without an alibi for the time Como was killed. If she's got one for Neshek . . . what's that look?"

Tamara answered. "We had her and her brother over for dinner last night."

"Her and her brother?" His jaw suddenly clamped down, Hunt looked from Tamara to Mickey, and back again. "Why did you do that?"

"Because they're good people," Mickey said. "I wanted to have them over. We're starting to be friends."

"I'm happy for you," Wyatt said evenly. "But they're also — or at least she is — a suspect in a murder investigation, unless she's got an alibi on Monday night."

Mickey and Tamara shared another furtive look.

"What now?" Hunt said.

Tamara let out a breath. "She slept out in her car by the beach Monday night. Got up early to surf Tuesday morning."

After a pause, Hunt asked, "What beach?"

Mickey took it. "Ocean. Out by Seal Rock."

Hunt hesitated again. "Did I tell you where Nancy Neshek lived?"

"No." The defensive pose sitting heavy on Mickey now. "Where?"

"Just above Phelan Beach, well out that way."

Mickey was shaking his head. "There is no way Alicia killed anybody, Wyatt. If you talked to her, you'd know that in five minutes."

"How would I know that?"

"Because you could tell. You could just see the person she is."

Hunt just barely did not snort. "I don't think I've got to remind either of you how unreliable personal reactions can be. People can hide things, really for truly. They can fool you even with who they are." He pointed a finger at each of them. "All of us know this firsthand, so excuse me if I'm not overly enthusiastic about Alicia's overtures to become your friend."

"She hasn't made any moves, Wyatt. I asked her over to dinner."

"That's true," Tamara added.

"I'm sure it is."

Mickey, getting a little hot now, "What do you mean by that?"

Hunt held up a restraining palm. "Nothing. I'm just cautioning you to go slow and be a little wary. And neither of you should be socializing with these people. Really."

But Mickey couldn't let it go. "She didn't do anything, Wyatt. I *know* she didn't."

"All right," Wyatt said, "but let me ask you this: Did she tell you that Dominic Como had fired her on the last day of his life?"

The siblings exchanged another glance. "Who told you that?" Mickey asked.

"Mrs. Como. Who heard it point blank from her husband."

"Maybe she was lying to you. Maybe he was lying to her."

"Maybe both," Hunt admitted. "But maybe I'm going to ask Alicia about it today, if she's at the service. Not at a nice friendly dinner. And while I'm at it, I plan to ask her, and Al Carter if I get the chance, if either of them know where they store the tire iron in a Lincoln Town Car."

"Why would that matter?"

277

"Because we know the weapon that killed Dominic Como was a tire iron. And we know that the tire iron from his limo isn't there anymore."

"We do?" Mickey asked. "When did we find that out?"

"Yesterday afternoon. Juhle and Russo went out to Sunset and looked. And they're probably looking for more in it now even as we speak."

After a minute, Tamara brought up the usual objection. "That doesn't mean the tire iron that killed him came from that car."

"Good, Tam. No, it doesn't. Not automatically. But on the other hand, there's nothing says it isn't either. It certainly could be. And, Mick, just consider this: Your friend Alicia, who might have just been jilted by him, and fired at the same time on the last day we know he was alive, had easy access to it. And then certainly had access back to him."

Mickey was sitting back, his mouth set, his hands clenched in his lap. "This is bullshit."

"No, Mick. These are facts we have to deal with." Hunt slowed himself down with a breath. "Look, I'm not saying she's guilty of anything. She might be the nicest person in the world. But she's in this until conflicting evidence or an alibi gets her out, okay? You can't become friends with her, and probably not with her brother either. I'm sorry, but you just can't." He looked from one of them to the other. "Neither of you."

A heavy silence settled in the tiny reception area. Mickey and Tamara shared a few more looks, until at last Mickey came back to Hunt, his voice again under control. "So. What do you want me to do?"

"Look around up at Sanctuary House. Nancy Neshek's place. That would be a start. Juhle and Russo are going to be futzing with the limo and crime scene stuff from last night all morning. This gives us a small opening before anybody in Sanctuary has a chance to get their guards up."

"So you're going to talk to Al Carter?" Mickey asked.

"Yeah. If he's at the service, which he should be. What about him?"

A shrug. "One of my lunatics yesterday, Damien Jones? Maybe he wasn't actually off on everything. He said we should look for somebody, probably with the Battalion but maybe not, up at Sunset. Which, by the way, my grandfather agrees with. Meanwhile, just so you're clear that Al Carter's another guy with access to the tire iron. Also the last known human to see Como alive. I

279

don't know about his alibi, if any. And he hasn't told us very much about Como's mysterious last appointment either."

"Yeah. I'll talk to him. That's a good thought. But listen" — Hunt leaned his lanky form forward, his elbows on his knees — "the main thing for all of us — even you, Tam — is to be careful here. Whoever it is, this killer's now done it twice. Let's not force a third. All we're trying to do is collect information and pass the valid stuff along to Devin. That's all."

Mickey shook his head. "Nice try, but it's gotten bigger than that, Wyatt," he said. "A whole lot bigger."

The address of the administrative headquarters for the Sanctuary House for Battered Women was on Potrero Avenue near San Francisco General Hospital. Unlike the other service-oriented nonprofits he'd visited in the last few days, for obvious reasons Sanctuary did not shelter, educate, or test any of its clientele on-site — instead, they were assigned, often with their children, to one of the organization's seventeen secure locations within the city limits. Because of this, Sanctuary's footprint here on Potrero was so small as to be nearly invisible. Mickey drove by what should have been the address twice before he realized that the office must be somewhere among the buildings that made up the much larger hospital complex.

Fifteen minutes after he'd finally managed to park in a handicapped zone in the hospital's main but still woefully inadequate lot, he found the place — one of many apparently identical offices on the ground floor of the hospital's Admitting and Triage Building. It was a typical overused bureaucratic medical landscape — already at nine A.M., long lines had formed at each of the glass windows, with the chairs in the main lobby filled with mostly older and poorly dressed patients. Although there was still the usual complement of mothers with their coughing or sleeping children, spaced-out young adults, and obvious derelicts, all waiting in numb patience while the clammy fluorescent lighting lit the area and reflected up at them from the greenish tile flooring.

The only indication of Sanctuary House's presence was the name of the organization stenciled onto the glass doorway, now open at the farthest extent of the lobby. Mickey stood in the doorway for a long moment. In front of him, a counter bisected most of the room across the front, and behind it were mazes of green and gray filing cabinets and a few desks. Venetian blinds over the high back windows. To his left, the counter made a right angle, and behind it more of the ubiquitous green-tinged glass separated out the two or three other offices.

He heard low voices, apparently coming from one or more of those offices, but saw no one, so he stepped forward and, following instructions, "Please Ring for Assistance," pushed the little hotel bell that someone had duct-taped down to the peeling wooden counter.

In five seconds, a tiny and tentative bespectacled young woman appeared from between one of the banks of filing cabinets, wearing what looked to Mickey like a thrift-store cotton dress and a devastated and yet somehow impatient expression. Beneath her wire-rimmed glasses, her eyes were red and swollen. Mickey at once realized two things: that the employees had heard the news about their executive director, and that maybe this should have been an assignment for Tamara — the vast majority of the time, Mickey supposed that men here were going to be the enemy; it came with the turf. Still, he dredged up a look of respectful solicitude.

"Can I help you?" she asked.

Having done his homework, Mickey knew

the name of the associate director. "I'd like to speak to Adele Watrous," he said, "if she's in."

"Is there something I can help you with?"

"Are you Ms. Watrous?"

"No."

"I was hoping to talk to Ms. Watrous."

"It's Mrs., and she is having a difficult morning. I'm afraid we all are. Can I tell her what this is about?"

Mickey's heart went out to this young woman, but he was here to get information — specifically if Nancy Neshek had mentioned to anyone here the question she'd wanted to ask Hunt — and the further down the food chain he went with the staff, he thought, the less likely the result. "I'm afraid it's about Ms. Neshek, which I can see you already know about. I'm very sorry."

She opened her mouth to reply, but no words came out, and then she closed it, nodded twice, then again, and finally disappeared back into the maze. After another moment, a grandmotherly woman appeared. Her snow-white hair was disheveled and she, too, had clearly been crying, but she spoke in a crisp, no-nonsense manner. "I'm Adele Watrous," she said. "Is this about Nancy? How can I help you?"

"I'm working on the investigation into Mr.

Como's death," he began, "and now Ms. Neshek's. Nancy's. She made a call to our office on the night she died, and I was hoping to talk to you about whatever she might have told you, if anything, that might shed some light on her death."

Nodding wearily, Mrs. Watrous lifted the flip-up portion of the counter and motioned him inside into the office proper, then led him beyond the first door they passed and into the second one. Once they were seated, the door closed behind them, she templed her hands at her mouth and blew into them a time or two, regaining her composure.

"When did you hear about it?" Mickey began.

She sighed. "This morning. The phone started ringing around six-thirty. One of our women out at the Jackson Street facility heard it on the news. After that . . ." She opened her hands. "Everybody." Then, suddenly, in a kind of a double take, she seemed to focus on him more clearly. "You said you were investigating Dominic Como's death?"

"Yes."

"And you think Nancy's is related to that?"

"We don't know. What we do know is that Nancy called the hotline at our office after the reward was announced on Monday and said that she had a question, an important question. And would we please call her the next day, here at your offices, or at her home? She said she'd be at one of the two places, definitely, but never answered at either."

"No. She never made it in here on Tuesday." She paused. "But that wasn't by any means unusual. I mean, she'd often get called out to one of the sites and have to stay until whenever. . . ." Trailing off, she shook her head in obvious dismay and confusion.

Mickey gave her a minute. "Were you both here when the reward on Mr. Como's death was announced?"

"And when was that, exactly?"

"Around four in the afternoon."

"Well, then" — she considered carefully — "I'm sure we were here, yes, both of us. But I don't remember hearing about it here. I know we didn't talk about it."

This was more or less what Hunt and Mickey had expected, but that didn't make the bare fact — that Watrous had no information about why Neshek had called the Hunt Club — any easier to accept. He pursed his lips in frustration. "Might Nancy have spoken to anybody else here about it? Did she stay late, for example?"

Again, Mrs. Watrous gave the question its time. And again she shook her head no. "She left right at five on Monday, or a little after. I stayed on till a little past six."

Grasping at straws, Mickey asked, "Was that also usual, that she left work right around five?"

"No. Usually she stayed much later. Unless she had a fund-raiser or some event or something like that. The work here is never finished, so we tend to put in some long hours."

"So" — Mickey barely daring to hope, but here at last was a possible opening — "was there something Monday night, then?"

She started to shake her head again, and then abruptly stopped. "Well, yes . . . I mean. Oh, God, I hadn't even thought of that."

"What's that, Mrs. Watrous?"

"They were having a COO meeting at City Hall."

"COO?"

"You know? The Communities of Opportunity. Oh, and speaking of which, did you see that thing in the paper this morning, the CityTalk column? That's what they must have been going to talk about, that report coming out."

"Who was that? Besides Nancy, I mean."

"Well, I suppose all or most of the beneficiaries. Us, Mission Street, Sunset, Delancey, all the others." Now, her color suddenly high, Adele Watrous tapped impatiently on her desk. "People don't realize. It's harder than it looks. You've got to put on a song and dance to get people to come out and give you money for these projects. You see what's in the paper today, you think it's all about throwing this foundation money away on music or public relations consultants or other nonessentials, but you've got to spend money to make money, especially in these times, in this field. Mr. Turner understands that. There's no other way to do it."

"I believe you," Mickey said, keeping his calm. The mention of Len Turner's name in this other context suddenly put his brain on high alert. "So you're fairly certain that Nancy was planning to attend this meeting?"

"I'm sure she was. But you can find out if she did easily enough."

"You're right, Mrs. Watrous, we can. Well" — Mickey started to get to his feet — "I want to thank you for all your help and cooperation here today. I know this news must have been brutal."

"It was. I still can't make myself believe it.

287

And you know what's really so terrible, almost the worst part?"

"What's that?"

Suddenly her weariness seemed to overcome her. She sighed again and closed her eyes briefly. When she opened them, she shook her head in what Mickey took to be resignation. "The worst part is that we're so used to terrible news here. We get terrible news here every single day."

18

Due to the late night they'd both spent at the Neshek home, neither Juhle nor Russo got into work until just before Hunt arrived to make his statement to them. In Nancy Neshek, they had a fresh homicide to begin investigating, and the crime scene analysis and report to review, but Russo wanted to go down and finish up whatever work remained with the limousine first. After all, they'd gone to all the trouble of getting a warrant and having the Lincoln towed to the impound lot, and that lot was only just across Seventh Street, adjacent to the Hall of Justice, where they currently found themselves anyway.

"But Hunt's going to be here to make his statement any minute." Juhle was at his desk in the homicide detail, a wide-open room filled with desks on the fifth floor of the Hall of Justice. "We're going to want to talk to him about that and find out what else he knows or knew about Neshek. I'd bet you he's also going to know about those City-Talk numbers —"

But Russo cut him off. "I don't even want to talk about Wyatt Hunt."

"Sarah, come on. It was late. What were we going to accomplish by taking him downtown?"

"We were going to accomplish the mandate of our job. We were going to accomplish what we're supposed to do to somebody who discovers a body in any kind of a compromising manner. How about that?"

Juhle shook his head. "He didn't kill Nancy Neshek."

"No? How do you know that? How do you know he didn't contaminate the crime scene? How do you know what he did before you got there?"

"Look, Sarah, Hunt isn't going anywhere. If his statement's squirrelly in any way, we haul his ass back here and grill him till he's well-done. But that's not going to happen. He was up at her place because she'd called with a question about the reward and . . . well, we've been through all this."

"Yes, we have. And for the record, it still fries my ass. I don't care what time it was. We should have hauled Hunt down here. And if Marcel" — this was Marcel Lanier, head of homicide — "if Marcel gets wind of this and goes ballistic, I'm laying the whole goddamned thing off on you as my senior partner who made the final decision. And meanwhile, just so I'm not tempted to lock up Hunt on general principles if he shows up here when he's supposed to, I'm going to stroll on out of here and take a look at the guts of that limo right now. You and your pal can play patty-cake in the interview room and I'll catch the rerun on the tape later."

Sighing, Juhle got up from his chair. "You were way more fun when you were younger, you know that?"

"Not really," she said. "People just think I must have been." And she turned on her heel.

When Hunt got to homicide to make his statement, Juhle was waiting for him. After wrestling with the decision, Hunt decided that his job was to pass relevant or potentially relevant evidence along to Devin and Sarah. So he included an account of Alicia Thorpe's completely unverifiable and somewhat provocative alibi for Monday night.

Hunt finished with Juhle, then grabbed both his sport coat and a tan overcoat against the still-gusting and cold north wind that he could hear whipping up the street. When he got back into his office, he waited for Tamara to finish her call and hang up, and asked about her progress with his potential pool of part-timers.

"We're in luck. And more than that, you might be happy to hear that the downturn in business over the last six months might not all have been fallout from Craig."

"What makes you say that?"

"Well, my first call was to Willard White" — another local private investigator firm — "and Gloria said I could have her whole staff for a few days if we could put 'em to work. Beats her having to lay them off, she said."

"Really? How many people she talking about?"

"Up to five."

Clearly, the number surprised and pleased Hunt. After Mickey had gone out again this morning for his interviews, Wyatt had spent some time with Tamara going over the notes he'd taken yesterday on the work he'd acquired. He'd estimated that load at close to two hundred hours. Five stand-ins would bridge the gap nicely. And from what it sounded like, they and perhaps even their bosses might all be available to fill in on standby if he kept hustling future work. "Why don't you see if you can get all five of them down here later today, and maybe even Gloria and Will themselves, say two or two-thirty, and call me on my cell and let me know?"

Tamara snapped him a salute. "Will do, *mon capitaine.* Oh, and we also did get one more reasonably intelligent-sounding reward call, finally, from Hang-up Lady, real name Linda Colores. She was walking home from work — she's one of the floor people at the Pottery Barn on Chestnut — and she heard a man and a woman having an argument on one of the streets down by the Palace. She thinks this was last Tuesday night, but she's not sure exactly."

"Did she get anything they actually said?"

"I didn't ask her that. I didn't want to step on your toes. But I got her vitals if you want to go out and talk to her, although she works all afternoon starting at one. Or I could ask her to come in here in the next hour or so and I could talk to her."

Hunt, standing in front of her desk, shook his head in admiration. "Has anybody recently told you how fantastic you are?"

Tamara blushed and looked down briefly, then back up. "Thank you. It's good to be back working. I didn't know if I could do it anymore. Or do anything, really."

"I wasn't worried about that. In fact, it never crossed my mind." He came forward and put his palms down on the desk across from her. "You can do anything you put your mind to, Tam. You know that, don't you?"

She couldn't meet his eyes. "I used to. But then I kind of got convinced I was fooling myself."

He was standing looking down at her, but she couldn't seem to commit herself to raising her eyes. "Hey."

When he reached across, touched her chin, and gently lifted it, she looked up and gave him a half-broken smile. "You know," she said.

He shook his head. "You weren't fooling yourself, Tamara. You were amazing. You are still amazing, okay?" Waiting, still touching her chin, he held her gaze on him. "Okay?"

And at last something gave way in her and she nodded. "Okay."

He pulled his hand away from her chin and straightened up. "That's settled, then. Once and for all."

She saluted again. "Yes, sir," she said. "Once and for all."

"You want to talk to this Linda Colores?"

"I could."

"Okay," Hunt said. "Go for it."

Nearly the size of a football field, the Green Room at the San Francisco War Memorial was on the second floor of the stately marble building next to the Opera House on Van Ness Avenue. Floors and pillars in the vast room were of marble. The ceiling was at least twenty feet high and the featured colors were gas chamber green trimmed with gold. The room was earthquake rated for 1,300 people, though it easily could hold many more than that. For Como's memorial, city employees were on hand at both sets of doors to turn mourners away and prevent the room from getting overfilled.

Hunt got there early enough to get in without any problem and he looked around to see an oversized photograph of a smiling Dominic Como hung from the wall behind the podium. Hunt had already walked by one of the long tables piled high with brochures of the Sunset Youth Project, the Battalion Special Corps, and pledge cards for the reward fund. The large portable screen up against the front wall indicated that the service was also going to include a video or a slide show.

Hunt was beginning to wonder what he had hoped to accomplish by coming here today at all. Not only was this going to be a difficult, if not impossible venue in which to hold even the most cursory of interviews, he did not yet know many of the players by sight. The only people he had actually met in connection with Dominic Como were his wife, Ellen, and Len Turner.

Now Ellen was surrounded by a mob of well-wishers and fellow mourners — perhaps some of them family members, but also a large host of mostly African-American men, women, and teenagers who Hunt assumed were Como's associates, fellow workers, and many of the beneficiaries of his charitable work over four decades.

But then in the sea of faces, Hunt spied a familiar one on the outskirts of the group surrounding Ellen, and he gradually made his way up near the podium and touched the arm of the man who'd discovered the tire iron in the lagoon.

"Mr. Rand?" he said, extending his hand. "Wyatt Hunt."

Rand recognized him right away, shook the proffered hand, and said half-jokingly, "You ain't here to tell me I already got that reward, now, are you?"

Hunt grinned. "No, sir. I'm afraid not. But now that you mention it, we've learned that it was in fact the murder weapon. I don't think that's been in the news yet. They found some of what may be Mr. Como's hair on it that didn't get washed away. So if that information leads anywhere, I'd have to say that you're still in the running, at least for part of it. Are you waiting to talk to Mrs. Como?"

"Not really. I never met the lady. I'm just payin' my respects." He raised a hand and mouthed a hello to someone he knew and then came back to Hunt. "Good to see this kind a turnout. 'Specially after all that in the paper today. I don't know where they got all that, make Dominic look like some kind a . . . I don't know what. You see that?"

"I did."

"So what'd you think?"

"I think Jeff Elliot usually gets his facts right."

"So you think Dominic was skimmin' some a that?"

"I don't know what to think, to tell you the truth. I didn't read it so much that he was skimming something for himself as that he was only supposed to use certain money for certain things, and maybe he didn't care so much about that."

"You got that right. He just put it where they needed it. And all that about his car and people runnin' for him, that's just the way he done it, drivin' folks around, taking people where they's needed." Rand waved a finger around at the crowd. "You just look around in this room and now tell me Dominic Como didn't help a whole lot more people than most anybody else ever *meets.* You hear what I'm saying?"

"I do."

"You do things first, you ask permission later, that's how he was. An' nothin' wrong with that, you ask me."

"You feel the same way about Len Turner?"

The name alone cast a shadow over Rand's face.

"You got a problem with him?" Hunt asked.

Rand shrugged. "Don't hate him. Different breed of cat, that's all."

"How do you mean?"

"Well, I mean, like Dominic, he one of us, one of the people."

"And Turner's not?"

This brought a tolerant smile. "You go have a word with the man. You find out soon enough."

"I already have, and I will again. And I believe you." He turned to where Rand had glanced and finally saw Turner with a small knot of other mourners in somber conversation. "You know those other people over there with him too?"

"Some. That big, good-looking woman behind Ellen, talkin' to him now, that Lorraine Hess, Dominic's number two. Next to her is Al Carter."

"Dominic's driver."

Rand nodded. "One of 'em. Then the couple holdin' hands, that's Jimi and Lola Sanchez, from over at Mission Street."

"Those are a lot of my reward people," Hunt said. "I'm going to mosey over there and say hello. Good talking to you, Cecil." He'd gone two steps when he stopped and turned. "Oh, and as soon as I know anything on the reward, I'll get back to you."

Rand showed some teeth. "I be waitin' by the phone."

When he got close to the Turner group, Hunt hung back for a minute to listen. As opposed to the scathing CityTalk column, the death of Nancy Neshek hadn't made it into this morning's newspaper. But still, from radio, television, phone calls, and the Internet, word had obviously gotten out, and now this core group of nonprofit professionals was discussing her death.

Hunt waited for a lull in the flow of the conversation, then stepped in. "Excuse me for interrupting," he said, "but I thought I'd come by and introduce myself."

Turner took over and made the introductions all around, and when he'd finished, Hunt said, "I couldn't help overhearing what you were talking about."

"Nancy can't really be dead," Hess said. "I can't believe that. It can't be true."

"I'm sorry, ma'am," Hunt replied, "but it's an absolute fact."

Turner asked Hunt, "You think this is connected to Dominic?"

"How could it be?" Hess asked the group at large. "How could any of this even be happening?"

Carter, calm but firm, put a hand on Hess's arm. "Lorraine. Think about it. How could it not be connected to Dominic?"

"Nobody knows about that one way or the other," Hunt said. "Cause of death was the same. Blunt force trauma to the head. Beyond that it's all conjecture."

"So you're saying someone killed her?" Turner asked.

Hunt nodded. "Without a doubt."

"Lorraine's right. This is unbelievable." Jaime Sanchez put his arm around his wife and drew her in closer to himself. He looked to Hunt for an answer. "Do you have any idea what this is all about?"

"No," Hunt said. "The timing suggests a

300

connection with Mr. Como's death. Plus, Ms. Neshek called my offices on Monday night with a question about the reward."

"What was the question?" Turner asked.

"She never got to ask it. She wanted to talk to me in person, but never got to it."

"And this is why we're paying you?" Len Turner asked. "This and the *Chronicle* story this morning?"

The question was so unexpected and so hostile that for a moment it stopped Hunt in his tracks. But not for too long. "I knew nothing about the CityTalk column until it came out this morning. And even if I had known about it, I would not have been able to stop it. Jeff Elliot writes what he wants. We are doing what you're paying us to do, Mr. Turner. We're following up leads as quickly and efficiently as we can."

Turner was fuming. "Well, I trust, Mr. Hunt, that you'll also do the other thing that we're paying you for, which is to keep us well-informed of the progress of your investigation. That seems to have become a problem."

Lorraine Hess interrupted. "So you're saying these murders were about the money? They had to be about the money."

"Not at all," Hunt said. "I don't know what they're about, though I do believe they're connected."

"Nancy and Dominic ran very different operations, Mr. Hunt," Turner said. "You've admitted that any connection between them was conjecture. Don't you have anything specific to report to us in the way of progress?"

"No, sir, I'm afraid I don't. We've had lots of phone calls and several interviews, although I don't believe the police are close to an arrest yet. On either case."

"But poor Nancy." Tears had overflowed onto Hess's cheeks. "And you're saying the police haven't found anything at her house either? Nothing at all? I mean, this isn't a situation like Dominic, found four days later floating in the lagoon. There must be something."

"I don't know," Hunt said. "They only discovered the body last night. I'm sure they haven't gotten through sifting everything they got. Something may turn up."

"This just seems so hard to imagine," Jimi Sanchez said. "Nancy and Dominic were the last people you'd ever —"

But he was interrupted by what sounded to Hunt like a strangled cry right behind him.

Turning, Hunt was still only a few feet from Ellen Como, who was standing now as

302

if transfixed, her hand extended outward, her eyes focused on a spot somewhere in the back of the room. Following her line of vision, Hunt didn't at first notice anything unusual, the large crowd mostly milling in front of one of the brochure- and pledge-card tables, until he heard Ellen's voice again. "How *dare* that slut show her face in here!" And then raising her voice even further, speaking to no one and to everyone, Ellen Como went on, "Put her out! Put her out on the street where she belongs! Get her out of here now! Now! Do you hear me?"

The suddenly silent crowd seemed to separate and open a corridor through the room and Hunt, standing right beside Lorraine Hess, found himself looking at a very attractive young woman in a plain black dress that hinted at an exquisite body beneath it. She was standing perfectly still with one hand held over her heart. Her eyes were wide in surprise at being thrust into the spotlight by this unexpected reaction, and this, if anything, made her, if possible, even more luminous.

On the other side of Hunt, Al Carter spoke in a matter-of-fact tone — "I'll get her" — and moved at the same time to escort the young woman, who Hunt immediately knew had to be Alicia Thorpe, out of the room.

The exterior of the 2006 Lincoln Town Car was spotless and shone with a high gloss. The black leather seats, likewise, might as well have been brand-new. The trunk contained a spare tire, but no tire iron or any other tools or debris. It looked as though it had been vacuumed within the past day. All the nonleather internal soft surfaces — dashboard, steering wheel — had recently been wiped down with Armor All, which, as all cops and many miscreants know, does not readily yield fingerprints. Russo and Juhle stood by while the crime scene personnel lifted the front rugs on both sides and found nothing under them. The CSI team had also already shone their flashlights and used their whisk brooms under the nonremovable front seats. The entire exercise had so far yielded one paper clip, nearly hermetically wedged into the seat-belt connector on the driver's side.

The police impound garage doubled as a maintenance shed for city-issued cars, and looked very much like the service area of any gas station. Russo, on her knees, her own flashlight in hand, watched while crime scene personnel now felt around under the passenger-side track that allowed the seat to move forward and backward. The technician, in her surgical gloves, worked something back and forth gently until it came loose from its perch under the seat. The woman straightened up, cricking her back, held up for their inspection an unopened condom in its wrapper.

"Eureka," Russo said. "Getting warm now."

"Oh, yeah." Juhle's enthusiasm less than genuine. "That ought to break the case wide open."

"You wait."

After she placed the condom in a Ziploc bag, the tech opened the back door of the limo, waited for her partner to do the same on his side, and then the two of them lifted the backseat. Russo turned her flashlight beam to the area under the seat cushion itself and it illuminated what looked like a multicolored rag of some kind scrunched into a ball and caught there.

"What's that?" Juhle asked.

The tech was extricating it with some care from the springs under the seat. She finally brought it out and held it up by one end so that it fell open and revealed itself as a silk head scarf in reds, yellows, and oranges. But all of it did not fall out; several folds in the silk appeared to be stuck to each other.

The inspectors watched and waited while the technician pulled one of her standard tools — a Wood's lamp — out of her kit and shone it on the scarf. Under its ultraviolet light, a smear of characteristic stains appeared as fluorescent.

She made a face and held it out at arm's length.

"Semen," she said.

19

Jim Parr got outside, then, noting the weather, immediately went back in and up the stairs to his place to get his heavy pea-coat. And so by less than a minute he missed his first chance to catch the N-Judah bus to downtown. As he rounded the corner to the bus stop, he saw it pulling away and took the opportunity to dust off several of his favorite underutilized profanities.

The next bus put him in the thick of the last-minute crowd rushing into the War Memorial building. He was standing in the middle of the crush of humanity at the bottom of the stairs when word traveled down that the Green Room had reached its capacity and that no one else could be admitted. Over the next twenty minutes, those members of the crowd who chose to remain, including Parr, managed to push themselves upstairs, where they got backed into the hallway that led to the doors inside of which the memorial was to take place.

Jostled back and across the entire hallway and now near the entrance to the elevator, Parr had just about decided to call it a day when he saw his old acquaintance and successor Al Carter approaching him, shouldering his way through the mass of people gathered between his spot and the Green Room's door, his arm protectively around a tearful and perhaps frightened Alicia Thorpe.

"Al!" he called out. "Alicia!"

Carter raised a finger in acknowledgment.

On an impulse, Parr pressed the button for the elevator. When it opened, he stepped back into it and held the door open as a few of the overload of mourners filed in before Carter and Alicia finally made it too.

"Going down?"

"Anywhere," Carter replied, his arm still around Alicia's shoulder wrap.

Though she was clearly shaken, Alicia's hooded expression barely allowed her to nod at Parr before she leaned her head against Carter's chest. The doors closed in front of them and the elevator began its descent.

On the ground floor, Carter stayed around long enough to exchange a few pleasantries with Parr. Then he turned to Alicia. "Are you sure you're okay?"

"I'd like to kill Ellen," she said, "but otherwise . . ."

"You got a way home?" Carter asked.

"I'm good," she said. "I drove myself down."

Parr cleared his throat. "You wouldn't by any chance be going back my way, would you? Save me another Muni adventure."

"Sure," she said. "Done."

Carter had made sure the guard at the door he'd exited upstairs knew he'd be coming back in. He was certain that he'd be readmitted, so he could afford these moments of pleasantries with Jim and Alicia, but clearly he wanted to get back up. After a few last encouraging words to Alicia, Carter left them both in the lobby and disappeared again into the elevator.

When he was gone, Alicia turned to Parr. "Let's get the fuck out of here."

Now they were speed-walking together on Van Ness into the teeth of the misty north wind. Alicia had parked a few blocks away and the walk to her car wasn't much conducive to conversation.

Once they were both in her car, the doors slammed shut and quickly locked behind them, they sat for another moment in silence, breathing heavily. Alicia fumbled in her purse, found her keys, turned the ignition on, and blasted the heater and then the fan all the way up.

Parr still wore his heavy coat over his dress suit and it had cut the wind and cold to some extent. But Alicia — in her flimsy dress and woolen shawl — hugged herself with her hands up and down on opposite arms and took deep breaths and long exhales until she had gotten herself back to some sort of comfort.

Eventually, she reached out and put her hands on the steering wheel, then gave Parr an apologetic smile. "Sorry. I didn't mean to get so cold."

"I'll forgive you this time. Are you all right?"

"Yes. Just cold."

"Maybe not just that, huh? What happened back there?"

For an answer, she just shook her head. Her hands gripped the steering wheel at ten and two, her knuckles white. She turned away from Parr to study a green light's worth of traffic as it passed outside her window. Slamming the car into gear, she released the parking brake, turned the wheel, again checked the traffic.

Then, abruptly, another shudder of cold or something else went through her, and she shifted back into neutral and set the parking brake. She stared into some middle space somewhere out in front of her. "Fucking Ellen Como," she said.

"What about her?"

"She saw me and went ballistic and kicked me out of there. She thinks I had a thing with Dominic." She paused. "Which I did not. Thanks for not asking."

Parr shrugged. "None of my business."

"I'm not that kind of person, not with married men anyway. I just don't get involved that way anymore. It's nothing but trouble, you know?"

Parr chortled. "Full disclosure. It's not a big problem in my life."

"And Dominic wouldn't have been any part of that anyway, no matter what. That wasn't who he was either. You knew that, too, didn't you?"

Parr stopped looking at her. He folded his arms over his chest.

"What?" she asked.

"I didn't say anything."

"Yes, you did."

He hesitated. "People can change," he said. "I believe that. I did."

"What does that mean?"

"It means that the Dominic I knew maybe wasn't the Dominic you knew."

She brought her hands down off the steering wheel, onto her lap. "You're saying he used to play around." Her startling green eyes took on a glassy brightness, as if tears were starting to form in them. She turned to face him. "Regularly? Often?"

Parr shrugged.

"And if that's true, you don't believe me, do you?"

"Listen to me, darling. You tell me to my face that you walk on burning coals, I'm going to believe you. I'm just saying that for Dominic, the Dominic I knew, it might have been a little out of character if he didn't even try."

She took a long beat and waited. "Did Mickey know that Dominic too?"

"Mickey? I don't know where Mickey —"

She shook her head in impatience. "Come on, Jim. What I'm asking is if Mickey is assuming that I slept with Dominic too? The way everybody else is?"

"Well, first, not everybody else is."

"That's not an answer!" Her voice taking on a panicky tone. "Did you tell him that you thought I probably was?"

"Easy, hon, easy. Mickey and I never talked about it. Not at all. I had my business with Dominic and Mickey has his life. He never asked about my opinion on any of this we're talking about, and I wouldn't have told him anything because I didn't know anything. Now I do, but only because you've told me. And it's still none of my business. Or his."

"No. I think it is his."

"How's that?"

"It's just that Mickey's investigating who killed Dominic. And I already told him what I told you, that Dominic and I were close but not that close, and if he thought that wasn't true, then not only would I be a liar, but I'd have a motive, you see?"

Parr reached over and patted her on the hand. "You're overthinking this, darling. Mick's not that complicated. You want an old man's opinion, I'd say that he's thinking about you and him, not about you and Dominic. And I couldn't exactly say I'd blame him."

She all but blushed. "You're sweet, Jim. That's a sweet thing to say."

"I'm a sweet old fart all right. But the point is Mick's on your side. We all are."

She let out a deep sigh. "I can't tell you what a relief that is, Jim. Especially after what Ellen . . . what she did in there. I can't have Mickey thinking I did this too. I didn't. I really didn't. You'll tell him that, won't you? And he's got to believe me and you,

313

too, then, right? To stand between me and the police. You see that, don't you?"

" 'Course I do, darling. Even a blind man could see it."

"Well, all right then." Taking another breath, she picked up Parr's hand and kissed it. "Now let's get you home," she said.

She pulled out into the traffic lane, got up a couple of blocks to California Street, and hung a left, heading west.

"You know, if you don't mind," Parr said after a moment, "it's out of the way, but maybe you could drop me out at Sutter."

"What for?"

"I thought I'd talk to some people, see who's hanging around, who knows what."

"Mickey said he was going to be out there talking to Al Carter."

Parr scratched at his cheek. "That's Mickey and Al, and Al's back there at the memorial. So I don't think I'll be in anybody's way, not for a little while, at least."

"So what are you looking for?"

"I don't know exactly, except I'll know it if I see it or hear it. Somebody always knows something, you know, even if they don't know what it is. And what else am I doing with my time anyway? That is, if you don't mind the drive."

"The drive's nothing. Driving's what I do.

314

I'll be happy to take you out there."

"Even you," he said after a bit.

She shot a glance over to him. "Even me what?"

"You drove Dominic that Tuesday morning, didn't you?"

She nodded.

"How long? Four hours? Five?"

"Something like that. Why?"

"You think hard enough, I bet you can remember something he said that would give you an idea about who he was meeting that night. 'Specially if you two were close, like you say. You talk about anything important with Dominic that morning? Anything unusual?"

Her hands were again tight on the wheel, her eyes straight ahead, her brow creased in concentration or worry. "No," she said. "No, I don't think so. Nothing I can remember, anyway."

Linda Colores, heretofore the Hang-up Lady, tried to make herself comfortable on the one wooden chair that Tamara had set up across from her reception station in the outer office. But it didn't seem to be working.

"Are you all right?" she asked.

Ms. Colores, perhaps twenty-two years

old, was a thin and stylishly dressed woman. She flashed a quick and apologetic smile, then raised a hand to her right temple. "I'm sorry. My head . . ."

Tamara had already opened her desk drawer. "I've got some ibuprofen, if . . ."

But Ms. Colores waved that off. "No. I'm sorry, but I know what it is. Food."

"Did you eat something that disagreed with you?"

"No. Not food that way. I shouldn't say food. I should say no food." She stole a quick glance at her watch. "Is that the real time, eleven-fifteen?"

Tamara checked her own watch, then the corner of her computer, saw that it was, and nodded. "Eleven-fifteen," she said.

Ms. Colores swallowed. "I'm so stupid. I'm out of bed at seven, I run five miles, I get ready for my appointment with you before I have to go and work all day, and I just forget one little thing. Actually, two. The first one is that I'm hypoglycemic. I don't eat, my head explodes, and other things. The second thing I then forget is to actually put some food in my mouth."

Tamara eyed her with some suspicion. "Are you sure you didn't talk to my boss or my brother? No, I'm kidding. But both of them are always on me to eat, eat, eat." She paused for a second. "Maybe we should go out and have a little bite. Would you like to do that?"

"I think I have to. I'm sorry."

Tamara pushed her chair back and stood up. "No more apologizing, okay? We go get something to eat, we talk about what you heard the other night. Good?"

"Yes, good," Ms. Colores said. "Thank you."

Fortuitously, Hunt's office was close to Belden Alley, just a block away. Mickey often said that Belden Alley alone, one short block in length, if it were the only street in the city, might make San Francisco qualify as a better-than-average-destination restaurant town, and then he'd list its restaurants like a carnival barker: "Brindisi Cucina di Mare, Voda, Taverna, B44, Plouf, Café Tiramisu, Café Bastille, and Sam's Grill."

Partially guided by expense, although none of the places would bust even Tamara's budget, she convinced Linda that Brindisi was what they wanted. Fifteen minutes later, during which they made small talk mostly about food and their brothers (Linda had two, both older), the waiter delivered Tamara's rigatoni with lamb ragout and artichokes, and Linda's grilled salmon

317

sandwich on ciabatti with lobster mayonnaise, salad, and fries.

"So," Tamara began, a few bites into her lunch, "what happened that Tuesday night?"

"Well, that's the thing," Linda said, then paused for a moment. "I feel really bad that I didn't do more, I mean when it happened. But then, I know it sounds bad to say I didn't want to get involved, but at the time it just seemed like a fight, and all I wanted to do was get away from it. And then at the store, they were talking about how they found the body right near where I'd been. And then at first I wasn't even sure it was Tuesday. I mean, I really didn't think about it at all as maybe connected to Mr. Como's murder until I heard about the reward — I know that sounds a little crass . . ."

"Don't worry about that."

"Still. I just thought about what if it might have actually been important. You know?"

"It's fine, Linda. That's why they put out a reward. Get people thinking about things that otherwise they might not really have registered. But now you're pretty sure it was Tuesday?"

"No. I'm completely sure." She dabbed a napkin at her mouth. "I have this little calendar book — I know this is pretty Type-A, but welcome to Linda Land, as my brothers say. Anyway, I kind of use it as a shorthand diary for everything I do every day — how much I ran, hours I worked, where I ate, who I went out with, movies, books. It's probably a disease, and I've definitely got it." She shrugged. "In any event, I checked back and realized it had been payday and Cheryl — she's my friend from work — and I decided to go wait at the A16 bar and have dinner there. Which, of course, took about three hours."

"For dinner?"

"Well, one and a half for the wait — totally worth it, by the way — then about the same for dinner. But the point is that I probably got out around ten, ten-fifteen, said good-bye to Cheryl, and then — remember, it was that warm week? — I was stuffed so I decided it was so nice out I'd walk some of the food off, so I headed down to the Palace of Fine Arts, which I love at night."

"Go on."

"So then I'm down by the lagoon, just really strolling, enjoying the night, and I get down to the parking lot by the Exploratorium and I hear these voices, a man and a woman, so I stop. It's not like I was trying to eavesdrop. Just ahead of me the trail turned and they must have been around the bend."

"You didn't see them?'

"No. Even if I had, it would probably have been too dark to recognize them. But anyway, it was obviously a fight, I mean just from the sound, but then I'm standing there and the woman goes, 'God damn you!' and I hear this, like, slap. And then she's all 'Oh, God, I'm sorry, I'm so sorry, I didn't mean that.' "

Clearly getting caught up in the emotion of her retelling, Linda Colores blew at a few of her hairs that had fallen in front of her face, then brushed them from her forehead. "So now I'm thinking," she continued, "I've got to get out of here, but it's like my feet are stuck to the ground. I'm just rooted there, afraid I'm going to make some noise if I move. I mean, I *really* don't want to be there, but . . ." Another shrug, followed by another sigh.

"So she hit him?"

Now Linda nodded. "And then there's this silence, and finally I hear him plain as day. 'Look,' he says, 'I'm sorry, but it's over. I can't do anything about it.'

"And she goes, 'You can. You can if you still love me.'

"And he goes, 'Aren't you listening to me? That's the problem. I don't love you anymore.'

"And then I hear her say, 'No, no, no, that can't be,' and then there's this kind of sickening sound, like a . . . I don't really know what it was like exactly. I mean, she kind of groaned with exertion or something and then there was this, this kind of dull sound — I even thought at the time it could have been somebody getting hit with something. I know I should have maybe gone and looked then. I mean, it sounded bad enough, but by then I was scared. I mean really scared. And then suddenly I start to actually feel sick and light-headed myself and I turn back and start walking away as fast and as quietly as I can. I really should have done something about it then, I think. I mean, called the police or told somebody. But when there was nothing about it on the news, not until Friday when they found the body, and even then I didn't immediately put it together. Although I guess I should have, shouldn't I?"

"You're here now," Tamara told her, "when a lot of other people wouldn't be. So I wouldn't beat myself up over it too much."

"I don't like to think I'm such a coward," Linda said, "or that I only came forward now because of the reward."

"I don't think that," Tamara said, "and I'm the only one listening."

20

Being thorough, Mickey stayed on at the Sanctuary House offices and spoke for a time with each one of the five other women who worked there to see if any of them had seen or heard anything from Nancy Neshek on the Monday afternoon of the reward announcement that might bear on the question she had meant to put to the Hunt Club. None of them was particularly helpful; all were shaken and tearful.

It was after noon when Mickey finally finished and left the admin office. From the hospital lobby, he called Hunt on his cell phone and left a message, thinking, *What's the goddamn point of having a cell phone if you don't take it with you or keep it turned on?* Hunt was supposed to be at the Como memorial. So was nearly the entire cast of characters from which he needed to find alibis for the past Monday night. So it was doubly frustrating that Mickey had just

322

learned that the Communities of Opportunity people had held a meeting on that night. Presumably — in fact, almost certainly — Nancy Neshek had been there along with many others of the nonprofit executive directors, associates, and certainly even Len Turner.

And Hunt, at this very moment, was in all probability with these people and didn't have that one rather critical bit of information. But then, getting to his car, Mickey realized that if Hunt spoke to even one of these people, he'd find out about the Monday-night meeting right away anyway.

Still, Mickey liked being the bearer of good news, especially when he thought it was good stuff and he'd discovered it himself. So he placed another call to the office to brag a bit to Tamara, but she didn't pick up there either. And what was that about? he wondered.

For just a brief moment, he found that his stomach had gone a little hollow. Where was his sister? Had he and Hunt been too cavalier about bringing her back to work, in assuming that's what she wanted, in giving her more responsibility? Or might Mickey hope against hope that she had actually, of her own volition, gone out for something to eat? It was, after all, lunchtime.

His phone still in his hand, without much forethought, he went to his favorites list and hit Jim's number, heard it ring four times, got his answering machine. "Give me a fucking break," he said aloud, and leaving no message, he threw his phone onto the seat next to him.

He knew who he wanted to call next. But really, what was he going to say to Alicia except that he had just loved her company the night before and wanted to see her again? Wanted to see her all the time, in fact. What she had called her nerd moment from the night before had struck Mickey as incredibly poignant, echoing as it did his own feelings. It had humanized her to an extent that had taken him by surprise. He really didn't need anything to help make her more compelling, but there it had been, unpracticed and sincere, a glimpse of the person under the package.

Beautiful there as well.

Still, he would have to wait. She was mourning Dominic Como. In fact, now that he thought of it, she was almost certainly at the memorial herself.

This was just swell, he was thinking. Here he was, all dressed up and no place to go. In the future, he would really have to try to remember to get more and/or clearer assignments from Hunt before he left the office for the day, which now stretched long and empty before him.

He turned the key in the ignition, the car started right up, and he pulled out of his space. When he got to Potrero, the traffic was heavy and unbroken going south to his left, but there was an opening turning right if he moved quickly, and so he jammed down on the accelerator.

That was the extent of the thought he gave to turning back uptown. It could have easily gone either way, since he didn't have a destination in mind.

Such a small, random decision. Such huge consequences.

The windows that overlooked the booth tables at Lou the Greek's were set high in the west-facing wall, their bases perhaps six feet from the floor. This unusual design feature wasn't due to some architect's skewed or artistic vision; from outside the building, all six of the windows sat level to the asphalt that paved a debris- and Dumpster-strewn alley. Lou's had been built about halfway underground. Patrons entering the building's front double doors could either go up the stairs to the first floor — Acme Bail Bonds, Florence Ward/Notary

Public, and Presto Dispatch (a document delivery service) — or down eight ammonia- or possibly urine-tinged steps, through a red-leather one-sided swinging door, and into the bustling netherworld of Lou's — "Open Six to Two Seven Days a Week/Full Bar/Daily Special."

When you walk in, the bar is to your right. If it's lunchtime, the bar is jammed, with all the stools taken, and behind them a couple of rows of standing room. If it's your first time here, you notice the high windows, under them the six old-fashioned four-person wooden booths, the low-slung acoustic tile ceiling, the faint odor of cooking oil, soy sauce, maybe spilled beer. The place squeezes twenty four-tops onto the floor, and six two-tops around the walls, and every weekday it serves over two hundred lunches, all the more remarkable because its menu every day, save the occasional bonanza of fortune cookies, is comprised of only one dish: the Special.

Lou the Greek's wife, Chiu, was Chinese, and for twenty-five or more years, she'd been honoring her and her husband's union by creating a new dish nearly every single day, always based on their two nationalities. Today's Special, for example, General Lou's Pork, was at once typical and unique: pita bread pockets stuffed with bright red Chinese barbecued pork, scallions, garlic, hoisin sauce, yogurt, and hot pepper flakes. A lot of hot pepper flakes.

Juhle and Russo sat sucking their iced teas through straws across from each other in one of the booths.

Russo set her glass down, swallowed, and blew in and out noisily a couple of times. "Holy shit," she said. "Lou calls this 'some spicy'? I'd like to see a lot spicy if this is some. This stuff is fire."

Juhle slid over the little jar of pure hot pepper seeds in oil. "You want to get serious, add some of this. Then it gets spicy."

"I pass." Russo sipped again, rubbed at her lips. "I mean it. Holy shit."

"You already said that."

"It's a two 'holy-shit' pita pocket."

Juhle took another bite, chewed contentedly, switched to another subject without preamble. "So how can it hurt? We're just talking to her."

"We don't know it's her scarf, Devin."

Juhle shrugged, sipped some tea, shrugged again. "We ask her. We show her that lovely color photograph you took and ask the lovely Ms. Thorpe if she's ever seen this thing before. She says no, we keep looking, maybe ask some other people if they ever saw her wearing it, or somebody else wearing it. On the other hand, she says yes, we're getting close."

"I'm not even so sure of that."

"No? Why not, pray?"

"Because even if it's hers, we don't know if it's his semen."

"Granted. But we will know in a couple of days. And?"

"And you just seem to want to be building this case on one flimsy lead after another. You really don't see this?"

"I see what you're saying, sure. First we get the tire iron. We know it's Como's hair on it, but we don't know it's from Como's limo, although the tire iron from the limo is missing. Right? Right. There are a lot of tire irons in the world. Close, but not proof positive. So then we search the limo and guess what? We find the scarf. And sure, it might not be the Thorpe girl's scarf, and it might not be Como's masculine essence on it, either, but —"

"Jesus, Dev, you think you could just say 'semen'?"

"I doubt it. I don't even say 'semen' when I'm talking to Connie."

"So what do you . . . no, never mind. Forget I asked. Go on."

"So I agree with you, is what I'm saying,

in theory. We've got all these things we don't know for sure. Could be but might not be. The tire iron, the limo, the scarf that might not be hers, the semen — see, I can do it — that might not be his. But let's say — let's just say — that the elements of the trail I see here all turn out to go in our direction. I mean, it turns out the tire iron came from his limo. It's her scarf and his semen. Then, in that case, she's definitely lied to us, which tells us something new, doesn't it? Now, add to that that she had daily access to the limo, that he fired her that day —"

"We don't know that. Only maybe that he said he was going to."

"So we ask her that too. She tells us yes, she's got a motive. And all this is not even talking about Monday night, where she slept in her car out by the beach a couple of blocks below where Nancy Neshek breathed her last." Juhle took the last loud slurp from his iced tea, held up a hand until he'd swallowed it. "I'm not saying we're ready for an arrest here, Sarah. But come on. Put a little press on her, get another statement, see if she answers the same as last time. What have we got to lose?"

When the service was over, Al Carter hung back over in the corner of the downstairs lobby of the War Memorial building while Hunt corralled Turner, the Sanchezes, and Lorraine Hess into a circle off to the side at the bottom of the steps. Carter listened in while Hunt pinned down each of them in turn about their whereabouts the night of Neshek's death. It seemed to take some of the wind out of Hunt when he learned that they'd all been at a meeting with one another on the Monday night when Neshek had been killed. But then when he learned that Nancy Neshek had been there with them all, too, he picked up again. So, Hunt asked, what time did the Communities of Opportunity meeting break up? Where had every one of them gone afterward?

This last question got Turner hot enough that nobody wound up having to answer. Maybe, Turner had exploded, Hunt didn't realize that he was talking to the leadership of the philanthropic community in San Francisco. None of Len Turner's associates were suspects in either one of these murders. In fact, Turner himself had hired Hunt and these people had contributed to the reward. Weren't those the facts?

Hunt had had to admit that they were.

And then Turner went on the offensive. Carter had heard him do it before. He reminded Hunt that all of these executives had places to go and important things to do, and maybe Hunt could better spend his time following the leads he had already developed through the process they were paying him for rather than harassing them in this ridiculous manner, thank you.

After the executive group broke up, Hunt had waited until they'd all left the building, then he'd sat down on the steps and had a brief talk on his cell phone. By the time he closed the phone and slid it into its holster on his belt, Carter was standing in front of him, arms crossed over his chest, leaning back against the wall.

"That Len Turner, he's a force of nature, isn't he?"

Hunt stood up, nodded in acknowledgment through a frustrated grin. "Al Carter, isn't it?"

"Yes, sir. I had a talk with one of your people the other day out at Sunset. Mickey?"

"Mickey it is."

"And his grandfather is Jim Parr?"

"That's him. Do you know Jim?"

"I do. He was my predecessor and taught me some of the driving ropes. It's not all about steering and brakes and acceleration, you know. There's a significant political component as well."

"I'd imagine so. In any event, Mickey mentioned that he might be trying to see you again today, as a matter of fact."

Al Carter's wide, intelligent face closed down slightly. "He didn't make an appointment."

"No. I think he just planned to go out there and hoped he'd run into you."

"Did he mention what he wanted to discuss? Maybe you and I can take care of it here, whatever it might be. Although I must tell you, my ignorance about Mr. Como's movements that last night is near total. I dropped him off near his home, as I told your Mickey and the police, and had the limo back in the school lot by six-thirty. Then I went home myself. Can I ask you a question?"

"Sure."

"The police impounded the limo last night. Do you have any idea why?"

"I presume they wanted to search it more thoroughly."

"For what?"

"For whatever they find. You know they think they have the murder weapon?"

This brought a little snort. "Yes. Lorraine Hess told me. The tire iron."

"Not necessarily *the* tire iron from the limo, but a tire iron certainly."

332

"And are they sure?"

"Reasonably, yes. Unless there's some way Dominic Como's hair ended up on another tire iron that found its way into the Palace's lagoon."

"Yes." Carter's smile did not reach to his eyes. "That would be an impressive long shot. So, presumably I had access to the tire iron more than most. Am I then a suspect?"

"I haven't heard that from the police. I don't believe they have a suspect yet."

"Ah, I was forgetting. We don't have suspects anymore, do we? Only persons of interest. The vocabulary change affords me little comfort." Carter's lips pursed out, and then in. His facial muscles moved in a way that suggested he was trying to smile, but this time, his lips could not hold the expression. "Let me ask you this, then, Mr. Hunt. Among the potential suspects — people with access to the limo and the tire iron and so on — are there any other black men with prison time in their background?"

"Not that I know of."

"Can you appreciate why this might be a matter of some concern to me? Of more than average concern?"

"Obviously. Don't take this wrong, but might someone come to the conclusion that you had some kind of a motive?"

Carter's eyes closed down almost to slits before he opened them again as the broad expressive face fell into relaxation. "I've had the job eight years. I'm an ex-convict. All the demographics predict that I shouldn't have a steady job, much less an education, and yet I do. All compliments of Dominic, a generous and powerful man."

"But there was a price," Hunt said.

"If he wanted to go, if he *needed* to go, doesn't matter where it was, what time it was, how long you had to wait for him, whatever he was doing, you either took him and *took it* or he'd find someone else who would. This was unstated and intuitively understood. And an absolute job requirement."

"So you were essentially on call all the time? Even with the other drivers he used?"

This brought a mirthless laugh. "Again, I don't mean any kind of slur. Dominic was a great man. It was a privilege to work for him. But for the interns, the younger people without criminal records, the girls . . . there wasn't much in the line of actual driving, except to our work sites. Certainly they did not drive him to open-ended events, night-time meetings with partners and constituents, other things. . . ."

"Women?"

Carter's smile and gesture were ambiguous. "In any event," he said, "with the other drivers, the relationship was symbiotic. Dominic got good, presentable, inexpensive help, and then he placed that help with other people in the city who could help him. You want tickets to the Giants? The Warriors? The Niners? You want a parking ticket fixed? Or, more likely, a drug bust. You'd like the ear of your supervisor on a development issue?"

"But that wasn't you? You weren't in line for one of those jobs?"

"No. I was a lifer. I *am* a lifer. Except now, with him gone . . ." He spread his hands.

"And you're concerned that someone might take that as a motive? That you wanted out?"

"Perhaps unwisely, I mentioned it to a few people. And I don't really know if I did want that. What else would I do? What am I going to do now? But did I sometimes feel trapped? Yes. Might Dominic have heard about it and fired me? Perhaps. He didn't tolerate disloyalty, even the hint of it. He might even have fired me on Tuesday."

Hunt nodded. "Well, as motives go, I'd call that pretty weak. Even if anyone could prove it."

"I agree. But my so-called alibis for both

nights are also flimsy. I live alone and I was at home alone both nights. So, combined with my record, my race, the motive, the lack of alibi, and the fact that except for his killer, I was the last person to see him, the police —"

"I see what you're saying."

"Well, no, I'm not sure that you do, since I haven't said it yet."

Hunt waited.

"I've wanted to stay out of all of this to the extent that I could. Reward or no reward, I know how the police often go about their work. And I'm afraid — you see, it's already happened to me once before — I'm afraid that they might find in me a path of least resistance. That's the only reason I've decided to talk to you."

"You know something."

"Yes. And I only mention it with great reluctance because of everything I've told you about here today. I wanted you to understand me. If they don't have someone else, there's a likelihood they're going to come knocking at my door." He took a breath and held it, his lips again pursed and tight. "He fired Alicia Thorpe that morning."

21

"Yeah, we're sitting outside her place right now, hoping to talk to her," Juhle said. "Got any idea where she might be?"

Hunt was in his car talking on his cell phone, which miraculously had a strong signal two floors down in the City Hall lot. After finishing up with Al Carter, he'd half jogged through the thickening drizzle, gotten to his car, and punched in Juhle's number. "Sorry. I know where she was an hour ago, and that was here. But Ellen Como had her kicked out."

"She could do that?"

"It was her party, Devin. She could do anything she wanted. It wasn't very pretty." He paused. "So what did you get?"

Juhle ran down the latest link in the chain that was apparently beginning to close around Alicia Thorpe. "At least," Juhle concluded, "if it's her scarf . . ."

"Why do you think it's hers?"

337

"She's the only female driver. The scarf's in the limo. Hello? Anyway, at least it gives us something to ask her about. Not to mention Carter corroborating Ellen's story that Dominic fired her. You believe him?"

"Yep."

"On the very day? We got that right?"

"Tuesday morning."

"Did Carter change his story, then, about who Como was going to see?"

"No. He didn't know that. Dominic said he was meeting an old friend and didn't go into it. In truth, it might not have been Alicia. But Carter thought it might have been. So how long before you find out about the semen? If it was Como's."

"As opposed to whose?"

"I don't know, Dev. Maybe as opposed to any other guy who'd ever been in the limo getting some head from somebody wearing a scarf. Where'd you find it in the limo, anyway? The scarf?"

"Under the backseat. Why?"

"Just trying to picture the scenario that gets Dominic into the backseat."

"That's where people sit in limos, Wyatt."

"Yeah, mostly, I know. Except I don't think Como did. I read that somewhere. Or saw his picture. Something, maybe both. He prided himself on being a regular guy, sitting in the passenger seat up front. I'm sure of that."

"And what's that mean?"

"I don't know. Maybe nothing. So how long?"

"How long what?"

"Before you know the semen was Dominic's."

"DNA? About the same as the DNA on the tire iron. Round it off to four days, maybe six, multiply by the phase of the moon, divide by, I don't know, let's say fourteen. It's anybody's guess. But after today, we may not need it until the trial. We'll see."

"You think you're near an arrest?"

"We'll see."

"It would be great if you could say something else besides 'We'll see.' "

"It would, I know."

"Well, keep me in the loop."

"We'll see." Juhle's tone was distinctly ironic. "Hey, this could be her. Gotta run." And he broke off the connection.

Alicia pulled up to the curb outside the house where she rented her basement room and sat unmoving, staring straight ahead, in the driver's seat with the motor running, her hands locked onto the steering wheel.

She had her lights on and the windshield wipers swished back and forth intermittently.

"What's she doing?" Juhle asked.

"I don't know. Waiting for her favorite song to end? Meditating?"

Juhle gave her a full minute before his patience ran out. He got out of his own car, crossed the street, came up behind her, and knocked on the driver's side window.

Startled, Alicia jerked her hands away from the wheel and her head toward Juhle, who wore a practiced professional expression and held his badge open next to the window.

After a brief moment of what he took to be confusion, she moved one hand over to the door and the window came down.

"Yes?"

"Ms. Thorpe. Inspector Juhle, you may remember. I wonder if we could ask you just a few more questions?"

She dropped her head before lifting it back up again. Then she dredged half a smile from somewhere, said, "Sure," grabbed her purse, rolled up the window, and pushed open the door.

By this time, Russo had joined Juhle, and now the three of them marched across the lawn and down the side path that led to the entrance to her room in the back. The wind wasn't as strong as it had been downtown, although the mist and drizzle out here had intensified into true rain, falling straight down on them.

It didn't make any of them walk any more quickly.

When they got inside with the door closed behind them, Alicia hit the lights and adjusted the thermostat, then turned. "I'm just going to throw on a pullover, if that's okay." She crossed the room and took down a bright green knitted sweater that was hanging from a peg on the opposite wall, and brought it over her head. Coming back to them, she got to the table and pulled out one of its chairs, indicating that they do the same.

They all sat.

"I'm supposed to be at work in about an hour and a half. Should I call them and tell them I'll be late?"

Juhle and Russo exchanged a glance, and Russo said, "I don't think we'll be that long, but if we get close, you'll have that opportunity. Okay?"

"Fine." She looked from one inspector to the other. "So." She drew a breath. "What can I do for you?"

"Well," Juhle began, "as I said, we've got a

341

few more questions for you."

"About Mr. Como?"

Russo had gone solemn, and she nodded. "Him and a few other things, yes."

"Am I some kind of a suspect?" Alicia asked.

Juhle answered. "We haven't identified any true suspects yet, Ms. Thorpe. We're trying to fill in gaps in our understanding at this time. And hope you might be able to help us."

"So I'm not under arrest?"

"You are absolutely not under arrest," Juhle said. "You don't have to talk to us at all and can terminate this interview at any time."

"So I don't need to call a lawyer?"

Russo forced a conspiratorial smile. "If you want to call a lawyer, Alicia, that is your right," she said. "We could wait here for him or her to show up, or make another appointment later. But we are hoping to keep making progress on this case and thought you would want to help us keep it moving along to catch Mr. Como's killer."

"It shouldn't take us more than a half hour," Juhle added. "Maybe less."

"Okay," Alicia said. "In that case . . ."

"Great. Thank you." Juhle took out his pocket tape recorder and placed it on the table between them. "We'll just be taping what we say to preserve an accurate record. We did this last time, too, you recall?"

"Yes."

"All right." Juhle pushed away from the table and leaned back in his wooden chair. He crossed one leg over the other, his body language clearly stating that he was no threat to Alicia or to anyone else. "I apologize if we cover a few things we went through last time, but we've been talking to a lot of people and sometimes we lose track of the sources of certain information."

This was the purest of twaddle, and Juhle knew it. What he was really hoping was that Alicia would contradict her earlier answers, and thus give them substantial leverage. And of course, if Alicia had elected to wait to talk to a lawyer, she would have known this. But there wasn't anything she could do about it now. She didn't even seem to realize it might be a troublesome issue.

"Now, then," Juhle began, "you'd been driving for Mr. Como for how long?"

Tag-teaming, Juhle and Russo walked her through most of her earlier statement — her service at Sunset, her duties as Como's driver, her perceptions of some other key members of the staff at the Ortega campus — and finally got to her personal relationship with her boss, which she answered as she always had. They were close friends, but not intimate.

Juhle kept it casual. "So, once again, you did not have any kind of physical relationship with Mr. Como?"

"No."

"Never kissed him?"

She hesitated. "Not in a romantic way, no."

Russo picked up the distinction. "What other way did you kiss him, then?"

Alicia showed her first sign of true frustration, a sigh accompanied by a slight puckering around her lips. "More like a buss on the cheek, sometimes, when I'd first see him or when I was leaving."

"Both?" Russo asked.

"Sometimes."

Russo wasn't letting it go. "Usually?"

Pausing again, nodding, Alicia said, "By the end, yes. Most days. Just like friends do. Maybe a small hug and a little kiss hello."

"A hug and a kiss, then?" Juhle asked.

"Not a big hug. Really just like a greeting or a good-bye." She leveled her gaze at both of the inspectors in turn. "Come on, you guys. You know what I'm talking about. We usually kissed hello and good-bye, just like I'd do with my brother. It wasn't sexual. We had become friends, that's all."

Juhle asked, "And you were still friends on the day he was killed?"

"Yes, of course."

Russo: "You weren't having any troubles at work?"

"No."

"None?"

Alicia straightened up in her chair. "What's this about?"

Russo came forward, but did not answer her. Instead, she said, "You were at Mr. Como's service this morning."

"Not for long."

"We understand that Mrs. Como asked you to leave."

A bitter chuckle. "If that's how you want to put it."

Juhle asked, "How would you put it?"

"Were you there?"

"No, ma'am."

"Well, the way I'd put it is she had me thrown out."

"Why would she have wanted to do that?" Russo asked.

"Because she's a crazy woman," Alicia said. "She thinks I had something going on with Dominic, which I think we've been through enough, huh?"

"Were you aware," Juhle said, "that she

demanded that Mr. Como fire you?"

"That wouldn't surprise me. Nothing she did would surprise me."

"But Mr. Como didn't tell you that?"

"What?"

"That his wife wanted him to fire you."

"No. When?"

"Anytime. It never came up?"

"No. Never."

Sarah Russo, her hands clasped in front of her on the table, raised her head. "And he didn't, in fact, fire you?"

"No, he didn't."

"That last Tuesday was just another day at the office for you," Juhle said. "Is that what you're saying?"

"That's what I'm saying. God knows, I've thought about it enough, trying to remember any hint he might have given me while we were on the road about his appointment that night. But it was just a normal day."

"Tuesday, you mean?"

"Right. That last Tuesday."

"But you didn't come into work the next day?" Russo asked.

"Yes, I did. I went home when I saw Dominic wasn't there."

"And what about the day after that?"

"What about it?"

"Did you come in then?"

346

Alicia paused. "No."

"Why not?"

Alicia hesitated a moment longer. "Well, Dominic wasn't in, so there wouldn't have been anything for me to do."

Russo, on a scent, came forward. "How did you know he wasn't in?"

"What do you mean?"

"I mean — it's a straightforward question — how did you know Dominic wasn't in?"

"I don't know. I don't remember. I must have called."

"You must have called? Why would you have called? Did you call most mornings to see if he was at work before you came in?"

"No. Sometimes. I must have those days. Or I had heard he was missing. I think that was probably it. His wife by then had said he was missing." Alicia's eyes were bright with emotion, and suddenly she found a voice for it. "And while we're on that, listen," she said. "I've been sitting here letting you guys ask me all these questions, but don't you think — forget all these innuendoes about me and Dominic — don't you think it's just a little suspicious that his wife didn't even call to report him missing until he was already gone for a whole day? Isn't that a little hard to explain? Doesn't that bother you at all? Plus the fact that Mrs. Como is the one who was jealous, regardless of whether I gave her a reason to be or not. And I didn't. She's the one who thought Dominic was cheating on her, and if she thought that, she might have wanted to kill him for it. Doesn't that make more sense than sniffing all around me?"

Juhle raised his eyebrows at his partner. He wasn't here to tell Alicia everything or anything that they knew, or assumed: that Ellen Como had had no real access to the presumed murder weapon, that they had no indication or information that she'd ever ridden or even been in her husband's limo, and hence couldn't have left a possibly incriminating scarf there, that both Ellen and Al Carter, apparently independently, had stated unequivocally that Dominic had in fact fired Alicia on his last morning at work. Ellen's behavior and unsubstantiated alibi notwithstanding, she was not really their prime suspect. Although of course they had not totally written her off.

But Juhle only said, "We appreciate your perspective, but as we've told you, the investigation is ongoing. We're just trying to gather information."

"And to that end," Russo picked up, "I wonder if you could tell us what you did last Monday night."

If the question was meant to shake her up, it succeeded almost to the point of panic. Alicia's mouth turned down, her eyebrows came together over her eyes. She looked to Juhle as if verifying that this was what they wanted to know. "Monday night a week ago?" she asked. "The night before Dominic was killed?"

"No," Russo answered patiently. "This past Monday night, two nights ago."

"Two nights ago? Why?"

Juhle had his professional face back on. "If you could just answer the question, Alicia."

The official tone hit its mark and Alicia sat back meekly, holding her hands together in her lap. "Monday night, Monday night. Tuesday I was at a friend's for dinner, and then Monday . . . oh, I got it. Monday I slept in my car down by the beach. Ocean Beach. I wanted to go surfing Tuesday morning."

"And you were alone in your car?" Russo asked.

"Yes."

"And from what time?"

"I don't know exactly. I had a pizza with my girlfriend Danielle at Giorgio's. On Clement? I guess I left at around ten."

349

"And drove out to the beach?" Russo asked.

"Right."

"Did you talk to anybody out there?" Juhle asked. "Were they having bonfires that night?"

Alicia shook her head. "I went to sleep in my car. I've got a mattress I throw in and a sleeping bag. I wanted to be up early. What happened Monday night?"

Again ignoring Alicia's question, Russo threw a sharp glance at Juhle, then reached under her jacket and pulled a color photograph out of her breast pocket. She placed it on the table in front of Alicia. "Do you recognize this?" she asked.

Alicia's eyes lit up briefly, then closed down as she looked at Russo to answer her. "Yes. That's my scarf. I lost it a couple of weeks ago. Where did you find it?"

"Her name is Linda Colores." Tamara had Hunt sit down in the one chair across from her in the reception area as soon as he'd arrived back at the office. "The Hang-Up Lady."

"I'd forgotten all about her," Hunt replied. "What'd she have to say?"

"That she was out by the Palace on the night Mr. Como was killed. Like maybe ten

350

or ten-thirty. She was just walking by herself after dinner on the path by the lagoon and two people were having an argument right in front of her."

"Tell me she saw them."

"I wish I could, but she didn't. They were around where the path turns right down there at the end, near where Mickey found the body. But the point is that she heard them, really clearly."

"Okay."

"A man and a woman. The man telling the woman he didn't love her anymore. Then, maybe, the sound of her hitting him. At least this grunt of exertion and then this kind of sickening sound."

"So what'd she do then? Your witness."

"She got scared and turned and got out of there as quickly and quietly as she could."

"While our murderer," Hunt said, "made sure Como was dead, then got him into the lagoon and tucked him away in the roots."

"Linda didn't know anything about that, but I'd say probably."

"I would too."

"Anyway," Tamara said, "I don't know if that tells us anything we don't already know, or think we know, but it seemed important to me somehow."

"It's damned important," Hunt said. "If

only because that was really the end of it. If that's when Como was killed."

"That's what it sounded like to Linda."

"And if that's the case, it's not part of the money issues, is it? In spite of what Gina would have me believe."

"And it's also," Tamara said, "not a guy."

"Maybe not. Not unless our woman here hid Como away and then called somebody to finish up."

"So two of them?"

"Not likely, I admit, but not impossible. Alicia and her brother —"

"No, Wyatt, no."

"I'm just saying . . ." But then other possibilities sprang into his mind — Ellen Como and Al Carter or Ellen Como and Len Turner; or even Nancy Neshek and an accomplice who'd wound up then killing her. Then back again to Alicia and . . . almost any man who would do anything for her and her favors, which, after only a quick glimpse of her at the memorial service, Hunt figured would include most of the male population of the known world.

22

If Mickey had turned left, which was south, on Potrero, he would have gotten to Cesar Chavez Boulevard after only a couple of blocks, then immediately taken the on-ramp to 101 North and made it back to the Stockton garage at just about the time he figured Wyatt would be returning from the memorial service. They would have grabbed a bite somewhere, compared notes on their respective morning's adventures, and developed a plan for the rest of the day, or even week.

But as it happened he turned right, got up to Eighteenth Street, which reminded him of the tasty and tender goat he'd bought the day before at Bi-Rite Market, which happened to find itself on Eighteenth as well. So he turned left on Eighteenth, intending to get provisions for the homestead — whatever looked good, and something would — for the next couple of days. His plan was to keep cooking at home for as long as Tamara kept showing her renewed appetite.

The light was solid green for him to go when he got to Mission and so there wasn't any reason to slow down. He was thinking about special cuts of pork they might have at Bi-Rite and then after that maybe he'd go to his favorite burrito place only a few blocks over to his right on Mission.

He never even began to see the 2009 Volvo going, according to the accident records that were later filed in the incident, approximately thirty miles per hour. The car ran the red light and broadsided him on his passenger-side door.

The initial impact pushed his car sideways for exactly thirty-six feet until its momentum was stopped by a ten-year-old Chevy Suburban that was parked at a meter on the west-side curb of Mission. This second collision, on Mickey's side of his car just behind his seat, T-boned his Camaro, smashed his head against the side window, concussed him, broke his left arm and three of his ribs, and rendered him unconscious. His cell phone, which he'd thrown onto the passenger seat a few minutes earlier, and which held all of his contact information, got bounced around like a pinball inside the car and hit something hard enough to smash its screen and break it, making it use-less.

The parked Suburban, jumping the curb, killed a homeless John Doe everybody called Frankie who'd been a fixture begging at that intersection for the past seventeen months. The driver of the Volvo, who was wearing her seat belt and whose airbag deployed perfectly according to factory specifications, was a bit banged up but basically uninjured.

Hunt came out of his own office in the back and hooked a hip over Tamara's desk. She was working on a scheduling spreadsheet on her computer and kept tapping the keyboard for a second before, still typing, she turned to face him. "Yes?"

"I've been wrestling with it for half an hour driving back here and I've got to ask you a question."

She didn't miss a beat. "Almost thirty," she said, "but most people guess closer to twenty-five."

In mock chagrin, Hunt hung his head. "When am I going to learn?"

Tamara put on an empathetic face. "One day it'll just happen. You wait." She broke a smile. "Okay, what's the real question?"

"The real question is Mick. How serious

355

is he with this Thorpe woman?"

Tamara sat back. "Alicia, Wyatt. Her name's Alicia."

"I know what her name is, Tam. I'm a little worried about both of you using it, being on a first-name basis with her. I don't want you two getting too close to her."

"You said that this morning."

"I meant it then too. And I noticed it kind of pissed off both of you, Mickey maybe a little more. And that was before I talked to Al Carter and heard the latest from Devin. That's what I've been wrestling with. Whether I should even tell you what they said, either of them, either of you."

"Of course you should tell us. We've got to know what we're dealing with."

"That's true, but I don't want either of you shutting me out because I'm keeping an open mind on all the possible suspects."

"Are you?"

"As far as I can tell, Tam. You tell me where I'm not."

She touched his hand. "You don't have to get mad."

"You know, I'm afraid I can't help that. Six months ago, you'll remember, we had a little problem with —"

"This isn't like that."

"It isn't? Employee of the Hunt Club gets

involved with murder suspect who turns out —"

"Craig was never a suspect."

"No. That's true. We both know what Craig was, though, don't we? An actual murderer, too smart to get himself suspected. And he had everybody fooled. Even me."

Tamara flared. "Even *you?* I like to think that if there's an *even* there in that equation, it's *even* me."

"All right. I'll give you that. But that's not the point either. The point is Mickey and whether he's being blinded to the truth about somebody he obviously cares about. And if he is, what I'm going to do about it."

"And are you sure you know that truth?"

"No. Not ultimately. But I do know some truths, or probable truths, and I just learned what might be another couple of 'em. You want to hear them?"

Still pushed back away from her desk, Tamara, her mouth a grim line, folded her arms. "Go ahead."

"All right. Let's start with her relationship with Como. She admits they were close. In fact, real close. Mrs. Como says it was more than that — Dominic was in love with her. He admitted it. And even if he didn't, they

357

got themselves caught doing it in the of-fice."

"No, they didn't."

"Mrs. Como says they did. Lorraine Hess says they did. We call this corroboration. Besides which, I don't think a guy like Dominic Como gets in love with somebody if something physical isn't going on. You buy that?"

"I'm listening."

"All right. We know we've got a tire iron, probably from the limo, as the murder weapon. We know Alicia could have gotten to that anytime she wanted. Next, we find out from your witness just today — Hang-up Lady — that two people, a man and a woman, are having a violent fight at about the same time and in the same place where Dominic got hit. Good? Good. So then this morning an hour ago I'm talking to Al Carter and I'm not even asking him any questions about Ms. Thorpe and he *volunteers* information that exactly cor-roborates Mrs. Como's story that Dominic fired her on that Tuesday, the day he got killed. We didn't know that this morning when we all were talking. We just had Ellen's word for it. But now with Carter's —"

"What did she say? Alicia. When Juhle talked to her."

"What do you think? She denied it."

"And you think that was a lie?"

"I think that Al Carter and Ellen Como both didn't independently make up the same story, let's put it that way. They're not exactly bosom pals, you know? There's no indication that they've ever even talked to each other."

Tamara merely shrugged. "What else?"

"Well, since you ask, Devin's latest, from underneath the limo's backseat, there's the whole semen-on-her-scarf thing. And it is her scarf." Hunt straightened his back, eased himself off the desk and over to the window, letting the gravity of this last revelation work its way into Tamara's worldview. At the window, he turned around. "I'm not making that last part up, Tam. It's her scarf. She admitted it. It was stuffed into the limo's backseat."

Tamara uncrossed her arms. Her hands went to her belly, which she squeezed a couple of times.

"I don't mean for this to give you a stomachache, Tam. But I don't want you and Mick thinking you've got to stick up for her because you've all become friendly since this investigation started. And also, let's remember last Monday night. She's sleeping in her car a quarter mile from

Nancy Neshek's." He came back over to the desk. "I'm not saying she did it. Not yet. Although Dev and Sarah are getting pretty close to thinking so. But I am saying we'd be foolish — any of us — to just ignore these facts."

Now Tamara's hands had settled onto her lap. Her eyes stared before her without focus. "Does Mickey know all this?"

Hunt shook his head. "Not what I've found in the past hour or so. Carter and Devin's information. I tried to call him but his phone's off. He's probably still down at Sanctuary House. I left him a message, but just to call. I thought I'd tell him like I've told you, in person. See how he takes it."

Tamara blew out heavily. "So what about all the money stuff? Didn't you talk to all those people at the memorial too? Do they all have alibis for Monday?"

The clenched muscles in Hunt's face started to relax. He just barely allowed the corners of his mouth to turn up. "Well, that's the other reason I'm not a hundred percent with Devin and Sarah about Ms. Thorpe yet. I haven't eliminated too many other people either. But I'll tell you one thing — this Len Turner's a piece of work."

"Did you talk to him again?"

"Oh, yes. Definitely."

"Did you ask him about Monday night?"

"As a matter of fact, I did."

"Well?"

"Well, I asked and he didn't answer. Not him and not nobody else neither."

"Why not?"

"Because he clean cut me off."

"And how about Ellen?"

"How about her?"

"Wyatt? Monday night?"

Hunt met her eyes, shook his head in disappointment. "No."

"No what?"

"No. Never talked to her. Never even thought of it."

Tamara pulled herself back up close to her desk. "Do you want me to call her and make an appointment? Maybe if that's the only thing you're supposed to do, you'll remember."

"Maybe," Hunt said. "But I don't know if I'd bet on it."

Len Turner sat in a leather chair in his other spacious office, the one that housed his law practice on California Street. He was smoking a Cuban cigar and drinking Hennessey VSOP cognac from a cut crystal glass.

Turner didn't like the storm of bad publicity about the COO money, but he'd weathered worse. The plain fact of the matter, as he would explain to Jeff Elliot as soon as he could arrange an interview with the columnist, was that sometimes you didn't see tangible results for specific projects because there was just never enough money, period. And as in every other business, you had to advertise, market, put on shows to educate and generate enthusiasm for the cause, hire consultants and public relations experts, pay decent salaries to your executives so that you'd get quality people. This wasn't just the nonprofit world; it was the big wide world.

The biggest problem with the CityTalk column was that it conveyed the impression that because the COO program's specific objectives hadn't been met, Turner had mismanaged these funds. And this, in his honest opinion, was not the case. The simple fact was that the $4.7 million in private foundation money — really a pittance — that supported the COO over the past couple of years needed to be about double that, or maybe triple, if it was going to address the real needs of real people who lived in the impoverished areas of the city.

This was because nothing got done for free in San Francisco. It was a pay-to-play environment, and had been for all of Turner's lengthy career.

If you wanted to renovate a dump of a house in the Mission and turn it into a marketable or even usable property, first you had to buy it from the slum landlord who hadn't put in an improvement, including paint, since 1962. That landlord, of course, got a substantial write-off for the monetary loss entailed in "donating" his property to your charity. Then you needed your plans, and then your redone plans, approved by the Housing Department for a sizable fee each time through. Often, if not always, you'd need a zoning variance by the Board of Supervisors, which tended to be exquisitely sensitive to even the most remote and spurious objection to the project, brought to them by one concerned constituent or another.

A residential unit for drug rehabilitation, for example, because it was used in conjunction with the courts, was considered a public building and as such was subject to the strict enforcement of the Americans with Disabilities Act, so you often needed internal elevators, wheelchair access, and restricted handicapped parking spaces. All buildings in San Francisco, of course, now had to be retrofitted for earthquakes. Asbestos had to be removed.

Every step of this process demanded juice — some kind of payoff to someone, whether it was financial or political or, most commonly, both.

And none of this even included when the real fun began with the awarding of the contract to do the actual work. On a publicly bid job, for example, the contractor better have a woman or two and some gay people and a politically correct mix of Caucasian and African-American and Hispanic and Asian workers on the job. Oh, and some veterans, even better if they'd been wounded or maimed.

But the great thing about the fund-raising environment in San Francisco was that the very *idea* that somebody was going through the process of trying to get better housing and a better life for poor people, and even using rehabilitated drug addicts to do such meaningful work, tended to open the coffers of philanthropy. Never mind that the houses often didn't actually get made, the art classes and day care centers didn't get staffed, the theaters never put on a show because of all the hassles, the payoffs, the uncertainties. Still, the money kept coming in to support the efforts. And it came in at about the same rate that it was going out to advertise, educate, and promote.

Of course, Turner wasn't going to go into all of that with Jeff Elliot. It would be enough to explain the costs and benefits to keeping the programs running at all. The major foundation donors all understood the game, and would probably continue to give at pretty much the same levels that they always had. So he wasn't really too concerned about the COO section of the City-Talk column.

The AmeriCorps side of it, on the other hand, and Elliot's cavalier parting shot that the nonprofit game was a deadly one, was a cause for immediate and serious concern. First of all, although funding had been cut for only a year, this was federal money that, once withheld, might not ever be reinstated. California politicians had a lot of juice in Washington, Turner knew. California would get its share of the money, and San Francisco would always get a bite of that. But that didn't mean that Turner's organizations had to see a dime. There were ten others waiting to take up the slack at the first sign of his blood in the water. Further, though all the specific charges of misuse had been leveled at Como, Turner knew that if the feds were sniffing around Sunset for misappropriated funds, they could not be far from his own complicity and, worse, outright fraud.

Turner had cautioned Como about his largesse to most of the city's political movers and shakers, but the man had been a force of nature and did exactly what he wanted when the mood struck him. And now all that money was gone with nothing to show for it. The actual charges — having drivers and errand goers and paying his teaching staff out of AmeriCorps money — could all be explained away as accounting errors. In a busy place run by nonprofessionals, these things happened.

More problematic was that Turner hadn't been cautious enough himself. The legal fees he'd accepted from Como — and from all of the other AmeriCorps recipients that he represented — amounted to nothing less than straight kickbacks for helping these charities obtain their federal funding. Fifty thousand a year here from Mission, a hundred thousand there from Sanctuary House, a half a million over four years with Sunset.

Turner knew that he'd let his greed get away from him — he really didn't know why because he didn't need it. But the money was just there for the taking and it seemed ridiculous not to. And after the first few years, he simply came to believe that the government would never even look at where the money went, much less audit for it.

He'd been wrong.

And now the records were there should the auditors come around to him, looking for fraud. Given time, he could probably get that billing cleaned up. Como and Neshek were no longer around to testify against him, so he could pass off their excesses and poor bookkeeping on their own organizations. Fortunately, too, Turner was certain that he could control Jaime with the leverage of offering Sunset to him, and Mission back to his wife. Maybe it could still all work out for the best.

But then with this Hunt fellow nosing around . . .

Clearly Hunt had expanded the original mandate Turner had given him to simply monitor the reward calls for the police and, more importantly, to keep him informed as to the progress of the investigation. It seemed to Turner now that Hunt was actively investigating not just Como's but Neshek's murder. And nobody — certainly not the reward consortium — had hired him to do that.

Turner considered simply firing Hunt and getting someone more tractable to do the job. But on reflection, he decided to follow the old adage: Keep your friends close, but your enemies closer. It looked like, for whatever reason, Hunt was in this for good. So long as Hunt nominally worked for him, at least Turner could keep a close eye, and maybe even some control, on what he was up to.

And at that thought, Turner finally felt the knot in his stomach loosen. He took a long sip of his cognac, and a good pull at his cigar, then blew the fragrant smoke out into his beautifully appointed office.

He was going to have to put in a call to Mr. Hunt, remind him of their original understanding, the parameters of his role.

Get this last monkey off his back.

23

For all the reasons he'd elucidated to Wyatt Hunt, the only thing Al Carter knew for an absolute certainty was that he had to keep his profile as low as possible around the police. He was black, an ex-convict, the last person to see Como alive. As far as he was concerned, right there he had strikes one, two, and three and it might not be long before he was out. Strikes four and five, as if they needed them, were his easy access to the tire iron and his lack of alibis on the nights of either of the murders. The greater part of him was amazed, in fact, that the two inspectors hadn't already braced him and brought him downtown for questioning.

Somehow he — or maybe just the circumstances — had held them off for now, and maybe what he'd told Hunt about the Thorpe girl would slow them down for a few more days as well. He hadn't liked to do that to the girl, or to put himself into the evidence mix on any level, but realistically, what were his other options?

In the meantime, he'd been thinking about it nonstop for the past four days and he'd come to the decision that he needed some hard-core insurance. And finally, he thought he had a workable plan.

Now he sat alone in the very back booth in front of a cracked mug of steaming coffee at Miz Carter's Mudhouse on California. The Carters who'd run this establishment for years were no relation to Al. When the door opened, he raised his hand and caught the attention of the couple who'd just come in — his younger brother Mo and Mo's wife, Rae. They walked on back, greeting people they knew in the bustling coffee shop. They were childless, married for seventeen years, and regulars here. They were also solid citizens — a crucial criterion for Al's purpose today — the owners of Ebony Emery, the tanning salon and manicure place a few doors down in the Laurel Center. Meanwhile, Al slid out of the booth and was standing by the time they got back to him. He greeted Mo with a warm chest-bump and a tapped fist, and Rae with a chaste hug and an air kiss by her ear.

The original Miz Carter's daughter Penny

had a couple more cracked mugs of coffee (the place's funky trademark), small plates, and a big wedge of cinnamon coffee cake in front of Mo and Rae before they'd gotten their napkins unwrapped. Everybody made small talk, casual and loose, while Penny hovered and took orders. Al, on one side of the red leather booth, put in an order for a hamburger and a milk shake while his brother and sister-in-law on the other said they'd split the mac-and-cheese and the house salad. As he ordered, Mo was slicing the cake, giving some first to his wife, then serving himself.

When Penny went to place the order, Mo popped a bite of cake into his mouth, sipped from his mug, then put it down and raised his eyebrows. A question.

But now that the time had come, Al found his resolve weakening. He smiled to cover the sudden embarrassment — that's what it was — then put his own mug down, twirled it a couple of times. "You're great to come down."

Rae, thin and buxom, gave him a kind smile that animated her face and made it a thing of beauty. "It didn't exactly wear us out, Al." Then, in a more serious vein, "What's troublin' you, brother? This thing with Dominic?"

"At least that."

"What else?"

"Well, the Neshek woman too."

"I don't know her," his brother said.

"One of Dominic's colleagues. Got herself killed, too, this past Monday night."

"Good Lord," Rae said. "Two of 'em now?"

"Two of 'em," Carter said.

Mo came forward over his coffee and cake, put his elbows on the table and his hands on both sides of his face. The ridge over his brows was pronounced, almost hooded. "They got you involved?"

Carter blew out a long sigh. "Not yet, Bro-Mo, not yet."

"But you're worried?" Rae asked.

Carter bobbed his head down and up. "It seems to be my constant state lately."

"So what do they got on you?" Mo asked.

"Nothing. There's nothing to get." He met their eyes, one at a time. "I swear to both of you. There's nothing to get."

Rae reached a hand over the table and touched Carter's. "Well, then, sugar, what you worried about?"

His throat rumbled as though he were chuckling, but there wasn't anything funny in his eyes. "You got to ask?"

She looked down, picked at her cake with

her long fingernails. "No, I guess not, I think about it. You think they do that again?"

"They did it last time," Carter said. "Three and a half years for a crime I didn't commit."

His brother spoke up through his natural reluctance. "Hey, Al. Not that you hadn't done some shit."

"Okay, grant that," Carter said. "I was a dumb kid. I wasn't an angel. Maybe I'm still not, but I keep my nose clean. And I damn sure didn't kill Mr. Como or anybody else. Whatever I've done before, I've paid for it now. And that's not how it's supposed to work. You know that. They're supposed to send you up for something you actually did. Last time, they missed that little detail. I never went near that liquor store and —"

"Yeah, well," his brother cut in, "the problem was you shoulda remembered back then how we all look the same."

"Problem is," Carter said, "I'm remembering now. And there is no way I'm going back in on this."

"So what — ?" Rae stopped and started again. "Why did you need to talk to us? How we gonna help you?"

"I'm not sure you can, but —"

He stopped speaking as Penny showed up back at the booth with their orders. After she'd put the food down, she asked, "What's a fish say when it swims into a wall?"

They all looked up at her.

"You tell us, darlin'," Mo said.

"Dam!" And with a delighted giggle, she was gone back to the counter.

Al Carter couldn't help himself. The absurdity of the ridiculous joke while his life was in such turmoil had him chuckling. "Damn," he said, shaking his head. "Damn damn damn. That woman's been reading my mail." And suddenly the chuckling turned into real laughter. Extended laughter. Finally, wiping his eyes, Carter faced his relatives across the table. "Sorry. I don't know why that hit me."

"Me neither," his brother said.

Rae put a hand on her husband's arm. "Man's got to be under some stress." Then she looked across at Carter with sympathy in her eyes. "You got to get out more, sugar." She forked a bite of lettuce. "So how we gonna help you?" she asked. "But you not sure we can."

"What's it going to depend on, Al?" Mo asked.

"It's going to first depend on whether you two spent either Tuesday a week ago or Monday this week alone together."

Mo stopped his mac-and-cheese on the

way to his mouth. "Either or both?"

"Either would be good enough."

"Monday was what?" Rae asked. "Two days ago?"

"That's it."

Rae was already reaching for her purse, from which she extracted a small spiral calendar. She flipped the pages, stopped, flipped another one, went back to her first stop. "Last Tuesday, no. I had my book group. Went on till midnight." She turned the page. "Monday, I got nothin'."

"That's 'cause Monday is *Monday Night Football*," Mo said. "Raiders and Baltimore. You didn't see that game, Al?"

"Matter of fact, I did, Bro-Mo. Home alone." He pointed. "So you two watched it together, just the two of you? You're sure?"

"Romantic fools that we are," Rae answered. "So now what?"

Carter let out a breath of relief. He seemed to see his hamburger for the first time. Picking it up, he took a huge bite, sipped some milk shake, chewed some more, and swallowed. "Okay," he said, "this next part's where it gets tricky."

"We're here," Mo said.

"I know you are." Carter paused. "Here's my worry. It's all about these alibis. Last time, when they sent me down, you remem-

375

ber, here I was minding my own business by my lonesome, sleeping at my place — hell, it's two in the morning, how unusual is that? And that's what I told them. But, as we know, they didn't choose to believe me. How could I be home sleeping at the same time I'm robbing that damn store? See? So the alibi, even though it was the truth, wound up hanging me anyway."

Mo put his fork down. "All right. So?"

"So I'm not comfortable telling the man this time that I was home alone."

"Haven't you already told him that?" Rae asked.

"I did."

"Well, then . . ."

"Well, no. That's not going to do it."

"What do you mean?" Mo asked.

"I mean, I need something else. Something stronger."

"So you're thinking you're going to change what you told them?" Mo's brows had come together in a frown. "That is no kind of a good idea. They know you lied, they all over you."

"Right," Carter said. "Which is why I don't go to them and tell them anything. Everything just stays the same. Except if they come back on to me."

Mo's expression was pure confusion.

"And then what happen?"

"Then I tell them I lied."

The couple exchanged a glance.

"I tell them, Rae" — Carter took a tentative breath — "that I was with you. That's why I couldn't tell them the truth the first time when they asked. I didn't want it to get out to Mo. I *couldn't have it* get back to Mo."

Rae's frown matched her husband's. "So then they ask me? Then what?"

"Then they probably won't even ask, but if they do, you tell them, yeah, you were with me. Mo was home, having some beers and watching the game, you told him you were out with your girlfriends, your book club, whatever it was. But really you came to my place and stayed on till late." He took another sip of his milk shake. "You think you could go along with that, both of you? Make sure your brother doesn't have to go back to the joint?"

24

Tamara had handled the preliminary meeting to okay the staffing earlier in the day, but now at three-thirty, Hunt was still in the middle of his follow-up meeting with the Willard White people — Will, Gloria, and three of their staff — running down the tasks he'd need to have them perform for his law firm clients over the next week or two. They were all jammed into his small back office, with straight-back wooden chairs for the principals, the others sitting on the file cabinets. Though he had told Tamara to hold his calls while the meeting was in progress, suddenly the phone on his desk chimed and he glared at it, then excused himself and picked it up.

Mickey was propped up in a bed in a double room at San Francisco General Hospital. His ribs were bandaged. His left arm was in a soft cast. The area around his left eye was swollen and discolored. Groggy from the painkillers, he was otherwise reasonably coherent, managing a feeble smile when he saw his sister and then Hunt behind her. "You should see the other guy," he said, then grimaced.

He told them that because of the head injury, they wanted to keep him overnight for observation, but he was sure he'd be back to relatively normal in no time. He was, he said, actually very lucky — first, that he wasn't killed, and second, some cops had come by and told him that the woman who'd hit him and who'd been completely and unarguably at fault was insured to the hilt. He'd probably get a good used car out of his totaled wreck of a Camaro, and at least some, if not all, of his hospital bill would be paid. They might not even have to make a claim on the insurance he carried through Hunt's business. If all went well, they would let him out tomorrow — Tamara could pick him up in the old Volkswagen she hadn't driven in six months — and he might even be in at work by the afternoon.

"Don't push it," Hunt told him. "Whenever you're feeling better."

Then Mickey wanted to tell Hunt about what he'd learned at his visit to Sanctuary House that morning, and did Hunt know that many of the reward participants, including Nancy Neshek, had actually been to a Communities of Opportunity meeting together on Monday night at City Hall?

"That became clear at the memorial," Hunt said. "Although they all put on a good act that they'd barely heard about Neshek's death."

"You think that was bogus?" Mickey asked.

Hunt shrugged. "Hard to say." He gave them both a pretty much word-by-word account of everyone's reactions to Neshek's murder — Turner, Hess, Carter, Jaime and Lola Sanchez, it didn't take long — and then took a deep breath and came out with what he'd been avoiding. "But aside from them, there actually have been a few new developments."

"Which you're not going to like too much," Tamara added.

"What?"

Hunt filled him in on the latest news about Alicia, and Mickey brought up the same objections that Tamara had earlier.

"Well, I know how both of you feel," Hunt replied. "But I'd have to say at this point that Devin and Sarah consider her the prime suspect. And you both ought to know that. We'd be smart to think of her the same way. At least until we get something that positively clears her." Hunt's eyes went from Mickey around to his sister. "You think we can do that?"

"We can try," Tamara said at last, folding under the pressure of Hunt's gaze.

Hunt turned back around and leaned in toward the bed. "How 'bout you, Mick? Mick?"

But Mickey's eyes were closed, his breathing regular. For all the world as though the pain drugs had kicked in again and he had faded off to sleep.

At a few minutes after six, Tamara said good-bye to Hunt, got out of the car he'd driven her home in, opened her building's front door, checked her mail — mostly throwaway stuff except for the PG & E bill and the latest *Gourmet* — and climbed the stairs up to her apartment. Letting herself in with her key, she sang out a greeting, but not too loud, as her grandfather was known to take the occasional nap. "Hey, Jim. I'm home."

When he didn't respond, she walked over a few steps. His bedroom door was ajar. She pushed it open enough to see inside. His bed was still made and he wasn't in it. Well, he was probably hanging out with his friends, she thought. Usually he made it a point to get home by dinnertime, which tended to be around seven. She didn't give his absence a lot of thought.

She dropped the mail onto its spot at the top of the living room bookshelf, then turned and hung up her coat in the closet by the front door. On her way into the kitchen to check the refrigerator for something to drink, she passed the phone, saw the number "1" flashing, and pushed the button for playback.

"Hi. This is Alicia Thorpe and I'm trying to get ahold of Mickey. Mickey, your cell phone's not picking up. I think it must be not turned on or something, so I'm trying the other number you gave me. Could you give me a call as soon as you get this? Or Jim or Tamara, maybe you could get in touch with him and have him call me. I really need to see Mickey as soon as I can. The police came by again today and . . . well, I can tell Mickey all this when he calls." She left her number and continued. "I should be able to answer all day. I called in sick at work, so really, anytime. But sooner would be better. Thanks. Talk to you soon, I hope."

Tamara, her face now clouded over by concern and indecision, stood by the phone and pushed the button to hear the message again. This wasn't any social call. Clearly, Alicia understood that her situation had changed. Her voice was charged not just with tension, but with an undertone of desperation.

Conflicted by the recent and unequivocal instructions from her boss, Tamara remained standing by the telephone for another minute or so. After that, she continued on into the kitchen, opened the refrigerator, found some orange juice, and poured herself a glass. Bringing it with her, she went back to the living room and plopped herself down on the one stuffed chair they had by the back windows. She took a good drink and put the orange juice glass on the small table next to the chair. Then she came forward and clasped her hands.

She started to get up once, then — hamstrung by her indecisiveness — all but fell back into the chair. On her second try, she was more successful — she got all the way up and over to the telephone. It took her another minute before she played the message a third time. Then at last she picked up the receiver and punched in the numbers.

"Alicia, this is Tamara. . . . I got your message here at the apartment. . . . I have to

383

tell you that Mr. Hunt doesn't really want us to talk to you, either me or Mickey. . . . I know. . . . I think I agree, but the bottom line is he's the boss . . . but you should at least know that Mickey was in a car accident today . . . no, he's okay, they think, I hope. They're holding him for observation overnight. . . ."

Tamara had been planning to come back down to visit Mickey again with her grandfather when Jim got home, but by eight-thirty, a very long two and a half hours later, he had not arrived back at the apartment. Frustrated now and starting to get worried, she tried to call Mickey at the hospital, but San Francisco General Hospital did not provide telephones for individual patients in their rooms. In fact, the afternoon call to the Hunt Club that had informed her of Mickey's condition had not come from Mickey directly, but from a nurse in the emergency room, who placed the call on her cell phone as a favor to her brother.

On her first try, she got cut off when she pressed pound according to the instructions. On her second, she punched seven different numbers in the automated menu over a five-minute period. Each option provided a suitable wait before suggesting the next one. (The hospital, by the way, had chosen the mellifluous and relaxing tones of Eminem as background while you waited.) When she finally reached a human being at the nurse's station on Mickey's floor, she could tell immediately from the woman's sublimely indifferent bureaucrat's tone that it was going to be a trying few more minutes.

"I'm sorry," the woman said. "We don't deliver messages from the nurse's station. You can come and visit the patient and deliver your message in person until ten o'clock."

"How about if the message, though, is that I can't get down to visit him?"

"Well, then, there's a message center option in the menu that you can access by simply hitting the pound key."

"I tried that before and it didn't work. This time it's taken me about half an hour to get to talk to you." This was an exaggeration, of course, but it was what it felt like. "Aren't you near to his room? Mickey Dade. Number three twenty-seven. Couldn't you just go and tell him his sister can't make it down tonight and will pick him up in the morning?"

"I'm sorry. I can't leave the nursing station unmanned."

"Look." Trying to sound reasonable. "Aren't you only like twenty or thirty feet from his room? Can't you just walk across — ?"

"I'm sorry, but I'm not allowed to leave the nurse's station. You can just press pound and leave a message. I'm sure he'll get it."

"I pressed pound the last time and it got me disconnected."

"That's not really very likely. If you'll hold, I can just transfer you myself."

With great reluctance, Tamara found herself saying, "All right. We can try that. Thank you."

A click, then an ominous emptiness sounded at her ear for about five seconds before Tamara heard a chirpy three-toned, high-pitched ring, and then a metallic, disembodied voice: "If you'd like to make a call, please hang up and —"

"God damn it!" She slammed the phone back onto the receiver. Swearing a blue streak, she walked into the kitchen, made an about-face, came back to the telephone, picked it up about a foot, and slammed it down again. Then she turned and stared at the door to her apartment.

"And while we're at it," she said aloud to no one, "where the fuck are you, Jim?"

25

The drugs were beginning to wear off, but when Mickey opened his eyes, for a minute he thought he might be hallucinating. "Alicia? What are you doing here? Shouldn't you be at work?"

"Your sister told me what happened." She sat in a chair near the head of his bed. Beyond her, he caught a glimpse of the wall clock — eight forty-five. "You look really beat up."

"I wouldn't be surprised."

"Are you okay?"

"They say I'm going to live. But she really nailed me. The other driver, I mean." He closed his eyes briefly, opened them again. Yep, Alicia was still there. "You didn't have to come down here," he said. "I'm glad you did, but —"

"I had to see you," she said.

"Well, you came to the right place. I don't seem to be going anywhere soon."

"I have to talk to you. Can we do that?"

He abandoned the flippancy. "Of course. Why wouldn't I talk to you?"

"Because your boss told you not to?"

Mickey went to shake his head, but with the pain didn't get far. "He didn't exactly tell me not to. He just said it would be dumb."

"Why? Does he say I killed Dominic too?"

"He says he's keeping an open mind. But he does believe the cops are thinking that way. So Tam and I ought to watch out too."

"Mickey." She reached out and rested her hand on his arm. "I swear to you. I didn't have anything to do with that. Or with Nancy Neshek either. I promise."

"All right."

"Please tell me you believe me."

Mickey drew in a breath. Here, indeed, was the crux. He didn't need to consciously recall the many discussions he'd had with Tamara in the wake of the boyfriend who'd betrayed her and Wyatt Hunt and everyone else he'd known. Those conversations were by now part of his DNA. Even Mickey had considered Craig a good guy, possibly a future brother-in-law, and a fine choice at that.

And now here Mickey was, in an analogous situation with a woman for whom he had an attraction that was — no other word for it — dangerous. And still, knowing everything he did, he was thinking about committing in the same way his sister had committed.

More than thinking about it.

Almost without conscious volition, he found himself answering her. "I do believe you," he said. "You didn't kill anybody."

At his words, her eyes teared up and she put her head down, resting it against the side of the bed. Her shoulders rose and fell a couple of times before she looked up at him again. "How can I ever thank you?"

"Don't worry about that. The big question is what are you going to do now?"

"I don't know. I don't have any idea. That's why I came here. To ask you. I think they're going to arrest me. I can't let myself get arrested, Mickey. I really can't."

"You think they're that close?"

She nodded. "I don't know what they need, but they asked me if I had any plans to travel outside the Bay Area anytime soon. If you want my opinion, I think I'm their main suspect." She moved her chair closer in to the bed, and now spoke in a near whisper. "I didn't go in to work today. I didn't want them to know where to find me."

"You think they'd arrest you down there? At Morton's?"

"Why not? That's where they questioned me the first time."

Mickey hesitated, following the inexorable logic of what must have been true. "So you're out of your room too?" he asked.

She didn't seem surprised at the question. "I grabbed some stuff as soon as they left and threw it in my car."

"So where are you going to go from here?"

"Mickey" — she hesitated — "I don't have anyplace to go. My brother's the only family I've got, and I know they'd look for me at his place. I'd just been sitting out by the beach until I heard from Tamara. Then finally I decided I needed to come in here. To ask you to help me."

In spite of himself, Mickey's chest heaved as a bitter laugh began, then stopped with the clutch of his broken ribs. Wincing, he moved his right hand over to cover them.

"Mickey?"

"I'm okay, I'm okay." He puffed out a quick breath, then another. "Just enjoying the humor in you thinking I could help you. Especially how I am right now."

"But I know you can."

He closed his eyes and took a beat to think. She wanted him to help her, was begging him to help her. She was not who they thought she was, and he might be her only hope left. Opening his eyes, he met her gaze. "Look, Alicia," he said. "This is a little town. How long do you think you can hide from them if they really want to find you? A couple of days? A week? A month? And do you really think that doing that will make it better for you when they do find you? Even if you could avoid them for a little while, you'd just be making it worse."

"I don't care if it's days or a week, Mickey. I need some time. And they need some time to look at other suspects."

"So you were parked all day out at the beach?"

"Right."

"You don't think they've got the plates on your car?"

"I don't know." Then, realizing the obvious, "They would, wouldn't they?"

"You can bet on it. You might as well have gone in to work. You're in that car, they got you."

"I didn't think of that."

"Have you used your cell phone?"

"Sure. To call work and say I was sick. Then your house, and then when Tamara called me back. And then Ian, just to let him know where I was."

Slowly, now, slowly, against the pain, Mickey shook his head. "You can't use your cell phone, Alicia. They can locate you by that."

"They can?"

A small smile. "It's a rough environment for fugitives out there."

"But I'm not a fugitive. I'm not under arrest. Not yet, anyway." She brought her hands up to her forehead, rubbed it, brought her hands back down. "They're just not looking in the right places, Mickey. They can't be. They've got to be missing something. This was what we talked about when we first got together, you remember? You were going to investigate the murder, now murders, and not let them land, finally, on me. You remember that, don't you? That's what this was all about, right? Was I making all that up?"

The details still fresh in his mind, Mickey experienced again the rush of those moments when he'd determined that his plan could resuscitate the dying Hunt Club while at the same time give him an opportunity to get to know this woman. This remarkable woman. This woman with whom he could see himself.

Well, he'd done the Hunt Club part. It had its new clients and its reward billings.

His efforts had, at least for the time being, even brought his sister back from the edge of anorexia, returned to her some of her sense of self-worth. All that was left was in some respects, the personal respects, the most important part.

And now the person at the center of that was asking him if she was making all that up? Everything he'd promised her, had she just imagined that? Was it all merely a game for Mickey to toy with and then drop when it became inconvenient, difficult, even perilous? Was she, take away the self-serving rationalizations, just another pretty girl to him?

"Was I, Mickey?" she repeated. "Was I making all that up?"

He took his right hand off his ribs and laid it gently on her shoulder. "No," he told her. "That's still what this is about."

"Thank you," she whispered. "Thank you." She put her hand over his, then leaned over and kissed it. "So what are we going to do?"

Mickey, with some difficulty, pushed himself up on the bed. "First," he said, "we'd better find where they hid my clothes."

The clothes and valuables were hung in a plastic bag in the closet. Mickey's bed was one in a three-bed room, but the one closest to the door. The other patients in the room had screens pulled around those beds, and the one in the middle had three visitors, chatting away. After she brought over the bag of Mickey's clothes, Alicia went to the hallway door and stood in it, just inside the room.

Even moving slowly and with great care, it didn't take Mickey more than two minutes to get on his underwear and pants. He couldn't get his shirt over the cast, but thank God it had been a cold day and he had his jacket, which served. He called Alicia back to him and she helped him with his shoes, left untied. His socks were just too much trouble to even bother with. They went into his jacket pocket along with the shirt.

She took his good right arm and together they strolled out into the hallway.

The walk out of the hospital was challenging. Dizziness made him come to a dead stop three times. Beyond that, even though it was his left arm that was broken, his left leg had evidently gotten banged up badly as well. Both his hip and his knee throbbed with every step and his ribs were worse — constant pinching pain that kept him from standing straight. Once they cleared the building itself, just walking unimpeded out the front entrance, they hit the drizzle and the biting wind. Alicia was wearing her jeans and hiking boots and a water-resistant ski jacket over a pullover sweater, and she pulled her left arm out of the sleeve and wrapped the jacket over Mickey's shoulders, holding his right arm, pressing up tight against him.

Nevertheless, by the time they made it out to Alicia's car at the very far end of the darkened parking lot, Mickey was shivering, his teeth actually chattering, a general pain now diffused by the shaking throughout his body. Alicia opened the front passenger side door and got him into the seat, then spun out of her heavy jacket and draped it over him, tucking it in around him. She ran around the car, got in, turned on the ignition, and set the heater to max.

"It'll warm up in a minute," she said. "Then we'll jam the fan."

Still shivering, his teeth audible in the close space, huddled down inside the blanket, Mickey could barely get out one word. "Good."

Alicia revved the engine to speed the heating process, but kept her lights and the windshield wipers off. They were cocooned, the drizzle on the car's windows preventing them from seeing much outside. In less than a minute, she reached down and turned the fan onto high, and feeling the vent, she nodded. "Better than outside already."

Mickey, rocking almost imperceptibly back and forth, just shook his head.

Five minutes later, the car was warm enough that he didn't need her jacket and she gently helped him get it unwrapped from around him. His shivering had stopped and with the surcease of movement, the pain had noticeably lessened everywhere but in his arm and ribs. "No phones," he said. "In fact, turn it off completely."

"But what if we have to call somebody?"

"We'll borrow somebody's, or find a pay phone. We really don't want to use your cell. Starting now."

"Okay." She held down the button that turned her phone off. "I'm trusting you."

"That's a good idea."

She looked over at him. "So what are we going to do now?"

"Good question," he said. "Dancing's definitely out, though."

"Darn."

"I know. It's a disappointment. I'm a great

dancer, actually. You ever go to the swing clubs?"

"Not enough. Drawback of working nights."

"Well, when we get out of this, maybe some Monday or Tuesday . . ." He lapsed into a thoughtful silence.

And eventually Alicia broke it. "Mickey?"

"I'm thinking. You got any close girlfriends you can trust who live alone?"

She considered for a moment, then shook her head. "Not who live alone, no. I'm about the only one my age I know who does. What are you thinking?"

"I'm thinking you're going to have to lie low somewhere where the cops won't think to look for you, if it gets to that. Plus, we've got a car problem. This one might as well have a sign on it, so we've got to put it someplace where it can't be seen."

"But then we can't use it."

"That's right."

"So how do I get around?"

"Where do you have to go? That's not close to your biggest problem."

"Good point. But how do you get around, for that matter? You don't have a car any-more either. Plus, you can barely walk."

"There's that too," he said grimly. "You've got to give me a minute here." He gently probed at his head.

"Are you hurting bad?" she asked.

He glanced over at her and tried a smile.

In the living room of her Nob Hill condominium, Gina Roake sipped her Oban and said, "You've got a half hour to cut that out completely, buster. I mean it."

Wyatt Hunt, rubbing her feet on the ottoman between them, gave her a grin. "A half hour from now, I'm betting I'll have moved on to other things."

"Promises, promises."

"You wait and see."

"I believe I will." She sighed contentedly, leaned back, sipped her Scotch again. "So how close is our Inspector Juhle?"

"He's waiting until the DNA work comes in on the semen. But even if he gets a hit, it's still a long way to Tipperary. It all comes down to whether or not he fired her that morning." He nodded appreciatively at her. "And if you're paying attention, I believe that would be your influence at work on Juhle. It's going to be a while before he makes an arrest again before he's got the evidence."

"Let's hope. You'd think they'd teach that in cop school."

"They do. Then they get out into the real

world and need to make arrests. Especially when they know who did it, as in this case."

Gina sighed. "And in so many others."

"Well, yes. No argument there."

"So they're convinced it's this woman Alicia?"

"I'd say yes."

"What do you think?"

Hunt considered for a moment.

Roake softly kicked his hands. "It's not a trick question. You don't have to answer if it's going to make you stop."

"Apologies." Hunt's hands went back to work on her feet. "What do I think? I think it's highly unlikely that both Ellen Como and Al Carter independently made up the story about her getting fired the day he gets killed. I think that happened."

"What does she say?"

"She says not. But then again, she would, wouldn't she?"

Roake shrugged.

"So then I think," Hunt pressed, "that if that's true, if Como fired her, then she had a damn good reason to kill him. Especially if they were intimate."

"And the scarf establishes that?"

"Pretty much. If it's his semen."

Roake brought her Scotch to her lips. "Anybody ever see them together out of work? Maybe going into her place? Some motel? One of Sunset's residential units?"

"I haven't heard of that. At work, yeah, according to Ellen. But I don't think Devin and Sarah have gotten around to asking neighbors, if that's what you mean. Except, you know, you're alone together in a limo four or five hours a day, I'm willing to lay odds a determined couple could get in a little nooky from time to time. And it does appear, in fact, that that's what happened, doesn't it?"

"Could have happened. If it was actually Como. Or Alicia, for that matter. Although it might have been neither."

"Neither?"

"Neither. The driver — Carter, is it? — and his girlfriend, if any. Or one of the other young male drivers and somebody they were driving around on any given day."

Hunt stopped rubbing her feet again and chuckled. "Roake, you are definitely in the right field, you know that?"

"What does that mean?"

"It means that your devious defense-lawyer mind just automatically sees all the ways you can rearrange and argue the facts so that the most obvious explanation gets lost in the shuffle."

"Well, sometimes the most obvious explanation is wrong."

"Most of the time, though, not."

"Still. Enough to make the exercise worthwhile."

"From what I've told you, don't you think it's likely Alicia?"

"I have no idea." With a sigh, she pulled her legs back off the ottoman and sat up straighter in her chair. She put her glass of Oban down on the table next to her seat. "There is simply nothing I've heard that comes close to convicting her, Wyatt. If I were going to be exerting any energy here, I have to tell you I'm still liking Len Turner."

"Who I had a nice chat with this morning, you know."

Roake sucked in a quick breath, concern suddenly obvious in her demeanor. "You didn't do anything to make him feel threatened, I hope."

"No. He was surrounded by his gang at Como's memorial."

"Do you know what, if anything, Juhle and Russo are doing about him?"

Hunt shook his head. "No. Not much, I don't think."

"Looking into his alibis, if any? Trying to get a feel for his financial records? Asking Ellen Como or anybody else about personnel or financial problems that might have come up recently between him and Como? Seeing if Turner has any kind of special relationship with any of the Battalion members?"

"All of those would be included under the general heading of 'not much.' What about the Battalion?"

"Nothing, specifically. And again, just rumors."

"Why am I doubting that, Roake?"

She wilted under Hunt's gaze. "All right," she said. "Although it galls me if this is the way it has to get to Juhle and Russo. They should be looking in this direction already. If I didn't think you needed to know so you'll take Mr. Turner more seriously, I wouldn't mention it."

"Okay," Hunt said casually. "That's a good lead-in. What do you know?"

"I know and everybody knows that one of the Battalion's visible roles is that for only twenty dollars, they hand out little signs you put in your window that your business supports the Sunset Youth Project. You've seen them all over the city, right?"

"Right. So?"

"So what most people don't know is the percentage of contacted businesses of all types that support the SYP. You want to guess?"

"All businesses?"

"Right. Asian cleaners and restaurants, Hispanic mom and pops, Muslim shop owners, law offices, cigar stores, everybody. Take a stab."

Hunt shrugged. "Forty percent."

"Close," Gina said. "A hundred percent."

Hunt was silent for a long beat. "They're selling protection," he said.

"No, they couldn't be," Gina responded. "The city would surely bust them, would it not? Oh, except if they somehow had enough political influence to just let the practice remain a necessary evil, the cost of doing business here. The SYP is really doing a world of good for a lot of people, and that's true. So businesses should be glad to pony up twenty bucks for such a good cause. Plus, they get the nice sign in the window."

"That can't be the entire Battalion."

"No. It's not. It's only a few who go out if somebody doesn't pay. Trusted senior guys. In other words, professional muscle. On the payroll, and paid for by your tax dollars, by the way."

"And you think Turner's got access to these guys?"

"Not exactly. No."

"Well, then . . ."

"Wyatt, I *know* it. Fifteen years you're a public defender here, you learn a few things. These kids aren't angels to begin with, you know. Como gives them the jobs, strictly legit, tutoring and cleaning up at Ortega, passing out political pamphlets and like that. Eventually the promising ones are in the Battalion, moving up, getting paid decent money. AmeriCorps money, by the way. Life's good. Turner picks a few every year and just tells them if they want to stay on, they'll just do this or that. Break the window on this store, vandalize that flower shop, strong-arm some liquor store clerk. Otherwise, they go back to jail."

"And Como didn't know about this?"

Gina shrugged. "Maybe he did. I don't know. But he wouldn't have had to. Or maybe it was his cost of doing business and he thought it was a fair trade. Or maybe he just found out last week and he called Turner on it."

"You're saying Turner could have one of these Battalion kids kill for him?"

"I'm saying if I were Juhle or Russo, at least I'd try to rule it out. Oh, and if it turns out this is any part of it, I told Jeff Elliot I'd split the reward with him."

"I'll put that in my report if the time comes. With a strong recommendation."

"I've got a strong recommendation for you." Roake drained the last of her Scotch, and placed it down on the lamp table with finality. She reached over, took his hand, and stood up. "If you want to get the lights."

26

It was by no means the obvious choice.

In fact, it was risky and desperate, but Mickey couldn't think of another solution.

Alicia had abandoned her own digs. If Juhle and Russo were planning to put her under arrest, the next place they would look would probably be Ian's, who was listed at Morton's as her primary contact in case of an emergency. As she'd told Mickey, none of her girlfriends lived alone, so they were out. And once they realized that Mickey had disappeared from the hospital, they would undoubtedly come to his place. They could go to a motel, of course, but that was both expensive and impractical — they would have to register and he, with a black eye and his arm in a cast, would be easy to identify.

Eventually he formed his plan, and under his direction, she took the 280 Freeway to the Sixth Street exit and turned right onto

Brannan, then made a U-turn and pulled into the depressed curb space outside an industrial roll-up garage door to a good-sized and completely darkened warehouse. Mickey got out into the now frankly bitter night and pushed the button on the box next to the metal door adjacent to the garage's entrance.

When no one answered, he got back into the car and directed Alicia to turn right at the next corner, then to take another quick right into the alley behind Brannan. She pulled over and stopped by a low stoop under a darkened door that he knew to be painted bright orange by day. The light over the door, and all the windows in a row high along the wall, were dark. But Mickey knew where he was going as he got out of the car again and found the key right where it was supposed to be, tucked into a magnet case that was stuck against the upper inside edge of a floor vent on the side of the stoop.

He told Alicia to wait where she was. Then, opening the back door, he let himself into Hunt's warehouse on the residential side. He deactivated the alarm, and then, turning on lights as he walked through the kitchen, den, hallway by the bedroom, he let himself into the massive basketball court side, then crossed to the door next to the garage and unlocked it. Retracing his steps, in spite of his gimpy walk, he was in seconds back in Alicia's car, directing her down to the end of the alley, then through another couple of right turns back onto Brannan, and then waiting by the curb while he let himself in again, and pushed the button to raise the garage door. As soon as she was all the way inside, with Mickey getting her parked so she'd be out of the way of Wyatt's Cooper, another push of the button let the garage door down.

Alicia let herself out of the car and stood dumbstruck, turning all the way around as she attempted to take it all in — the half basketball court, the guitars and audio stuff, the computers against the opposite wall. "Where are we?" she finally asked.

"My boss lives here. Pretty cool, huh?"

"Unbelievable."

It may have been unbelievable, but it was also very cold on this side of the warehouse, and in another minute they were inside the living area, where the temperature was close to seventy degrees. Alicia found herself a seat in a leather-and-chrome reading chair in the den and Mickey went to help himself to a couple of beers from Hunt's refrigerator. He brought back the Pilsner Urquells and a corkscrew that doubled as a bottle opener. "I could open these," he said, "but I bet you could do it easier."

"I bet I could too." She opened both bottles, passed one to Mickey, who gingerly sat on Hunt's tan leather couch. "So did I miss something?" she asked. "Does your boss know we were coming here?"

Mickey tipped up his bottle. "I don't see how he could have, since I didn't know it myself until about a half hour ago."

"But —"

"Yeah, I know. It could be a problem, but I don't think so. Wyatt's a good guy and he's on the right side. Besides that, and more important, Juhle wouldn't ever believe that he'd be keeping you here. Not without telling him. And at least until there's a warrant out for you, there's no legal issue. You can stay anywhere you want."

"So we're staying here?"

"That's my plan." Mickey sipped more beer. "For a few days anyway. It's the safest place I can think of. Plus your car's off the street. Presto, you're disappeared."

"That's scary."

"Maybe. But a lot safer for you. And not just because of Juhle."

"What do you mean?"

"I mean whoever killed Dominic and Neshek. If they know you're a suspect and

409

you, say, show up dead, looking like a suicide, well, now, wouldn't that be convenient?"

"Now you are scaring me."

"Well, that's one of the reasons I thought of coming here. You're safe here. From everybody."

Alicia digested that for a long moment. "So when is Mr. Hunt getting home?"

"I don't know. Sometime."

"You don't want to call him and leave a message we're here?"

"I don't think so," Mickey said. He didn't want to give Hunt the option of ordering them out — not an impossibility — before he'd had a chance to argue for his position. "It might be better as a surprise."

"Nobody ever cooks for me," Mickey said, "except in restaurants."

"Well, I do now."

At ten-fourteen on this Wednesday night, Alicia was standing over a bowl of half a dozen broken eggs in Hunt's kitchen by his four-burner Viking stove. Mickey had stolen one of Hunt's short-sleeved sweatshirts and he and Alicia had maneuvered it down over his cast and now he sat — nearly reclined, actually — at the kitchen table. She'd already set out a couple of plates and

410

utensils and had bread going in the toaster. He held his just-opened third beer in his right hand.

Pouring the eggs into the skillet, she pinched some salt and pepper over them, then opened the spice cabinet over the kitchen counter and took down a small bottle of yellowish liquid. "Truffle oil? Normal people have truffle oil?"

"Don't leave home without it," Mickey said. "Sure."

"Should I put some in?"

"Every chance you get."

In a small stream, she added some of the magical stuff, gathered the eggs with a spatula, then turned off the heat as the toast popped up. After buttering it, she put a slice on each plate, ladled the eggs onto each, covering both pieces of toast completely, then topping the mass with another pat of butter.

Mickey picked up his fork and took a bite. "These are perfect," he said.

After they'd finished their eggs and Alicia had washed up, they were back in the den. Mickey had perked up when they'd first arrived, and that burst of energy had carried him through their meal. But now he sat slumped down in the reading chair, feet up on an ottoman, head on a pillow, covered with a blanket that Alicia had found next to the pillow on the top shelf of Hunt's bedroom closet. "The couch opens up." His voice sounded thick and groggy. "You can sleep there."

"What about you?"

"I'm good here. I'm almost asleep already."

"Sorry, Mick. You're mangled and battered. You get the bed. Period."

"Are we going to have a fight about this?"

She was already pulling the cushions off the couch. "No. You're going to get in the bed as soon as I get it made."

"And what about you?"

"I've got my trusty sleeping bag and pad in the back of my car out there." She pulled out the couch mattress, which was already made up for guests with a sheet and a blanket. Then, pulling down a corner of the blanket, she turned to face him. "Do you need help getting up?"

"No." But even as he said it, he winced at the attempt.

"Stop." She stepped over and took off his shoes, then held his feet up while she moved the ottoman out from under them. Next she removed the blanket and draped it over the bed.

With his feet flat on the floor, he took her hand with his good arm and lifted himself into a sitting position while she went to one knee in front of him.

"Okay," she said. "Good arm around my neck. Easy, easy."

Suppressing the urge to moan, he was up, still leaning on her.

She guided him over a few steps, then helped him down so that he was sitting on the bed. Finally, she put his pillow down where his head would be, lifted his feet, and turned him so that he could recline fully. She pulled the oversheet and both blankets over him and tucked them in. Then she lowered herself and sat on the edge of the bed. "How's that?"

Clearly, the movement had cost him. Any boost he'd felt when they'd first gotten here had dissipated with the adrenaline and the beer. Now a light sweat had broken on his forehead and he was breathing through the pain in his ribs, slowly and deeply through parsed lips. "Good."

"Would you tell me if it was bad?"

"Maybe." He broke a tired smile. "Probably not."

"You macho guys." She gently wiped his forehead with a corner of the oversheet, then tucked it back around him. After a minute her shoulders settled and she let out a long sigh. "I'm so sorry, Mickey."

"For what?"

"Getting you into this."

"You didn't get me into this. I got me into this."

She brooded on that for a long beat. "Not really. If I . . ." She exhaled heavily again. "Anyway, I don't know how I can thank you. I don't know what I'd be doing right now if it wasn't for you."

"You'd be fine."

"No. I'd be running, I think. Though I see now how dumb that would be."

He shook his head ever so slightly. "There's no need to run. Not yet. Maybe not ever."

"But I wouldn't have known that if not for you. I'd have just screwed up more."

Mickey put his hand softly on her thigh. "You haven't screwed up. You didn't do anything wrong. Look at me. Alicia, look at me. You haven't done anything wrong."

She turned to face him, but couldn't hold his gaze. Rather, her mouth trembled and she closed her eyes. She put her hand over his as though grasping it for support. For a long moment, neither of them moved. Mickey studied her face, on the verge of tears. And then heavy drops formed and fell

414

at the same time from both of her eyes.

"Hey." Mickey squeezed her leg. "Hey, now, it's going to be all right."

But she was shaking her head from side to side. "No. I have screwed up. I did do something wrong."

"No, you didn't. You just —"

"I did, Mickey, I did. I . . . I lied to those inspectors. I've even been lying to you." Now she looked straight down at him. "That last morning when I came in to work? Dominic's last day?"

"What about it?"

"He did fire me. He said I couldn't work at Sunset anymore. He couldn't see me anymore either. He said we could never see each other again." Her shoulders began to shake, and a deep wrenching sob broke from her throat.

Tamara got ready for bed and then turned on the television to watch the late news.

Generally preferring to read or, in the old days when she had a social life, to hang out with friends, she almost never watched TV. But tonight it was the only thing she could think of to keep herself from imploding with frustration, concern, and anger.

Mostly anger.

Jim Parr still hadn't made it home. Where

415

the hell had he gone, and why wouldn't he have called if he'd known he was going to be so late? But of course, he didn't have a cell phone, had never bothered to learn how to use one. As if this took some sort of special dexterity or brains. She had already decided that she and Mickey were going to buy him one immediately if not sooner. Of course, then he probably wouldn't pick it up when the damn thing rang on his belt. He had nothing but scorn for her and Mickey "being the slaves to technology" anyway.

Beyond that, she would be good and goddamned if she would try getting through the Gestapo switchboard at San Francisco General again to try to talk to Mickey. She did consider testing her Volkswagen and driving down there, but in the end decided that, since it was past visiting hours, she'd have less chance actually seeing him than she would talking to him on the telephone. And wasn't it just the perfect karma for today that Mick's cell phone had died in the accident so she couldn't call him directly?

That was really special, and further proof that God hated her.

And when Wyatt Hunt had dropped her off at her home earlier, he told her that he had a date with Gina Roake, and it was far too late to interrupt them, even if she thought Wyatt might have been able to help in some way. Which she didn't.

Finally, she knew she could call the police and report her grandfather as missing, except that it was decidedly premature for that. She knew from work that authorities would do nothing about a missing person report until that person had been missing for at least three days. Beyond that, Jim had been home most nights for the past six months since Tamara had lived here, but at least three times he'd wound up staying out somewhere mysterious and didn't seem to feel the need to explain where or to check in with his grandchildren. She'd thought it was just drinking and probably passing out at the apartment of one of his bocce-ball companions, but then she'd discovered the plastic container of Viagra (certainly not Mickey's) when she'd been cleaning up one day, and a little later had overheard him bragging to Mick that he'd "gotten lucky."

But, the whole tenor of the evening nagging at her, she thought she'd better at least check the late-night news to see if there was anything about a body of an old man being found in a ditch or somewhere. But though there was no shortage of murder and mayhem in and around the greater Bay Area, there was no mention of anyone who could have been her grandfather.

At the end of the program, the smiling weatherman informed her that the northern storm whose lower edge had arrived in the city this morning would really slam them tomorrow. It would be cold and wet, great news for a drought-starved state. And more good news — it was expected to drop up to four feet of snow in the Sierra.

Somehow underwhelmed by all the terrific weather and other news, Tamara hit the remote, pulled the covers over her head on the Murphy bed, turned onto her side, and went to sleep.

27

Hunt liked to run most mornings, but he wasn't a fanatic. When the weather turned this ugly, he thought he could let a day go by and not miss it too much. He'd pump some iron at home and maybe get in a sprint workout on the court and could still be showered and shaved, dressed, and ready to head for work by eight.

With his windshield wipers slapping away, at a few minutes after six o'clock Hunt depressed the garage door button on his car's visor and started to turn in, only to abruptly slam on his brakes. Just there to his right, parked along the wall, was a dark blue Honda Element. A frown creased his brow, and he considered jamming his car into reverse, backing out of there, and calling the police, telling them he had an intruder.

Instead, though, he scanned the open space in front of him. The Cooper's lights were still on, and he could see at a glance that no one was lying in wait for him, although someone could conceivably be using the Honda for cover.

His heart pumping in his ears, he pushed the visor button and heard the garage door beginning to close behind him.

Moving the Cooper forward, he next pushed the dashboard button to shut off his engine, pulled out his keys, and opened his car door. His car's beams now were out, and crouching low, he scampered over to the light switch next to the metal door and brought up the room lights.

Nothing. And nothing looked to have been touched. On this side of the warehouse, anyway.

Hunt owned a couple of guns. He generally did not carry them with him, and didn't have them now. They were locked into a hidden safe under a pull-up board in the floor in his bedroom.

Note to self, he was thinking. *When you're working on any aspect of a murder case, carry your piece. You just never know.*

But if that was today's lesson, it was too late to benefit from it now. Again he considered letting himself out into the downpour, using his cell phone, getting a police presence or some reinforcements. But again, something stopped him.

It was all so quiet. His alarm should have gone off.

Every nerve on full alert, he walked over to the Element and dared a quick look inside. Through the slightly tinted window, he could see that the backseats had been folded up to the sides. There looked to be a pile of clothes covering the floor. All but tiptoeing now, he crossed his basketball court and got to the inner door, which was unlocked, and opened it without a sound. The rooms on this side of the warehouse would only be naturally lit by the high windows in the far wall, and little of that light penetrated to this hallway, which was close to pitch-black.

Now he didn't hesitate at all, but picked his steps as quietly as he could into his bedroom. Dim light from the windows here relieved the blackness of the hall, but not by much. Over in the corner, he lifted the edge of the throw rug.

By now he was breathing hard and drops of sweat were beginning to stand out on his forehead. Somebody was still in or had been in his place. And if he was going to meet them, even if it was someone he might know from somewhere (enough that they knew about his alarm and its secret code), it was going to be on his terms.

He pulled up the floorboard and silently lifted it away. The last time he'd closed his safe, as was his habit, he'd set it so that the combination was mostly set and needed only a half turn to the right. This time, it worked as it should, and he reached in and lifted out his .380 ACP Sig Sauer P232. The gun was loaded and he released the safety and snicked a round into the chamber.

Then walked back out into the hallway, turning on the lights as he went.

Hunt was by no means over his adrenaline rush and his anger and he spoke in a whisper, all the more intimidating for its control. "You could have so easily gotten yourself killed. Both of you. I can't believe how stupid this is."

They were all sitting at the kitchen table. The gun, safety now back on, rested on the counter behind them. Mickey was still barefoot in his jeans and Hunt's sweatshirt, augmented by the blanket wrapped around his shoulders. Alicia, barefoot, wore her jeans from last night, though she'd thrown on a brown turtleneck sweater from the stash in her car.

Alicia raised her eyes to meet Hunt's. "I'll go if you want me to."

"No!" At his outburst, Mickey clutched at his ribs.

Hunt's expression dark, he turned to his employee. "That's not the worst idea I've ever heard, Mick."

"And where's she supposed to go?"

"How about back home? How about to her regular life?"

Mickey, very slowly, shook his head. "She's not going to have a regular life until this is over, Wyatt. Juhle and Russo think it's her. You told me that yourself."

"I also told you they're a long way from a warrant."

"That could change in a heartbeat. And besides, it's not just them."

"It's not?"

Alicia took the opportunity to break in. "Mickey thinks that whoever really did this might . . . might want to kill me too."

Hunt's mouth twitched in derision. "And why would they want to do this?"

"If she's the main suspect," Mickey said, "and then she kills herself, or it's made to look like she kills herself, the investigation goes away."

Hunt took a beat. "I've always said you've got a good imagination, Mick."

"This guy's already killed two people. Why wouldn't he kill somebody else if it would end it? You don't think that could happen?"

"A lot of things could happen, Mick. Do I think there's a likelihood?" He turned his gaze from one of them to the other. "No."

"Yeah? Well, I don't want to bet on likelihoods. Any likelihood at all is too much. You want to bet Alicia's life that something like that won't happen? We just can't do that."

Hunt blew out a heavy breath.

"Look," Mickey went on. "We took this job, among other reasons, to investigate this murder, now these murders, and try our damnedest to keep Alicia out of jail —"

"That's not why we took this job."

"Yes, it is, Wyatt. It is exactly. It's what I promised her before I even came to you about the rewards."

This unexpected information didn't make Hunt any happier. "It might have been nice to let me know about that a little sooner."

Mickey started to shrug, but the pain stopped him. "It's what I did, Wyatt. It seemed like the right thing. Alicia did not do this. Either of these."

Hunt's glance at Alicia made it clear that he wasn't close to sold on this story. He came back at Mickey. "So what do you propose we do, as opposed to what we've already been doing trying to investigate these murders?"

"Well, first," Mickey said without hesitation, "for her own safety, she stays here." He held up his good hand. "Look, there's no warrant out on her. Devin and Russo haven't even asked her to check in with them. So she's just hard to find, visiting a friend, however you want to spin it, if it comes up at all."

"What if they get a warrant? Or the Grand Jury gives 'em an indictment?"

"You told me that won't happen at least until they get the other DNA. And even with the DNA, where's the case against Alicia?" Mickey looked over at her, seemingly took strength from her expression of gratitude. "And if they come back with a warrant or indictment, then we ask Gina to come aboard as her lawyer."

For the first time, Hunt relaxed his fierce front. "And wouldn't Devin love that?"

"Wouldn't he?" Except Mickey wasn't done. "But that's not going to happen, Wyatt. Devin and Russo haven't even looked at Neshek yet. There'll be clues at the crime scene there, the investigation is going to open up. Something will break. Or else one of our reward people will come up with something. At least it'll move in a different direction, and then Alicia can go back to her life."

"And in the meanwhile, she's here?"

"Nobody's going to look for her here, Wyatt. She can sleep in her car. You won't even know it."

Hunt looked from one of them back to the other. "I hate this," he said.

But then, unbidden and unwelcome, he recalled the discussion he'd had with Gina the night before. All of the unanswered questions about the money, about Len Turner, about his connections, if any, to the Battalion. And Mickey was right — even forgetting the Nancy Neshek homicide, all of that was stuff Devin and Sarah had barely begun to look at.

Still, Mickey had without his permission moved a murder suspect into his home. Had essentially committed the firm to take her on as a de facto client, and one who didn't seem likely to come up with a retainer. But, even beyond all that, was Mickey's point that if the damned woman was in fact innocent, she might be at risk. And now he'd made it Hunt's business.

"You know what they say about fish and guests?" he asked. "After three days, both stink." Hunt's face had reverted back to where it had been all morning. Unyielding. "So three days. That's my best offer. Then we figure out some other accommodation."

He pushed back his chair, got up, grabbed the gun, and walked off down the hallway toward his bedroom.

The windshield wipers kept up their regular rhythm. Hunt, grim-faced, waited out the red light on Market. Finally, he turned to Mickey. "You're sure you're okay to be moving around?"

Mickey barely inclined his head. "I moved around more last night."

"That's not what I asked."

"I'll be all right. We've only got three days."

"It might be longer than that. You might want to prepare yourself. It probably will be, in fact, so don't get your hopes up. And then where does she go?"

"As you say, we'll figure something out. I've got some people I know from cooking classes who might let her crash with them."

"Yeah," Hunt said. "Make more friends."

The light turned green ahead of them. The line of traffic did not move. The driver behind Hunt laid on his horn, and Hunt said, "I wonder if he'd do that if he knew I was packing."

Mickey received this intelligence in silence, but he shot a quick look over at his

427

boss. Say what he would to the contrary, Hunt's decision to carry a gun on him marked a sharp escalation in his estimation of the dangers of this case.

"So," Hunt said. "When I got there this morning, you were both on the sofa bed. You want to elaborate on that? And in case you're wondering, it's not really a question of whether you want to or not. I need to know your relationship."

"Friends. But, yes, I find her attractive. I'm attracted to her."

"You tell her that?"

"I think she's probably figured it out. But nothing's happened. Nothing. She was nervous out in her car alone."

Finally, they rolled ahead about two car lengths. Six or eight cars ahead of them, the light turned red again. "So how do you know she's innocent? And you do realize, I hope, that you are betting your life, and maybe mine, on that."

"I think you can tell when someone is a good person. Some people. And I know all about what you're going to say about you and Tam and Craig, but Alicia is different. She's real, she's consistent. Just last night, she even told me the one thing she'd done that she felt she hadn't handled correctly in this investigation. And nobody made her tell me that. She just wanted to be completely honest."

"And what was that?"

The office door opened and Tamara raised her head and turned, her eyes wide with surprise. "Mickey! What are you . . . ? I was going to come down and get you at the hospital in a couple of hours. How are you . . . ?"

But in the palpable tension, she shut up.

Hunt, a couple of steps behind him, let Mickey step out of the way — just barely — and then, with a curt nod and no greeting, passed around Tamara's desk to his own door, which he opened and then turned back to her. "I'm not to be disturbed. Half an hour," he said. "No exceptions."

He closed the door silently behind him.

Mickey slowly and carefully lowered himself into the one client's chair. For a very long moment, the siblings just stared at each other. Finally, Tamara drew a deep breath. "This is going to sound like a ridiculous question since you've been in the hospital, but have you heard from Jim?"

"Have I heard from Jim?"

She nodded. "He was supposed to go to the memorial yesterday, though I don't know if he actually did. And in any event, he didn't come home last night. I've been worried sick about him."

28

Al Carter was reluctant to make too many changes in his habits lest he call undue attention to himself. So on Thursday morning he presented himself at the Ortega campus at eight-twenty, which was the new time he'd been coming in since Dominic Como had originally gone missing. Of course, there was still no limo, but he had to believe that things someday would return to normal; and when they did, he didn't want to have lost his place in the pecking order.

The day seemed to be getting off to a slow start again this morning following the closure of the admin offices until mid-afternoon of the day before for Como's memorial. Al had dropped by here after his meeting with his brother and sister-in-law at the Mudhouse yesterday. He stayed just long enough to let his presence register and to pick up a stack of a hundred or so pledge cards — newly printed with a recent photo of a smiling and vibrant Dominic Como. All the Sunset people had been urged to hand these out to acquaintances, friends, and businesses, so it was good form to grab a bunch and disappear with them, although in Carter's case, he simply tossed them into his garbage when he finally got home.

Now he closed his umbrella and walked through the empty, echoing lobby. The teachers' lounge, back behind the wide-open general offices area, seemed to have attracted everyone who'd so far come in to work today and it fairly hummed with low-key activity. Making his way through the desks and cubbies outside, when he got to the lounge door, he put on a confident and sober face, and waded into the crowd.

Younger Battalion members mingled here democratically with both the clerical and executive staff. Someone had brought in doughnuts, and of course there was regular and decaf coffee and hot water for those who wanted tea or hot cider. But in spite of the sweets and drinks, between Como's and Neshek's deaths, yesterday's CityTalk column, and the miserable weather, the mood in the room was decidedly somber.

Al slapped some backs and made small talk as he negotiated his way through to the refreshment table. Not for nothing had he worked all those years with the consummate politician that was Dominic Como. He finally found himself holding a jelly doughnut and a cup of coffee, on the periphery of a small group of women that included his nominal new boss, Lorraine Hess.

In a quick appraisal, Carter saw that the events of the past two weeks had played havoc with Hess's looks. When Al had first come on at Sunset, she'd been in her mid- to upper thirties and quite attractive, vivacious and upbeat, with a body that was a little short of spectacular. Over the years, she'd softened her image, and her body tone, considerably until she began to fit Al's description of the poster child for the aging female bureaucrat — large and gray. But especially when she smiled, which had until recently been quite often, her face had always retained something of its youthful glow and even beauty.

But not today.

Today she wore fatigue like a shroud that enveloped all of her. Her eyes, rimmed with dark bags, had sunk in over her hollowed-out cheeks. Even through the thick padding of imperfectly applied makeup, blotches were apparent on her forehead, on the imprecise, jowl-lined thickness of her jaw.

The conversation she was engaged in with the other women around her concerned the AmeriCorps improprieties and what they would mean in terms of immediate funding, whether there would be layoffs, how it would affect Sunset's ability to conduct business with the city. Hess, a master at these administrative and bureaucratic details, was holding her own against the onslaught, downplaying the threat, but Al could clearly see that on top of everything else she'd endured, these topics and her people were wearing her down.

He decided to rescue her. "Pardon me for butting in," he said, "but Lorraine's telling you the truth. It's not going to change anything. Dominic knew all about this long ago too. He was trying to get it all straightened out behind the scenes before they went public with it, but . . . well, we know what happened before he could do that.

"But the plain fact is, and we've all heard him say it a hundred times, that with government funding, when you get a difference of opinion, one side is going to say that the other is guilty of sin. That's discouraging, especially when we're set on helping others. But the thing we have to do now, all of us, is just to forget about all this bad news and go back about our work and not concern ourselves with things over which we don't have control. First of all, Len Turner and Dominic were already talking about appealing the suspension of funding, and next, when Lorraine takes over here full-time, she'll convince these auditors that all of these are insignificant issues that have, for the most part, been resolved. Isn't that right, Lorraine?"

She forced a weary smile. "Exactly. That's what I've been trying to say. This isn't the time to panic, but to buckle down and do our work. And, Al" — now the smile came to bloom — "for a minute there, you sounded like you were channeling Dominic."

"I think after eight years he may have rubbed off some."

"Well, keep him around if you can."

Al showed some of his own teeth. "I intend to."

The bell, indicating the first period of the school day, sounded, and Al more or less naturally fell into step beside Hess as she headed back toward her office. When they'd cleared the lounge, she took his arm and leaned in toward him. "Thank you for that in there."

He shrugged. "They're just worried. It's a hard time."

435

"Tell me about it. But I'm still very grateful for your help speaking up. It gets tiresome talking about it."

And then she was opening her office door and they were inside. Hess went around her desk and, sighing, lowered herself into her chair.

"I wanted to ask you," Al began, "any word on when we get the limo back?"

She shook her head. "Shouldn't be too long. Why do you ask?"

"Well, nobody's noticed too much yet, but I don't seem to have a job. I've been filling the hours distributing pledge cards, but . . ." He trailed off with a hopeful smile.

"But that's hardly the most productive use of your time."

"Well, yes, that. But more, I was wondering about . . . later."

"In what sense?"

"I mean, when you move up, the whole question of the limo. If you'd be doing the job the same way Dominic did. In that way."

From her reaction, it might have been the first time she'd considered that question. She cocked her head to one side, let the beginning of a small thoughtful smile hover at her lips for a moment. "If you're asking me will I be needing a driver," she said, "I can't imagine doing the job without one.

And I also can't imagine it being anyone but you, Al. Does that answer your question?"

He didn't want to appear either too grateful or too needy, so he simply nodded. "Yes, ma'am, it does. Thank you."

So great was Hunt's fury that he didn't trust himself to come out of his office and face Mickey again. After first verifying that Mickey had independent transportation around town — Tamara's Volkswagen — he gave his orders to Tamara by intercom that Mickey was to get the identity of everybody who'd been at the Monday night Communities of Opportunity meeting at City Hall, and then get all of their alibis: what they'd done after they'd left the meeting. That ought to take Mickey the rest of the day and maybe then some, Hunt thought, and it might possibly, though not definitely, keep Hunt from killing or maiming his young, gullible, dumb-shit associate.

When he was sure Mickey had gone, Hunt stood up, opened his door, went into the outer office, and put a haunch on the corner of Tamara's desk. "Did he tell you?"

"Uh-huh. Basically. She's at your place."

"If she hasn't stolen my goods and lit out for the border already. But did he also tell you about her lying to the police?"

Her brow clouded. "I think he left out that part."

Hunt filled her in. "And you know what this means, don't you?"

"I'm not sure."

"Well, forgetting the obvious obstruction of justice, and let's do that, this is the one bit of information that, if she tells it to Devin or Sarah, puts her in jail."

"Why?"

"Because getting fired on the last day of Dominic's life counts, believe me. If we only know about that from Ellen Como, it's just what she thinks Dominic intended to do. If we get it from Carter, it's what he thinks he overheard. But if it's an admission we get directly from Alicia, guess what? It's a fact." He slammed a palm on her desk. "Shit. Pardon the language."

"It's okay," she said. "You should have heard me last night."

"What were you swearing at?"

"The idiots at the hospital. You don't want to know. Oh, and then Jim. He never came home."

Hunt took a long beat. "Jim didn't come home? Till when?"

"So far, till the last time I tried to reach him, which is like ten minutes ago." She

438

gave Hunt the excuses she'd fed herself last night. He had been planning on going to the Como memorial. After that, he might . . . or he might . . . finally, she ran out of steam. "He just could have picked a better night," she concluded. "That's all."

"Let's hope that's all."

As soon as he'd said them, he regretted the words. And Tamara called him on it. "What do you mean, 'Let's hope that's all'?"

Hunt hesitated, wanting to avoid coming out with it directly. But there didn't seem to be any other way. "I mean, if he went to the memorial, Tam, maybe he met somebody there among our group of possible suspects. Which I wouldn't want to think. But you know, I was there, and I never saw him."

"Maybe he never got there."

"Or couldn't get in. The place was packed."

"Okay." She assayed a low-wattage smile. "Now we can say 'Let's hope that's all.' I just wish he'd turn up."

Hunt slid off the edge of her desk. "Me, too, hon. Me too."

Back in his office again, Hunt couldn't seem to get himself focused. As long as there was a question about whether Alicia had actually been fired that Tuesday morning, he could live with the presumption of her innocence. Knowing that Dominic had in fact fired her, and that she'd lied about it, washed a great portion of his personal doubt away.

And now this woman was staying at his home.

Also, he had to call Juhle, but how was he going to talk to him, knowing what he now knew? The subject would come up, and then Hunt would be withholding evidence in a murder investigation. Talk about losing his license. But beyond that, how did he justify it? How could he live with himself?

His brain kept running back to Alicia having free run of his place. Try as he might, he couldn't remember if he'd turned the combination lock on his gun safe when he'd closed it up after taking out the gun he was carrying. What if she did a thorough search? Had he folded the throw rug back down over the loosened board? Had he even made sure that the board was flush and secure? No matter what, he told himself, he'd have to go home and check that.

He had Tamara call and verify that she was still there. Yep.

And now the phone on his desk chimed. Gingerly, he picked up the receiver. "What's up?" he asked Tamara.

"There's two gentlemen out here to see you, sir. Mr. Len Turner and an associate. He doesn't have an appointment, but says you'll want to talk to him."

"He's right," Hunt said. Quickly, without conscious thought, he reached around and checked the weight of his gun, tucked into a holster attached to the center of his belt at his back. "Send him in."

Turner's African-American associate, whom he introduced first thing as Battalion Colonel Keydrion Mugisa, looked to be about twenty-five. He stood about six foot three and certainly weighed less than a hundred and seventy pounds. This lack of heft did not make him less intimidating, though. His handshake was cool, and in spite of its brevity, apparent effortlessness, and the polite accompanying nod for a greeting, it was crushing. Under his classic trench coat, he was well-dressed in light green slacks, a light brown dress shirt, a thin dark-brown tie, and an olive sport coat. He wore his hair Obama-style. The skin of his face was very black and smooth; his eyes dark brown, flat, unexpressive. A well-trimmed goatee surrounded a thin mouth that stayed closed.

In a thousand-dollar pinstripe business suit, Turner took Hunt's hand in both of his as though they were by now old friends. One of the flaws of Hunt's office was lack of seating space, but Tamara brought in the chair from outside, then closed the door behind her on her way out.

"So," Hunt began when everybody was comfortable. "How can I help you?"

"Actually," Turner said, "I thought I might be able to help you."

"That would be great. I can use all the help I can get."

"I think we all can. But after our discussion yesterday, I really came away with the impression that you may be widening the scope of your involvement in this matter in a way that nobody really intended when we decided to bring you on board. When we originally spoke, as I'm sure you remember, the idea was that your function would be to help the police analyze the quality of the information that came in on the reward hotline, and then turn the valid or promising leads over to them. Does that ring a bell?"

Hunt smiled cooperatively. "That's pretty much it."

Turner smiled back at him. "That's what I'd understood. And in fact it's why I agreed on behalf of the reward participants to take you on board. It seemed a valuable service worth the fee you were charging."

442

"Thank you. I think we've already saved the police a lot of needless legwork, and frankly, we've turned up some valuable evidence in the process. The probable murder weapon, for example. From one of our callers. They seem pretty happy with what we're doing so far — no complaints, anyway."

"Yes, but, well . . ." Turner crossed a leg. The hostile tone he'd adopted the day before was nowhere to be seen, although the presence of Mugisa, to Hunt, lent a tone of unstated threat to the meeting. "It seemed to me that yesterday you had taken that initial assignment and expanded it to include suspicions of some of us in the charitable community."

Hunt said nothing. He sat up straight with his hands clasped lightly on the desk in front of him. He adopted an inquisitive air, staring at Turner.

"My point," Turner said at last, "is that your fees for assisting us in this reward endeavor are adequate and acceptable to us, but that if you are diluting your efforts on our behalf in an independent investigation, perhaps we will have to reconsider our agreement. We need somebody whose loyalty is undivided, Mr. Hunt, and whose concentration is totally focused on the job

443

for which we're paying you. If you can't give us that loyalty and focus, we'll need to find someone who can." He held up his hand. "I am responsible for the administration of this reward fund. It's my responsibility to see that the integrity of the process is uncompromised."

After this little speech, Hunt nodded thoughtfully. "Nancy Neshek was one of the very first calls on the reward line, Mr. Turner. She was killed that same night, just after a meeting of your Communities of Opportunity. My staff and I are simply following up on her call to this office, a call that might have indirectly or directly led to her murder. The police think this is a reasonable assumption and, further, that her death is probably related in some way to Mr. Como's.

"I would think, Mr. Turner, that it would be in the interests of those who put up the reward to have us ensure not only that information is appropriately transmitted to the police, but that also they are not personally at risk because of their inadvertent connection to these terrible events. But of course, if it is your instruction that we not consider that possibility, then naturally we'll do as we are instructed. Do you think it would be better if I explain the situation

444

personally to the people who've put up the largest parts of the reward?"

Turner gave it a minute before responding. "I don't think so, no. I can take care of that. If you come upon anything that concerns you in this regard, you communicate it to me first and I'll make the decision on who, if anyone, we need to contact. How's that sound?"

Sounds like a stalemate, Hunt thought to himself. He couldn't do anything Turner told him not to do. But Turner couldn't very well tell him to ignore any possible threat to the people who had put up the reward. In other words, he could keep doing what he'd been doing all along and remain on the payroll. "It sounds like it ought to work," he said. And then, losing his stomach for this circumlocution, Hunt cut back to his point. "So did Como and Neshek have a personal relationship I don't know about?"

"Not that I'm aware of. They were professional colleagues, no more."

"So the two of them being killed within a week of one another, and she on the day she called our reward line about his murder, that was a coincidence?"

"Possibly, though you're right, it doesn't seem likely. But looking for an answer among the professional community I work with is not going to get you anywhere, I can guarantee you."

"What I'm doing is looking for an answer anywhere and everywhere. And to that end, here's one I'd like now, if you can give it to me: What did you do last Monday night after your COO meeting?"

Turner's eyes flared briefly. He glanced over at Mugisa, who, during this entire discussion, might as well have been a block of stone. Finally, back at Hunt, he shook his head in apparent disappointment. "I don't think you've heard a word I've said, Mr. Hunt, but for the record, I stayed on at City Hall with some members of my staff, including Keydrion here." He turned to the young man. "We left at about what time, Key, nine?"

"Nine."

"So nine. I live with my wife and two children on Seventeenth Avenue near California. I got home at nine-fifteen, nine-twenty at the latest. My oldest, Ben, had five friends over making a float for their homecoming parade in my living room and all of them greeted me when I got home. How's that?"

"That's good," Hunt said. Then he looked to Turner's companion. "How about you, Keydrion? You go straight home after you dropped him off?"

Turner shook his head again in apparent disgust. "Let's go, Key," he said.

Hunt brought the visitor's chair out of his office after they'd gone. He put it in its normal place across from Tamara by the window. "Any word about Jim?" he asked.

Mute, she shook her head.

"He'll turn up."

"This isn't normal, this late."

Hunt sighed, scratched at his cheek. "What do you want to do? You want to go home and wait?"

"No. What good would that do?"

"Probably none. But if you want, it's an option."

"No. I'll just wait here. Maybe if Mickey checks in, I can send him out looking at the usual haunts. After he's done with your stuff, I mean."

"That's okay, Tam. You could call him now if you're that worried."

"No, I can't. He doesn't have his cell phone. He's got to call in."

"Well, if he does." Hunt looked down at her. "So you know, I mostly just sent him out on these errands to get him out of my sight."

"You're really that mad at him?"

"Pretty much, yeah."

"He's trying to do what he thinks is right."

"If I didn't think that, he'd already be fired. But he's got me in a potentially terrible bind with Devin and Sarah, just when we're getting back in their reasonably good graces, and also not so good a place in my own home. I really don't like feeling that I could open my door and be looking down the barrel of one of my own guns."

"Wyatt. Come on. She's not going to do that."

"Well, as I said to Mickey when he said the same thing, I hope you're right. But I won't know for sure, though, will I, until it happens or not?"

"It won't."

Hunt shrugged. It either would or it wouldn't, and talking about it wasn't going to make any difference. "So listen," he said, "I was supposed to call Gloria White twenty minutes ago and then Turner showed up. So I need to touch base with her now or sooner. Meanwhile, can I bother you to call Devin, set up a time we can get together? I don't think they know yet about the Monday-night meeting before Neshek got killed, and it wouldn't hurt if they were following up on that too."

"Plus, that gets them off Alicia for a while."

"Secondarily. I thought you might notice that."

"Softie," she said, with an approving smile.

"Don't get your hopes up," he told her. "It's probably temporary. Anyway, see if Devin can run some kind of a sheet on a Keydrion Mugisa? He'll have to guess on the spelling, but that's why they pay him the big bucks. He'll do it. In any event, the kid said exactly one word that whole time, you realize that? Which makes me think he wasn't really there to add to the meeting."

"Why, then?"

"To let me know Turner could do more than just fire me if I got too far out of line."

29

Aside from his physical pains, which remained substantial, Mickey felt sick to his stomach at Hunt's response to what he'd done. Driving out through the rain once again to the Ortega campus, shifting the Volkswagen, an inordinately difficult task with his steering arm in the cast, he kept revisiting his decision-making process from the time Alicia had appeared at his bedside. Maybe the Vicodin had played a role and affected his judgment, he told himself. Nevertheless, he wished he'd brought some of them with him from the hospital. His head pounded with every beat of his pulse, every bump in the road.

And then there was the psychic pain as well. Mickey knew that Hunt was an experienced and intelligent guy, not given to extremes of emotion or flights of fancy, and Hunt didn't think much of Alicia's basic story. Clearly, Hunt had read Alicia's admission of her lie to the police completely differently than Mickey had. To Mickey, it had been the baring of a burdened soul, utterly believable. To Hunt, on the other hand, this confession had pretty much sealed the deal that she should be considered the prime suspect in Como's death. And in Neshek's.

Although every fiber in his being rebelled at that thought, Mickey couldn't get it out of his mind. What if she was just playing him for a lovesick dope?

He kept hearing himself explaining to Hunt, replaying the words in his head, that he could tell when someone was a good person. If anyone else had said them, Mickey knew what his response would be because it was the same one he had to his own words — what a tool.

Of course you couldn't tell when someone was a good person. Or a bad person. Or anything. You just saw enough of someone that over time you came to trust what appeared to be their essential character.

And even Mickey would not argue that once you had the essential-character thing down, anomalies could occur. Good people did bad things all the time, sometimes by mistake, sometimes because they'd lost track of themselves in an altered chemical or alcoholic state, sometimes because smart, good people do foolish, wrong things. So to say that you could tell if someone was a good person was not only inherently idiotic, it was irrelevant to anything. It certainly couldn't explain or predict guilt or innocence.

That said, though, he could intellectually give his assent to a slightly different, though related, proposition: Alicia Thorpe might be a good or a bad person (and she'd at least told one big whopper of a lie in a crucial setting), but there was no way in the world he could imagine her brutally killing not just one but two people.

And with that, he kept returning to another fundamental question: Why would she have come back to him, instead of just simply blowing Dodge? What, he asked himself, would be in it for her? Mickey's involvement with her could not keep her from getting arrested if the cops came to that. If anything, he reasoned, the fact that she had come back to Mickey argued that she desperately wanted the killer to be found. Otherwise, why wouldn't she have fled after her last interview with Juhle and Russo? Instead, she'd found out he was in the hospital and she'd come running to him.

Why would she have done that if she didn't believe he could save her? She was truly innocent and she would put her trust in the one person who absolutely believed in her, that's why.

Of course, there were other, more disturbing, possible answers. But let Wyatt Hunt agonize over them, Mickey wasn't going to.

Even if it meant infuriating his boss, and it did.

Even if it meant his job, and it might.

The bottom line was that it was a matter of faith. And for good or ill, Mickey believed her. He believed in her. If she were lying and betrayed him . . .

But he shook his head. That wasn't happening. He wasn't going to go there.

Russo and Juhle were parked outside of Alicia's house again.

"I've got this amazing sense of déjà vu," Juhle said. "Wasn't she not home yesterday at this time too?"

"It was later, but yes."

"Where does she go?"

"This is probably mostly when she kills her victims. Except those days she's surfing."

"She kills people before she goes to work?"

"Right. Usually. If she's not too busy surfing, or if the waves suck. And then, remember, she's got to get cleaned up afterward, either from the killings or the surfing, or both, if she's got to be dressed up to greet the carnivores."

Juhle, nodding sagely, looked at his watch. "How long you want to give it?"

They'd already been parked here for nearly a half hour. They had been on their way out to Nancy Neshek's to canvass the neighborhood, but the idea of slogging to mostly empty houses through the rain to try to talk to rich people who didn't look out their windows had persuaded them both to take another stab at interviewing Alicia Thorpe. After the scarf identification yester-day, both of them thought she was close to breaking, and now Russo was of the opinion that even though they didn't know definitely whose semen it was, they could drop the news, which they'd held back yesterday, about its presence on the scarf and see if they could break her at last.

Yesterday, she'd remained strong in her insistence that she'd lost the scarf a few week ago, but that, too, was something they had on tape that she could possibly contra-dict, and once that happened, their leverage would increase exponentially. Neither of them had much doubt about her factual guilt, and they felt that they needed just one small break to have an excuse to put on the handcuffs and take her downtown, and once that happened, the confession was pretty much just going to be a matter of time.

"Ten more minutes," Russo said. "Then we get something to eat and come back one time on our way out to Seacliff."

"The quality of decisiveness," Juhle said, "is not strained."

"What?" Russo asked.

At that moment, the cell phone on Juhle's belt went off with a ringtone from an old-fashioned telephone that was so loud it made them both jump.

"You gotta change that," Russo said.

But Juhle, already on the call, didn't even hear her. "Yeah," he said, and then again. "Yeah, but we'll be in the field most of the day. Nothing so far, but if he's interested, he can catch us down at the Hall when we get back in. I'll be on this phone. Right." He listened for another few seconds, then said, "You could tell him that maybe he ought to be checking those himself, but I wouldn't waste too much time on it if I were him." He rolled his eyes over at Russo. "Because we've already got a person of interest with no alibi for that night, as he knows . . . no . . . no . . . no, we like thorough, that's fine. All right. Just a sec, I need something to write with." Resting the phone against his ear, he pulled out his little notebook and the pen from his pocket. "Okay, shoot. You want to spell that? All right, you're not sure, it's phonetic. Got it. We'll try. Okay. Fine. Later."

Hitting the disconnect button, he said to Russo, "That was Hunt's girl, and —"

"You mean his secretary?"

"Yes, of course. What could have gotten into me that I said 'girl'? You'd think that after all those weeks of sensitivity training . . . what I meant to say was that was Hunt's executive assistant, is what I was saying. He wanted us to know that Turner's Communities of Opportunity, including Neshek, had a meeting at City Hall on Monday night before she was killed."

"Okay."

"And he wanted us to check everybody's alibi. I told her to tell him we already had Alicia's lack of one and liked it a lot, but if he got a better one, he should let us know."

"I heard you. So what'd she have you write down?"

"A guy's name." Juhle looked down at his pad. "Keydrion Mugisa or something like that. He'll have a sheet somewhere. We'll find him. One of Len Turner's people. I'm thinking probably not Irish."

"What about him?"

"I don't know. That's what Hunt's asked me to find out."

"We gonna do it?"

"Might as well. I don't see how it could hurt."

Al Carter was sitting in the lobby at a fold-up lunch-style table among a large group of what Mickey had come to recognize as Battalion members — mostly young men, but some young women as well, all reasonably well-dressed and well-groomed. A hum of comfortable, loose banter floated out across the lobby all the way to the door where Mickey entered.

He was here mostly to see Lorraine Hess about her whereabouts and activities on Monday night, but when he saw Carter, Mickey thought of a question he wanted to ask him and headed over that way first. They were working from boxes filled with perforated forms — pledge cards — that they were tearing into thirds, organizing in some way, and then sending the oblong mailing through a Pitney Bowes automatic postage machine. When they'd gone through that, another few of the Battalion kids packed them into a growing pile of open-topped white cardboard boxes that Mickey guessed would soon be on their way to the nearest post office, or possibly even all the way down to the main station at Rincon Annex, if the mass mailing was big enough.

Mickey got about two-thirds of the way there when Carter saw him. After an infinitesimally brief look of confusion or maybe impatience, the older man rearranged his face into its natural and neutral expression and pushed himself back from his folding chair. Closing the now-small distance between them, he extended his hand. "Al Carter," he said, reintroducing himself.

"Yes, sir. I remember. Mickey Dade."

"Well, Mickey Dade, what happened to you?"

"I got hit by a car. Or rather, my car got hit by a car. It looks worse than it is."

"I'm glad to hear that. 'Cause if it was as bad as it looks, you'd be dead at least twice. You want to sit down a minute?"

"That'd be good."

They got over to the wall by the administrative offices and sat down where a few extra fold-up chairs had been set up. "I met your boss yesterday at Mr. Como's memorial," Carter began. "Hunt. So what brings you down here to these environs again?"

"I've got a few more questions for Ms. Hess, but then I saw you and I thought I'd ask —"

Carter stopped him by replying, "I already told your Mr. Hunt about Mr. Como firing Alicia that last morning. I don't know what I can add to that."

"That's not an issue," Mickey said. "Or not the issue I was talking about."

"All right." He cocked his head to one side, a question.

"Last time I was here, you told me you'd known my grandfather, Jim Parr."

"I did. Reasonably well."

"Well, I know there were a lot of people at that memorial, but you didn't by any chance run into Jim there, did you?"

"As a matter of fact, I did. Why?"

Mickey took a deep breath and released it. "He hasn't come home. He didn't come home last night."

Carter straightened up, his face now thoughtful, his frown pronounced.

"What?" Mickey asked.

"Well, I didn't just see your grandfather yesterday. I don't know if you heard about Mrs. Como when she saw Alicia . . ."

"She kicked her out."

"Yes, she did. Or rather, she asked that she be removed. I don't know if you'd heard that I stepped in and became the remover."

"No, I don't think so."

"I went over to her, put an arm around

her, got her outside, and the two of us ran into your grandfather. I was surprised that they knew each other."

"Yeah. We'd had her and her brother over the night before."

"So I gathered." He paused and looked sideways over at Mickey, obviously conflicted about going on. "You know," he said, "when we first talked about the reward last time you were up here, I didn't want any part of it. I didn't want to make any profit out of Dominic's death. But since then . . . well, it's a hell of a lot of money. It's life-changing money."

"It might be. But I don't see what you're getting at."

"I'm getting at what I told your boss yesterday, about Alicia. Getting fired. If that turns out to be what the police need, for her arrest, I mean. I'd just want you and Mr. Hunt to remember where you heard it."

"There's no chance we'd forget, sir. But I don't see what Alicia being fired has to do with her and my grandfather."

"I don't see that either. Not specifically. But I just have the same feeling I had yesterday when I felt like I was pointing the finger at her. I don't mean to do that. I like the young woman very much."

"But . . . ?"

"But I know what I know." His vision lasered into Mickey's face. "She told Jim she'd drive him home."

"Alicia did?"

He nodded. "That's who we're talking about, isn't it? Jim had come down on the bus, and was going to take it home, but she said she was going by his way, and she'd take him. Wouldn't hear otherwise." He shook his head, uncomprehending. "And now you're telling me he never made it home. You hear what I'm saying?"

The sudden pounding of his heart into his broken ribs threatened to double Mickey over with pain just as an explosive throbbing expanded behind his eyes. He brought his good right hand up to his forehead and squeezed at both temples. "Give me a minute." Dry-throated, he barely got the words out. "I just need another minute."

It took him more like fifteen minutes, and when he got his breathing and the pain back under control, he was still at a complete loss as to how he was supposed to proceed. Al Carter, having made sure he was basically all right, and with nothing else to tell him, left Mickey and went back to his supervision of the pledge-card mailing.

When his head had sufficiently cleared, Mickey's first inclination was to call Alicia and simply ask her.

But he found that he couldn't do it. Some psychic barrier had arisen. He didn't know what it meant yet, but for the first time now the weight of all the evidence against this woman he had believed and cared for had tipped the scales out of her favor. He didn't immediately leap to the conclusion that something bad or, God forbid, tragic, had happened to Jim, or even that, if something had, Alicia had played a role in it. But the possibility loomed large and ate at his guts. Along with the stark reality that so far as he now knew, Alicia had been the last person to have been with Jim, who'd known where he was. And with all of that, suddenly — very suddenly — he found himself reluctant to give her any more benefit of his doubt. And that, more than anything, shook him to his depths. He found himself unwittingly back in Hunt's camp, reinterpreting not only Alicia's confession, but nearly everything she'd told him about herself and about her relationship with Dominic Como.

Doubting.

Was she truly the kind of person Mickey had heard about but never met, a bona fide psychopath — nerveless, emotionless, a consummate actor, absolutely capable of cold-blooded murder whenever it suited her convenience?

Doubting and doubting.

In the cascading maelstrom of his thoughts, his next idea was to call Tamara and Hunt and tell them the basic facts, even to warn them about his suspicions, such as they were. Although he realized that the warning would be something Hunt wouldn't need. He was already on his guard. Still, this new information was too important to ignore.

How could Alicia have been with him all that time last night and never mentioned the fact that she'd driven Jim back from the memorial? Granted, they were engrossed in his strategy for her safety. Mickey himself had never been out of pain. They hadn't exactly been chatting aimlessly about life and its vicissitudes, but he'd have thought that the bare fact of Jim's transportation would have come up, at least tangentially, casually. "Oh, by the way, I saw your grandfather today and . . ." But there had been nothing.

Gradually, the pain subsided and his head cleared. He told himself — a thin whisper in the howling storm of his cogitations — that this latest information about Alicia need not have any sinister element. It was entirely within the realm of possibility that she'd dropped Jim off at the apartment, or even — more likely — at the Shamrock or another of the neighborhood bars. Once there, as he'd done quite recently, he'd gotten himself loaded and pitied by a barman or, amazingly enough, some lonely woman. And that he was even now, as Mickey fretted, sleeping it all off.

Meanwhile, Mickey was here to do a job. In the time it took him to talk to Lorraine Hess about her Monday-night activities, Jim could be back home and the fact that Alicia had driven him yesterday would simply be a favor she'd done. The new information had taken him by surprise, that was all. He'd take a figurative deep breath, not do anything out of panic.

So he stood and walked across the lobby and knocked on Hess's door and a woman's voice told him to come in.

She clearly couldn't place him immediately, so he said his name again and the light came on. Looking fatigued and haggard, Hess nevertheless put her empathy for Mickey on her sleeve — the cast, the black eye. She stood up, matronlike, clucking and asking questions about his injuries, coming partway around her desk to make sure he got settled into his chair, asking if he'd like anything to drink or eat — they might have doughnuts left over in the lounge.

Mickey, somewhat to his own surprise, since he normally didn't eat two doughnuts in a year, told her he wouldn't mind some coffee, black, and maybe a doughnut, and she placed the order to someone over her intercom.

In a moment, someone knocked on the door and it opened to one of the Battalion members — a young teenage girl — bringing in coffee in a paper cup and a couple of round, sugared mounds of doughnut on a paper plate. Looking for permission from Hess, and getting a nod, she placed the items on the front edge of the desk, then actually curtsied and left, closing the door behind her. Mickey pulled his chair up to be within reach and took a bite of the pastry. "Oh, my God," he said, "custard-filled. I'm in heaven."

His enthusiasm brought a small smile to Hess's face. "They're my favorite too."

Mickey washed down his bite of heaven with a sip of coffee, then held the paper plate out to her. "Have the other one."

She shook her head no. "Can't. I've already had two this morning, which is one over my limit, and should be two over it." A beat. "So you should be in the hospital, but you've got too much work to do. And you're here. So your work has to do with me?"

"Actually, with all the people who were at the Communities of Opportunity meeting at City Hall a couple of nights ago. Just basic legwork to eliminate people, really. How many of you were there, by the way?"

Her face became contemplative. "All told, let's see, maybe twenty. Do you want just the professionals, or everybody? Some of us had staff with us."

"I think just the professionals, unless you think one of the staff might have had issues with Nancy Neshek."

"Oh, of course," she said. She sat straighter abruptly, suddenly struggling against a wave of emotion. "This is about her, isn't it? Was that the night she was killed?"

"Yes."

"So after the meeting?"

"That's right. We're going on that assumption, although it could have been the next morning. She was down close to room temperature when she was discovered, so it had to be fifteen, maybe twenty hours, before . . ."

But Hess was holding her one hand, putting the other over her mouth. "Please," she

466

said. "I don't mean to be squeamish, but . . ." She exhaled heavily, closed her eyes, came back to him. "These details. I go a bit light-headed when I think about the reality of them. Of Nancy. I mean, the person who was Nancy. To think of her as lying there at room temperature." She shook her head from side to side. "I'm sorry."

Mickey waved it off. "It's all right. I shouldn't have been so descriptive. But the point is we're trying to eliminate individuals who the police won't have to interrogate at all, and the best way to do that is establish who had alibis and who didn't."

"Alibis for what? The night Nancy was killed?"

"Right. As I say, in most cases, just a formality."

The confusion on Hess's face gave way to a frown. "But at the service yesterday, your Mr. Hunt said they were assuming that the same person killed Dominic and Nancy."

"That's right."

"But that means . . . you think . . . I mean, on any level, do you think I might have done these things? That there's even the remotest possibility?"

"No, ma'am. It only means that if you can account for your time when either one of the murders was committed, you're auto-

467

matically and completely eliminated, probably from both of them. Have the police asked you about the night of Dominic's death yet?"

A hand pressing into the scalp at her hairline, she was still shaking her head slowly back and forth. She seemed about to break into tears. "I can't believe this." Taking a breath, getting herself together, she finally looked across her desk at Mickey. "I don't know about the individual days, one by one. But I have a twelve-year-old boy, Gary. He's a special needs child. He's just started seventh grade and he's not having an easy time of it. With his medical bills and the economy being what it is, I had to let go one of his tutors, so we've been doing homework together every school night for at least the past three weeks. A lot of homework. Every single school night, Sunday through Thursday, and even a little bit on the weekends. I've also had to cut his caregiver back to half-time. But I'm sorry. This isn't about me. You can ask Gary if you need to. He'll remember. I know he'll remember. It's been grueling. He won't need any reminding."

"So you went to this meeting on Monday night?"

"I did. But it was over at eight or so, and I

was home by eight-thirty. Not much later, I'm sure. Where does Nancy live? Do you know?"

"Not exactly," Mickey said. "Somewhere out in Seacliff."

Hess spread her hands, palms out. "I live on lower Telegraph Hill. I would have had to drive pretty fast."

"Well, there you go. That wasn't so hard, was it?"

She put both hands over her mouth for a moment, then lowered them so she could speak. "It's just that I'm so lost over this. Over everything that's happened. It just doesn't seem possible."

"I know," Mickey said. "It's hard." He placed his coffee cup back on the desk. "While I'm here, could I trouble you to write me down a list of everybody you remember at that Monday meeting? It looks like I'm going to have a long day."

She sighed. "All right. I'll try to do that. But I can't really believe it was anybody who was there. I mean, everybody loved Nancy."

"I'm sure they did," Mickey said. "I'm sure they did."

Armed with his list of names, many with phone numbers, of those who'd been at the

469

meeting, Mickey sat with Hess's permission in one of the free cubicles in the large open staff room at the Ortega campus. Making conversation while she'd drawn up the list, he'd let drop that he didn't have a telephone, and she'd offered him the use of theirs. Save him a lot of driving. Beyond the five he'd heard of — Turner, Hess, Neshek, and the two Sanchezes — there were seven other nonprofit professional executives.

His first call wasn't to any of these people, though, but back to his own apartment, where he listened to the answering machine. Next he called the office and got his sister on the first ring. "Any word on Jim?" he asked.

"Still nothing."

"Maybe I should drop by the apartment."

"He'd pick up the phone, I think, if he were there. And I've called about ten times already."

"Yeah. I just did too."

"I'm really worried here, Mick."

"I know. Me too." He took a beat. "Is Wyatt still there? You think he'll talk to me if I told you it might be important?"

"He'll talk to you, Mick. You got something important?"

"I don't know. Maybe. You tell me."

He told her.

470

30

Hunt listened on the telephone as Mickey gave him the play-by-play on his interview with Lorraine Hess, such as it was. Down to the cute Battalion-member who delivered the custard-filled doughnuts, through her essentially rock-solid alibis and her son Gary's homework load. By the time Mickey relayed Hess's degree of her upset about being considered any kind of a suspect, her question about where Neshek had lived, and her joking comment about how fast she had to drive from there to Telegraph Hill after the Monday-night meeting, Hunt knew that Mickey was stalling and interrupted. "Not that all this isn't fascinating, Mick, but Tam said you had something important."

Mickey had already practiced the casual tone he wanted to use when he'd told Tamara, and now he said, "Well, I don't really know how important it is, but I ran into Al Carter down here and asked him if

471

he'd seen Jim at the memorial yesterday, and he told me he had. When he took Alicia outside after Mrs. Como —"

"I know all about this," Hunt said.

"Well, maybe not." He hesitated. "Carter told me that Alicia offered to drive Jim back home to our place."

After some seconds of silence, Mickey said, "Wyatt? You still there?"

"You're saying that your Alicia drove Jim home?"

"She offered to anyway. I don't know if she actually did."

"Have you asked her about this?"

"Then I'd know, wouldn't I?"

"Don't be a wiseass. Have you talked to her or not?"

"No."

Hunt let out a breath. "You're sure?"

Mickey didn't respond.

More silence.

"Wyatt?"

"I'm thinking. You haven't talked to her about anything since we left her this morning, including this?"

"I just said I didn't."

"I know you did. I didn't want there to be a misunderstanding between us again."

"Again?"

"You know. Like the last time I told you I

472

didn't think you should be hanging out too much with her, just to be on the safe side since she was a potential murder suspect, and the next thing you'd moved with her into my place. That kind of misunderstanding."

"I haven't talked to her. I called you."

"Yes, you did. Good move. Do you think you'll be able to keep yourself from talking to her until I get a chance to?"

"If that's what you want."

"That's what I want."

"So when are you going to do that?"

"Pretty damn soon."

"Okay."

"Mick?"

"Yeah."

"Tell me the truth. I know you want to believe her. And loyalty's a wonderful thing as far as it goes. But is this doing anything to your worldview?"

It took Mickey some moments to answer. "It's trying to."

Hunt paused, too, and let out a sigh. "If it does, just let it happen. Don't fight it the way your sister did with Craig. Put it someplace you can deal with now, then bring it into the open and sort it all out later. All right? That's my advice. We may have to do something about her sooner than the next three days. And I may need you with me for that. If it comes to it. You hear what I'm saying?"

"I think so."

"I want you to more than think it. This is not me making stuff up. This is not anybody wanting to believe something that didn't happen. Did she tell you about the scarf Juhle found? Her scarf?"

"Yeah. In the limo. That's when she decided to get out of her house. She thought they might come back for her. But she'd lost that scarf a couple of weeks before."

"That's what she told Devin too."

"You don't believe that either?"

"Some things are harder to believe than others."

"What makes that one hard?"

"Well, mainly because she left out one little teeny tiny part. You know she's always said she didn't have an intimate relationship with Como?"

"I do believe that. She didn't. I'm sure she didn't."

"So she says. Just like she said he didn't fire her that morning, huh? And she wasn't intimate with anybody else out there at Sunset, either, was she?"

"There's no sign of that, Wyatt. Like who?"

"Like anybody. But in fact I'm guessing Como, and so is Devin."

"And what's that got to do with her scarf?"

"This is another thing you're not going to want to tell her, and another reason you shouldn't talk to her at all. We're clear there, right?"

"Right. We've already done that. I won't talk to her at least until you do. Promise. But what?"

" 'What' is that somebody came on that scarf, Mickey. That's what."

When Hunt hung up, he raised his head.

Tamara was standing in his open doorway. "Just because Alicia dropped Jim off, that doesn't mean —" she began.

"Don't start. I don't know what it means or doesn't mean. But if on top of everything else, we're looking for Jim, too, I'm going to ask her what she knows, if only to get some kind of a timeline on him. In fact" — he checked his watch, started to push away from his desk — "enough of this. I'm going over there right now. At least find out where we stand."

"I need to go with you."

He shook his head. "I'm not going to let you do that, Tam."

"If you're really worried about her that

way, Wyatt, you should just call her."

"If I do that and spook her, which any of my questions just might do, she runs again and we're lost, aren't we?"

"I still really don't think she's going to do that. I don't think any of that's going to happen."

"Good for you. But it's my call, okay? I don't like even the remote chance of something happening to you, not now that I've just got you back." He patted her on the arm and gave her a quick buss on the cheek. "You just hold down the fort, okay? I predict the Willard White gang is going to be calling in all day needing your guidance. Meanwhile, I'll call you the minute I know something."

She sighed. "All right. Oh, and, Wyatt?" she said. "Also Jim. Don't forget about him."

"No chance, Tam." He was putting on his coat. "He's at the top of my list."

"That was that same detective with the Hunt Club," Lola Sanchez told her husband after she'd shut the door to his private office at the Mission Street Coalition. "He wanted to know what we did after the COO meeting. And then he asked about last Tuesday, a week ago, the night Dominic was killed. He didn't say so, but I'm sure he'll be calling you, maybe next."

Lola, tightly wound even when she was at her most relaxed, was in nowhere near any kind of a calm state at the moment. The color was high in her strong, attractive Aztec face; her black hair, normally swept back and up, had come out where she'd pulled at it during her call with Mickey.

Jaime was up and around his desk before she'd even finished. He got her down on the couch against the side wall and sat next to her, holding both her hands in both of his. "You don't need to worry, love. Len will not let anything happen to us. We have an understanding."

"Yes, but we've had understandings with him before. He really looks out for no one but himself. You know this. We know it. We've seen it."

Jaime, poker-faced, squeezed his wife's hands. Without question, Lola was right, and Len Turner's character worried him deeply, but the ugly truth was that if you wanted to be in the game in San Francisco, Turner was your go-to guy. He controlled much of the money and enforced most of its distribution.

But of more immediate concern was his wife's propensity to panic. Jaime himself didn't necessarily believe that because a private investigator wanted to know what they'd been doing on the nights of the two murders, he had any actual suspicions. And beyond that, a private investigator was not local or federal law enforcement. No one had any real reason to be looking at anything he or his wife had done, but Lola's temperament was always a consideration.

According to plan, she was going to be running Mission here in a few more weeks or months, and by the time that happened — if it was going to happen — she was going to have to learn to carry the weight of that responsibility without letting it crush her. Sometimes in this business, Jaime knew, you had to play fast and loose with some of the rules. You had to work with the Len Turners and even the Dominic Comos of the world, difficult though they could be. This was the big leagues, and coolness in the face of challenge and adversity was one of the hallmarks of leadership. And success.

He leaned in and gave her a light kiss. "Just forget about Len Turner," he said. "The main thing is that you and I don't contradict anything that either of us says. We have a consistent story and no one will even think to question it. So what did you tell this person you'd exactly done Monday after the meeting? So that I can say the same thing. I do hope and trust that, whatever it was, you said you were with me the whole time. *¿Sí?*"

31

The rain had stopped.

As Hunt drove back to his place, he caught sight of a line of blue in the sky to the west. Normally, the coming improvement in the weather would have elevated his mood. But today it could have suddenly turned balmy, bright, and warm and he might not have noticed at all. Instead, as he drove with his jaw clamped shut, he couldn't help but be aware of the dampness of his palms, a dry mouth, the pinch of the gun he still had tucked into his belt at the small of his back.

At some point, he reached behind him, got ahold of the gun, and laid it on the passenger seat beside him.

By the time he pressed the button to open his garage, he was breathing deeply through his nose, all of his senses on full alert, his world closed down in an immediacy to the here and now that would have surprised and possibly embarrassed him if he'd been aware of it. Which he was not.

Even before he actually entered, just as he was turning off Brannan, he saw that Alicia's car was still parked up against the right wall of the building, where it had been when he'd come in this morning. He sucked in a lungful of air and let it out in relief.

Again, his eyes scanned the space in front of him. Seeing no movement, or even a shadow that he could not account for, he shut off the car's engine, at the same time pressing the button on his visor to lower the garage door again. He opened the door to the Cooper and listened for a moment. Nothing. The screen savers on his three computers, all beach and ocean scenes, glowed over across his basketball court. Grabbing the gun, he stepped out of the car and closed the door behind him. Taking off the safety, he started walking to the house, his gun hand in his jacket pocket.

It occurred to him, now much too late, that maybe he should have called to see if Devin and Sarah were nearby at the Hall of Justice, and could come by — it was only a few blocks — to accompany him when he went in. Gone from his mind was the slightest thought of providing her sanctuary from the police any longer.

But he'd already announced his presence by opening his garage. There was nothing for him to do now but press ahead. When he got to the door that led to the part of the warehouse he lived in, he knocked, and almost at the same instant, the door flew open in front of him.

"Oh, God." Alicia's hand at her mouth, her eyes wide. "Thank God it's you," she said. "I heard the garage and was just standing here inside, afraid to move. Scared to death, really."

Hunt released the tightness of his grip on the gun in his pocket. "You and me both," he said.

"I can understand me being frightened," she said. "But what are you afraid of?"

"Lots of things. But right up there at the top is coming into my home when I know it's not empty."

"Yeah. That could be creepy. I could see that."

"I'm sure you could. But in this case it's not hypothetical."

When Hunt's meaning hit her, her face clouded over. "You're not saying you're really afraid of me, are you?"

"I don't know if *afraid* is exactly the right word. For the time being, let's go with *cautious.*"

"But that doesn't make sense."

"By the same token, it's not something that you're going to talk me out of."

"You can't think I killed Dominic."

"I can't? Why not?"

"Just because . . . because you can't. I didn't."

"That's what Mickey says too."

"Well, Mickey's right. You ought to believe him, if not me."

"It's not a question of believing."

"It's not? What is it, then?"

"It's opportunity, motive, access to the murder weapon, or weapons."

A brittle, small laugh escaped into the space between them. "Oh, so I'm a suspect in two murders now? Dominic and Nancy, I suppose."

"While we're at it," Hunt said, "maybe three."

"Sure, why not?" she snapped out, then shook her head in a very convincing show of disgust. "Please."

But Hunt wasn't in any kind of conciliatory mood. "You want to step back and let me in? Then we can continue this discussion."

She backed away from the door, pulling it along with her. Hunt stepped over the threshold, threw a quick glance first over her shoulder down the hallway to the right, then over to his left. "Okay," he said, reaching for the doorknob and closing it behind them.

"Who's the third murder victim?" she asked.

"We'll get to that," Hunt said. "Meanwhile, what I'd like you to do is go down to the TV room and sit there for a minute and wait for me. I'll be right with you."

"Has someone else been killed?" she asked. "If somebody was killed last night, I was with Mickey the whole time. I couldn't have killed anybody."

"Maybe not," Hunt said. He pointed. "TV room. Please."

She crossed her arms and stared at his face with ill-disguised hostility for a couple of seconds, then let out a frustrated and angry guttural sound and turned back down the hallway, disappearing where Hunt had asked her to go.

As soon as she'd gone, Hunt went to his bedroom, where, with a mixture of chagrin and relief, he saw that his rug had apparently not been disturbed. Nevertheless, he crossed to the corner of it, pulled it up, and lifted out the board that covered his safe. He twirled the combination wheel, which turned easily, signifying that it was locked.

But, wanting to be sure, he dialed the combination and opened it again, saw his second gun where he'd left it earlier, and then closed and made sure he'd locked it up one more time before he stood and reversed his actions with the board and the rug.

As soon as he appeared in the doorway to the television room, she looked up. Scrunched over as though she had a stomachache, her elbows on her knees and her hands clasped in front of her, she appeared suddenly small, waiflike. And all the more beautiful for her apparent vulnerability — her doe eyes threatening to overflow, the color high on her cheeks.

For a moment, even in his highly skeptical, antagonistic state, Hunt felt something akin to awe at the power she could wield over men, if only she knew.

But of course she knew, he thought. How could she not know?

"Has someone else died?" she asked. "Please tell me no one else has died."

Taking her very seriously indeed, wishing to minimize the chance that she would try to play him by mere proximity, Hunt sat in the chair farthest from her across the room. "Al Carter says that you offered to take Jim Parr home from the memorial yesterday,"

485

he said. "Is that true?"

She dropped her head as though someone had cut the tendons in her neck. When she looked back up, the tears had broken from her eyes. "Is Jim all right?"

"No one knows," Hunt said. "He never made it home."

She closed her eyes, shook her head back and forth a couple of times. "I didn't take him home," she said. "He didn't want to go home. He wanted to go out to Ortega. That's where I dropped him off."

This news, whether or not it was true, sent a jolt of electricity up Hunt's back. "What time was this?" he asked.

"I'm not sure exactly. One, one-fifteen, somewhere in there."

"What did he say he wanted to do there? At Ortega?"

"He didn't say specifically. He just wanted to walk around and talk to people. He still knew a lot of people out there. One of them might have heard something or seen something, or just knew something, that might help Mickey. And you. He really wanted to help get the guy who'd killed Dominic if he could, and he thought there might be some chance up there. But when we got there, the place was all closed up — we realized for the memorial, of course. The staff was downtown."

"So what'd you do? With Jim, I mean."

"I told him I'd take him home. But he wanted to stay out there."

"In the rain?"

"There's a pizza place down on Irving, near Nineteenth. I dropped him down there. He said he'd wait it out and go back down to Ortega when the building re-opened. I tried to talk him out of it, that he should just go home, but no luck."

"So you left him at this pizza place? You're saying somebody might remember seeing him there?"

"I don't know how long he would have stayed, but somebody'd probably remember. One of the workers. Maybe you could call there and ask if an old guy came in alone a little after lunchtime? See how long he stayed." She met his gaze with a hard one of her own. "And I know you could say that I hung around and picked him up when he came out, but I didn't do that, Mr. Hunt. I went home and got ambushed by Juhle and Russo and then, when they left, I threw my clothes into my car and called in sick to work and got out of my apartment and went to find Mickey. That's what I did. I left Jim at the pizza place."

Hunt had to admire her skill and tenacity.

This was another perfectly plausible scenario — albeit a very difficult one to verify definitively — that she'd pulled together on the spot, all the while flawlessly acting out her part as a damaged and falsely accused victim. On the other hand, it might after all be the truth. Hunt found himself fighting against the temptation to believe her. "Do you remember the name of this pizza place?" he asked.

"I'm going to guess Irving Pizza."

"And creativity still flourishes," Hunt said.

He pulled his cell phone out, punched in 411, and in a moment had gotten connected. Though it was lunchtime and there was a lot of background noise, the manager found time to come to the phone and listen to Hunt's question, preamble and all. "Yeah," he said. "The old guy was here all right. Came in a little after the lunch rush, ate a small pepperoni, and had most of a pitcher of beer. Nice guy. Jim something, I think. We shot the shit for an hour or so. He left under his own power. Is he all right?"

"We're trying to run him down," Hunt said. "Thanks for your help."

When he hung up, he looked across at Alicia Thorpe.

"I'm not lying," she said. "Not about any of this."

Hunt said, "You lied about Dominic firing you. Did you forget that one?"

She shook her head. "I was afraid. But I told Mickey about that. I told him why I did it. I'd never gotten grilled by the police before. I thought they'd arrest me because it might give me a motive to have killed Dominic."

"No 'might' about it."

"But it wasn't like that. And it wasn't like I even needed the job. I've already got a job, you know. I mean a real, paying job, not that it's making me rich. But I'm okay with that for now. Besides, Dominic didn't just kick me out. He explained the whole thing about Ellen to me. He was really sorry, but he just couldn't deal with his home life anymore with our relationship making Ellen so crazy, even though there was nothing sexual to it."

"Nothing sexual?"

"That's right. Ian can tell you, I —"

"Who's Ian?"

"My brother. He can tell you, I don't do sexual with older guys anymore, especially married older guys. In fact, I don't do much sexual anymore, period. It screws everybody up. Not to mention that it screws me up. I'm kind of hoping I get an actual boyfriend someday, then maybe start over with that stuff. But nobody seems to want to take the time, find out if we get along first. You know?"

"I've heard stories," Hunt said. But this was what he'd steeled himself against, this urge to connect, to believe her. And before he got to that place, he was going to take another shot at breaking her story. "But let me ask you something else: If there was nothing sexual going on with you and Dominic, how do you explain the fact that there was semen on your scarf?"

Again, if this was acting, it was brilliant. She straightened up, her face a mask of confusion. "Is that true?"

"Yes."

"The police didn't tell me that."

"No. They sometimes don't tell you everything they know all at once. They're hoping maybe you'll slip and tell them first, before you were supposed to know."

"Well." She did not hesitate, did not even seem overly concerned. "I don't have any idea about that. How am I supposed to know what happened to my scarf after I lost it? Doesn't that make sense that I don't?"

Hunt realized that her relentless apparent guilelessness was wearing him down. She had either thought all of this through to a degree that would have been unique in his experience, or she was in fact telling the truth. Mickey believed her, Jim Parr had believed her, Tamara couldn't bring herself to think ill of her.

"You know what I wish?" she asked him.

"What's that?"

"That I'd just never met Ellen. Then I'm sure none of us would be going through this. At least certainly not me."

Hunt felt an unexpected little frisson of interest at these words. They made him recall his first meeting with Ellen Como, when she'd set his own mind — and by extension Juhle's and Russo's, since Hunt had passed it along to them — onto the idea that Dominic had been in love with Alicia, certainly a believable scenario given his reputation and her desirability. But what had never quite registered with Hunt was he had accepted this bare fact — Dominic's love of Alicia — because he'd taken Ellen's word for it.

The other bare fact — from Hunt's personal experience — was Ellen's enmity toward her husband, and her rage and jealousy at Alicia for being young and beautiful.

"How did you even meet her?" Hunt asked. "I'd heard she didn't have much to do with Dominic's work."

491

"She didn't. But one of the causes she did believe in was the Sanctuary House — battered women and their kids. And back when I first came on, Nancy Neshek had their big yearly do at her place and it was my night off and I thought — well, Dominic thought also, since I was just starting to work on my networking — that I ought to go. Besides, the rest of the Sunset professional staff was going, too, so I wouldn't be all alone with just people I didn't know. It would be fun, and great food — always a good thing.

"But then Dominic, just being his usual charming self, you know, he kind of pulled me away from Lorraine and the other Sunset women and escorted me over specially to introduce me to Ellen as one of his new drivers, trying to make me feel at home, and I could just tell from the second she laid eyes on me that she was going to make trouble if she could. I mean, I was wearing this nice simple black cocktail dress — totally appropriate since it's this like formal party — and Ellen looks me up and down and says something like, 'Oh, hello, dear. Is that the new driver's uniform?' or some such bullshit. I could tell she wanted to scratch my eyes out, and this was long before Dominic and I had any relationship at all. So later, when we got to be friends, I guess he'd mention me sometimes, and she didn't forget. She wasn't going to be happy until I was toast."

As he listened to this, Hunt's eyes had gone vacant and faraway. For one thing, almost without his conscious assent, he found that he had crossed over the line regarding Alicia. She sat facing him with no agenda and no sense of drama, just telling him what she knew as an unadorned truth.

And something else besides.

"Mr. Hunt?"

"I'm here."

"Is everything all right?"

"No," he said. "Not everything. Do you think Jim went to Sunset after he got finished at Irving Pizza?"

"Absolutely. If he made it. But it's only a few blocks, so he should have."

Hunt made the quick count in his head. San Francisco's east-to-west streets run south through the avenues in alphabetical order; Irving at Nineteenth was therefore only six blocks from Ortega at Nineteenth. An easy walk, even for an old man with a beer buzz in a light rain.

"Mickey's out there now," Hunt said. "At Sunset, using their phone to check some alibis. I've got to make another phone call."

32

"I'm here with her now," Hunt told Mickey. "She's fine."

"Did she drive Jim home yesterday?"

"No." Hunt paused. "She drove him out there."

"Where?"

"Where you are right now. Sunset."

"But he promised me . . ." Mickey stopped midthought. A promise might be a promise, but another cliché holds that a promise is made to be broken. And Mickey knew which one Jim had accessed yesterday. "That wily bastard. So where is he now?"

"That's what I'm calling you about. We still don't know. He hasn't come home as of a half hour ago. The campus was closed when they got there, him and Alicia. So she dropped him off at a place called Irving Pizza. . . ." Hunt filled him in on it.

"And you believe that?"

"It happened," Hunt said. "I called the

494

place. The manager corroborates it. He remembers him."

Mickey hesitated. "So . . . you believe *her?*"

"Starting to. Maybe."

"Whoa. Rein in that enthusiasm, Wyatt."

"It's under control. But what would really help is I need to talk to Al Carter, as soon as you can find him. Is he up there today?"

"He was. He might still be."

"Okay. So find him first, then see if anybody up there saw Jim."

"No." Lorraine Hess was in the middle of a celery-and-carrot-stick lunch at her desk. "I never saw him. And I would have loved to have seen him, since apparently I missed him at the memorial too. He's a wonderful man. Are you sure he was here?"

Mickey shook his head. "No. I know where he was at around two, maybe two-thirty, but not if he ever actually made it down here. Would you mind if I ask around?"

"Not at all. Do whatever you need to do." She took a quick nibble of carrot. "Most of the staff didn't get back here until closer to three, though, just so you know. We opened up again at around three-fifteen. So maybe he got here and didn't want to wait. Especially if he was outside in yesterday's weather."

"I realize that," Mickey said. "And all of this may be a false alarm anyway. Jim's been known to stay out overnight before. He also promised me he wouldn't come out here asking questions and bothering people, so maybe on his way his conscience started to eat at him a little. Though, knowing him, that's unlikely."

"He always did have a mind of his own." Hess spread her palms, gave him a sympathetic smile. "Well, if there's anything I can do, anything you need . . . you're sure you're up to all this running around?"

Mickey tried without much success to put on a reassuring face. "My head's felt better, but I'll be fine."

"Somebody out in the cubicles might have some painkiller."

"I appreciate that. Maybe I'll just go and see what I can find."

He walked out into the lobby and noticed that the makeshift table where they'd earlier been preparing the pledge-card mailing was now doubling as a kind of study hall for half a dozen pairs of tutors and their students. Limping over to them, head truly pounding again, he knocked at one end of the table. "Excuse me," he said, as twelve pairs of eyes turned to him, "did any of you notice an older guy hanging around here yesterday afternoon, inside the building or out? About six feet, skinny, maybe seventy years old?"

A sea of blank faces stared back at him. Not much of a surprise.

On his phone call, Hunt had told Mickey to locate Al Carter if he could and ask him to give a call. After he'd done that, Mickey was to abandon his alibi search and phone calls to COO members and devote his time to trying to discover what had happened to Jim. His disappearance, Hunt had made clear, was now looking more and more as though it might be somehow related to this investigation, and this was anything but good news. In fact, the new development had seemed so immediate and important to Mickey that he'd totally forgotten that his boss had told him — first — to find Carter and give him the message to call Hunt. Then Mickey was to start looking for Jim, getting a line on where he'd gone after Irving Pizza if he could.

Suddenly Mickey realized he'd forgotten the first part of the assignment. Back in the administrative cubicles where he'd been making his phone calls, he got some aspirin and learned that Carter was back in the parking lot — the city had returned the limo and he had gone out to make sure they hadn't damaged it too badly.

Mickey found him sitting alone behind the wheel, apparently sleeping in the new-minted and welcome sunshine. The front windows were down and Mickey hesitated, then started to walk with his halting steps up to the driver's side. When he was about five feet away, Carter spoke through his closed eyes. "The sound of your walking gives you away. Tell me I got the reward."

"Sorry. Not yet. But my boss would like you to give him a call. You might be getting close."

Mickey punched in Hunt's number on Carter's cell phone and handed the instrument back. He then moved away, out of earshot, and sat on the asphalt, his back up against the building, and settled into a drowsy semi-numbness in the warming sunshine. In spite of himself, he dozed off. Seconds, or minutes, later, he started awake with Carter still on the phone, his side of the discussion consisting mostly of a series of yeses and noes. Except for his closing phrase, when Carter said, "I never thought of that."

Then Carter walked over to where Mickey sat, and with a shrug, handed the phone down to him.

Hunt's voice shimmered with intensity as he gave Mickey his new marching orders, and whether it was that or the short nap he'd slipped into or the aspirin kicking in, Mickey felt a sudden sense of clarity and purpose.

Hunt knew that Jim had already been drinking when he left Irving Pizza. Then the rain had come on at least close to the time that he was supposed to have started walking down to Ortega. It wasn't unreasonable to assume that a shower had caught up with him and driven him inside again, to another bar on the way. Hunt had Googled bars in the neighborhood and had located seventeen of them within walking distance of the Ortega campus. And now he gave Mickey those names and addresses.

At least these were places to look.

When he rang off, Mickey looked up at Carter and asked, "So what'd he say to you?"

And Carter replied, "He told me not to tell you."

Devin Juhle, Sarah Russo, and Wyatt Hunt met at Lou the Greek's, where they took an empty booth in the back. During their lunch in their car, Sarah had decided to phone Morton's. That call had revealed that Alicia

Thorpe had called in sick with the flu. She'd be out at least through the weekend, which, with her normal days off, meant until the following Wednesday. To both Juhle and Russo, this was a good enough sign that she'd gone underground or fled, and so the inspectors canceled their canvassing of Neshek's neighborhood and arranged this meet with Hunt. Now the priority was to turn up the burners under Thorpe and bring her in for questioning, if they could find her.

"Hey," Hunt said, "people get sick."

Russo, a deep frown in place, took a good pull at her lemonade. "True," she said, "but she's not home in bed trying to get better. She's not at her brother's. She's not in the hospital. We're assuming she's not with your boy, Mickey, either."

Hunt kept his head down and refrained from comment.

"So what's that leave?" Juhle asked. "She's on the run."

"Maybe you scared her off yesterday," Hunt said. "She knew you had the scarf. It was only a matter of time."

Juhle was tearing his cocktail napkins into tiny pieces. "Shit."

Russo nodded. "Shit is right. We had her."

"She'll turn up," Juhle said.

"Maybe in our lifetime," Russo retorted.

Hunt noticed the obvious tension between the two inspectors, perhaps brought about by Juhle's reluctance — due to his recent history, mostly with Gina Roake — to haul Alicia downtown to talk to her in one of the homicide interrogation rooms, where, due to the intimidating setting, results were often easier to obtain.

"So we wanted to get you and Mickey and even his sister on it too," Russo added. "All of them know a lot of the same people, don't they? We need you to put out the word."

"Absolutely," Hunt said, "we'll get right on that." Then, changing the subject, "Meanwhile, while we're all here having such fun together, you manage to dig up anything on Keydrion?"

"Ah, Keydrion," Juhle said. "How did you get to him?"

Hunt shrugged. "He's a colonel or something in the Battalion out of Sunset, but he's hanging around with Len Turner, and I was kind of wondering what his role was. You get anything on him?"

"He's clean," Juhle said. Then added, "As an adult. 'Course, he's only been out off the youth farm for seven months, so he's barely had time to get his sea legs back. As a kid, though, he was reasonably badass. Went in for manslaughter when he was sixteen, though there was some question about maybe it should have gone down as murder one. The DA almost charged him as an adult, but I hear our friend Mr. Turner applied some influence and suddenly Keydrion needed rehab and consolation."

"You think Keydrion is somehow involved in all this?" Russo asked.

"Not impossible," Hunt said. "But I wouldn't mind knowing for sure."

"I wouldn't mind knowing anything for sure," Juhle said.

Hunt didn't miss a beat. "Anthony," he said.

"What's Anthony?"

"My middle name. Something you can be sure of."

Juhle just shook his head while Russo gave Hunt a dead eye. "I appreciate that you're worried about him, Wyatt, but Keydrion's a low priority for us," she said. "We're looking for Alicia Thorpe, and if you want to be any help to us, you'll be doing that too."

"You putting out a bulletin?" Hunt asked.

Russo's head slowly tracked its way back and forth. "Can't. Not yet. Not officially. Officially, we just want to talk to her again."

Juhle said, "But first we've got to find her."

Hunt nodded. "All right. I'm with you guys. We'll see what we can do."

Hunt sat in his office with his stomach in a knot. After the last half hour, if Juhle and Russo ever found out, even after the fact, that Alicia was or had been at his place, he was dog meat. It was not impossible that he could face charges for obstructing justice or anything else they wanted to throw at him, and earn himself some jail time. And that's if he was *right.*

If he was wrong — if the inspectors were right and Alicia was in fact a multiple murderer, as he himself had believed until only a couple of hours ago — it might be much worse than that.

But he hadn't been able to come clean with them. He couldn't even include them in his slowly forming plan, because that plan depended on what Mickey discovered — on what he *had* to discover — and Hunt hadn't yet heard back from him. From where Hunt sat right now, from what Alicia and then Al Carter had told him, he only had a strong inkling of the truth, not a forged linkage that could withstand any assault.

He had to wait. He could only wait.

And the waiting was doubly excruciating because if Mickey came back with the answer Hunt was hoping for, the result he expected, it was the last thing he actually wanted, because it almost assuredly meant that Jim Parr was dead.

"Come on, Mickey," he said aloud. "Come on."

Another cleverly named place on Noriega Avenue, the Noriega Lounge, was the closest bar north of the Ortega campus, only one block away. Unfortunately, it wasn't on Nineteenth Avenue and couldn't be seen from that main thoroughfare, and Mickey had decided to be his usual thorough self and start all the way south by San Francisco State University and move north to Golden Gate Park.

He'd already made eight stops by the time he got to the Noriega at four o'clock. Mickey thought that although it was rather generally unsung, the place might in fact be the location of "San Francisco's Happiest Happy Hour," which would formally begin in a half hour — two-for-one drinks, nothing over two bucks, and free hors d'oeuvres. A decent mixed crowd was getting itself in the mood to get more in the mood, a loud sound system with a very strong bass boost played disco music, and two silent televisions — one featuring Oprah, and the other ESPN — vied for space and attention over the bar.

Every stool was taken.

Mickey found a spot suitable for standing between two stools and sidled himself up into it. His cast brushed up against his left-hand neighbor, a black-leather-jacketed, bearded biker with chains hanging off his belt loops.

Whirling on his stool, he started with "Hey, watch —" and then caught sight of Mickey's eye, the cast. " 'Scuse me," he said, moving down a few inches and giving Mickey a little more room. "You okay, dude?"

"Hanging in there," Mickey said. "Car wreck."

"Fucking blind four-wheelers," the biker said. "Never watchin' out for the other guy. Hey, Claudio!" he yelled down the bar. "Set my pal up here." He stuck out his hand. "I'm Ivan. What are you drinking?"

"Mickey. Just a Coke's fine. I'm working."

Ivan laughed heartily. "You're working *here?* I want your job. I just about live here, man, and nobody's offering to pay me." The bartender appeared across the smooth cherry plank. "Claudio," Ivan said, "this here's Mickey. He's working. Give him a Coke." Then, back to Mickey. "What are you working on?"

"Trying to find somebody," he said. He pulled out his wallet and flipped to the one picture of Jim that he happened to have. It was eight years old, taken at Tamara's graduation, all three of them in the photo.

"I'll take the babe on the right," Ivan said.

"She's not missing," Mickey said. "She's my sister."

"All the better. And I mean it," Ivan persisted. "I'll meet her anytime."

"I'll give her the message," Mickey said. "But who I'm looking for is the old guy in the middle. Might have stopped by in here for a drink yesterday about this time, maybe a little earlier. Maybe alone. Maybe with somebody."

Ivan turned on his stool and took the picture out of Mickey's hand, held it up to catch a little more light from the window behind them. "I can't really say for sure. He's a little familiar. But, hey, half of us in here today were here yesterday too." So he yelled again down the bar. "Hey, Claudio! Get your ass down here. Check out this picture, in the middle. Isn't this the guy got all fucked up in here yesterday?"

33

"Mrs. Como? Hello. This is Wyatt Hunt."

"What's happened? Tell me they've arrested her."

"If you mean Alicia, no, ma'am. Not yet."

Hunt heard her sigh. "I can't imagine what's taking them so long when it's so clear to me."

"Well, that's why I'm calling. The inspectors share your frustration. Especially when they think they've got almost everything they need to get it sewn up."

"Then what's the delay about?"

"That's the question. I saw them this afternoon and they thought maybe they could move things along a bit more quickly if you and some of the other witnesses would agree to meet with them again in one place and all of you go over the information you've given in a little more detail."

"I don't know what that would be. I've already told you everything I know."

"I realize that. But as you say, you told me. Which means the police got it second-hand. I might not have asked you all the right questions. Or put together the information from all the other sources." Hunt paused. "We're not talking much more than an hour or two."

"And what other witnesses?"

"Al Carter. Lorraine Hess. Jimi and Lola Sanchez."

"What about them?"

"Well, they've all cooperated with the police to some degree or another."

"With information against the Thorpe girl, you mean?"

"I can't absolutely confirm that until the arrest is a done deal, Mrs. Como. The inspectors don't want to have the news get out before the suspect's in custody, which I think you'll agree is understandable."

"Well, yes. I suppose it is."

Hunt wasn't sure that he had her yet and thought he saw a way to sweeten the deal. "There's also the issue of the reward," he said.

A silence hung on the line.

"What about the reward?" she asked.

"You'll remember that in our interview, you said that if the information you provided proved useful to the investigation, you wanted to be sure you were in line to stake a claim to the reward? Well, it turns out it looks like there are going to be multiple claimants. You know Len Turner is administering the distribution?"

"Of course. I gave him my money, too, you might recall."

"That's right. Well, Mr. Turner thought, and I agree, that it would be worthwhile if the major potential claimants talked on the record with the inspectors present so there wouldn't be any dispute later about the relative value of the respective contributions to solving the case. But where I don't agree with Mr. Turner is that he didn't seem to think that your information about Ms. Thorpe's relationship with your husband and her subsequent firing on that last day rose to the level of real evidence."

"That's ridiculous," she said. "What could be more real than that?"

"Of course," Hunt said. "That's my feeling too. Which is why I thought you'd want to be down here to defend your position. Maybe I shouldn't tell you this, but I think you need to be aware that Mr. Carter corroborated the fact that your husband fired Ms. Thorpe on that last day, so he'll be making a reward claim on much of the same information you gave us first."

"That's just not right."

"No, ma'am, it's not."

"So where is this meeting? And what time?"

He told her, and then he hung up and looked around his kitchen table at the group he'd assembled — Alicia, Mickey, Al Carter, and Gina Roake to act as Alicia's attorney should the need arise. "Well," he said, "that's number three. Two to go. Then Devin."

"Sometimes it worries me, Wyatt," Roake said, "how easily you manipulate, cheat, and lie."

The comment was simply meant to break the tension, and to some degree it worked. At least it brought the beginning of a grin to Hunt's face. "It's a concern," he said, "but I try not to let it get me down."

Hunt said, "Pick up, Devin. It's important."

After a few seconds, the inspector's voice came on. "In the middle of dinner, Wyatt, this better be good."

"Good enough," Hunt said. "What if I were to tell you I've found Alicia?"

"Have you?"

"I'm asking you. What if?"

"I'd say keep an eye on her until I can get to where she is and put some cuffs on her.

Where is she?"

"You'd arrest her? Even without the DNA on the scarf?"

"We got that just before I went home today. It's Como's. So we got her."

"Except, as it turns out, you still don't know where she is."

"But you do."

"I never said that."

"Don't get wise, Wyatt. Where is she?"

"I could get her to come here."

"Again. Where?"

"Here. Home. The warehouse."

"Okay. So do that."

"I will try." Hunt paused. "Provided you promise you won't arrest her."

Juhle's laugh exploded in the phone. "And why, pray, would I agree to that?"

"Because I'm also going to have your murderer."

"You are, are you? And who's that?"

"I could tell you, but it wouldn't do me or Alicia any good."

"She's Alicia now, is she?"

"She's also my client."

"She's *what?*"

"You heard me."

"When did that happen?"

"That doesn't matter either. Not to you. What matters is you promise you don't arrest her."

"Until when?"

"Until I get you the murderer."

Another small bark of humor. "Well, I'm going to say 'hell, no' to that, Wyatt. I have evidence against Thorpe and if I see her, I'm going to arrest her."

"Then all bets are off."

Juhle paused for a long beat. "You're saying you know who the killer is?"

"I am. I do. And I'm saying if you want to find out, you promise no arrest. End of story."

"And what if you're wrong?"

"I'm not wrong."

"So we take Alicia downtown, then if you prove we're wrong, we let her go."

"Nice try, Dev. But what really happens is once you get her booked, it's almost impossible to arrest anybody else. Why? Because not only have you just given your second suspect a built-in defense — 'Oh, it was Alicia Thorpe last week, Your Honor, but this week it's *really* my client X who did it' — but also because a second arrest for the same crime makes you and Sarah both look stupid."

"No, that wouldn't —"

"Bullshit. Listen to me. You arrest her now, Alicia's charged with specials" —

multiple murder special circumstances — "and gets no bail. The DA says she can argue some other dude did it at her trial. But meanwhile, once Alicia's in jail, your real killer is tipped to all the evidence and can make their own story tighter, if in fact they don't leave town. That's what really happens, Dev, and you damn well know it. So I can't tell you who the murderer is. You'll just say 'thanks for playing' and arrest my client. I've got to show you. And I can do that. But first I need your word. No arrest. Nonnegotiable."

A long silence. Then, "Last, best, and only offer, Wyatt. You get your dog and pony show. I'll come over, but if I do, somebody's going to jail. I'm thinking it's Thorpe, but I'll give you a chance to convince me it's someone else." After another short pause, he asked, "Where is she now?"

"Doesn't matter," Hunt said. "A secret place. Mickey found her. But the point is I've got him bringing her down here."

"Why would she do that? Come down there?"

"Because Mickey's convinced her this is the safest place she could be. She believes Mickey."

"Shit."

"You keep saying that."

"You know why? It keeps being appropriate. Shit shit *shit.* What am I supposed to do about Sarah?"

"I'm not sure she could agree to the conditions."

"So now I cut my partner out of it. I know you're not a cop, Wyatt, but that kind of behavior is frowned upon down at the Hall."

"Yeah, well, I appreciate that. But what's happening is happening now. This is all the warning I can give you."

Wyatt heard the soft exhale of resignation and decision. "Okay," Juhle said. "Twenty minutes, half hour."

"That ought to work," Hunt said.

By eight-thirty, Hunt had the place arranged the way he wanted it, with a nice democratic circle of eleven folding chairs set up on his basketball court. In the end, he'd cajoled, connived, or otherwise convinced all of the principals to converge on his warehouse at nine o'clock so that, depending on what Hunt had told them, they could provide more detailed information, or argue for their portion of the reward, or fortify their alibis, or simply get caught up on the progress of the investigation to date.

Or, finally, in the case of Devin Juhle, to

514

arrest the real murderer.

Now Hunt went back into the residential side, to his kitchen where Roake, Carter, Alicia, and Mickey remained seated at the table with a palpable air of tension surrounding them. "Almost time," Hunt said lightly. His own nerves were stretched to the breaking point, but he couldn't show that, not now. "Everybody still loose and ready to have some fun?"

In fact, nobody looked that way. They all looked like they'd been talking about deadly serious issues among themselves while he set up his chairs. Roake, the group's obvious spokesperson, looked around the table, then up at him. "We've been thinking it might be better after all if Alicia wasn't here, Wyatt."

Hunt drew a short breath. "If she's not here," Hunt said in as reasonable a tone as he could dredge up, "she gets herself arrested anyplace they find her outside. Here I've got Devin's word he won't touch her."

"And you believe that?" Carter asked.

"Absolutely."

With a deep frown, Carter shook his head.

"Just imagine, though, Wyatt," Roake said. "What if he called Russo and told her? She didn't make you any promise. She comes in with him and he just shrugs and says it's out of his control."

"That's not what's going to happen."

"But what if it does, Wyatt? And Alicia goes downtown. As her lawyer, I don't know if I can in good conscience let her stay here."

"As her lawyer," Hunt said, "you've got to let her stay here. It's her best chance to stay out of jail."

"But, Wyatt," Mickey put in, "she won't get arrested if we go hide out again someplace else."

"Guys, understand. The second she's not here, she's back as the prime suspect, and then it's only a matter of time." Hunt straightened up to his full height. "We've been through this already," he said. "I appreciate all of your concerns, but Alicia has to be here for this to work. If Juhle gets here and she's gone, he walks out and the whole exercise becomes futile. The only reason he stays is because if my idea doesn't work, then and only then he handcuffs Alicia."

"Swell," Mickey said.

"But that's not going to happen," Hunt said. "If everybody shows up, this is a lock."

"And if they don't?" Alicia finally found her voice. "What then?"

"I've motivated them all sufficiently," Hunt said. "They can't *not* come."

"That's the other thing," Gina said. "If

you're right, one of these people you've invited here tonight has already killed twice. You don't think there's an element of risk?"

"There's an element of risk to crossing the street. I've got to believe we've got strength in numbers here if any one person starts to get out of hand. And remember, Juhle will be armed. And," he added, "so will I."

Roake rolled her eyes. "So you do think something could happen?"

"I know something might happen, Gina. Something unexpected could always happen. But here, tonight, I doubt it's going to be violence. I'm carrying my gun because I want to make sure it's as close to foolproof as it can be. Just covering the bases, making sure we've got these contingencies thought through."

"Thinking a plan through doesn't necessarily prevent it from falling apart."

"No," Hunt said, "I know that. Of course not. But this is our best chance to get Alicia out from under this cloud of suspicion and get on with her life. We all agreed on this a couple of hours ago. This is the way it has to go down. And it has to be now. Alicia" — he turned to her — "are you still with us?"

She forced a weak smile. "With everything you've said, I don't see that I have another choice."

"That's the right answer," Hunt said.

The buzzer at the back door sounded, loud as a klaxon in the enclosed space of the kitchen. Everyone at the table reacted with a start — even Hunt had a reflexive jump and then smiled at his nerves. "Here we go," he said, walking across to check the peephole, and then opening the door to Devin Juhle, all by himself.

Juhle hated this.

He imagined himself in front of the Police Commission, explaining how he had gotten involved in this half-assed operation. And without his partner or any other backup. This was not how it was done, fraught with risk and uncertainty for everyone involved. He wondered, and sincerely doubted, if any other cop he knew would make the kind of promise he'd made to Hunt; if any other homicide inspector, with an imminent arrest of his prime suspect in his pocket, would have postponed the moment and agreed to this amateur-hour charade. His only consolation was that when Hunt's scenario failed — as it surely would — he would then pick up the Thorpe woman. Of course, the fact that Hunt had invited Roake along would complicate that arrest, but not

518

impossibly so. Still, it galled Juhle that Hunt had never even mentioned Roake's presence here as Thorpe's attorney during their phone call. In fact, everything about this felt wrong to him. But, he told himself, that's what happened when you believed your friends.

And people wondered why cops grew so jaded over time. It was because you were either in the brotherhood or you were not. You played by the rules or you didn't.

Somehow Hunt had persuaded him that he had no choice. And that, more than anything else, added to his fury and frustration.

Almost as soon as Juhle had arrived, Hunt suggested that they all come out now to the basketball court. Now Roake, Thorpe, Mickey Dade, and Carter sat together in consecutive chairs while Juhle stood behind them, arms crossed and his shoulder holster unbuttoned, where he could keep his eye on them as well as on whoever entered through the Brannan Street door. The lights were up; the temperature fairly cool, in the mid-sixties, the way Hunt liked to keep it.

They weren't in there and settled for more than three or four minutes when the doorbell for this side of the warehouse rang and Hunt crossed to the door by the garage entrance, opened it up, and said hello to Len Turner and a tall, thin, well-dressed young black man that Juhle guessed must be Keydrion Mugisa.

Inside his jacket, Juhle's hand went to the butt of his duty weapon.

Hunt hadn't invited Keydrion to attend this meeting with Turner, so they had to bring another chair over to add to the circle. Turner, after a barely cordial greeting to Hunt, fell into the role of his voluble and friendly self after he recognized Carter and Juhle. Lorraine Hess had met up with Jaime and Lola Sanchez outside on the street and they came in together a few minutes after Turner. The last arrival, and the only one to make any kind of a stink — when she saw that Alicia Thorpe was in attendance — was Ellen Como. But Hunt got her calmed down and seated her next to him on his right. Juhle took the left seat. So around the circle, it went Juhle, Roake, Alicia, Mickey, Al Carter, Lorraine Hess, Jaime and Lola Sanchez, Turner, Keydrion, Ellen Como, and Wyatt Hunt. In the relative chill, all of the latter arrivals kept their coats on.

The low hum of conversation gradually faded to silence and all eyes went to Hunt. "I would thank all of you for coming down here tonight," he began, "but the truth is that none of you actually did so because I asked you to. In fact, you're all here for your own very good reasons, and they're all about your own self-interest. Some of you — Mr. Carter, Mrs. Como, Ms. Hess — want to make your claim to all or a portion of the reward. Some of you — Mr. Turner, Mr. Mugisa, Mr. and Mrs. Sanchez, and again, Mr. Carter, want to make sure that the police understand and believe your alibis for the night of the two murders, and let's make no mistake, the same person killed Dominic Como and Nancy Neshek."

"That's right. And she's right here," Ellen Como blurted out. "We all know that." Looking across to Juhle, she pointed at Alicia. "I don't know why you're not arresting her, Inspector, why you haven't done it already. Can there be any doubt? We all know what she did and why —"

Hunt held out a hand toward her. "Mrs. Como, please."

"No, she's right, Hunt," Jaime Sanchez said. "What the hell?"

Hunt shot his gaze around the circle. "Inspector Juhle is here to make an arrest tonight, all right, but he's promised it's not going to be Alicia Thorpe unless we fail to provide him with somebody else."

"What are you saying?" Turner demanded. "That one of us — ?"

"I think you can figure that out for yourself, sir," Hunt said.

Next to him, Ellen Como stood up. "I didn't come down here to have to take this kind of abuse. I'm the victim here. My husband was the one who was killed. Doesn't anybody care about that? I'm not going to be any party to this." She turned toward the door and pushed her chair out of her way.

"Mrs. Como!" Hunt spoke up. "No one's accusing you of anything. Sit back down. Please. We need every one of you here if we're going to get to the truth."

Straight across from Hunt, Lorraine Hess said, "Are you really saying that one of us killed Dominic? And Nancy too?"

"Yes, ma'am," Hunt said. "One of you."

"But I was . . . I was with my son. . . ."

"I didn't say you, Ms. Hess" — Hunt took in the group — "or all of you. I said one of you."

"And you intend to prove this," Turner said, "to Juhle's satisfaction? Right here, right now. How do you intend to do that?"

"By comparing the stories you've told and seeing where they don't agree. But also, a little bit," Hunt replied, "by the process of elimination. You, for example, Mr. Turner. Mr. Mugisa drove you home right after the COO meeting on the night Nancy Neshek was killed. You've got your son and your wife and the other kids who were there building their homecoming float who will swear that you were with them until you went to bed. No one's suggested that you've done anything different, and you can prove that. So you didn't kill Ms. Neshek, and therefore you didn't kill Dominic."

Turner sat back, shaking his head in derision. "Well, of course I didn't. The idea's ridiculous."

"The whole concept is ridiculous," Jaime Sanchez said. "Lola and I went to dinner after that meeting, and then home together."

"Where did you go to dinner?" Hunt asked.

"The Hayes Valley Grill. We walked there from City Hall. They know us there. I'm sure I'll even have a credit card receipt."

"And after that?"

"Jesus Christ!" Turner raised his hands as if in exhortation. "Inspector Juhle, is this the kind of questioning that Mr. Hunt thinks is going to get us anywhere? Do you have any reason to believe that Jimi and Lola Sanchez are any kind of even potential suspects in either of these murders?"

Juhle said, "No, sir. No, I don't." He turned to Hunt. "If this is your idea of breaking the case, Wyatt, maybe you should send these good people home and let me go about doing my job, which is arresting my suspect."

Hunt kept his cool. "Mr. Sanchez," he said, "my apologies to you and your wife. I was using you as an example of Mr. Turner's point about the process of elimination, which I think we can all agree is not too satisfying. Far better is the question of the information we've received, and where what one person told us is contradicted by somebody else." Now Hunt turned in his chair. "For example, Mrs. Como. You told me that your husband was in love with Ms. Thorpe and that —"

Ellen cut him off and snapped back at him. "He was. He told me. There wasn't any doubt about that."

"No, not about that bare fact. Your husband was in love with her, okay. But Alicia swears that they didn't have a physical relationship."

"Well, she's lying. What do you expect?"

"I'm not lying," Alicia said, as Roake put a restraining hand on her arm.

Hunt turned to Ellen and went on. "How do you know Alicia's lying?"

"Because they were caught in the office."

"Making love, you mean?"

"*Fucking,* is what I mean. Fucking is what they were doing, not making love. Don't try to dignify it."

"And where were they doing this?"

"What? What do you mean?"

"I mean, physically, where were they having sex in the office when they were caught?"

"I don't know. How would I know?"

"So how did you know about it in the first place?"

"Well." Her brow clouded, then cleared. "Lorraine told me. I think I even told you that, didn't I, Mr. Hunt?"

"Yes, you did. So, Ms. Hess." He came around to face her. "Let me ask you. Where in the office did you discover Mr. Como and Alicia having sex?"

Hess had straightened in her seat, her hands on her lap. "I don't know." She shook her head. "I wasn't the one who saw them. It was one of my people, one of the young women."

"Do you remember who, exactly?"

"No. It seemed like everybody knew kind of all at once. You know how offices are."

"So you, Ms. Hess, didn't really know for sure firsthand about this physical side to

Alicia's and Dominic's relationship?"

"No. Not firsthand, no."

"And yet you gave this information to Mrs. Como?"

"I thought she needed to know."

Ellen Como spoke up again. "I did need to know, God damn it."

"Yes, well, and Ms. Hess made sure that you did, didn't she?"

"She's a friend. Of course she did."

"Of course." Hunt took a breath, shifted again in his chair. "Mr. Carter, as Dominic's driver, you must have been privy to many of his private thoughts and even secrets, isn't that true?"

"I like to think so."

"Did you ever have occasion to hear him talk about Alicia Thorpe?"

"Yes, frequently, since she started driving him mornings."

"Was he in love with her?"

"Yes. At least, that's what he told me."

"And did he also tell you any details about his love life, if any, with her?"

Carter came out with a dry chuckle. "Only the fact that he didn't have any love life with her."

"That's not true!" Mrs. Como exclaimed. "I know he —"

"No, ma'am. It is true as I know it."

Warming to his topic, Carter brought in the rest of the circle. "He laughed about it, how he had this pure love that neither of them were going to do anything about. They talked about it. How seeing her every day, not being able to touch her, knowing he was never going to be able to touch her, it was just breaking his heart."

Again, Ellen Como couldn't take it. "Bullshit, Al!" she said. "That's just bullshit."

"No, ma'am. That's what he told me."

"Okay, Al," Hunt said. "Let me ask you this. In your eight years driving Dominic, did you ever know him to see other women?"

At this, Carter hesitated, looking first at Ellen Como, then over to Lorraine Hess. "Yes," he said. "Many times."

"Shit! That bastard. That fucking bastard!"

Hunt pressed. "Anybody else at Sunset?"

Another pause, this one lengthy. Finally, Carter looked over to his left again and shrugged. "When I first came on, he and Lorraine were in the middle of a thing."

Ellen Como exploded, *"What? Lorraine."* And stood up.

Hess shot out of her seat, held her arm out as though fending Ellen off. "That's a lie, Ellen! That's a damn lie, Al!"

Juhle was on his feet, arms out to either side as though he were a referee at a boxing match. He pointed to Hess. "Sit down!" and over to Como. "You, too, please, ma'am, right now."

But neither woman sat down. Instead, they stared at each other across the circle. "Lorraine," Ellen Como asked in a near-whisper, "is this true?" She turned. "Al?"

The driver nodded somberly.

Hess was shaking her head. "No, no, no." Pointing at Alicia, her voice quivering with rage, Lorraine Hess went on the attack. "She's the one who was sleeping with him. They were screwing in the car. I know they were. If you look, you'll know I'm telling the truth."

"If you mean look in the limo for evidence, Lorraine," Hunt said, "the police already did that. And they found what you planted there."

"I didn't plant anything. What are you talking about?"

Hunt didn't respond to her, but turned to Carter. "Al, what's the first thing you do every day at work?"

Carter nodded. "Like I told you today, we clean out that limo for my shift. Polish the car, wash the seats, vacuum the rugs."

"And that includes under the seats,

doesn't it?"

"Yes, sir."

"And did you do that the day after you dropped off Mr. Como for the last time?"

"Yes, sir."

"And was there a condom in the car, or a scarf?"

"No, sir. Nothing like that."

"But" — and here Hunt came back to Hess — "in fact, those items are exactly what the police did find. So the reason you were so sure there was evidence in the car, Lorraine, was that you put it there, didn't you?"

Hess seemed rooted to the floor, unable to reply.

"My only question," Hunt went on, "is if you stole the scarf intending to kill Dominic, or if you simply found it later and decided to use it to frame Alicia."

"Lorraine?" Ellen Como asked a last time. "It's you. Could it really have been you?"

Hunt, standing next to Juhle, took a step in Hess's direction. "Do you want to tell us about the federal money, too, Lorraine? Dominic's private safe? He not only broke it off with you, he discovered you'd been taking the money, too, didn't he? He was going to let you go out at Sunset as well."

"This is all wrong," Hess said. "You don't

know this. You can't prove any of it."

"I don't have to prove it, Lorraine. The police will have all the proof they need when they get a search warrant for your bank account, won't they? When they find all the unexplained cash deposits. And when they talk to all the extra help you hired for your son, they're going to find you paid with a lot more cash than you can explain, aren't they? And even if you've got more cash stashed in other bank accounts, they're going to find that, too, aren't they?"

Lorraine Hess put her hands in the pockets of the ski parka she was wearing, then lifted out her right hand, in which she was holding a revolver. Juhle, caught completely off-guard, went to reach for his shoulder holster.

Hunt motioned for Juhle to stop, then turned and spoke calmly to Hess. "What are you going to do now, Lorraine? Kill us all? And then go on the run? Who's going to take care of your son? And how long do you think it's going to take the police to find you?"

Hess stood holding the gun in both of her hands, aiming it squarely at Hunt's chest. Her eyes flitted over to Ellen Como, to Juhle, to Carter and Alicia, and then back to Hunt. No one seemed to be breathing.

But then at last, something shifted in Hess's position, and she slowly began to lower the gun, then finally dropped it with a clatter onto the basketball court's flooring at her feet.

Now staring with a pathetically blotched face at Juhle, she hung her head, wagged it disconsolately from side to side, then looked back at him. "Thank God," she said. "Thank God. It's finally over." She met Juhle's eyes. "I never meant . . . but it doesn't matter what I meant now, does it?"

Hunt had crossed the circle and gotten his hands on the weapon. Now, that threat removed, he looked up at her. "Lorraine," he said. "Jim Parr. Where's Jim Parr?"

For an answer, Hess turned vaguely, almost wistfully, to Juhle. "I wonder if you could send somebody to see if my son Gary's all right? I always worry about those pills I give him when I need him to sleep, that I might have given him too many."

34

Juhle hated this.

He imagined himself in front of the Police Commission, explaining how he had gotten involved in this half-assed operation. And without his partner or any other backup. This was not how it was done, fraught with risk and uncertainty for everyone involved. He wondered and sincerely doubted if any other cop he knew would have made the kind of promise he'd made to Hunt; if any other homicide inspector, with an imminent arrest of his prime suspect in his pocket, would have postponed the moment and agreed to this amateur-hour charade. His only consolation was that when Hunt's scenario failed — as it surely would — he would then pick up the Thorpe woman. Of course, the fact that Hunt had invited Roake along would complicate that arrest, but not impossibly so. Still, it galled Juhle that Hunt had never even mentioned Roake's presence here as Thorpe's attorney during their phone call. In fact, everything about this felt wrong to him. But, he told himself, that's what happened when you believed your friends.

And people wondered why cops grew so jaded over time. It was because you were either in the brotherhood or you were not. You played by the rules or you didn't.

Somehow Hunt had persuaded him he had no choice. And that, more than anything else, added to his fury and frustration.

Almost as soon as Juhle had arrived, Hunt suggested that they all come out now to the basketball court. Now Roake, Thorpe, and Dade sat together in consecutive chairs while Juhle stood behind them, arms crossed and his shoulder holster unbuttoned, where he could keep his eye on them as well as on whoever entered through the Brannan Street door. The lights were up; the temperature fairly cool, in the mid-sixties, the way Hunt liked to keep it.

They weren't in there and settled for more than three or four minutes when the doorbell for this side of the warehouse rang and Al Carter, who for some reason Hunt had designated to greet the guests, crossed to the door by the garage entrance, opened it up, and said hello to Len Turner and a tall, thin, well-dressed young black man that Juhle guessed must be Keydrion Mugisa.

Inside his jacket, Juhle's hand went to the butt of his duty weapon.

The doorbell rang again. As instructed, Carter opened the door again.

Quite clearly, Juhle heard him say, "Hello, Lorraine."

And then he heard the voice of Lorraine Hess as she said, "Hi, Al, you dumb shit."

And then the enormous boom of the shot.

Hunt was over by the residence side of the warehouse and broke for the door, jumping over Carter's prone form. He got outside just as Lorraine Hess was running to get to her car, sitting and idling there at the curb fifty feet up the street, a couple of seconds after the unmistakable report.

"Hold it," he yelled. "Stop!"

Stopping and turning in her tracks, but without any hesitation, she raised her arm and fired another shot. Hunt, seeing her arm coming up, dove sideways away from the building and heard the bullet ricochet off something back at the corner.

Hunt by this time was lying on the pavement, leveling his gun out in front of him, but he found that he could not fire. She was not then firing at him and it was bad luck to shoot in the back even an escaping murderer. To say nothing of the fact that under those conditions, it was nearly impossible to claim self-defense.

Even if it was. Even if she'd just shot at you.

Lorraine Hess got to the door of her car and again he saw her extend her arm, and again he rolled as the shot pinged off the pavement behind him.

Still on the ground, he squeezed off a round in the general direction of her tires. Off to his left, coming out his door, Juhle had his own weapon out, extended in both hands. He got off two quick shots that cracked the windshield before Hess got the car moving, and then Juhle had to jump backward inside the warehouse as she slammed it into gear and tried to run him down, smashing her front bumper into the side of the building, then bouncing off and coming on, faster now and off the curb.

Hunt, in her path now as well, rolled out into the street and the car passed him, missing him by no more than a few inches. He turned to see her disappear around the corner with a squeal of her tires, heard the diminishing roar of the engine as she sped away, and, lying there on the street, then heard Juhle's professional voice talking urgently into his cell phone. "I'm calling to report a shooting victim at around Sixth and Brannan. Ambulance required immediately. Urgent, repeat, urgent."

And then, as he closed up the phone, "Son of a bitch."

It was one week to the day after the arrest of Lorraine Hess.

Wyatt Hunt put down the pages and looked across Gina's small living room to where she sat with her Oban, her legs tucked up under her. "A twenty-two doesn't make an enormous boom," he said. "More like a 'pop.' "

"Everybody's a critic."

"And besides," Hunt went on, "that's not what happened."

"I realize that. But it's damn sure what very easily could have happened, and forcing you to take a good hard look at the other possibilities was kind of my point in doing the exercise. Because actually, it could have been much worse even than this. In my first draft of this, she runs you over and you die too. But then you'd be out of your misery, and I didn't want that."

"You wanted me to suffer?"

"Just a little more. I wanted you to see where this so easily could have gone." Her smile was fleeting, laced with portent. "But just for fun, let me count the ways." She held up a finger. "First, Lorraine doesn't confess and goes home and realizes that she's finished and she shoots her son while he sleeps and then takes her own life. And meanwhile, of course, Devin arrests Alicia."

"Don't be such a softie," Hunt said. "Have something bad happen."

"Something bad is coming right up," she said. "Because maybe you've forgotten about it, but that first shot, Lorraine's first shot as soon as Al Carter opened the door? In my little version of the story, it killed him and he's lying dead on the floor of your place. And guess who the mildly angry Inspector Juhle is going to blame for that homicide — hint, it's not just Lorraine, but the person who set up the encounter in the first place. So the good news is that nobody cares what he thinks because he's going to lose his job for getting involved in this at all. But the bad news is you can't give him a job because you lose your license at least, your shop gets closed up, and you maybe even go to jail. Next, in her ongoing rage and plain old embarrassment at having somebody shot to death in her partner's presence when he was right there to stop it and she would have been there if you hadn't sandbagged him, Sarah Russo comes after me for conspiracy or obstructing justice or some trumped-up charge and I lose my "license too."

"And," Hunt added, "we become another of San Francisco's prominent homeless couples, living out of a Dumpster."

"Laugh if you want, Wyatt, but all of this was *this close* to happening, and I don't see you realizing that."

"That's because it didn't. . . ."

"Oh, and the last thing . . . because Lorraine killed herself when she got home, see above, she never could have told us where she had dumped Jim Parr at Lake Merced after she shot him, and he would have undoubtedly died too."

"And still may."

"True. But maybe dead, or as Billy Crystal would put it, mostly dead, is far preferable to completely and officially dead. They've done studies."

"All right." Hunt crossed a leg and sat back in his chair. "Yep, those all would have been bad things, I agree. But what else would you have had me do, in some future case where I'll be able to apply all these important lessons you're trying to teach me from this one?"

"How about you just call Juhle — or whoever the relevant police figure may be in the future — and tell him what you'd figured out?"

"And then what? In the first place, he doesn't believe me. He thinks I'm blowing smoke at him to protect Alicia. Then, even if he buys what I'm telling him, he's still got no evidence. So he's going to play it by the book. He shows up with twenty-five cops, the SWAT team, a tank, and a helicopter and scares Lorraine away. Or worse, he simply goes and talks to her and she denies it and not only is she on her guard because she knows she's a possible suspect, but Juhle's back at square one —"

"Not exactly. He could have found witnesses at that Noriega bar. Or after they found Jim, dead by this time, he could have gotten a warrant to look for the gun."

"But once she knows they're looking at her, she ditches it."

"They'd eventually have gotten to her, Wyatt."

"I'm not so sure. And in any event, it wouldn't have been soon enough. All of his focus, and Russo's, too, was on Alicia, you remember. At the very least they would have brought her downtown — even with you there lawyering her up — and put her through a very bad time. And she was our client. She was my first responsibility."

"That's another thing, Wyatt: How did she get to be your client?"

"Mickey brought her on. He committed us."

"For how much retainer?"

"I know," he said.

"So how weak is that?"

"Very. Admittedly. But it's what I acted on. Which, in my defense, worked out okay."

"I grant that. But what I'm trying to tell you is you didn't have to take all those risks, to bring all of us together like that."

"I did. I needed Alicia for Devin, Carter for Hess, you for Alicia. Ellen for Hess's lie about seeing Alicia and Dominic doing it. Turner and the Sanchez couple for verisimilitude and to convince Hess it was a charity business meeting, me and Mickey for the party favors. I'd probably do the same thing again under the same conditions."

"Which, luckily, are not likely to recur." She tipped up her Scotch, set the glass down on the end table next to her, then got up and crossed the room, where she leaned down and kissed him. "I'd just like you to try to think about it. Is that asking so much?"

With a straight face, he held up his right hand. "I hereby promise to think about it." He tapped the pages he still held in his lap. "These words have not been in vain."

Still leaning over him, her arms on the

arms of his chair, she looked him full in the face. "I believe I've mentioned," she said, "how it worries me that you lie so easily."

"I'm in therapy for it." Hunt grinned. "Honest."

Jim Parr, in an extremely drunken haze by the reed-lined water's edge at Lake Merced, and thinking they had gotten themselves to this private place so he could get himself fellated by the still reasonably-hot-by-his-standards Lorraine Hess, had taken the .22 brass-jacketed bullet point-blank in the chest. It had passed through his heavy pea-coat, slowed down considerably, nicked his sternum, and been deflected down and slightly to the right, where it had missed a lung and lodged behind a front rib. It had not hit any of his major organs or, more importantly, any arteries.

Nevertheless, between the drink and the bullet, he had gone down like a dead man — enough to fool Hess, anyway — falling back into the muddy reeds, where he lay unmoving and progressively more comatose for the next twenty-eight hours until a police unit found him exactly where Hess had told Juhle he'd be. His pulse was a bare flicker, his body temperature ninety-two, and the paramedics had to resuscitate him twice in the ambulance when he flatlined on the way to the ER at the Kaiser Hospital on Masonic and Geary. His doctor said that his survival was a flat-out miracle, but offered his theory that the exposure and low body temperature had probably saved him. He didn't even have a theory about how he survived the gunshot wound.

For the first few days, Tamara and Mickey had come in to visit him every day and night, but he remained in the ICU, basically unresponsive, and Mickey had stopped coming by at every opportunity, since he truly hated hospitals and Jim wouldn't know he was there anyway. Tamara, though, wanted to be around for when her grandfather woke up, as she believed he would, and she visited whenever she could.

Now, Thursday, six days after Jim's admittance, during the later evening visiting hours, Tamara was sitting by her grandfather's bed a few blocks from their apartment, holding one of his cold hands in both of hers when he opened his eyes for the first time, saw her, squeezed her hand, and smiled feebly.

He started to say something, but could only manage a guttural gurgle.

"It's okay, Jim," Tamara whispered through her enthusiasm. "It's Tam. You're going to be okay." He closed his eyes again for a moment and in that time Tamara pressed the call button by the head of the bed.

Almost immediately a nurse was next to her, checking his vitals, glancing with concern at the monitor.

"He's awake," Tamara said. "He just tried to talk to me." And Jim opened his eyes again. "Maybe he could have some water?"

"Water's always good," the nurse said. She poured a glassful from the pitcher near his bed, put in a straw, and directed it to Jim's mouth.

After swallowing two or three times, he lifted his head slightly and the straw came out. "Where are we?" he asked.

"Kaiser," Tamara said. "You got shot? Do you remember?"

Shaking his head no, Jim closed his eyes again. His chest rose and fell under his blankets. When he opened his eyes again, Tamara thought she detected some vestigial sign of his old spark. "I thought she hit people on the head," he said.

"You do remember."

An infinitesimal nod. "Lorraine."

"Right."

He sighed. "Como and her."

"Yep."

"I thought I remembered that. But I didn't want to say until I was sure."

"You remembered right."

"Mickey told me not to go. But I had to find out."

"That's all right. Don't worry about that now."

"He's gonna bust my ass."

"Probably."

He paused to take a weary breath or two. "But a gun?"

"Her ex-husband's. After the first two, she thought it would be cleaner."

A small ripple of what might have been laughter, or at least ironic amusement, shook him. "And look at me. How do you like that?"

"A lot, Jim. I like it a lot."

He closed his eyes as if savoring the moment. "So where is she now?"

"In jail."

Again, he nodded. Closed his eyes.

"He's tired," the nurse said. "Maybe that's enough for today."

"Okay." Tamara wasn't going to push it. She squeezed his hand again and felt the small but definite response. His mouth creased upward marginally. She stood up and leaned in to plant a kiss on his cheek. "I'll bring in Mickey tomorrow," she whispered. "Meanwhile, you keep getting better."

She started to take her hand out from under his, but suddenly, he squeezed hard enough to hold her and opened his eyes one more time. "Tam?"

"Yeah?"

"You still eating?"

"Every day, Jim. Every day."

"Good. Don't stop that again."

"I won't."

He patted her hand. "That's my big favorite girl." With a final small nod, he closed his eyes once again, and the pressure of his hand holding hers went away.

Watching him, she stood still long enough to see his chest rise and fall a few times, then pulled her hand out from under his and turned for the door.

35

Various legal technicalities and the perennially overcrowded San Francisco court docket held up the arraignment of Lorraine Hess, but Hunt was in the Department 11 courtroom that Friday morning and listened to her plead not guilty and not guilty by reason of insanity to two counts of first degree murder, one count of attempted murder, and assault with a deadly weapon.

Just after she was led back to the holding cells, Hunt walked across the lobby of the Hall of Justice. Outside, he stood on the steps in the windy sunshine and debated with himself whether he should go back inside and try to talk to Juhle. But he was reluctant to put himself in the position of seeming to apologize for his unorthodox ways.

After all, in spite of even Gina's concerns that he'd acted recklessly, he had delivered Dominic Como's and Nancy Neshek's murderer into Juhle's hands without even a minor scuffle. In the process, he'd saved his friend, and Russo as well, from another false or, at best, deeply flawed arrest.

If Juhle didn't like the way Hunt had done that job, that was just too bad. When you're at the table and your hand comes in, you've got to bet it and play it now, and that's what Hunt had done.

Sure, it could have gone differently. Granted, there were more risks involved than Juhle and even Gina felt comfortable with, but the fact was that Hunt was not a cop. He was a private investigator and didn't have to abide by the written and unwritten rules of the police force. If Juhle didn't like that, he'd have to get over it.

He checked his watch, scanned the traffic as it flowed by him on Bryant, then descended the steps and jaywalked across the street, to where Lou the Greek's was probably just starting to serve the day's first orders of the Special, whatever that might turn out to be.

If Hunt went right down now, he could get a table with no wait.

He was halfway through his Yeanling Clay Bowl, sitting at a two-top that faced away from the entrance and the bar, when a shadow crossed his table and in the next second Juhle was in the chair across from him.

"I saw you in there," Juhle said without preamble. "I love that she pleaded not guilty."

Hunt shrugged. "How does she do that after she confessed?"

"Happens all the time," Juhle said. "You'd be surprised." He pointed at Hunt's food. "Yeanling Clay Bowl?"

Hunt nodded. "And the yeanling today is especially fresh and tasty."

"Do I have time to get some and talk to you, or are you running out to solve another crime?"

"I've got no crimes on the agenda. I'm back to litigation work. Not that I'm complaining. There's suddenly a ton of it."

"Getting your name in the paper never hurts."

"Yeah, there's that." Hunt shrugged again, twisted a forkful of the noodle contingent of his dish. "What else do you want to talk about?"

"I've been thinking about it for a week now. It's driving me crazy. I don't know how you knew."

Hunt chewed. "I didn't. Not till the last minute. Before that, I was wrong on every guess. Turner, Ellen, Alicia. I was all over the money. I never even looked at Hess."

"So what changed?"

"She snagged herself. At Como's memorial, she pretended she had barely heard of Neshek's death, but then a few minutes later, before anybody had said anything about it, she asked me if the cops had found anything at Neshek's house."

Juhle spoke up. "And she shouldn't have known that soon that Neshek had been killed in her own home."

"See? You can figure things out, after all. But I didn't figure it out. At least not then. I just thought somebody might have included that detail before I went over to talk to them. You know, 'Did you hear Nancy got killed at her house last night?' kind of thing. So I didn't put too much on it. She possibly could have known. So I gave her the benefit."

"Okay."

"Okay, so the next day, Mickey's up at Sunset talking to her about her alibi for Monday night and she tells him she's got a son she's helping with homework all night, but then she lets drop that she doesn't even know where Neshek lived. So I get this little 'ding ding ding' in my brain and wonder how likely that is. I mean, she's worked with

Dominic like for a decade and all these execs go to the same functions." He raised a hand and stopped one of the waiters going by. "You ordering?"

Juhle nodded and told the waiter he was going to walk on the wild side and have the Special and a Diet Coke, and then he came back to Hunt. "So she said she didn't know where Neshek lived?"

"Right. At the same time, she tells Mickey how she's hurting for money. Big bills, medical stuff. But somehow before that she had the money for a full-time caregiver and a tutor. Anyway, that sticks with me a little bit. But still, I mean, possible, I suppose. And she's still got her kid as an alibi. Plus, there's absolutely no hint of a motive, so I let it pass again. Strike two."

"All right, the oh two pitch."

"I'm talking with Alicia Thorpe, trying to bust her story wide open, and she tells me that she'd met Ellen Como at a Sanctuary House benefit at Neshek's place."

"Ellen Como? Am I missing something?"

"No, hang on. So Alicia's talking about this first meeting with Ellen and then she lets slip — I mean, really just an aside, pure luck — that Dominic pulled her away from the Sunset staff to introduce her to Ellen. And she mentions Hess specifically, at

Neshek's house."

"Better."

"Getting there. Then it occurs to me that the reason Ellen is sure that Dominic is screwing Alicia is because Hess told her so. She said she caught them in the act a couple of times. Now, there's no doubt that Dominic was screwing around. How likely is it he's going to get caught in his office not once, but a few times? So I'm starting to wonder, if Hess isn't telling Ellen the truth, what's she got against Alicia? Bringing me, of course, to the oldest motive in the world."

"You got her."

"Not yet. I've got some thoughts and some definite issues, but nothing solid for Como and no reason in the world for Neshek. So I'm stuck."

"Until?"

"Until I remember Al Carter, who's worked there for eight years and presumably knows everything. And he's uptight because he's black and he's got a record and thinks you guys are going to come after him."

"That's bogus, Wyatt. We don't do that. We never even gave him more than a passing look."

"I'm not the guy you've got to convince, Dev. Anyway, whatever, Al wants to help us find whoever did Como if he can, and not just for the reward either. So I have Mickey find him and we have a talk and I ask him, one, if, back in the day, did Lorraine and Como have a thing? And guess what? Not just back in the day, evidently, but back up until a few months after Alicia came on. In other words, until a few weeks ago."

"And Carter didn't think to mention that to anybody?"

"He thought Lorraine had no problem with it ending. She was cool. It wasn't like passion anymore, he didn't think. She'd gotten old."

Juhle's Diet Coke arrived and he took a long drink. "That's pretty much what she told us, motive wise. And you might like to know that what happened Monday night with Neshek is that she came up to Hess after the COO meeting and actually asked Hess if she should talk to you, Wyatt."

"Did she say why?"

"She was in Dominic's office one time and saw a concealed safe full of money. Wouldn't it be better for COO, she asked Hess, if they came forward with the money the feds claimed was missing? Or would it just tarnish Dominic's reputation and the work they were trying to do? Hess thought that what Neshek was really saying was that she knew that Hess had taken the money. So she killed her."

"So that would be the money you found in Hess's house?"

"Five hundred eighty-seven thousand, six hundred and eighty dollars, but who's counting? Not, by the way, in small bills." Juhle drank again. "But I still don't see you making your call to Hess, even if you had all of that — the contradiction about Neshek's house, the motive."

"Right. Still not enough. So I had a hunch. I knew that Jim Parr was on his way to Sunset, but either he never got there, or he got there and ran into somebody he knew who got him away."

"Hess."

Hunt nodded. "Hess. So I asked Carter if Hess had come back to Sunset that day after the memorial. He'd definitely been there and he'd know, and he told me she hadn't. But she'd told Mickey she had."

"There you go."

"Well, again, there was a luck element. Mickey found the bar she took him to like a block around the corner from Sunset."

"Okay, but why kill Parr?" Juhle asked.

"Basically same as Neshek. Jim knew from the old days that she had been doing Como. And he knew about the cash and the safe from his driving days too."

"But Al Carter knew all of that, too, and she knew it."

"So why didn't she kill him too? I don't know. Lack of opportunity? Or maybe she thought she'd convinced him — in fact I think she had — that she had nothing going with Como anymore. If it's any consolation, Gina thinks that she would have gotten around to Al next. By this time, she was ready to go off on anybody who got close."

"Actually, Wyatt, when you look at what she did, why she killed these people, maybe the insanity plea isn't so far-fetched after all."

"Why do you say that?"

"Well, the blunt instrument murders argue that she's crazy. I mean, women don't kill people with blunt instruments. They're too unpredictable. Plus, you've got to swing really hard."

Hunt chewed a moment. "Actually, I've thought about that, Dev, and it seems to me it's more an argument for premeditation than insanity."

"How do you figure that?"

"Well, I couldn't figure out, if Hess had a gun, why she'd use a tire iron. I mean, on the face of it, as you say, that's insane. But it's not insane if you want to kill Dominic and at the same time make it look like Alicia did it because you hate her for stealing him from you."

"Tire iron, limo, scarf."

"Bingo. Alicia's access to all of them. And by the way, it almost worked."

"But not quite," Juhle said.

Hunt let Juhle have his small face-saving moment. "And still, you know," he added, "it came to getting her down to my place. She might have just blown off everything and waited it out, let you arrest Alicia, maybe get out of Dodge with her boy. It was then or never. I had to move, Dev. Had to."

"Ever breathe a word of this to my partner, Wyatt, and I'll deny it to my dying day, but I'm secretly glad as hell that you did."

Wyatt Hunt heard what appeared to be lighthearted conversation as he mounted the stairs that led up to his office just after his first appointment of the day, which had been over at Gina Roake's firm.

Now it was close to ten o'clock, and he had no appointments that he knew of scheduled for his office. Opening the outer door, he caught Tamara in midlaugh at something. Across the room from her, two middle-aged African-American men in black suits, white shirts, and black ties filled up the tiny reception area. They both stood when he entered, and now he was shaking both of their hands. "Mr. Carter, how you doin'? Good to see you again, Mr. Rand. Welcome to the Hunt Club, such as it is. What can I do for you gentlemen?"

The visit by these two men was a surprise, and far from an unpleasant one. Hunt had last seen them together during the small but very well-covered ceremony at City Hall where the mayor had presented the reward distribution money — two hundred thousand dollars to Al Carter, and fifty thousand each to Ellen Como, Cecil Rand, and Linda Colores. Though Lorraine Hess was still a long way from actually being convicted, there was no doubt that she had killed Dominic Como, and on this basis, Len Turner decided to release the reward funds before he was technically committed to do so.

It seemed that Al Carter was the spokesman for the two of them, and after a few more pleasantries catching up on life, they sat again on their chairs while Hunt perched himself on the side of Tamara's desk. But no sooner had he sat than Al Carter halfstood again so that he could get at his wallet, which he extracted and from which he then produced a couple of business cards, which he handed over to Hunt.

Hunt looked down at the beautifully designed card, light blue with a colorful logo of a toucan, and the words "Toucan Limousine Service."

"We realize that this is short notice, but we were hoping, Cecil and I, that since this is the first formal day of our new business — I don't know if you've heard we've gone into partnership with two brand-new Town Cars — maybe we could drive you and your lovely associate here to the place of your choice and take you both to lunch."

"We go by convoy," Rand added. "All the way out to the Cliff House you want."

Hunt half turned back to Tamara. "This is a tough call, but I'm thinking we need to close up for the afternoon, Tam. How's that sound to you?"

She made a mock pout. "You're the boss. If we have to."

Hunt straightened off the desk. "You drive a hard bargain, but you gentlemen have got yourselves a deal. When do we go?"

"Tout de suite," Carter said. "As soon as you're all ready."

Tamara was on her feet. "I'll be right back. Just let me go and freshen up."

As she disappeared back through Hunt's

557

inner office, Carter said, "There's one other thing, Mr. Hunt. We've discussed this, Cecil and I, and we'd like to offer you free service in town if you need it, whenever we're not driving paying clients."

Hunt sat back down on the desk. His first thought being that this was like the old deal he'd had with Mickey when he'd been driving a cab, but better. And his second, that he couldn't accept it. "Guys," he said, "that's extremely generous, but you'll need your clients."

"And we'll get them," Carter said. "But in the meanwhile, we're at your service."

"Would you let me at least pay for gas?"

The two men exchanged a glance and a quick nod. "Gas would not compromise our position too badly," Carter said. "You can pay for gas."

"Thank you." Hunt shook hands with them again. "So what's with the name?"

Both men smiled and Rand said, "Toucan."

"Right." Hunt still not seeing it.

"Mr. Hunt." And then Carter said slowly, "Two con."

Mickey had missed six weeks of cooking school because of his broken arm. He'd had the last soft cast finally removed earlier this week and though he was still stiff, he could at least raise it and move things around in the kitchen. And this morning, he was so anxious to get started that he woke himself up at a few minutes after six, had his coffee, and started his cutting — onions, celery, fennel root (why not? he'd thought), green beans, Brussels sprouts, potatoes — a cornucopia of just-purchased fresh produce overflowing the counter on both sides of the sink.

He'd gone down to the Ferry Building last week and ordered a fourteen-pound Diestel family Heirloom turkey that he'd picked up yesterday and soaked in the *Chronicle*'s famous "Best Turkey" brine. Truth be told, there really wasn't much to cooking a turkey, as long as you didn't overcook it, and even that was easy to time and guarantee with an instant-read thermometer. To his mind, the trick to the great Thanksgiving dinner was the stuffing, and since everybody had different tastes, he was making several kinds — prune, chestnut, oyster, bread, and sausage, and what he and Tamara had always called "plain old," with celery, onions, stock, and poultry seasoning.

He was cutting the onions when he heard a scratching noise and he stopped and listened again. There it was again. A scratch and a soft tap.

Going out into the living room, he went over to the front door and opened it.

"I know it's too early," Alicia said, and then added all in a rush, "and the last thing I want to do is intrude on you or your kitchen, but I know how much you were doing today and I figured that since we were going to be eating here, our combined families, I mean, what there are of them, the least I could do would be to help you out a little, even if it's early, although I haven't really had much practice with exactly what to do on Thanksgiving, I mean, they've all been so different when we've even had them at all, and since Ian and I haven't really ever had one exactly together, this one's going to be at least one we can remember even if it's the last one we ever . . ."

She stopped talking and just stood in front of him with her hands down by her sides. She took a deep breath and let it out, her eyes beginning to go glassy now. "And one other thing." She reached up a hand behind his neck.

"I've been waiting for the right time," she said, "and I so don't want to be wrong, and I'm not completely sure if this is it yet." She took another breath. "But unless you tell me not to, I'm going to kiss you."

He beat her to it.

ACKNOWLEDGMENTS

While casting about for an idea that would drive this book, I was hoping to be able to include an element or two that was more or less pure fun. I have found that when you're writing about very serious issues, such as abuse of charity funds and murder, it adds to a book's readability and enjoyment if there's something else going on besides the heavy stuff. My muse (aka my wife, Lisa Sawyer) suggested I include a whole bunch of restaurants, San Francisco being such a great restaurant town. This struck me as such a good idea that I considered naming this book *Thirty Restaurants* and setting every scene in an eating establishment. Fortunately, I didn't carry the conceit that far. But I did decide that my main character, Mickey Dade, wanted to be not a private eye, but a chef. Since cooking has long been one of my own passions, I knew I could bring a certain authority, and definitely some fun, to that approach.

But there is a nearly unbridgeable chasm between recreational cooks and professional chefs. Since I am definitely one of the former, I didn't have a good idea of the mind-set and ambitions demanded of the latter. I was mentioning this to a friend, Laurie Lovely (her real name!), at my workout club, and she suggested I take a look at Michael Ruhlman's *The Making of a Chef.* It was a terrific book and set me well on the way to knowing who Mickey Dade was and what he was made of. I wish I could have incorporated more of the fascinating life of a chef-in-training in this book, but my story was after all about murder and corporate malfeasance and I didn't want to burden my readers with too many distractions.

Serendipity then intervened again in the guise of an article by Terri Hardy that ran in the *Sacramento Bee* about some questionable practices with the bookkeeping and business practices of a well-known charity that I won't name here. But I did call Terri and speak to her at length about her research and discoveries, and I'd like to thank her for providing the key that unlocked the door to the real meat of this novel. I'd also like to thank another journalist, Michelle

Durand, columnist and reporter for the *San Mateo Daily Journal,* who contributed some anecdotal information on ducks and ground squirrels (really!) that got the book off and running.

As in all of my books, Al Giannini continues to contribute mightily from the planning stages right up through the final editing. Al knows just about everything about criminal law that there is to know, and is unstinting in his generosity in sharing that knowledge with me. If these novels read like they're written by somebody who knows the ins and outs of the criminal justice system, and I hope they do, it is due largely to Al's efforts and insights.

Other friends who added to this novel in one way or the other include Max Byrd, John M. Poswall, Don Matheson, Peter J. and Donna Diedrich, Dr. Mark Detzer, and Bob Zaro. Peter S. Dietrich, M.D., M.P.H., has once again vetted the book for medical issues. And my assistant, Anita Boone, continues to lighten my days and my workload by being among the most competent, efficient, and cheerful people on the planet. In ways too numerous and too intangible to mention, my two children, Justine Rose Lescroart and Jack Sawyer Lescroart, play a huge role in the gestation and creation of all of these books. Thank you.

This is the tenth book of mine to be published by Dutton, and I couldn't be happier in my "home" here. So many people at this company work diligently to see that these books find an enthusiastic, loyal, and large readership, and I'm grateful to one and all. The professionalism, style, and taste that are the hallmarks of the organization are second to none in the publishing industry; and more than that, the people here are just simply a joy to work with. So once again, I'd like to shout out a thanks to my publisher, Brian Tart, the marketing team of Christine Ball and Carrie Swetonic, Melissa Miller, Signet/NAL paperback publisher Kara Welsh, Phil Budnick, Rick Pascocello, and the mega-talented cover designer Rich Hasselberger (who has outdone himself on *Treasure Hunt*). My editor, Ben Sevier, is smart, sensitive, insightful, and fun, and I hope nothing more than that we get to keep doing these books together for a very, very long time.

Karen Hlavacek and Peggy Nauts both were fantastic in catching those last little mistakes that so badly seem to want to creep into books even after a hundred people have read and edited them. Thanks to both of you for making the final book as clean as it can be.

Mick and Nancy Neshek have generously contributed to the naming of one of the characters in this book on behalf of the Sacramento Library Foundation.

Finally, Barney Karpfinger remains my great friend and tireless supporter. He is also, not incidentally, the finest literary agent there is. I am humbled and grateful to be working with him.

I very much like to hear from my readers, and invite all of you to please visit me at my Web site, www.johnlescroart.com, with comments, questions, or interests. Also, if you are on Facebook, please join me on my official page.

ABOUT THE AUTHOR

John Lescroart is the author of twenty previous novels, including *A Plague of Secrets, Betrayal, The Suspect, The Hunt Club, The Motive, The Second Chair, The First Law, The Oath, The Hearing,* and *Nothing But the Truth.* He lives in northern California.

The employees of Thorndike Press hope you have enjoyed this Large Print book. All our Thorndike, Wheeler, and Kennebec Large Print titles are designed for easy reading, and all our books are made to last. Other Thorndike Press Large Print books are available at your library, through selected bookstores, or directly from us.

For information about titles, please call:
(800) 223-1244

or visit our Web site at:
http://gale.cengage.com/thorndike

To share your comments, please write:
Publisher
Thorndike Press
295 Kennedy Memorial Drive
Waterville, ME 04901